SOULBREATHER

SOULBREATHER

BOOK ONE OF THE SOULMIST SERIES

HELEN GARRAWAY

Published by Jerven Publishing

Cover designed by MiblArt

Paperback ISBN: 978-1-7399344-7-7

Sign up to my mailing list to join my magical world and for further information about forthcoming books and latest news at: www.helengarraway.com

First Edition

ALSO BY HELEN GARRAWAY

For Blitz Abrego
A co-worker and a fan

CONTENTS

1

MAV

EIDOLON

Not all that was good was in the light; there was good in the dark too, if you bothered to look. *At least that was what my father had once said,* Mav thought as he crept around the edge of the field, his senses questing. Nothing. What should be a flood of information was met with silence. An emptiness that grated on his nerves. What was he thinking? Why was he making a stand? These children needed a protector. Instead, they had a fallen angel, who lacked the sense to know when his time was up.

But not just yet. He had made a promise, and even if it sounded hollow, he stood by his word. The kids had tried so hard. He couldn't let them down.

Peering through the damp mist, he ignored the filmy tendrils snaking around his ankles as if they could snare him in place, and listening intently, he strained to pick up hints of anyone approaching. Nothing. Ice cold water dripped on his head, making him flinch, and a sense of foreboding shivered through him as the hairs on his arms rose; he knew they were coming even if he couldn't see them.

Around him, empty fields lay fallow; once, they were

brimming with crops, but not anymore. Now it took a team of people to tame the heavy soil, which clumped into unmanageable sods. Much too unwieldy for the youngsters, currently sheltering in the rundown house at the edge of nowhere, to cultivate. He sighed out his frustration.

The gloom-misted lands of Eidolon concealed much in the shadows. Maybe that was what his father had wanted him to discover? A lesson for a fallen angel. A sudden longing for his sunny rooms in Puronia shook him, and he clamped the memory down. No point torturing himself with things he couldn't have.

Jagged branches loomed out of the mist like grasping fingers, and then the swirling haze that suffocated the land closed in again. It was as if the sky pressed down on him, the grey mass above squashing him into the dirt and not allowing him to rise.

Mav shook off the dreary image and scowled as he approached the wooden dwelling, which looked like it might collapse at any moment, and climbed the steps to the veranda. "Shandra, I can see you. Get yourself behind the barrier, now."

A low snarl was the only response, but she disappeared from view, and he crossed the wooden boards on silent feet. He squeezed through the loose slats into the front room, avoiding the door, because it squealed like a rampaging boar. Enough of a warning that someone was entering, if they needed one by then.

"They are approaching. Remember! Save your arrows until you have a clear shot; don't waste them."

A scruffy lad rolled his eyes, the whites startlingly bright against his grubby, brown skin. "Mav, you've told us already. Quit worrying."

But Mav couldn't. Having backed them into this corner, his high ideals were now crashing down around his ears. He wasn't sure why the kids still trusted him. He hadn't made their lives any easier.

"After the first barrage, retreat to the second defence. Once in position, take the toddlers out through the tunnel."

"We know, stop repeating yourself. Anyone would think you don't trust us," the scruffy lad replied, a wry grin on his lips.

Mav huffed. "Kerris, I trust you more than anyone in this world; I have no idea why you trust me."

"Because you tell the truth, even if you know we don't want to hear it," Shandra interrupted, checking over her quiver again. "And anyway, this is our house. They have no right to invade it. Pa would be doing what you are doing if he could, but he can't, so you are next best."

Mav rubbed a grimy hand over his face. How did he manage to get into these scrapes? He had only been passing by, searching for information about the politics of Eidolon, trying to discover who was exploiting these poor people and maybe find out how he had ended up here. Instead, he had found four abandoned children and a lost chicken. His lips quirked at the memory of the cranky bird that had led him to Shandra's home, along with the children he had collected, who were now scattered around the house, intent on defending it. Abandoned urchins trying to hold together a homestead, and he couldn't leave them.

Soulless youngsters gravitated to the rickety house as if it was a beacon in the shadows, gathering in the hope of some redemption, even though they weren't sure what they needed forgiveness for. Instead of information about his downfall, he'd found out more than he wanted to about how children were cast out, betrayed, and abused. And in the collecting of their stories, he discovered the darkness he had been searching for.

His gut roiled with anger. That his own kind, or those

who had once been his own kind, had caused such suffering was despicable. That they would condemn a child, steal their soul, and cast them into Eidolon was beyond his comprehension. The children's desperate tales touched a cord deep within him, a sense of betrayal so buried that the answering throb of pain was muted by layers of suppression.

Why he was suppressing it, he had no idea, but at least it enabled him to review the information dispassionately enough that he recognised the thread that linked them. The common denominator that gave him his next target. A seraphim who had come to the conclusion that Eidolon was his pot of gold.

For years, Mav had been scouring the shrouded lands for proof that those people without souls could be redeemed. Just as his father had charged him to do, before everything went so wrong. That piece of the puzzle still defeated him. Mav had no idea how he had ended up in Eidolon, without a soul, beaten and confused. But before he began the tired old ritual of running through all the things that had gone awry and he couldn't fix, he stiffened at a shout from outside.

Anger rippled through him again; that angels would stoop to exploitation and monetary gain when they already lived in such luxury and opulence. That they wanted more than they were entitled to; that they ignored the core mandates for their existence. When had it all gone so wrong? Why had his father allowed so many to suffer when he could have, *should have*, prevented it? How had angels within the citadel become so corrupted that they could con his father and the archangels all these years?

Sighing out a breath, he rotated his shoulders, trying to relieve the tension tightening his muscles. He had miscalculated the response from the syndicate peddling the kids and he was about to pay the price. But he had been upfront with his current batch of fledglings. This had been his chance to find out who was at the root, hopefully all the way up to the ruling body in the citadel.

He had to create a diversion to centre all the approaching men's attention on him so the children could escape to the fall-back shelter he had set up in case they were discovered. They needed to slip away unseen while all eyes were on him.

Flicking a glance around the room, he noted the kids' positions; the eldest were all upstairs, the youngest at the bottom, prepared to flee at his word. His brow darkened at the sight of them, armed and ready. Shandra—an ethereal shadow, her tangled blonde hair tied away from her sharp face; she should be a true fledgling. Kerris—a gangly lad, bright and too intelligent for his own good; a scribe in the making. Muntra—the strongest, muscular and determined, who should be training as a cherubim. And Bailey—a cherub if ever there was one, with his blond curls and angelic face. They should all be safe and nurtured under his wing.

His lips clamped into a straight line and he prowled up the stairs. Each vantage point had a child prepared to deal death. What was he doing? He was an angel, for god's sake, and here he was, encouraging children to kill, to embrace the shadows of their existence and fulfil that which the blind believed of them. He took a deep, calming breath. No, not kill, defend.

"Bailey, on my signal, remember?"

The slender young boy nodded, thrusting out his chest, obviously proud that Mav trusted him with the most important job of all, ensuring the youngest children got away safely.

Mav settled in a shadowy corner, peering out over the misty landscape. Movement rippled through the clumps of bushes edging the yard, and without looking down at his quiver, he grasped an arrow and nocked it. Memories of another life flashed through him, and he gritted his teeth as he aimed.

"Bailey, now," he said and released, arrow after arrow. He lost track of time until his fingers grasped empty air. No more arrows. He glanced around at the clatter of feet on the rickety stairs.

"It's just you, Kerris, Shandra, and Muntra left. We gotta go," Bailey said.

"You go on. We'll be behind you," Mav said as he discarded his bow and peered out the window. Shadowy forms advanced towards the house.

"Mav!" Shandra's cry sent an icy shiver down Mav's spine.

Deep voices outside on the veranda echoed his name, but Mav ignored them, rushing down the stairs. The wood groaned but held as the men outside tried to force the barricaded door open. The crunch of splintering wood warned that others were battering down the slats covering the windows. Muntra lay on the floor, pale and shaking. Shandra tugged at him, pleading with him to move.

"You're too heavy, Muntra, you have to get up."

"Get down the stairs," Mav snapped to the others as he knelt beside the boy. He clamped a hand over the wound. "It's just a graze, you'll be fine." He pressed down hard as the boy groaned. "You have a choice," he said, his voice low as he wrenched the lad upright. "You can die here or you can get your arse off the floor and down those stairs."

Muntra shuddered, glazed eyes staring at him as Mav stuffed a cloth under his shirt and slapped Muntra's hand against it.

"Time to go. Bailey is waiting for you." Mav stilled at a shout from outside.

"Demavrian? Is that you? Is this where you got to? Really?"

Fear fluttered in Mav's stomach as the voice continued. It wasn't the slave traders after all; it was someone even worse. He ignored the flare of pain and betrayal that the familiar voice evoked. How had Julius found him?

"Don't look back," Mav murmured as he pushed Muntra towards the trapdoor and turned to face the oncoming threat, surprised that Julius hadn't just barrelled in. What was he waiting for?

Julius' voice grew sharper. "I suppose I'm not surprised. You always were trouble. Why would it be any different here?"

"Julius?" Mav pictured the elegant captain of what he supposed was now his brother's Heavenly Host. A man he hadn't seen in nearly five decades. What was he doing here? In Eidolon.

"Surrender and we'll let the kids go. We don't want to harm them; it's only you we want."

"That's big of you, Julius. I would never have thought you would stoop so low as to traffic children. Where is the honour of the Heavenly Host?"

"You are a murderer; you have no right to speak of honour."

"Murderer? Julius, how could you? You wound me."

"I'll do a lot more than that when I get hold of you," Julius replied, his voice harsh.

"But trafficking children? I think your honour is much more tainted than mine. How do you face yourself each day? How long have you been searching for me? Too many decades to count, now? Don't you ever get bored?"

"Never." The swift retort was cold and bitter.

More footsteps clattered on the veranda, and Mav spared a last glance down the stairs. The cellar was dark and empty. Closing the trapdoor, he pulled the rug back over to hide it and sent a silent prayer after the kids who had put their trust in him.

"Heavenly Father, protect your children in this time of need," he murmured as he drew his sword up in salute. A last memory of his oathsworn, Eladriz, criticising his stance flickered through his mind and made him smile. His smile became a snarl as soldiers rushed out of the kitchen as the front door splintered, and he launched himself at the men supporting such a foul business.

2

SOLANJI

PURONIA

Sheer beauty sealed the deal, and a shady deal it was too. Every eye was drawn to the balcony where the golden-haired angels stood waving their hands as if they were the deities they should all worship. Solanji muffled a snort of disdain as she watched the expression of adoration spread over mindless faces. Just because the angels were heart-stoppingly beautiful, didn't mean every word from their lips was gospel truth.

Take the current announcement, for example. Archdeus Amaridin had announced that his brother, Demavrian, would be formally pronounced dead on the fiftieth anniversary of his downfall, clearing the way for an archangel to rise to the angelic height of archdeus. One step away from becoming a god. The decision rang through the sunny streets and passages of the city of Puronia like a death knell, or a celebratory accolade, dependent on your point of view.

This was history in the making.

"An archdeus has never fallen before," a young woman in pink and gold silks said, grabbing the arm of the man standing beside her. "Who do you think will replace him?" she asked, her eyes sparkling with anticipation.

"Got to be Archangel Serenia, hasn't it?" her companion replied. "Did you see how lovely she and Amaridin looked together on the balcony? Both blue-eyed and golden-haired." His eyes went dreamy. "And so beautiful! They would make an ideal couple."

"I suppose it's not surprising that Demavrian fell. He looked just like his uncle, Kaenera. Dark and deadly. Must have followed in his footsteps."

Solanji stopped herself from rolling her eyes. People were so predictable, making snap judgements based on few facts. Just because an angel had black hair, didn't make him evil like Kaenera.

"But Demavrian was just as handsome. He was a gorgeous man," the man said on a sigh.

The woman snorted. "Amaridin is far better looking. He just glows!"

Solanji moved on. She didn't see why they needed another archdeus when there was no proof that the other one was dead. Yes, he was fallen, but that wasn't the same. It was true that no word had been heard from him for years, but angels and their oathsworn were immortal, weren't they? Solanji sniffed. That was if you could believe the myths, maybe the son of a god was immortal, but their oathsworn too? She doubted it.

Why would they replace him now? You never saw them. Their god, Veradeus, had been absent for years. Veradeus had distanced himself from the mortals he oversaw, saying his people were perfectly capable of managing their daily lives. He had left it to his two sons, Archdeus Amaridin and Demavrian, and their hosts to rule in his stead, along with Archangel Serenia, who led the citadel council. Veradeus returned on occasion to offer advice and guidance to his sons and to glance over his world, before leaving again. That was until Demavrian had disappeared, accused of murder and worse, and Veradeus hadn't been seen since.

Ignoring the somewhat premature celebrations, Solanji continued on her way. Pausing at the street corner, she observed the people who strolled through the square. So relaxed and unconcerned. Their colourful robes and scarves fluttered around them, gilded by the golden sun, like the wisps of ephemeral soulmist that trailed after them. Bright sunlight lit the market, revealing the wicker chairs scattered under the vibrant green vines that grew across the woodwork and curled over the fret work arching above them.

Sheltered alcoves embraced the people as they sat and drank a fragrant bannoe, the popular infusion of bannen leaves sourced from Eidolon. So carefree. Solanji scowled as the delicate scent drifted on the air, reminding her that she couldn't afford it.

She glanced around, checking to see if any of the lesser angels, the seraphim, were in the crowds. The seraphim were the administrators who freely moved through Puronia and the rest of Angelicus. She huffed out her breath. They were probably the ones who did all the work, and certainly the ones she needed to avoid. She didn't want the citadel finding out she could touch souls.

Clearing the expression off her face, she strolled across the square, unable to resist trailing her fingers through the strands of soulmist, which she couldn't avoid as they quested towards her.

Images flickered before her, their uppermost memories, which she perused without a second thought. If they couldn't be bothered to shield them, then she wouldn't feel guilty reading them. Light and happy, they thought only of their own pleasure—purchasing a new scarf or material to make a gown, making plans to meet again on the morrow. Ah, there was one a little darker; loneliness. She knew what being lonely felt like.

Even in this sunny world without the threat of shadow, protected by the archangels and the seraphim, there was still loneliness and suffering. Predominantly ignored, as who could be unhappy surrounded by such beauty and colour?

Once, in a time lost in history, the archangels had mingled with the general public, but nowadays, they kept to the citadel, the glowing building at the top of the rise. Solanji peered up at the golden walls, softening the glare that the white marble would have radiated. They gleamed in the constant sunlight, elegant columns providing an eye-catching landmark. She had never been inside. Few knew what it looked like; there was just rumour and conjecture. Most of the population weren't bothered, didn't care to know. Solanji shivered. The only reason anyone would get a close-up view was if they were brought before the Justicers for some crime and the Justicers sent them to the SoulSingers.

It was an effective deterrent. Solanji was constantly aware of the concealed threat that hovered over them like a benevolent parent waiting for their child to take one false step.

SoulSingers were rare humans who could touch souls. Once identified, they were bound to the citadel. Solanji shuddered at the thought. It was supposed to be a life of luxury in return for removing souls at the Justicers decree. To Solanji, it sounded like torture. Without a soul, you couldn't live in the sun-drenched land of Angelicus. The only place you could go was across the divide to Eidolon, and from there, you had no hope of return. It was, in effect, a death sentence, especially as there were no SoulBreathers left to restore your soul after the SoulSingers took it.

Solanji rotated her shoulders against the sudden tension. Eidolon itself wasn't a bad place. It was just dreary and cold.

A place where the sun didn't shine. A land of shadows and the unknown. No one knew how big it was, though conjecture stated it was much larger than Angelicus. It was the thought of being banished and never able to return that was frightening; to never see your family again.

She exhaled a breath and drew in her wandering thoughts, and with some reluctance, returned to her inspection of her prospective clients. She needed one plump in the pocket; her rent was due and she needed to send her mother some money.

Her smile hardened at the thought of the cosy house in the coastal village that her family had struggled to hold onto since her father had died. Her mother held their small family together with unrelenting determination. Brennan, her younger brother, was a mischievous nine-year old, already scampering about the boat that her elder brother, Georgi, now worked on to support their mother and brother.

If her mother knew that she had resorted to working the black market and on occasion conning people out of a few coins, she would have been horrified, but she had promised to send money home, and she wouldn't break her promise.

She had heard on the grapevine that the Fixer was looking for a courier, and he usually paid well. It was worth the risk to avoid working for Jolee's pleasure house.

A wave of hatred swept through her, making Solanji falter.

"It will be mine, all mine. I can take his soul and then I can kill him." A strident mind voice cut across her meanderings, and Solanji nearly tripped at the spite that dripped from the thoughts. *"Gods, this is such a disgusting place."*

A second, more uncertain voice filled her mind. *"Shit! Shit! Shit! What am I doing? I should have known better than to trust a seraphim. This is not going to end well. I bet they'll blame me. Why did I agree to this?"*

Solanji searched the smiling faces of the people milling around her, trying to find the one whose thoughts she had sensed. But their expressions were all open and serene, focused on their enjoyment. The searing hatred faded, and she took a deep breath and encouraged the flowing crowd not to notice her. She adjusted her silken hood to cover her face and slipped down a side alley towards the Golden Host, a more salubrious ale house off the Shambles.

Angels fighting angels? Solanji shuddered at the thought. It had been two hundred years since the last angelic battles. Peace pervaded the lands and the angels reigned supreme, most of the time. She wrinkled her nose as she headed for the narrower streets and yelped as someone grabbed her arm and yanked her back.

She bounced off hard muscles with a gasp, and the man's hand shot out and grabbed her other wrist, his bony fingers biting her skin.

"Who are you?" he snarled.

Solanji jerked back as if bitten, but he dragged her forward, closer to his face. Piercing blue eyes raked her from head to foot as if judging her right to exist.

"I'm nobody," she stuttered as she took in his golden hair and smooth complexion. Even his breath, which was hot on her cheek, smelt sweet. A seraphim. His soulmist was familiar, tinged with anger. Had the man in the square felt her touch and followed her? Her gaze skittered up and down the alley. Only the man's fidgeting aide stood within earshot.

"Everyone is somebody, and you," he sniffed as if he could determine what she was from smell alone, "are not nobody."

"Sir, we don't have time for this," his aide squeaked out. "We're already late!"

"You can touch souls," he said, disbelief tingeing his voice as he continued to observe her.

"N-no, I can't. I have a high empathy rating. I work at a pleasure house. Please, let me go. I've done nothing wrong."

The man eased his grip, and Solanji twisted her wrist and stepped back. "I-I pick up on emotions, nothing more," she whispered.

"Sir, you'll miss your ride. You can't afford to annoy…"

"Yes, yes, I know." He moved away, allowing the aide to usher him back into the sun-drenched square. His blue robes swirled around him as he peered back over his shoulder, his scowl still in place. Solanji heaved out a sigh, absent-mindedly rubbing her wrist as the seraphim turned the corner.

Taking a steadying breath, she slumped against the wall, trying to calm her frantic heart. It beat so fast, she thought she might pass out. The seraphim had felt her touching his soulmist. She had nearly been caught. His soulmist had been so loose, she hadn't been able to avoid it. She hadn't meant to touch him.

Resting her hand on her chest for a moment, she pushed away from the wall and, after a quick glance around, started walking back down the passageway.

The Shambles were a delight and one of Solanji's favourite places. A hodgepodge of buildings leant against each other to hold themselves up. Wooden beams decorated the exterior and the dim interiors. Small boutiques, shops, and cafes rubbed shoulders with eateries, bakeries, and alehouses. It was the thrumming heart of this golden city, cooler as the buildings blocked the sun, but they still lacked shadows.

The Fixer kept shop at the back of the Golden Host. Even in this glowing city, there were those who helped redistribute the wealth, as the Fixer phrased it. Business was plentiful, if you looked close enough, especially if you were prepared to cross the divide.

A quick glance down the street assured her that no one

was paying her any attention, and she darted down a side alley. Checking the discreet pockets in her leather trousers, Solanji relaxed as she slid her fingers down the slender blade concealed in the seam. Her neck prickled, and she glanced around her, but as usual, people were hurrying about their own business. Still, she pulled her cloak tighter and hurried down the narrow alleyways, eventually arriving in the court-yard of the Golden Host.

For such a dazzling city, it was surprising how many shady establishments could be found in Puronia. Not that there were any shadows, it was just the air of dilapidation and disrepair; a corner of this bright city that was overlooked and thrived out of sight. The underbelly of the righteous, even present in the realm of Angelicus.

Inside the inn, the interior was dim, a relief from the blazing light outside. It managed to be grimy and worn but comforting in a way. Bright perfection wore on the nerves after a while, and Solanji relaxed into the soothing absence of expectation. No one here expected anything of her, except maybe the Fixer.

Wending her way through the hooded clientele, Solanji searched for the man she sought out when ends no longer met and she was willing to risk crossing the divide. She found him seated at a corner table, shrouded in his tattered ruby red cloak. She adjusted her hood as she sat and splayed her hand on the table before her.

"I was hoping you wouldn't turn up," the Fixer said, his voice deep and gravelly. He spread his much larger hand next to hers. Raised veins wriggled as if alive across the back of his hand as he waited.

"Oh?" Solanji replied, removing her hand.

"A young lass like yourself. Better suited to working in one of those fine houses, I would have thought."

"You know better than that. I am no slave to be pushed around."

"Pity. You might live longer."

Solanji rolled her eyes. "I am quite capable of looking after myself. After all, I have for the last twenty-five years. Why should it change now?"

The man shifted in his seat. "I admit, you've never let me down, but it pains me to send you off into the unknown."

Solanji stared at him. The Fixer wasn't usually considerate of others. "What have you heard?"

The Fixer shrugged. "Nothing you don't know already, which is why I have a job right up your street."

"And which street would that be?"

"The one that pays well and is ideal for invisible couriers, such as yourself."

A chill stole over Solanji's skin. "You must be desperate if you resort to compliments from the off," she replied.

The Fixer's chuckle rasped like a whetstone on steel, and Solanji's chill deepened. She tried to repress the shiver.

"You should know I don't deal false coin, no matter what the ignorant say," the Fixer said.

"I didn't know they said that."

"They only say it once."

Solanji nodded, unsurprised. "So, what's the job?"

"A well-paying one. Three halos for a trip across the divide."

Three? Solanji's heart quailed. What could they want for that much money? The divide was the border that separated Angelicus and Eidolon and kept those who were good and had souls and lived in sun-drenched cities like Puronia from those who had committed some crime and were now soulless and destined to remain in the shadowy depths of Eidolon forever.

"What are they expecting? Instant delivery?"

His rasping laugh made the hairs on her arms rise. "Not quite. The job is no questions asked and deep into Fidolon. You will be met at the crossroads by a man called Joran. This is his likeness. He will take the package onwards."

Solanji glanced at the piece of paper that he slid towards her; a crude sketch of a brute of a man, and she gave a small nod. The picture disappeared. "The crossroads? That's at least two days into the shadowlands."

"Which is why they are paying so well. You'll cross via the curio. It's best you're not searched, you won't want to be caught."

Solanji's breath whooshed out. "What?" She couldn't help the squeak that accompanied the word. She had used the tunnel only once before and she had sworn never to again. It was an experience she would prefer not to repeat. She shuddered at the memory of dark tunnels and confusing dead ends. The journey under was not for regular folk; only those with shadier dealings took the underground passage.

Official crossing places into Angelicus were scarce and controlled. The steep single-track road clinging to the side of the escarpment was a continuous ribbon of paler stone wending its way up the cliff face. No one knew how it had been carved from the rock. Most attributed it to their god, it was a feat beyond mortal men. Travellers took nearly a day to descend or climb the escarpment. The Heavenly Host, the soldiers of Angelicus, guarded the crossings zealously, ensuring those without souls remained in their rightful place, at the base of the cliff.

The Fixer grinned at her, his square chin jutting out from his hood, a blue-grey shadow marring his grimy skin. He splayed his ropy hand on the table again, and Solanji hesitantly placed her hand next to his. Her slender hand looked fragile and delicate, a healthy brown against his pale, papery skin. He slid a small round disk under her palm. "Your token. Grants you two crossings, there and back."

"Deadline?" She managed to keep the shake out of her voice.

"None. As long as it takes. The client accepts that Eidolon can be…difficult."

Difficult? Now that was an understatement.

"Joran will check the inn at the crossing every day for the next week. If you don't meet, bring the package back."

"Payment?"

"One halo before and the rest after."

"Transport?"

"Your advance should cover your needs."

Great, she had to take her expenses out of the fee. The Fixer slid a flat box, maybe a finger's width deep, and a small pouch across the table. Solanji swept it away before prying eyes could identify it. She tucked the package into an inner pocket with the token and checked the pouch. Gleaming coins greeted her, brilliant in the dim light, and she pulled the drawstrings shut and hid it in another pocket.

"Always a pleasure," the Fixer said in dismissal, pulling his hood lower.

3

SOLANJI

Sunlight blinded Solanji as she left the tavern, and she hesitated in the courtyard, watching strangers, checking for anyone interested in her. Her mind was spinning, considering and discarding options as she hovered. Not seeing any threats, she walked out of the gate and into the busy streets.

Dropping her hood, she ran a hand over her coiled hair. She hated tying her hair up in knots, but it was just a black cloud of curls, untameable and noticeable if she left it loose. Satisfied that it was still in place, she squared her shoulders. Swirling her amber-coloured cloak around her, she strode down the alleyway, back into the main thoroughfare and the bright and gaudy populace on display.

Her silk cloak had cost far too much, but it hid her leathers and helped her blend in. She would not need it in Eidolon; she had a grungy green, woollen cloak for those journeys. Combing her fingers through the trailing soulmist straggling after the people who passed by eased her tension, and her shoulders relaxed. The tingling sensation flushing through her veins heightened her senses and made everything sharper.

Reaching her destination, she entered the hostelry and, inhaling the aroma of fresh straw and leatherwork, strolled down the stalls. She paused to rub the pointed noses of the inquisitive calopes that stuck their heads out as she passed, hoping for treats.

Stroking a patchy brown and white calope with molten copper eyes, Solanji opened the gate and ran her hand down his flank. Calope didn't have souls like people did; they hummed instead, a vibration that tickled the senses and gave Solanji a warm and hazy hug. She smiled as the feeling intensified, and she nodded. "Very well. One like you will do."

Once she had paid her returnable deposit, and the fee for two week's rental commencing the following day at a hostelry she knew over in Eidolon, she was twenty lumins lighter. A fifth of her advance gone, but at least she should get two of those back. Next, she needed to make arrangements with Jolee to keep an eye on her room and her calmers. In her line of work, it was a bit silly having dependents, but she found them soothing. Their constant movement in the water-filled tank in the corner of her room were a bane to her frazzled nerves.

Soulmist was like a drug, and she was addicted to it. Extending her soul fingers through that mist satisfied her craving and filled her with energy as if the soulmist was what nourished her. But she had to be so careful; no-one could know or they would ostracise her. Everyone was afraid of the SoulSingers, those who could separate a soul from the body and yet still leave the person existing and banished to Eidolon. They were more typically called the more derogatory name, SoulSuckers. Hated and feared. *For good reason*, she thought. You could only live in the realm of Angelicus if you possessed a soul; the soulless were lost and forgotten in the belly of the world, one step away from oblivion.

As such, she couldn't reveal to anyone that she could see and touch souls. She could never take a soul from someone deliberately, ever. She clamped down on the memory of the one time she had accidentally done so. Just the thought of it made her feel ill. Imagine doing that every day? They would force her to strip souls if they found out; SoulSingers were rare and much sought after, and SoulBreathers, those who could manipulate souls back into a body, were extinct.

As she left the stables, her thoughts drifted back to Eidolon, the shadowy land across the divide.

Solanji couldn't help the flash of fear that caught her breath. Her friend, Sal, had been accused and sentenced for stealing. Sal had been arrested, soul-stripped, and shipped out so fast, Solanji hadn't had a chance to speak to her. Only to see the terror in her beautiful brown eyes as they'd carted her off to Eidolon. It was a one-way trip once you were stripped of your soul; a life sentence with no hope of parole. Solanji had never seen her again. She had never managed to find her in the expanse of Eidolon on the rare occasions she had travelled there.

Pausing at a junction, Solanji glanced around the square. Spotting Matti sitting on the steps of a fountain, which had stone cherubs cavorting in the spray, she hurried over. The sultry air was cooled by the fine mist spouting out of the cherub's mouth, which was why, Solanji thought, Matti sat there. The elderly woman was dressed in ill-fitting silk robes, which revealed too much sagging skin and gave her a desolate air. If the guards from the Heavenly Host came by, they would move her on or arrest her for loitering.

"Matti, you can't stay here," Solanji whispered as she slipped a coin in her gnarled fingers. "Go find a café and a nice cool drink."

Rising, Matti gave a short laugh. "There's no law against sitting in the sun," she replied as she shuffled off towards her favourite inn. Solanji watched her leave and sighed. Once you lost your youth and vigour and there was no longer a demand for your services, there were few establishments prepared to take on one such as Matti. Jolee tried to keep an eye on her, but Matti was stubborn about accepting offers of help.

Solanji's thoughts drifted back to her own problems as Matti disappeared through the open door. If she didn't need the money so bad, she might have let the job go. But it wasn't cheap to live in Puronia, and her family relied on the money she sent them. Her brother may say they didn't need it, but she knew better. There was no way she was going to let them slide into debt. Not with the Justicers so quick to judge.

Arriving at the Strutting Peacock, Solanji made her way around to the trade entrance. She did not want to be confused with a paying customer, even if she did have enough coin for a leisurely tryst with one of Jolee's very skilful employees. A tempting thought, but she didn't have time to waste, and her money would be better spent elsewhere.

Relaxing in a dusky-rose velveteen upholstered chair, Solanji considered how much to tell Jolee. She often acted like her mother; an unspoken need to treat those younger than her as unschooled children, or more likely the innate commander who moved her employees around like troops. Considering Jolee wasn't that much older than Solanji, it was quite a liberty, but seeing as Jolee was the only person, other than the Fixer, to have ever taken an interest in her, Solanji didn't complain.

The swish of silks preceded the Madam of the establishment into the ante chamber, and Solanji rose. Jolee was diminutive in stature, but large in personality, and she filled the room. "Solanji, my dearest girl, where have you been?"

"Working," Solanji replied as she submitted to being kissed on both cheeks.

"Bah! Work. I told you, I could place you here no bother. You have such a stunning figure and an exquisite complexion. I'd have clients falling over themselves to get to you, and those leathers would drive men and women wild. Such a waste. You'd be highly paid, my dear, and very popular." She studied Solanji. "And you'd be much safer," she said.

"Safer from what?"

"Whatever terrible deeds you have been doing, my dear. The streets are not as safe as they once were. You need to be more careful."

"There is no need to worry; I can look after myself. Could you keep an eye on my room for me? I'm going out of town for a while."

"You're not crossing the divide again? Solanji, I told you, it's not safe. It's even more dangerous on the other side."

"Who said anything about crossing? I am going to visit my family in Bruatra."

Jolee tapped Solanji's smooth, brown cheek with a slender white finger. "Don't lie to me, child."

Solanji raised an eyebrow. "Lie? Me?"

Chuckling, Jolee sat in one of the opulent chairs, her fingers tracing the gilt accents. "Child, you do nothing but lie. It's time you accept who you are and stop hiding. You would be much happier and richer," she added. "Your empathy skills would raise your price; you know what a client wants before they do."

Solanji snorted. What would Jolee know? She deeply regretted her short month at the Peacock. Indulging herself in all that soulmist had almost overloaded her senses and given her away. So many heady sensations had overridden her control, her diffidence, and she had nearly been caught planting suggestions. She had certainly been riding on a high for weeks. "Will you feed the calmers for me?"

Jolee waved a hand. "Of course I will. Bring them over tonight." She leaned forward, her bright blue eyes sparkling. "Have you heard? There is to be a new ascendency. A new archdeus is to be named as Archdeus Demavrian has not been found."

"They are eager to replace him, aren't they?"

"But it's not been proven that he is dead." Jolee's voice dropped to a whisper as if just saying the words were blasphemous.

"I've always thought that was strange. Wouldn't our god know if he's embraced his son on his final journey?"

"The scriptors say Demavrian has fallen beyond redemption. There is no way back for him."

"How would they know? Do you believe everything those tattlers say?"

"The word is that Archdeus Amaridin suggested it. He has announced that unless Archdeus Demavrian returns to his seat in the citadel by year end, he will be confirmed fallen and no longer eligible to ascend." Jolee's voice was hushed. "Such a decree has never been made before."

A chill stole down Solanji's back. "Who is making the challenge?" she asked, her voice just as low.

"The money is on Golaran. He has been waiting."

Solanji curled her lip in disdain. "He can keep on waiting. Veradeus will intervene; it is his word that confirms or denies, not those who inveigle above their station."

"Solanji, hush!" Jolee's eyes were wide. "Do not say such things; someone will hear you."

"In perfect Puronia? Someone will be listening at our door?"

Jolee's gaze flitted around the room. "It is said that the seraphim can hear every conversation."

"That is a scaremongering tale to keep the populace under control. It is quite obvious that it is not true, else the underbelly would be riven by now. Instead, it is flourishing. If the archdeus were so wonderful, we wouldn't *need* an underbelly, now would we?"

Jolee sighed. "The world is changing, Solanji. Don't get caught in their machinations."

Solanji laughed. "Me? What does any of it have to do with me?"

"Nothing. I'm just telling you to keep it that way."

Eyes widening, Solanji sat back in her chair. Jolee was serious. Did she know? Could she have some inkling of Solanji's...differences? "I promise, I will keep out of their way," she said slowly.

Jolee gave her a sharp nod. "Good. Make sure you do."

Leaving the opulent Strutting Peacock and returning through the city streets to her room above a busy laundry, Solanji opened her door and frowned at the folded piece of paper on the floor. She snatched it up and, recognising her mother's handwriting, quickly read it. Her stomach plummeted as she read it again. Her brother had done what? Her legs gave way as she collapsed to the floor. Her younger brother had been caught stealing and sent to the Justicers? She didn't believe it. Why? She sent more than enough money home.

Squeezing her eyes shut, she opened them again and read the letter a third time, hoping it would say something different. Her mother expected her to go to the Justicers and plead for her brother's life. To offer to pay a fine, to indenture him into the citadel, to offer anything to get her brother back.

Crumpling the letter up, she glanced around the empty space she called home and sifted through the conversations she'd had with the Fixer and Jolee. Both had been concerned for her, if for different reasons. It looked like they had been right.

Tossing the letter aside, she rushed back down the stairs and ran through the city streets to the Justicer's office set into the base of the citadel walls. How long had it taken for her mother's letter to arrive? Had Bren arrived in Puronia? Had he already been sentenced?

Her stomach was heavy as she joined the queue, and as she jiggled from foot to foot, she slowly progressed into the building. By the time she stood in front of the person in the booth, her limbs were trembling and her brain was almost incapacitated by fear.

"Yes?" the bored clerk asked, not bothering to look up.

"I'm looking for news of my brother, Brennan of Bruatra. Caught s-stealing. I need to know if he is here and what I need to do to get him released."

"Stealing, you say? He will be sentenced to Eidolon."

"But he's only nine. He won't survive on his own. Can you tell me if he is here?"

"We do not give out that information."

"But I'm his sister. I'm family."

"Makes no difference."

"I'll do anything you want. Tell me what it will take for me to return him to his mother's arms. Please. He's just a child."

"He should have known better than to steal, then, shouldn't he?" the clerk said, her gaze already moving on to the next in line.

"No, that can't be it! What if it was your son, your

brother? Would you let him be abandoned? Please, there must be something I can do. My name is Solanji. I live here in Puronia. I'll pay his fine, help work off his debt. Anything." In desperation, Solanji lowered her voice. "Please. I'll do anything, just don't send him to Eidolon alone."

"Anything, you say?" a man said, and a shiver ran down Solanji's spine as she recognised the voice. Raising her eyes, she met the cold blue eyes of the seraphim she had collided with in the city.

4

SOLANJI

Stiffening, Solanji stared at the angel. For such a beautiful man, he had the coldest eyes. Chips of blue ice, which pierced her body and inspected every inch of her. The angel gestured to the side, and Solanji followed as the clerk called for the next person.

"I have need of one such as you."

The words filled her mind: *such as her.* The way he said it, with such derision, made her skin crawl. He detested those who could touch souls. If that was so, then why speak to her?

"Perform a task for me and I'll ensure your brother is released."

Solanji's heart leapt, but then common sense doused her sudden flash of hope and she observed the angel with growing suspicion. If he knew who she was and what she could do, then he should report her to the Justicers. Stomach fluttering, she asked, "What task?"

"I have need of your skills," his lips tightened, "for a guest of mine. You will meet me in Eidolon at the inn on the crossroads in three days."

"To do what?"

"I'll tell you later." His smile was predatory as he watched her, and she knew she didn't have a choice. Perform some unknown task or let her brother be abandoned in Eidolon.

"How do I know you will release my brother?"

The man stiffened as if she had insulted him. "I am seraphim. My word is heeded."

"I want to see my brother."

The seraphim shrugged. "He hasn't arrived yet. Today's delivery has been delayed." His gaze leisurely ran over her as if he was talking about a delivery of milk. "You did say you would do *anything.*" Gaze was too polite a word, leer might be a better description, Solanji thought as she gritted her teeth.

"I want your written assurance that he will be released if I complete your…task," Solanji said, trying to keep the bite out of her voice.

"My word is sufficient. There will be no written docket. You will perform my task or I will not only ensure your brother is cast out into the most barren part of Eidolon, but I will also report you to the Justicers as an undeclared SoulSucker."

Solanji held the man's eyes as a vice tightened around her chest, but she had no choice. She didn't know who he was, but he knew who she was, and it wouldn't be hard for him to find her. "Three days," she snapped. "At the crossroads."

The man's smile followed her out of the office, and she cursed under her breath every step of the way. His eyes bored into her back, and she wanted to throw her dagger at him, just to wipe that smarmy smile off his face.

Scowling, Solanji slumped in the only chair in her room; why furnish a room when she was the only one who used it? Shivering, she rubbed her arms as a cold chill settled in her stomach and worked its way through her bones. Her gaze fell on the sketch of her brothers, and she snatched it up. They looked so alike. Brennan, a miniature version of Georgi, with his thick black hair and round face. Solanji smoothed a trembling finger over the image of her younger brother. He looked so sweet and innocent. There was no way he had been stealing. She didn't believe it.

She tried to ignore the sense of helplessness that threatened to overwhelm her, but it was impossible. Stomach churning, she held her head in her hands. The journey to the citadel must have been terrifying, and where were they holding him now? He would be all alone, and he wouldn't know she was trying to help him. Her mother would be distraught, frantic.

Anger shook her. That the Justicers would act so inhumanely to a little boy. How could they? It was all so unnecessary, and now she was in this angel's clutches, and it was doubtful he would ever let her go. She closed her eyes and massaged her temples. Her head was going to explode.

That seraphim expected her to meet him at the crossroads in Eidolon and perform an unknown task that could get her into even more trouble. Nothing about this whole situation felt right. At least she could still do the Fixer's job and then meet the seraphim. The need to move was a physical pain, and she was wasting time. The sooner she left, the sooner she could save her brother.

Decision made, she moved swiftly and efficiently, bagging up the few things she would take. A quick glance at the room confirmed its impersonal nature. She had never even changed the colour of the walls. She ruthlessly thrust away the longing to have somewhere she could call home, even if she had invested in those sleek, star-shaped creatures, which slowly undulated through the water in a continuous ripple of mesmerising sparkles.

She peered at them through the glass bowl, nose to nose with the largest calmer, who approached her. It rippled, and Solanji smiled. "I have to go away for a while. Jolee will look after you for me." The other calmers came up to the glass, and then they all turned away at the same time in a flash of brilliant colour. She grimaced and rose. "You'll be fine," she said, more to reassure herself than the calmers.

Having dropped the calmers off with Jolee, Solanji hurried down the street towards the city walls. Near the gates there were a variety of shops and market stalls, eateries, and inns. All jumbled together, striped awnings shielding the customers from the unrelenting glare and offered a treasure trove of goodies, all laid out to persuade the visitors to part with their money.

A mile down the road, the market stalls petered out and the small shops and eateries offered much less tempting wares, rubbing shoulders with dark warehouses and empty fronted shops, boarded up against curious eyes. Not that many people bothered to walk these streets, unless you were on the more desperate end of the citizenship. The end that was ignored and hidden, unacknowledged, housing those who clung to their souls and little else. Those prepared to break the rules in the hope of some coin and a brief relief from the unending grind of poverty. The poverty that the citadel refused to acknowledge even existed.

Solanji tugged her cloak tighter and narrowed her eyes as her gaze swept the silent street. She flipped the token the Fixer had given her, over and over between her fingers. She gripped a dagger in her other hand, concealed under her cloak. After another quick glance over her shoulder, she slipped down a shadowy passageway that shouldn't exist in sunny Puronia. The passage was cool and damp. Tendrils of leafy vines trailed from above her and snagged in her hair, making her curse as she untangled it before following the path down. She passed grubby windows, dank and dark buildings, and grey stone walls and continued into darker shadows until she reached a solid wooden door, in much better repair than the building surrounding it.

A small sign jutted out from the wall; a black cat sat next to a candlestick. She pushed open the door, and her gaze flicked around the room, taking in the tables and cabinets of curios, bits and pieces once precious to someone and now discarded in a jumbled heap.

Carefully shuffling between the randomly placed furniture, she curled her fingers tight around the token and dagger to prevent herself from touching anything. If she did, she would have to buy it, and the price would be more than she could afford. She knew that without asking. This was the last place she would ever be tempted to shop in.

The owner, Faythe, was normally lurking at the back of the shop, waiting to force some unsuspecting soul to buy something. You didn't enter the Curio without the intention of buying something. Solanji was sure Faythe made it so, no doubt charming the items to glisten and tempt, to make sure you parted with your money. Her eye caught a flash in one of the cabinets, and she steeled herself not to look. *Keep moving*, she told herself, eyes on the patterned carpet.

"Not so quick, my sweet," a soft voice spoke from the shadows, and Solanji's heart sank.

"I'm just passing through, Faythe," Solanji said, flashing her token. It should give her free passage.

"I see a disturbance around you, my sweet. You upset the balance, and my treasures speak to me," the woman continued as if she hadn't spoken. She stepped out of the shadows and into the dim lamplight. "Especially one of them." She winced. "Actually, it is roaring at me."

Faythe was a tall woman, with a voluptuous body draped in silk robes. Even her head was wrapped in silken scarves, not a hair in sight. Her long face was a deep brown, darker than Solanji's and much more wrinkled. Black, beady eyes observed her.

Solanji remained silent.

"It is insistent that you are its rightful owner. Now, why would that be?" Faythe asked, a purr in her voice as she approached.

"I don't know," Solanji replied. "Do your treasures often talk to you?"

"From time to time."

Shrugging, Solanji held up her token again. "I am not here to buy; I am just passing through."

"Ah, but you see, they don't work like that."

"Who doesn't?"

Faythe smiled, revealing pearly white teeth. "The gods."

"I have no idea what you are talking about," Solanji admitted, warily.

"The gods," Faythe said, raising her arms. Her sleeves slid back to her elbows, displaying black inked tattoos that swirled across her skin in intricate patterns. "The gods," she repeated, deepening her voice, "have decided."

Solanji drifted back towards the door. "Decided what?" she asked.

"The players, of course. They have been waiting for you. The set is now complete."

"What set? I don't know what you are talking about."

Faythe's eyes blazed, and she pointed. "You will choose." Golden soulmist flared around her, spiralling up into the air and then arching back down towards her.

"Choose what?"

"Your decision will be final, so say the gods." The light dimmed in her eyes and she stared at Solanji, her chest heaving. She slowly pointed at a glass-fronted cabinet. "Take it, it is yours."

Solanji followed her finger and caught her breath as ruby red eyes flared, and she was ensnared. She stepped forward and placed her hand on the door, before common sense reared its head. "What is the cost?"

Faythe grinned. "The choice you make will be payment. Choose well," she said, "our future depends on it."

Solanji opened the cabinet door; it was stiff, and the hinges screeched as she forced it open. A golden ring gleamed, a sinuous dragon with sparkling ruby eyes engraved on the flat surface.

"I cannot afford such a piece," she whispered, unable to look away.

"The price is already paid," Faythe said from behind her shoulder. "Take it. It is calling you."

"I don't hear it," Solanji replied, reaching for it. Golden soulmist swirled around her, enveloping her, encouraging her. Her fingers clasped the gold band, and a blinding flash whited out her vision. She froze as a large marble walled room coalesced around her, a woman lying on the steps, bright red blood staining her golden robes and the marble floor, a dark-haired man leaning over her, clasping her in his arms.

"Go…" the woman whispered, and Solanji shivered at the anguish in her voice.

"I can't leave you here like this," the man replied, his soulmist swirling in agitation.

"You must. I n-need…" her voice faltered, and she struggled for breath.

"Who did this to you?"

"Go…g-go…" Her fingers trailed through his brilliant soulmist.

The man cried out, "Athenia, no!"

"I-I must. I am sorry. You will s-see…" She spooled his soulmist in, and her voice strengthened as she stole his soul. "You must…" She gasped again, her face paling. "For me and for you…" Her eyes glazed as she cupped his cheek. The ring on her finger flared, ruby eyes blazing, and drew his soulmist within.

"Go…" she whispered. "G-go…"

He keened as he bent over her, his handsome face distraught, a red stone pendant dangling from his throat. A Vendetta stone. The vision faded as guards rushed into the room.

Solanji stepped back with a gasp. The ring shimmered, the ruby eyes watching her, and then it dissolved into golden mist and slithered over her wrist and up under her sleeve. Solanji slid her sleeve up her arm and stared at the golden tattoo bound around her forearm. The gold ink gleamed, and the red eyes flared before the dragon settled, watching.

"W-what?" Solanji shook her arm as if she could flick the tattoo off and then rubbed her fingers over the image. It was raised and hot to the touch. Her fingers tingled, responding to the soulmist within it. Her mother was going to kill her. A tattoo?

"See, it was waiting for you," Faythe said, tapping her thin lips with a bony, brown finger. "Why you?" she asked, her eyes sharp, a frown on her face as she observed Solanji.

Solanji turned to her, eyes wild, breath short and gasping. "What just happened?"

"What the gods ordained. It is time you left. You've a crossing to make, haven't you?"

"But, but…" Solanji couldn't form the words.

Faythe patted her shoulder. "Let it settle. You'll come to understand what you need to do in time."

"What?" Solanji's voice cracked in horror.

Faythe laughed and led her towards a small wooden door,

about half Solanji's height, but with a pointed arch at the top, which meant she wouldn't have to bend too far down to pass through. A symbol about the length of her hand was burnt onto the wood. A blurry image of a cat staring up to the sky. Beneath it was a circular hole, the size of her token. Solanji slotted the token in the space, still in a daze, and there was a resounding click. The door slowly began to swing open, and velvety darkness greeted her. Taking a deep breath, she stepped through the doorway. This was her second visit. There would be no flame, no candle. Only shadows to greet her.

The dark pressed in on her, and she shuddered. Walking forward, the sound of a spinning coin echoed around her, and she held her hand out. Her token dropped into her palm, and a soft, damp breeze blew across her right cheek. As she turned towards it, the door closed behind her. She followed the corridor, balancing herself against the rough wall as she tripped on a wooden ridge, a warning that she was about to descend the stairway leading her under the divide.

A dull glow grew, illuminating the never-ending view of stone steps that led down into more shadows. She began descending, her mind spinning, grappling with the vision of the woman lying on the marble steps and the man hovering over her.

Who were they? And why had the woman taken his soul when she was obviously dying? Had she been a SoulSinger? She didn't know.

Hours later, her thighs aching from the steep descent, the bottom of her feet burning, her fingernails scratched and bloody, she stumbled into another dead end blocking her way. "Never again," she muttered under breath. "I don't care how much money is offered, never again." Scrabbling around her, she found the gap and proceeded down yet another passageway. This tunnel began to slope up, and she breathed a sigh of relief to be finally ascending out of this dank, hellish hole.

As Solanji climbed, her thoughts drifted back to the conundrum of Faythe's shop. Situated in shadows that should not exist, it concealed the entrance to a secret passage that led under the divide. The only reason Solanji knew about it was because of another job the Fixer had hired her for. She wondered who the Fixer was to know such things. And if the gods were involved, maybe this should be the last time she accepted a job from him. She supposed she shouldn't be so surprised. It would have taken a god to cut this tunnel in the first place. No man could have hewn through so much stone for so long without the tunnel collapsing.

At the thought, Solanji peered around her. The air was stifling, and the rock crowded in on her, though she couldn't see it. The sheer weight of all the stone above her was suddenly oppressive.

Tripping over a coarse rope, which ran down the middle of the tunnel, Solanji grabbed it in relief and began to climb up the steep steps, leaning back slightly as the rope took the strain and led her up, out of the ground. She licked her parched lips, breathing heavily as she rested for a moment. The passage was getting steeper, and she was glad of the rope, even if her hands were burning. It was better than crawling on her hands and knees.

Resuming her climb, she looked up as a stronger waft of air flowed through the tunnel. Fresh, clean air. Not dank and damp like she had been breathing for the last however many hours. A renewed sense of purpose rushed through her, and she sped up. The breeze strengthened into a powerful swirl of wind the closer she came to the exit. A dull glow lit the end of the tunnel, growing larger as she approached. It coalesced into an echoey cavern, empty but for a wooden barrel and a bucket with a ladle beside it. Exactly the same as the last time she had used the crossing. Her booted footsteps echoed as she stumbled forward and collapsed to her knees by the barrel. Scooping out a ladle of water, she drank deep. The liquid slid down her throat and through her innards like a piece of ice through red hot flame, a brief and precious flash of refreshing coolness before it was gone.

It did the trick though, revitalising her enough as she dipped her hands in the bucket and let her burning palms cool. Rubbing damp hands over her face, she finally turned to the exit. A muffled snort made her freeze, and her heart rate spiked as she fumbled for her dagger. There should not be anyone else in the vicinity. Her token was supposed to guarantee safe passage.

Breath hitching, she flattened herself against the cavern wall and slowly inched her way forward. Peering around the corner, she came face to face with gleaming black eyes, and she swore as she stumbled back in shock.

5

MAV
EIDOLON

Burning hot flames flashed through him, and Mav nearly lost it, the edge of pain an exquisite reminder that he still lived, that he wasn't dead, no matter how many times they tried to tell him he was. He bled, a lot, and it still surprised him that he had any blood left to lose after all this time. Time was immaterial. All he knew was that Julius had betrayed him, and now…now he was in his own personal hell. Chains bit into his wrists, the warmth of his blood running down his skin a reminder that he wasn't finished yet. He didn't know how long he had been trapped in this purgatory; he only knew it was too long. He wished for the soothing shadows of oblivion. His burning back, shredded repeatedly, drained his ability to heal, but he did heal, just enough so that they could whip him again.

He coiled tighter, gripping his faltering determination; they wouldn't break him. Shielding that last spark of divinity which they sought, he clung to the shreds, forcing it deeper, hiding it in the shadows that swirled around him. They had already taken his freedom; let that be enough.

Piercing white-hot agony almost made him relent. Almost.

His right knee shattered as the spear penetrated through his skin and bone and into the rock, pinning him to his prison. More blood rushed out, pooling around him and painting the stone floor red. His wings flared as the pain consumed him and they went up in flames. The pure white feathers, an iridescent gleam in the dim cavern, curling and writhing as the greedy flames spread, destroying the last shred of what he used to be.

Leaving him teetering on the edge until he embraced what he had become.

He was no more.

The flames banked and died in his core, sealing the remnants of a tiny spark, hidden and secure.

Too many times they had flayed him to near death.

Too many times his wings had gone up in flames.

They had laughed.

No more.

6

SOLANJI

EIDOLON

Solanji exhaled, berating herself for imagining monsters. A calope waited, patiently tied to an iron ring in the outer cavern wall. He shifted, his brown hide dappled by the shadows, the gleam of his eyes giving him away. The animal snorted again as he scuffed his foot in the scattered straw beneath him. Another calope snoozed in the stall next to him. The other bays were all empty, the animals already hired out. She had forgotten the tunnel came out in the back of a hostelry located at the base of the escarpment, two days ride south of the official crossing. She had paid extra to have a mount waiting for her in the hostelry.

Striving to still her thrumming heart, she rested her hand against the forehead of the nearest animal and relaxed at the gentle vibration that ran through her. "Stupid, that's what I am," she murmured into his skin. Straightening, she searched the cavern, empty but for the calopes and a sack of feed. Tying the bag to the saddle and then filling the water-skin from the barrel, she hesitated, debating for a moment.

There was no 'night' as such in Eidolon. It stayed the

same, day and night, always shrouded in gloom and shadow. No sunlight broke the monotony. Therefore, it was difficult to tell what time of day it was. What she did know was that the quicker she reached the crossroads and delivered her package, met the angel, and completed his task, the sooner she could return to Puronia and her brother.

It would take at least two days to reach the crossroads. Two days of travelling through the most populated part of Eidolon. Populated with the dregs of Puronia, those who had been banished and not yet found their footing in their new world. Those who would be desperate and ruthless. After all, they had already lost everything. What more was there to lose?

There was safety in numbers. Solanji needed to join up with a wagon train as soon as possible. If she joined the Crossing Road, she could travel with others who had crossed legitimately. Leading the calope out of the dim stable, she flashed her token at the man waiting by the door. His grizzled face was lined and wrinkled, but his hooded eyes were sharp, and he nodded, allowing her to pass without question. Mounting her calope, she wriggled in the saddle to get more comfortable and unfolded her map on the cantle.

Squinting at the faint squiggles in the gloom, she calculated she was probably at least a league from the nearest main road. Within a few hours, she should reach safer roads, if they could be called such. Folding the map, she tucked it away and urged the calope north.

Dreary fields passed either side of her. Grey and dull in the persistent gloom. Rain fell, a gentle sift of fine droplets penetrating her cloak after a few miles. Her hair frizzed in the damp air, and she tugged her hood forward as she wiped her face. Wooden huts, dilapidated and sad, lined the road. Filthy children squatted in the doorways, and she urged her mount on, avoiding their empty eyes. She wished she could give them some money, but she couldn't afford to draw any attention.

Once a person lost their soul and was banished to Eidolon, there was no return to sunny Angelicus. They were destined to live under the oppressive clouds forever until they died, and begged their way past the Gate Keeper, Kaenera, and through the Oblivion Gate.

Scowling around her, she fingered her knife as she wondered why the people stayed here. If Eidolon was so big, wouldn't it be better to leave and find a piece of land just for them? Somewhere they could start a new life? Away from the daily reminders of what they had lost as merchants and travellers ventured into Eidolon to exploit anything they could from these desperate people.

Why had she ever agreed to come here? She was mad, taking such a risk. Jolee was right; she should find a safer profession. If she survived this trip, maybe she would take up Jolee's offer? Maybe. The thought made her heart quail as much as the sight of the surrounding squalor.

Three halos. The job was worth three halos. Enough money that her brother could be apprenticed to a boat to keep him out of further trouble. She could spend time with her mother and have some to spare. She breathed a sigh of relief as the junction with the Crossing Road came into view, and she turned onto it, hurrying to catch the end of a wagon train. Her breath plumed in the air as she exhaled, relaxing her tight muscles as she moved up the wagon train to the group of riders in the centre.

There were five men, hooded and cloaked against the rain. One of the men was grumbling a constant stream of complaints directed at the slighter rider beside him.

"It is not my fault, sir. I booked everything as instructed," the slight young man replied.

"Excuses. If you weren't the son of…well…you'd be out of a job by now. I do not ride through Eidolon."

"If you had been on time, sir, there would have *been* no need to ride."

"I was unavoidably detained."

"The dragonair couldn't wait. They have a schedule to keep, sir."

Solanji jerked upright, recognising the voice. It was the seraphim she was supposed to meet at the crossing. How did he rate a dragonair? The only dragonair in Puronia was bound to the citadel; a dragon and its rider, a magical beast only commanded by the gods. They were creatures of myth and legend that only answered to a god's purpose, and there was only one god, though he had two children who spoke in his name. Well, one, as the other was fallen. Who was this angel to be eligible for a seat on such a beast? And he had missed it? Her lip curled. What an arrogant fool.

"Did you not tell them who I am?" the man demanded, quivering with resentment.

"Yes, sir. The captain said she didn't care if you were Demavrian Deusson himself. She wasn't waiting."

There was a stark silence.

"She said who?" the man demanded, his voice sharp as a blade.

"D-Demavrian Deusson," his companion stuttered, flinching away from the angry man. "You know, that fallen angel; the one cast out for murder. They whisper he roams Eidolon, not having anywhere else to go."

"He's dead."

"That is just a rumour, sir. No one has been able to prove it."

"His name is blasphemy. It should be banished, as is he. Don't ever mention him again."

"No, sir."

A wave of hatred flowed through Solanji, and she gasped. Flashes of satisfaction and cruelty, tinged with pleasure, followed swiftly, along with the vision of a man hanging in chains, whipped bloody and raw.

The image was gone just as quick, and she hunched low in her saddle, dropping back to avoid the golden trails of soulmist following the seraphim riding in front of her. She had accidentally ridden through them in her haste, though to be honest, it was unavoidable, the way they trailed loosely after him. It was too late, and the angel stiffened, whipping around to stare at the other riders.

He was the beautiful angel from the Justicers. Golden curls framed a soft, round face. Hard, sky-blue eyes searched the faces of the other riders and landed on her. A cruel, satisfied smile curved his lips and then he turned forward, ignoring her. His muscles rippled beneath his fine cloak as he turned, promising an equally beautiful body.

Solanji exhaled in relief, her heart beating rapidly. Angels, Solanji mused, didn't often travel. They'd rarely leave the citadel, let alone ride into Eidolon. Where was he going that a dragon would have taken him? And why did an angel, even a lesser angel, have images of a tortured man in his thoughts? They were supposed to be good and pure, yet this angel had horrible memories.

Solanji shuddered, trying to banish the searing image hanging in front of her eyes. The tang of blood flooded her mouth, and she swallowed, forcing the rising bile back down. She fumbled for her water skin and took a gulp, clearing the taste from her mouth, and she sighed in relief as the image faded.

She rubbed her fingers over her new tattoo as the gleam of golden ink caught her eye. How she would ever explain that away, she didn't know. Rolling down her sleeve, she covered it up. Better no one saw it. Less questions that way.

Taking care to avoid the angel, Solanji joined one of the camp fires when the wagon train finally stopped for the night. She offered fresh bread and slices of seasoned pigley to the fare of vegetable soup and potato cakes, happy to share. The cook, a grizzled man of middle age, fell on the meat and diced it up, adding it to the soup.

"Just what it needed, lass. A bit of seasoning."

Solanji smiled and spread her blanket on a dry piece of tarpaulin that had been laid around the fire. The ground was soft under foot, and it hadn't taken much for hooves and wheels to churn it up, but at least it had stopped raining.

Being in Eidolon was good and bad. Good because few people had souls and she wasn't tempted to trawl her fingers through a stranger's soulmist, and bad because it was like having withdrawal symptoms and she yearned to touch the soulmist of anyone she saw possessing it.

In the short time she had worked at Jolee's, she had once accidentally taken a man's soul. It had been so luxuriating, heightening her senses as she'd brought the man to his climax. Surrounded in golden soulmist, she had coaxed and caressed and pulled it into herself without realising what she was doing. The man had stiffened, a glazed expression replacing the former ecstasy on his face, and she realised what she had done. In a panic, she had pushed the soul back into him, no idea if she had returned it correctly, but she had unentangled herself and soothed him to sleep.

Two hours she had waited for him to wake, pacing the room in terror. What if he hadn't woken up? What if the soul hadn't returned to him? What if he knew what she had done? As soon as he woke, remembering only the bliss, she had left the room, unable to be anywhere near him. After that, she had refused to work for Jolee again, and it had taken months for her to be able to touch soulmist again. Even then, it hadn't been deliberate, and now she tried to avoid it, only trailing her fingers through the edges when she could no longer resist it. It wasn't worth the risk of being exposed, nor the risk of her condemning someone to death. If she took their soul and they remained in Angelicus for more than one day, they would die, and there was no way she could confess what she had done.

Just the memory made her go icy cold, and she shivered. She was not only a SoulSinger, able to take souls, but she was able to return them, even if she wasn't quite sure how she'd done it. Thanks be to the god, Veradeus, she'd been able to give the soul back. She had no intention of ever taking one again, and yet the soulmist called to her, a need to touch that never ceased to torment her.

She eyed a man and a woman who were surrounded in scintillating soulmist, fortunately seated at a distance from her on the other side of the fire. The young man settling on a rug was long and lean with a youthful face framed with soft, blond curls. He spoke to a much larger woman who was travelling with him. She had thick, muscular arms and thighs and yet moved with a silent grace. *Someone trained to fight,* Solanji thought as she discreetly observed them. Catching the odd word, it sounded like the young man was complaining about sleeping rough, and Solanji smirked as the woman's hard voice cut off his complaints and recommended he make the best of it.

"How far do you travel?" Solanji asked the cook as she made herself comfortable.

"We turn south at the crossroads, heading down to Merapol."

"Merapol?"

"Yeah, town down on the southern coast. We have a regular trading route and carry messages," the cook said as he stirred his pot. "That is the saddest part of this world, I think. Splitting up families."

"Do you have people in Merapol?" Solanji asked, hearing the pain in his voice. She thought of her family in Bruatra, they could soon be in a similar position if she couldn't save Bren.

His lips tightened and then he glanced at her from under bushy brown eyebrows. "Where is a young lass like yourself going?"

"Just to the crossroads, no further."

"Travelling alone?"

There was a wealth of questions in those two words, and Solanji ignored them. "At the moment. My brother was supposed to escort me, but he is late. Hopefully, he will catch up tomorrow."

"Not much of an escort," another wagon driver growled as he passed her a mug.

Solanji sniffed it and then sipped, smiling as the warmth of the bannoe spread. "Brothers can be a little unreliable," she agreed, and the men laughed.

The man and woman opposite her paid them no attention, though they did stiffen when they saw the seraphim settling himself at another camp fire, his strident voice carrying on the air. After a low, hurried conversation, the young man glanced around him and then rose. He pressed his hand on the woman's shoulder and shook his head, and then he disappeared into the shadows. The large woman stared after him, a frown on her face, and then as if aware of Solanji watching, she smoothed her expression and met her gaze.

Solanji immediately dropped her eyes, shocked at the woman's penetrating glare. She spent the rest of the evening focussing on her food and listening to the men chat.

After a tasty bowl of soup, Solanji snuggled down in her blanket, relieved the men hadn't pressed her further. They had accepted her explanation a little too easily, but she supposed it made no difference to them. The young man didn't return and the larger woman settled down on her blanket, though her gaze often rested on the seraphim across the camp when she wasn't watching Solanji. Uncomfortable with those sharp eyes on her, Solanji stayed awake as long as she could, her dagger gripped tight in her hand, but she eventually fell asleep to the deep voices surrounding her.

The next morning, when Solanji awoke, the large woman and, Solanji assumed, her young companion, had already left. Solanji reluctantly remounted her calope, her aching bottom protesting after a day in the saddle. She hadn't had the chance to ride for ages, and she was out of practice.

Sten, the cook from the previous evening, had offered her a seat in the wagon, but Solanji hadn't wanted to spend a whole day talking to him. He was too perceptive. Lagging behind, Solanji followed the wagons, curling her fingers tight and avoiding the other riders. Their golden soulmist beckoned and tantalised, but Solanji ignored it as she huddled in her saddle. The damp day was depressing. Why anyone *wanted* to travel into Eidolon was beyond her.

The mis-matched couple were nowhere to be seen, and Solanji was relieved not to be at the receiving end of those penetrating stares.

As Solanji thought she might finally fall out of her saddle, a shout came from ahead, and word was passed down the wagon train that the crossroads were near. Solanji sat upright and peered over her calope's head. Wagons were beginning to speed up at the thought of a comfortable bed for the night, for those who reached the tavern first.

"Don't worry, lass, there will be enough room for all!" Sten shouted over his shoulder as he urged his calopes onwards.

Solanji observed with interest as they approached the crossroads. She had never been this deep into Eidolon before. The wagon rumbled over the low, wooden bridge crossing the wide river. Solanji watched the slow-moving water wending its way south and then drew her gaze back to the crossroads.

The crossroads were just that. The junction of two main roads crossing each other. One running east to west, the other running north to south. An imposing tavern with adjoining stables and barns took up most of the land to the north of the road, and a jumble of hodgepodge stalls and wagons surrounded it. A tent city spread around the edges, of all shapes and sizes. From large white marquees, with colourful pennants flapping in the breeze, to small, pointed tents big enough for two people and no more.

Voices rose, hawking their wares. Aromas of roasted meat and honey mead tainted the air, smoke rising from many individual campfires dotted amongst the tents. It could have been any marketplace in Angelicus, if the sun had been shining.

Wooden corrals held calopes, pigleys, and other livestock. Bartering was in full flow as the owners showed off their animal's paces. Solanji stared around her in amazement, and she reined her calope in next to Sten. "Where do they all come from?"

Sten huffed out a laugh. "Where do you think? Eidolon is no different to Angelicus, really. We're all the same people, lassie. Some are just more fortunate than others."

"But I thought people were banished to Eidolon as punishment for their misdeeds."

"Nay, lass, it was a place of second chances, once," he said, his voice dying in a sigh. "A place to redeem yourself and reclaim your soul. At least, it was supposed to be." Sten stared out over the camp, his face sad. He shook himself and his reins, urging his calopes off the road. "We've arrived," he said with a slow grin.

"So I see," Solanji said as she dismounted. She looked up into his kindly face. "Thank you for your company."

Sten nodded. "You take care now, lass. Second chances are few and far between these days. Don't do anything silly."

"I won't," Solanji replied as she led her calope towards the tavern.

7

FELATHER

EIDOLON

F elather snarled as he followed Eladriz, or Adriz as she preferred to be called, down a muddy road away from the crossroads and the obnoxious seraphim stalking into the tavern. He was over-tired and irritable, a combination that Adriz would not tolerate for very long.

Heaving a deep sigh, he shifted in his saddle and tried to ease the tension trying to strangle his neck. He rolled his head from one side to the other, trying to soothe the ache. He had spent the previous evening up a tree, balanced above the seraphim's campfire and straining to hear every word.

It had been a complete waste of effort. The seraphim had spent the evening complaining to his aide and issuing impossible instructions that the poor man had no chance of completing. The seraphim was a whiny, spoilt, sack of shit, and Felather wanted to punch him in the face.

Years of searching had worn him down, and now they were running out of time. Something he thought he would never have said, seeing he was oathsworn to an archdeus. He was now immortal, along with Eladriz and Ryvalin,

Demavrian's other oathsworn. The only three still loyal and determined to find him.

Demavrian had to be in Eidolon; he just had to be. They had spent the last forty-odd years searching Angelicus and then with some dread began searching the shadowy lands of Eidolon. Methodically combing the villages, the outlying farmsteads, the projects, and the factories.

His gut churned as concern rushed through him. In all that time, they had not found a sign of him, though they had found many other questionable things that they had periodically reported back to the citadel. Although Eidolon was much larger than Angelicus, they should have still found something. Rubbing his chest, he shifted in his saddle again. Demavrian was alive, somewhere, and he needed his oathsworn.

"Stop fidgeting," Adriz growled over her shoulder. "We are not stopping for a least another three hours."

Felather glared at her broad back. The woman was huge, with muscles upon muscles. Her thick arms and legs could break him in half without a thought. She was also as frustrated and distraught as he was, though she hid it better.

Well-worn leather armour moulded to her body, the leather smooth and burnished from use. Her huge sword poked above her head from the sheath on her back. Back straight, she rode on, ignoring his discomfort.

"It was your idea to do it all by yourself," she said for about the fifth time, and Felather rolled his eyes. She was pissed that he had slunk off without her, but Adriz was noticeable wherever she went, whereas he could blend in.

"Kyrill is a bastard. He could have tried to pull rank if he had seen us."

Adriz snorted. "He could have tried."

"And it would have tied us up in unnecessary delays, preventing us from being here," Felather replied, waving his hand at the dreary view. His calope splashed through a puddle, and he winced as the cold water penetrated the material of his trousers. He urged his calope up beside Adriz. "I don't understand how there is no sign of him. Someone must have seen Mav. He is so distinctive."

Adriz shrugged. "Eidolon is huge. Sparsely populated. If he chose, he could avoid people."

"But why would he do that? That makes no sense."

"None of this makes any sense. Why run? He painted himself guilty by running."

Felather ground his teeth. They were repeating a conversation they'd had many times over the years, and they still couldn't answer the questions. They couldn't prove Mav's innocence because no one knew what had happened. The only witness was missing.

He ran his hand through his damp hair, fingers snagging in the tangled curls. He wrenched his hand away, hissing at the pain as he ripped strands of hair out.

Adriz came to a halt and grabbed his arm. "Stop it. Hurting yourself won't help."

Tears smarted in Felather's eyes and he blinked them away, throat tight. "Where is he?" he whispered.

"We'll find him," Adriz said, her voice hard, her grip tightening on Felather's arm. She released him and urged her calope forward.

8

MAV

"Still here? If I had realised you were unable to save yourself, I would have come sooner," a silky-smooth voice murmured next to Mav's ear.

Mav didn't have the energy to react, and he hung motionless in his chains, no longer concerned with the vagaries of angels and dybbuks. They only took and gave nothing back.

The man tutted as he walked around him, a shadow in the darkness. "I can sense your murderous thoughts. Have you finally decided to come and join me, Demavrian? I think I have waited long enough."

Mav ignored him. If Kaenera thought he would ever descend into his destructive, lost cause of a realm, he was mistaken.

"Now don't pass the opportunity by so quickly. I could get you out of here, stop this pain." Kaenera grasped one of the chains, and Mav hissed as his muscles spasmed and the metal links bit into his skin. "I heard you wishing for oblivion, for this to end. You called me here; the least you could do is acknowledge me."

"And you're going to help me out of the goodness of your blackened heart," Mav growled to the floor, panting as sharp spikes of pain flashed through him, bringing him to the edge of absolute awareness. The beat of his heart resonated in his chest and reminded him that he still lived.

"There you are! I knew you were still in there. But you wound me. My heart is not black. No, I am here because I want what's best for you. You suffer for no reason. You know you hover in my doorway. It's time for you to take the step. You know you want to, deep down in your heart. You couldn't stay away. I know you've been visiting. Keeping to the shadows as if no one could see you. I can feel the coils of resentment, of betrayal. It's your destiny, Demavrian. You were always promised to me. Why do you think your father sent you here?"

"No," Mav whispered.

"No one is coming to rescue you. You are a sacrifice. Surely, you've realised that by now? You've trespassed into areas you shouldn't have and paid the price. You suffer for no reason, and you will suffer until you submit…to me. Remember that," Kaenera said, and then his hot tongue licked the blood from Mav's skin, leaving heated breath behind, and Mav shuddered.

"Exquisite," Kaenera breathed. "I am the only one who can save you. There is no one else, so why resist?"

"You lie," Mav ground out. His throat was so dry it came out as a rasp.

Kaenera laughed. "I have no need to lie. I think the evidence hangs before me. What a sorry state you are, and yet, still so beautiful." He ran his hands down Mav's chest and back up again, gripping the back of his neck. "Even your own have cast you out, made you suffer." He bent his shadowed face close and inhaled and then huffed out a laugh in delight. "Demavrian, you hound. How did you keep that quiet? No soul?" Kaenera released him and clapped his hands. "How delightful. I will be waiting to embrace you. But you need one last push, I think."

"Doesn't mean I'm lost."

"Oh, my dear nephew. Of course you are. There is no way back, only down. And you know I'll be waiting for you."

Mav grit his teeth and ignored him. Kaenera stroked his skin again, trailing his fingers over his shoulder, leaving a trail of burning heat, which dispelled the clammy damp that clung to Mav's body. A suggestion of possession.

"So strong, still believes. So much power. You still have far to fall, but at least you know I'll be there, prepared to catch you. There are few others I would make the effort for, but you, you're special. I promise I'll be waiting."

Kaenera's voice faded, and Mav knew he was alone. What had he done to deserve his uncle's regard? Kaenera paid little attention to the people of Eidolon. He didn't care what happened to them, not going by the behaviour of his dybbuks, who ran amok and terrorised the innocent. Kaenera was only interested when the soulless fell into despair and made that final journey into his embrace.

His uncle had once graced the halls of the citadel before his own spectacular fall, centuries ago. Mav barely remembered what he looked like, but that oily voice was ingrained in his memory. An insufferable, overbearing man who had fallen out with Mav's parents and been banished. Mav didn't know what Kaenera had done to deserve such punishment; his father never spoke of it, nor his brother.

Once, Mav had thought Kaenera's interest was in Amaridin, his golden-haired brother, but no; Kaenera had whispered in Mav's ear that they were the same and his place was beside him, not his father. Mav had set out to prove him wrong.

He snorted as he gently rocked. And look where it had

got him. Kaenera was right. He already had one foot through the door. The only place he could go was through the Oblivion Gate. Though it didn't sound like Kaenera planned oblivion for him.

No one knew what was through the Oblivion Gate. No one who entered ever came back. What Kaenera allowed you to see was not what it was. Having searched the shadows for many years, Mav doubted it was anything good. Kaenera didn't instil a feeling of welcome and happiness.

There had to be an alternative. An eternity of torture at the hands of the Oblivion Gatekeeper was not in his plans.

He continued to rock gently. What was his plan then?

9

SOLANJI

Entering the ramshackle building hogging the north corner of the crossroads, Solanji squinted in the dim light of the interior. The inside was as disreputable as the outside, with dark wooden furniture, battered and scratched, scattered around the room. A few tables were occupied by silent men, who watched her suspiciously, but none looked like the description she had been given, so she found a corner table and made herself comfortable. Ordering the daily special and a tankard of cider, she settled in to wait.

Scanning the other occupants, she sighed out her breath at the shifty nature of the clientele. Dissent was in the air; she could feel it. Someone was rooting for trouble, and she hoped she would be able to steer clear of it.

A disturbance by the door made her sit up more alertly as a man entered, flanked by what could only be his aide. The hooded man swept in, raising his head as he sniffed the air and wrinkled his nose. "Are there no nicer inns?" the man asked, turning to his assistant, who scuttled off to the bar. Solanji recognised his voice and silently groaned; she had been hoping to avoid the angel for a bit longer, at least until she had handed over her package. What was he doing in a place like this?

She stiffened when the man sat at a table near her, and she curled her fingers tight to avoid his trailing soulmist. The golden cloud flared around him as if trying to escape, and she leaned back in her chair, reluctant to receive any further images from him.

A server slid her plate of roasted meat and vegetables on the table, followed by the tankard, and she pulled it closer. The aroma wafted past and her mouth watered.

"I'll have what she's got!" the angel snapped.

As Solanji tucked into her food, she wondered if the man was ever happy. For an angel, he seemed to walk under his own storm cloud. She inspected him out of the corner of her eye.

He looked like any other man she had met, though with prettier face and clothes. It was a shame his sunny appearance didn't extend to his disposition. He wasn't a very good advert for angels. Her gaze drifted to the man beside him. He was dressed in a dull grey tunic, which reached his knees and was belted with a maroon cord, the same colour as his trousers. Short brown hair framed a round face, plump and perspiring. Pudgy fingers fidgeted with the tassel from his belt.

Solanji drank her cider, pausing to savour the unexpectedly rich flavour. Peering around the room, she couldn't see her contact. She knew he wasn't in the tavern. Her fingernails tapped a nervous beat on the edge of the table as she considered her next move. Although she preferred not to waste her money on a room for the night, it was probably the safest place for her to sleep. Concern that the angel would expect her to start his task before she completed her delivery rippled through her. She could have another two days to wait.

Golden soulmist wafted past her nose, and she sneezed. A brief image of a blood-spattered stone cavern and a sense of satisfaction flashed through her. Her nerves thrilled at the soulmist's touch, and her fingers inched across the table of their own volition. It was like a drug she couldn't resist, seductive and warming; she wanted to lose herself in its embrace.

The thud of plates on wood made her jerk back, clenching her fingers into a fist. She knocked her cider back and rose, intent on reserving a room. Anything to get away from these people. As she passed the angel, he grabbed her arm, and she flinched as she was assaulted by more images of the torture chamber, crimson blood spreading out over the rocky floor. Her stomach heaved.

"I thought as much," the angel said, tugging her nearer. "You will remain here until I am ready to leave."

Solanji flinched. "And when will that be?"

The angel smirked. "When I'm ready and not before. Sit back down."

She wanted as little to do with him or his soul as possible, but she didn't have the chance to tell him, as a huge, broad-chested man with thick arms entered the inn. He glanced around, spotted Solanji and the angel, and his eyes narrowed. It was the man from the Fixer's picture, Joran.

The angel was oblivious. "Carna, tell her the rules."

His assistant, Carna, sweated some more as he watched the huge man cross the room, but he did begin speaking as instructed, ticking off each point on his finger.

"One. You are hereby honoured to be one of the Seraphim Kyrill's fledglings.

Two. You will not consort with any other angel.

Three. You will not consort with any other fledgling.

Four. You will obey your master without question.

Five..." his voice trailed off as he looked up.

"You have something of mine," the hulking man said. "Release her."

Seraphim Kyrill raised a golden eyebrow. "I doubt that, my good man. Run along now."

"I don't belong to anyone, and I am not one of your fledglings," Solanji said and tried to pull away, but the angel tightened his hold. Heart racing, she faced the two men.

"Better to be a pampered pet than some raggedy stray," Kyrill replied with a sneer.

"Your offer did not sound that welcoming, and I decline." Solanji swayed towards the larger man, still trapped in the angel's grip. "I am no man's pet."

"You can't decline," Carna said, his voice a high-pitched squeak.

"I have and I did. I said I would do a job for you, not sign my life away."

"I have made the claim," Kyrill said as he rose.

"Let go of my arm." Solanji tried to twist free. He was going to break it if he didn't stop. His grip was so tight, she couldn't feel her fingers.

"You can have her once I've concluded my business," the large man said, and Solanji scowled at him.

"If you think this golden ass has any right over me," she spat but was interrupted by the angel again.

"She is soul-touched, and I have claimed her. You have no business with her." Voices rose around them as their growing audience gasped over the angel's words.

Solanji seethed. They were talking over her as if she wasn't even there. She reached for the assistant's golden soul-mist and suggested a sense of urgency, a deadline drawing near.

"S-sir, the dragonair will be waiting for us. We really ought to be leaving," the aide began.

What? Solanji's heart stuttered at the mention of a dragonair. Huge beasts that could eat a man whole. She froze, releasing the soulmist. They still had a ride reserved? She groped for the strands surrounding the hulking giant. *"You have business to complete,"* she breathed.

Joran leaned forward, jutting his chin belligerently. "My business comes first, then you can have her."

Kyrill scowled, the creases marring his beautiful face, and his aide hurried to speak. "We don't have time for a protracted argument, sir. Let them conclude their business and we can be away. You can't afford to miss the dragonair again."

Solanji opened her mouth to assert her non-existent authority when the huge man grabbed her arm and jerked her towards him. She snarled as the angel held on and she was caught between the two of them. "Give me the package," he demanded in a low voice.

"Give me a proof of delivery," Solanji replied, twisting her arm out of the man's grip and sliding her fingers down her leg for her knife. Her heart sped up as she tugged out metal, and she gripped the comforting weapon.

Joran grunted under his breath. "No chance. I don't want my name in his hands."

"Then how do I prove delivery to the Fixer? I won't get payment without it," Solanji protested, feeling her halo windfall being ripped from her fingers. She knew it had been too good to be true.

"You don't want him getting his hands on the package. You'll be worse off if he does. Give it to me."

"Not without payment."

"You stupid bitch! He's running out of patience. Choose. Life or death."

Solanji narrowed her eyes. "Tell me what is in the package."

Joran ground his teeth and cast a worried glance over her shoulder. "A soul," he muttered. "Now give it to me. Don't waste the number of lives it took to get it, please."

Solanji gasped. The man was practically begging.

"Please," he whispered. "The angel will destroy it."

"How do you know he's an angel? Who is he?"

"Seraphim Kyrill. The protégé of Archangel Golaran. Kyrill's an archangel-elect. He's been here before, now give me that package." Joran snatched the package out of her fingers, and Kyrill brought an ornate staff down across the man's arm. The man roared as he clasped his broken arm to his chest and turned on the seraphim as the package skittered across the floor and under the tables.

Taking advantage of Kyrill's distraction, Solanji wrenched out of his grip and dropped to the floor.

"Tch! tch!" Kyrill said. "I wouldn't if I were you." He glanced at the man, a sly smile tugging at his lips. "A soul you say? You sure that's what she carries?"

The man cursed under his breath, a hint of desperation leaking into his expression.

"Retrieve the package," the seraphim said. At his clipped words, the tavern erupted. Men overturned tables, drinks went flying along with their fists as utter chaos reigned, everyone in the tavern desperate to grab the soul for themselves. An opportunity no one would ever have thought possible. Solanji's contact dropped to the floor and scrabbled through the soggy sawdust and broken mugs, searching for his package. Solanji launched herself after him, hoping he knew where it had gone, because she didn't.

A soul? She hadn't sensed it in all the time she had been carrying it. Who's soul? Why? And then she thought, *How did they get it?* Solanji's thoughts spiralled out of control as she scrambled after the man. She scrunched up her nose at the filth on the floor, liquid dripping through the wooden planks into the spaces below.

Table legs flew through the air, and she ducked as mugs smashed against the wall. Gunk seeped through her leathers, and she cursed. Cleaning them would be a nightmare, and she hated the smell of stale beer.

"There it is!" hissed her contact, and Solanji barrelled into his broken arm and grabbed the package as the man roared in agony.

"Enough!" a commanding voice reverberated through the tavern, and silence fell as everyone turned to the door.

The grey-haired woman would have been impressive enough, clothed as she was in golden armour, but it was the large iridescent dragon's head peering over her shoulder that brought everyone to a frozen standstill. It filled the doorway. The dragon's head was larger than the woman and barely fit through the door. It wasn't one colour, it was all colours; hues of reds and blues, purples and greens, yellows and oranges flickered through its scales as it tilted its snout so the faceted eye could observe the room. Curved horns sprouted from the top of its head, and pointed spines trailed down its long neck, and possibly further, but the doorframe blocked the view.

Solanji held her breath as the observant gaze passed over her, paused, and continued.

"Kyrill. You are late. Again," the woman said, her voice cold. "We are not here for your pleasure. We do not respond to your whim. This is the last time we answer your master's request. Never ask again." The threat hovered in the air.

Smoke drifted from the dragon's tooth-lined jaw as it hissed in agreement. The scent of ash and ancient stone wafted across the still room.

Kyrill's mouth tightened as his face paled and then

flushed. "My profuse apologies, Honourable Ryvalin and Eminent Xylvin." He gritted his teeth and bowed his head to the dragonair. "My business is finished. We are at your disposal."

"I am pleased to hear it," Ryvalin snapped, and the dragon removed its head so the woman could leave.

Kyrill turned his furious gaze on Solanji, strode over to her, and grabbed her arm, dragging her out of the building after the dragonair. He plucked the package out of her hand and tucked it in his robe.

"That was mine," Solanji said as she dug her heels in and tried to twist out of his grasp. "Where are you taking me?"

"You are mine. You owe me," he growled. "You've lost me my transport."

"I did no such thing. You did that yourself," Solanji snapped as she raised her dagger, and the angel laughed.

"You think that will make a difference?"

"Let me go."

Kyrill snapped his fingers and her hand spasmed, her dagger dropping to the dirt as he dragged her onwards. She peered back over her shoulder. That had been her favourite blade! "Don't you know anything?" he snarled.

Solanji gulped a retort down. Obviously not. "I thought the job was here in Eidolon?"

"It is. Let me explain what you will do." The angel tightened his grip on her wrist and towed her towards the dragonair, his voice a needle piercing her skin and leaving his indelible mark. "I know you are an undeclared SoulSinger. I know what you can do. You will take a soul and then you will help the man escape or I will expose you to the world and your brother will die." The threat shivered through her as he continued. "You will befriend this man, a fellow prisoner escaping, and persuade him to return to Puronia. No matter what, you will bring him to me in the citadel."

Hissing out her breath, Solanji faltered. He wanted her to do what? "If he's in your prison, why do you need me? Why can't *you* take him there?" she snapped, her gaze riveted to the huge dragonair taking up most of the field.

"Do this and your brother goes free. Or would you prefer he is cast out all alone in the depths of Eidolon?"

"No," Solanji whispered as her stomach dropped. Gritting her teeth, she glared at the angel. Once she figured how to get out of this tangle, he would regret messing with her. He owed her three halos, not to mention the deposit she would lose on her calope.

Solanji stared in awe at the dragonair looming over them. It was huge, taller than the tavern, and it dwarfed the woman standing next to it. The multi-coloured hues continued over all its scales, down to its sleek tail, which split into five feather-edged fronds, which gently thumped on the grass like a person tapping their fingers, one after the other.

"Honourable Ryvalin. My apologies for delaying you. I assure you, it was not my intention," Kyrill said, giving the woman a small bow.

Ryvalin sniffed. "Get on. I'm not waiting any longer."

Solanji peered up the side of the enormous beast. Its feet were bigger than Solanji's body. And those talons, curved and wicked, were longer than her hand. Fear flashed through her, and she swayed.

"I'm a she, not an it," a soft voice said in Solanji's mind. *"My name is Xylvin. What's yours?"*

Why was the dragonair talking to her?

"Why shouldn't I? You can hear me, can't you? Not like some." Smoke trickled out of her nostrils as she snorted at Kyrill.

Ryvalin thumped Xylvin's side. "Let them board," she said, her words short and sharp.

"B-board?" Solanji managed to stutter, her heart fluttering in her throat.

"How else do you intend to get on?" Muttering a curse under her breath, Ryvalin glared at Kyrill. "Only two passengers."

Kyrill snapped his fingers at his companion, who still hovered by his shoulder, giving Solanji the evil eye. "Make your way back to the citadel. I will meet you there. Have the report ready for my return."

"Yes, sir," Carna replied, his mouth tightening.

Kyrill tightened his hold on Solanji's wrist and spread his wings. They were beautiful, dove-soft, and the palest of greys. He began to rise as he flexed his wings. Solanji gasped, her heart lurching as her feet left the ground. She dangled, held only by his grip on her wrist. What if he let her go? The ground wavered in her eyes as it receded, a green blur mottled with brown. And then there was warmth between her legs, and leather riding straps twined around her waist and arms, trapping her in place. Heat radiated off the drago-nair, but she couldn't get enough slack in the straps to allow her to touch the majestic creature. What kind of soulmist would a dragon have? Did it have a soul? She couldn't see one. Her mind skittered from one thought to another in her panic, unable to hold a thought still enough for her to answer it.

"Sleep," Xylvin's soft voice whispered in her frantic mind, and her eyes closed as she fell into a deep slumber.

10

SOLANJI

Blood. Cloying and sickly, it drenched the air and Solanji's senses. A metallic tang flooded her nostrils and her mouth, and her eyelids fluttered as she tried to process where she was. She was sprawled awkwardly on a cold stone floor, her muscles stiff with the chill emanating from the walls. The sharp odour of blood was everywhere. Was it hers? Stirring, chains clinked next to her, and opening her eyes, she focused on the coil of silver links beside her and threaded through a metal pin hammered into the rock.

Solanji cursed under her breath. Stupid, stupid, stupid. She was stupid. Why hadn't she stayed clear of that angel? Stupid, she muttered again, trying to twist her wrists out of the restraints, but they were unresisting. She clamped her lips shut in frustration.

A torch flared and illuminated the stone walls of a cavern. Squinting at the burning flame, she barely noticed her surroundings, or the open ledge opposite. She only saw the naked man hanging from the chains in the ceiling. The image she had caught from Kyrill. His skin had been flayed and shredded, and blood ran freely down his back, down his bare buttocks. He hung limp and still.

Eyes wide, she glared around the cavern. What was going on?

Just her luck; the seraphim wanted a SoulSinger. How did he know she could touch souls? What had given her away? Just because she could caress their souls, make them feel, did that make her a monster? It was fortunate they didn't know what else she could do, and she wasn't about to tell them, not for anything. She wasn't even going to think it, in case Kyrill was able to mind read.

"About time." Clipped words echoed above her and someone kicked her legs. "Stand up." A brutal-looking guard leered down at her, his coarse face cold and threatening. Tugging her chains, he forced her to her feet and shoved her closer to the man hanging limp and silent in his own personal hell. Threading her chains through a loop of metal protruding from the rock floor, the guard grabbed her face and squeezed her chin, forcing her to look at the flayed and pulpy flesh.

"No," she gasped, trying to pull away. Her stomach roiled as bile rose, and she thought she might vomit with sheer horror. Acid burned her throat as she stared at the man. Whatever she had done, she did not deserve a punishment like that.

The guard released her with a low chuckle devoid of any humour. "You're next," he whispered, running his cold finger down her cheek, and then he left. She stiffened as a soft panting began as the man disappeared back down the corridor.

The bleeding man was still conscious? After everything they had done to him? His blood continued to leak from his wounds, spreading the red puddle around him. He was going to bleed to death in front of her. There was the slightest movement, like he was rocking himself to soothe the pain. The agony he must be in.

A grimed and bloodied piece of cloth covered his eyes, and Solanji shuddered. Had they blinded him? He canted over to one side, and then she saw the spear that had been driven through his knee, pinning him to the floor, the source of most of the blood. She was thankful she couldn't see his face, shadowed as it was, hanging between his upraised arms. What could he have done to deserve such torture?

Was this the man Kyrill wanted her to help escape? He couldn't be serious. The man was near death, and in his condition, with the wounds they had inflicted, he wouldn't be able walk anywhere.

She shuffled as near to the open ledge as her chains would allow and peered out. The frigid air cleared her nose of the aroma of blood and made her sinuses ache. They were so high up. An unfamiliar snow-tipped mountain chain curved away in the distance, under a starlit sky. More shadows spread out over the darkened landscape, masking it from view. There was no moon in this sky. No moon? She was still in Eidolon.

Chains clinked behind her, and she peered at the man dangling like a slab of meat at the slaughterhouse. The cloying scent of his blood assaulted her again, and she swallowed. He had braced his other leg to take his weight and was trying to…what *was* he trying to do? How was he even moving? As she watched, he stiffened, cocked his head as if he heard something, and then gingerly relaxed back into limp despair, hanging from the chains.

The guard appeared with a bucket in his hands. He threw it at the man's back, sluicing the blood off. Pink trails of water ran over his taut muscles, down his lean body, and dripped to the floor. With a gasp, Solanji shuffled back towards the man as she realised the wounds were closing, slowly, and blood had stopped leaking out. Appalling red weals now crisscrossed his back, his legs. His muscles bunched as he took his weight again on his left leg, the spear still pinning him to the floor.

"Well, well. A sorry sight. I see your healing powers haven't deserted you yet. Though you're slacking. You haven't got the spear out." Solanji flinched at the harsh voice behind her, and she twisted round. Kyrill stood on the open ledge, surveying the scene, before he approached the man, carefully holding his robes above the blood-soaked floor. He grasped the spear, and the man shuddered and hissed his breath out.

Solanji froze, watching. The seraphim glowed, his grey wings flaring slightly in anticipation. He was the epitome of elegance, of beauty, and yet here he was in this ugly place, torturing an already tortured man. The injured man was broader across the shoulders, more muscular, dark-haired. At least, she thought he was dark-haired; it was difficult to tell with all the blood still coating most of him.

"You never learn, do you? You were sent here for a reason. That means you don't come back. You are not wanted. You're dead to us. But you persist, don't you? After all these centuries, you still keep trying." Kyrill twisted the spear, and the man cried out, a hoarse cry of agony that seared through Solanji. The seraphim suddenly turned on her and snapped his fingers. "Here."

She shuffled nearer and shivered as the seraphim circled her. He smelt of herbs and incense, sickly sweet incense. Pale blue robes draped his slender form, and when she looked up into his perfect face, her heart stuttered. His piercing blue eyes drilled into her. "If you want to live, you'll do as I said."

Solanji nodded and clenched her jaw when he smiled. His brilliant beauty was deceptive as concealed beneath it was so much brutality it stunned her. "You will trawl his thoughts and take his soul."

"He doesn't have a soul," she blurted. It was the first thing she had noticed. The absence of any soulmist within the shadows that wreathed around the injured man. He was the antithesis of this beautiful being.

The seraphim stilled, and the man in the chains tensed.

"It's not possible. He only lives here; he is not *of* Eidolon. Therefore, he has a soul," the seraphim said, and he stalked back to the man. He gripped his prisoner's hair, raising his face, now oblivious to the blood staining the hem of his pristine blue robes. "What did you do with it?"

The man didn't answer, and the seraphim leaned forward. "So that's why they were trying to steal a soul. They thought they could give it to you, the fools. Who did you speak to? How did they know?" Kyrill shook the man's head, and speckles of red splattered on his sleeve. He hissed out his breath and released him as he continued to speak. "The box was empty, a con, nothing in it. They were wasting their hard-earned coin on dreams, just to try and save you. Are you worth it?" Kyrill wrinkled his nose at the lack of a response. "We have an eternity, you and me, and I will make you suffer every minute of every day until you tell me."

Still no answer.

The seraphim grabbed the thin leather cords around the man's neck, yanking him forward, and Solanji's eyes widened at the sight of two vendetta stones. One a deep virulent red and one cerulean blue. They couldn't be removed, by anyone, until the oaths had been fulfilled.

A vendetta stone was a curse, a life sentence. And two? Two was a death wish. Who was this man?

The tortured man hissed out his breath, spraying bubbles of blood over the seraphim, and the seraphim let go of him as if he'd been burnt. The man dropped his head again as if too exhausted to hold it up. Stalking back to Solanji, the seraphim gripped her chin with his blood-smeared fingers. "You will watch until his wings flare and then you will take his memories. I want to know where he's been, what he knows, who he's been in contact with." The seraphim lowered his voice. "And you will bring him to me."

Solanji nodded, not knowing what else to do. Her stomach twisted as uncertainty gripped her. Wings? This man was also a seraph? The seraphim left to be replaced by two brutal guards holding a lash of knotted ropes, with shards of metal tied into the ends. The barely healed skin shredded in moments, and the man's screams rang around the cavern and sliced through her mind. Her own soul cringed in horror and disgust until the man hung lifeless and silent.

"H-he didn't flare any wings," she stuttered, as the guards turned to her.

The larger guard glared at her. "Then maybe you'd better make him? Maybe you can stimulate him a bit? Isn't that what you're good at? Or do you want to join him?"

Dear god above, who were these people? "Did you see any wings?" she asked, backing away as far as her chains reached.

They released her chain and dragged her over. The man was imitating another slab of meat, limp and bloody. "Your reward for tonight. Make him flare his wings. Grab his memories and we'll let you go."

Up close, the chained man looked even worse. Eyes wide, Solanji inspected his skin. It was a mass of fine scars; scars upon scars. How long had they been doing this for? Her throat tightened as tears welled and her vision blurred. The smell of his blood was overpowering, and it ran freely, puddling around her feet. She yelped as another spear pierced his skin, pushing him against her, passing through his side and grazing her arm. He moaned, spraying her shirt with more of his blood as he twisted on his chains, helpless and barely conscious.

When he had pressed against her, he had felt so hot, as if he was burning from the inside out. She placed a hand on his chest, the only unmarred piece of skin, and his flesh was cold and clammy to the touch. Shadows curled around her hand, and she snatched it back. This man was beyond her help. He had been reft of his soul, and he barely existed.

"There you go," the guard said, his voice coming from a distance as she stared at the steel point protruding from the chained man's body. "That should keep him down for the night." He gave her a lewd wink and left.

The man shuddered and the shadows began to spread, curling over his skin as if they could shelter and protect him. As Solanji watched, more blood leaked from his wounds and pooled around her feet. She didn't know where to start.

His black hair was matted with blood and threaded with glints of silver. It was long enough for her to run her fingers through it, and the thought of caressing those long silky strands was an unexpected temptation. She curled her fingers and then drew her hands up before her. Her wrists were free; they had forgotten to rechain her in their eagerness to hurt him.

He stirred, his chains clinking.

"Are you alright?" she whispered and then cringed. "Don't answer that, of course you're not. How can I help you?"

A better question, though not by much. He was beyond help.

His only answer was a low groan. He hung awkwardly, still canted over but now twisted in on himself. He must be in agony.

"Shit, shit, shit," she muttered as her hands fluttered in front of him, hesitant to touch him.

Unchain him. If she could release him, it might relieve some of the discomfort. She scuttled to the ring on the floor. Her nimble fingers made short work of the chains holding her ankles; locks were no problem for her. She shoved the pin she used as a lock pick back into her mop of dark curls.

Should she remove the blindfold? Of course she should, what was she thinking? She moved around him and picked at the knot. The cloth stuck to his skin, but she managed to peel it off, though she wasn't sure it was an improvement. His long lashes fluttered, and he screwed up his eyes against the dim light. How long had he been blindfolded?

Which side should she unchain first? If she released his right arm, all the weight would go on his right knee. No, no. The other arm first. She tugged at the heavy chain; his weight was pulling it taut. She hovered in front of him, wringing her hands. "Umm, can you lean to the right for a bit? I can't ease the chain with your weight on it."

"You should leave while you can." His voice was low and hoarse, his throat raw from screaming.

And leave him here? Like this? Just the thought set her on edge.

"Just for a moment, it won't take long," Solanji said, and she cupped his cheek. He raised his head, swaying slightly at the effort. His face was grey and taut, as if hewn from the stone surrounding them. Gaunt and ravaged, it was still beautiful, delicate even. High cheeks, a stubborn chin covered in a grey specked beard, and black eyebrows arched over... Solanji winced.

His eyes. Blood filled them. She couldn't tell what colour they were supposed to be. Solanji doubted he could even see. But he did, with an indrawn breath, ease over to the right.

He trembled, and Solanji rushed to release the chain. "Ready?" she called as she began to lower it.

He spasmed as the strain on his arm and shoulders was released, and he half folded over on the floor. Solanji wasted no time and released the other side. He was bent over, head resting on the stone, body braced as he shuddered. Solanji tried to ignore the pure muscle rippling across his blood-streaked back as she began massaging his shoulders, easing the knots and the spasms. He groaned under her hands, deep and guttural. His skin had begun to close again, though it still looked raw and bloody.

"Pull it out," he said, his voice low and harsh.

Swallowing, Solanji circled him. She winced as she inspected his still shredded back, his buttocks streaked with blood and the two spears piercing his body.

"Which one?" she whispered.

"Both of them."

"I-I can't."

"Yes, you can. When I pass out, don't stop."

"P-pass out?"

The man looked up, his gorgeous face strained. "I don't deny, I can take some pain, but I doubt I'll survive that. It'll be less painful if I'm unconscious, and I can't move unless you take them out."

"But it's impaled in the stone."

"We'll do it together," he said.

"What?" Solanji's voice rose.

"I'll help while I can, but at some point…" His voice trailed off and he shrugged. His shoulders were almost healed now, and the wounds further down his back were beginning to close, knots of scars covering his golden skin.

Solanji took a deep breath as her stomach fluttered. What was she doing? He was right, she should have run long ago before the guards came back and started this all over again. She knelt beside him, trying not to look down, and gripped the point of the spear impaling his body. Thankfully, it was a short spear, not like the one impaled in his knee.

The man's slender fingers covered hers. The other hand braced him off the floor. His wrist was swollen and bloody beneath the shackle still cinched so tight. "On three," he whispered. "One…two…three." They both pulled and the spear slid out with a rush of blood. So much blood. All his, everywhere. He swayed, his face paling, though he remained conscious. He had bitten through his lip, and bright, red blood trailed down his bearded chin, vivid against his pallid skin.

"Don't you think I should know your name?" Solanji asked, trying to distract him as she clamped her hand over the wound. She hadn't thought that far ahead. A glance around the cavern revealed it was empty. He didn't have any clothes, so she would have to use hers. She shrugged out of her leather vest and her shirt. Goosebumps rose across her bare skin in the frigid evening air, and she hurried to put her vest back on.

Struggling to rip up her shirt, she cursed as the fabric refused to split. Grunting with frustration, she managed to tear it in two and folded it into a pad to press against his stomach. She placed his shaking hand over the cloth and moved around to his back and pressed one over that.

"Just 'cos I'm naked doesn't mean you have to join me." His voice was low and strained, but at least he was trying.

Solanji chuckled. "Don't be getting any ideas now."

"I think you're safe," he whispered. "You'll have to come back another day when…"

Without any warning, Solanji heaved on the spear in his knee. It popped out of the stone with a crack, and the man passed out, slumping to the floor. Snapping off the end of the spear as close to his leg as possible, she hesitated and then rolled him over. He was so darned heavy; all that muscle. She couldn't avoid looking at him, and despite the state he was in, heat rushed through her as she admired his sculpted body, long and lean, with hard muscles, though his rib bones did jut out a bit as if he had lost weight, which was not surprising. She could just imagine him saying, *Had your fill? Now it's my turn.* Flushing, she concentrated on pulling the spear out, retching as white muscle and bone clung to the wood. His kneecap was shattered, destroyed. Pushing the cartilage and muscle back together, she bound it as tight as she could with the remains of her shirt.

The distinct lack of clothes, or material of any sort, was becoming a problem, and she took a deep breath and left him slumped on the floor as she cautiously picked the lock to the cell and eased the barred gate open. The passageway was deserted, though voices echoed up ahead. Creeping to the base of the stairs, she slowly climbed them.

At the top, a rough-hewn cavern was dimly lit by candles and two guards sat at a wooden table playing cards. They passed a bottle between them, the glass chinking as they topped up their glasses.

"She was quite a looker, if you like them sort," one of the men said.

"Not worth it. Can't trust them. How'd you know she wouldn't steal your soul? And then what?" the other replied, shifting in his chair.

"Why would she? Just 'cos she could, doesn't mean she would."

Solanji grimaced and crept closer, and after a moment's hesitation, she reached for the golden soulmist trailing across the floor. *"Sleep. You are so tired,"* she encouraged. Her fingers caressed the golden swirls, and she relaxed into the welcoming embrace. The men collapsed over the table, soft snores drifting on the air.

Exhaling, she scanned the room and continued out to the next corridor. Peering in doors, listening for any other guards, she searched the storerooms until she found enough clothes that might fit the man and a shirt for her.

Returning to the guard room, she encouraged the guards to sleep deeper and longer and then returned to the torture room. The man was still laid out, unconscious on the cold stone floor. Pulling his head into her lap, she smoothed her fingers over his cheek. His dark lashes were a delicate fan against his unnaturally pale skin, the sharp angles of his face reinforcing the notion that he was angelic in some shape or form. He was so beautiful, he had to be.

It was an hour or more before he stirred. She had spent it struggling to remove the shackles from his swollen wrists and bandaging them as best she could. A pile of clothes sat beside him, a shirt covering what needed to be covered, his head still resting in her lap. She had washed as much of him as she could, though he was a blood-smeared mess. At least his back had healed over and his stomach wound was only sluggishly bleeding. She had bound the pads with strips of cloth she had found, but the material was already blood-stained and needed replacing.

Her arm stung from the spear tip, but it was nothing to what this man had suffered. And she still didn't know who he was. Well, that wasn't completely true. She assumed he was a seraphim, if he had wings. The only problem was, she didn't remember any of the seraphim being cast out in her lifetime, or even the last century. Could he really be the outcast archdeus, Demavrian? Alive and soulless? No, it wasn't possible.

He groaned back to awareness, stiffening in her lap.

"Just take a moment," she said. "The guards are asleep. No rush."

She had watched, mesmerised, as the dark shadows had

curled about him as he slept. They weren't truly black. A sliver of silver glittered in their depths, sparking over his skin, smoothing the angry weals closed. The wounds were still pink and raw, but given time, she knew they would fade to the fine golden lines that covered his body. He had been repeatedly tortured, though it seemed that he was still immortal even if he was fallen. They hadn't managed to kill his body; she wondered what was left of the mind.

He stirred in her arms. Black lashes fluttered against pale cheeks, and she was suddenly pinned by a pair of amber eyes that were bright and clear. The irises were flecked with glinting gold, and she couldn't look away. No longer blood-drenched, they saw straight through her, and her heart thudded at his achingly vulnerable expression before the lashes swept back down and hid his deepest emotions. Her arms tightened around him when he stiffened as his body's woes bombarded him, his soft intake of breath the only other indication of the discomfort he must be in.

11

MAV

Pain. Jagged, all-consuming pain radiated through his body. His right knee burned, a hot ball of flame that threatened to consume him. His side ached, his muscles hurt, his skin stung. Head pounding, he opened his eyes and stared up at the exquisite face hovering above him. Huge, black eyes watched him with concern. A mess of soft brunette curls tumbled over the woman's shoulder, framing her sweet face and complimenting her smooth brown complexion. Trying to swallow, he caught his breath as it felt like swallowing glass shards, and he closed his eyes.

Images raced through his head. A different woman with a mass of strawberry-blonde curls. A large marble hall with a blood-coated body lying across the steps, his perfect wings going up in flames, stumbling through rain-drenched fields, the searing agony as his friend died in his arms, skin shredding, and more pain. So much pain.

Panting, he tried to rein his memories in. They battered him, waves of guilt and anguish mixed with confusion and anger.

He stiffened as the woman gripped his shoulder, and he

realised he was lying naked on a stone floor and his head was resting in her lap. It was freezing, and his bare skin was going numb where it touched the ice-cold rock. At least it was no longer sore.

A quick sweep through his body told him that it was slowly healing. His healing ability was nearly exhausted, drained by almost continuous use. The lack of food or water meant he'd not only had to heal himself, he'd had to sustain himself as well, and he had to admit, he wouldn't have lasted much longer. He hoped the woman wasn't injured, because he could only heal himself, not others, another barb in his already deflated ego. Most of the wounds on his skin had closed over, leaving raw welts. The worst injury was his knee and the wound in his side. Both of which were still sluggishly bleeding into the crude bandages.

"Drink," the woman said. She raised his head and tilted a mug against his lips.

Blessed water trickled into his mouth, and he gulped greedily. The almost forgotten sensation of liquid in his mouth nearly made him choke, but it soothed his raw throat. He vaguely remembered screaming and heat slowly flushed his cheeks.

Who was this woman? Why had she helped him? Where was that seraphim? Questions flew through his mind, tumbling one after another as he carefully flexed his limbs. Flames flared in his right knee, and he gasped. It took a few moments for him to regain control and force out some words.

"Why didn't you leave?" His voice came out as a deep and gravelly whisper, his throat still sore from screaming. The woman shivered.

"You needed help," she replied.

"I won't be able to protect you."

"I can look after myself."

He sat up and swayed as nausea swept through him. He swallowed and took a deep breath and then, spying a pile of clothes beside him, grabbed a pair of trousers. Awkwardly, he stood, and heat flared through him as he realised he couldn't bend his knee. Thankful for the bracing arm the woman supplied, and with much difficulty, he stepped into them.

His fingers strayed to his throat, an unconscious gesture he caught himself repeating. They were still there, both of them. How he had acquired two vendetta stones, he had no idea. Between being knocked unconscious and awakening on the side of a muddy road in Eidolon, he had gained a red and blue vendetta stone. Two separate oaths he had unknowingly accepted. One for life and one for death, always a balance. Until he fulfilled whatever the oaths were, he wouldn't be able to remove them; nor could anyone else. Seemed like he would have them for the rest of his life, seeing as he had no idea how to fulfil them.

Ignoring his blood-smeared skin, and careful not to dislodge the bandage around his waist, he struggled to pull on a shirt, discarded it, and tried a larger one. It wouldn't reach all the way across his broad chest, but it was better than nothing. He tugged a leather vest over the top, sucking his breath in against the cold material. At least it should warm with his body heat.

The woman had found a smaller shirt and vest, but they both hung down to her knees. She was much slimmer than him and a bit shorter, but she was toned and limber. He vaguely remembered her stripping off at some point. He wasn't sure if that was real or a dream, but the image of her smooth, lean body was vivid in his memory.

When she handed him a sheathed short sword and a dagger, he glanced at her in surprise but quickly belted it around his waist before she changed her mind. Wondering where she had got it from, he spotted the knives she had sequestered about her body. He peered down at his bare feet sticking out of too short trousers.

The woman shrugged. "Best I could do. You couldn't walk through this place in just your skin."

"No complaints," he replied and cocked his head. It was eerily silent. "Where are the guards?"

"I encouraged them to go to sleep."

He raised his eyebrow. She had done what?

"I'll explain later. We need to leave, unless you can fly," she said and gestured to the open ledge.

Anguish overwhelmed him, stealing his breath. After a moment, he shook his head. "No. I can't fly."

"Shame," she murmured and indicated the corridor. "We'll have to walk, then." She held out her hand. "I'm Solanji."

He hesitated and then shook her hand. "You can call me Mav."

12

SOLANJI

Trying to stifle her impatience, Solanji slowed her pace as Mav struggled to keep up with her. His skin may have healed, but his body had lost an inordinate amount of blood, and he was weak. He limped heavily, still unable to bend his knee, and she feared he would never be able to again. He supported himself against the wall as he swung his leg forward and hopped after her. His beautiful face was strained and grey but determined.

She bit her lip. What was she complaining about? The man had been half dead an hour ago. It was a miracle he was even walking. Absently, she scratched at an itch on her arm, and looking down, scowled at the tattoo. She had forgotten the golden dragon, but now it glowed in the dim light. She rubbed the tattoo again and dragged her sleeve down to hide it.

Peering around the bend, she listened for heartbeats. The one behind her was barely noticeable. If she hadn't known he was there, she wouldn't have thought anyone was. She glanced back at him. He was leaning heavily against the wall, sweat glistening on his skin.

"Do you know where we are?" she whispered.

"Some angel's damn torture chamber."

Solanji scowled at him. "And where is that?"

Mav chuckled, though there wasn't much humour in it. "The back of beyond, that's where. Miles from anywhere."

"You're not helping."

"Sorry. We must go down to get out. We need a ride. Head for the stables. He'll have some good beasts we can take."

"And I suppose we just add stealing to the list of things he wants to kill you for?"

"Well, if it's being added to the list, we'd better make sure we take the good ones."

Solanji gritted her teeth and took the left-hand fork, aware of him close behind her. Normally having someone that close to her would have made her jittery, but not Mav. He felt right.

She paused as two heartbeats approached, and she extended gentle fingers to stroke the fine mist swirling around them.

"God, it's been a long shift. I'm beat," one said as the other yawned.

"Me too," the other replied, and they veered off to a downward corridor.

Solanji shivered as Mav rested his chin on her shoulder and breathed in her ear. "What did you do? I felt something in the air; a ripple or something."

"Nothing, I was waiting for them to pass."

His expression said he didn't believe her, but he limped after her as she moved off. They stopped twice more as guards conveniently went another direction, and then the scent of straw and livestock drifted in the air. Dim lights revealed an open courtyard, lined with uncomfortable cobble stones. Large double doors barred the entrance to what Solanji assumed was the stables.

They were halfway across the courtyard when the clatter of boots made Mav spin towards the threat. "Wait," Solanji whispered as he inserted himself between her and the oncoming guard. Mav blocked the guard's punch and slipped on the slick cobbles, his knee giving way as he sprawled on the stones with a deep, pain-filled groan. The guard's follow up strike met clear air, and as he righted himself, he sneered down at Mav. Solanji threw her dagger, swift and sure, and the guard collapsed on top of Mav.

"Get him off me," Mav grunted.

"I said wait; there was no need to fight him," Solanji said as she tugged the body off him.

"Instinct," Mav replied.

"I don't need protecting."

"So I see. Who taught you to throw a knife like that?"

"My brother. He wanted to make sure I could defend myself after my father died."

"Sounds like a good brother."

"He is."

Once upright again, Mav exhaled slowly, and bracing his leg, he hobbled towards the stables, dragging the guard behind him. Pulling the heavy doors open, Solanji peered in, and not seeing anyone, she beckoned him inside. Releasing the body, Mav limped over to the nearest stalls and worked his way down, inspecting the inhabitants. Solanji scowled as she remembered her rented beast she had left at the cross-roads. More money lost, along with the rest of her payment, even though she had completed the delivery.

Mav smoothed a hand down the brown flank of the nearest calope. "These are purebred calopes. You won't find any finer. I wonder why there are so many here?"

"No idea," she admitted. "Just choose us some." Maybe

she could recoup the loss of the rented calope by giving them back an even better one?

"In that case, you search for travel bags and rations, whilst I saddle them up," he said as he moved further into the stables. "See if you can find a flint or a compass, they would be useful, and any food. It will take a few weeks to reach the nearest town."

Solanji froze, her stomach clenching. That couldn't be right. "What? That's not possible. It took less than two days to reach the crossroads from the divide."

"We're nowhere near the crossroads. That is leagues to the south." Mav observed her for a moment. "So, you're from Puronia, are you?"

"Does that mean you're not?" she snapped back.

His expression hardened, and she regretted her sharp retort. He looked away. "Not anymore," he said, so quietly she nearly missed it.

She stalked off, angry at herself for snapping at him. He hadn't deserved that. She looked around, wondering where the stable lads were. Collecting a saddle bag, she began stuffing items in it from the well-stocked storeroom she found at the far end of the stable. She lugged the bag back to Mav, who now had a tall beast saddled. He took the bag and slung it over the calope's back. "Bedrolls and water," he said as he limped into the neighbouring stall.

Solanji was soon back handing Mav what she thought was a compass. He looked at it, grunted, and slipped it his pocket. "It's too quiet, I don't like it," Solanji said, watching him.

Mav lifted his head, and his amber eyes went distant. After a moment, he huffed in annoyance. "I expect they are occupied. Angels tend to cause a lot of work." He shrugged, and a slight smile escaped. "Which is to our advantage, and I am not complaining. Teach him to be so self-centred."

"Who? The seraph? Is he the one who brought you here? Do you know who he is?"

"No, unfortunately not. I was brought here by a captain of the Heavenly Host. A very persistent tracker. But I never expected him to turn me over to…" Mav's voice trailed off, his face tightening. "It doesn't matter," he said as he led her beast out of the stall. He slung the second bag that Solanji had filled over its back and tied on the bedroll.

"Your knee is bleeding," Solanji said suddenly. "You're trailing blood everywhere. You should have said." That the man was standing was amazing in itself, considering the horrific injuries he had received, even if he had healed most of them. Nausea swept through Solanji at the idea of handing Mav back to the seraphim to suffer more torture, no one deserved that, but her brother's life hung in the balance. Brennan was relying on her to save him, and she wouldn't let him down, no matter what she had to do.

"We don't have time. Deal with it later."

"You'll leave a trail; they'll follow us easily." She couldn't make it look too easy for them to escape, though the lack of any guards was suspicious.

He reached for a spare set of reins and wrapped them around his leg above his knee. Sliding a dagger between his leg and the leather strap, he twisted and tied it off. Grabbing an absorbent towel, he wrapped his knee and used the rest of the leather reins to tie it in place.

"Why isn't it healing like the rest of you did?"

"I'm tired. It's a complicated healing. I'll sort it later."

Solanji darted back out of the stable; she had seen some bandages and some salve. She stuffed them in a satchel, which she slung crosswise over her body. Glancing around, she grabbed a folded map. He might know where they were, but she didn't.

By the time she returned, he was waiting impatiently by the mounting block.

"Get on," he said. "We need to leave."

Solanji climbed on the block and swung her leg over the calope. Mav led a larger beast up to the block and clambered on, his injured leg sticking out straight. Her animal followed him as he led the way out of the stable yard and down a track behind the castle. The stone walls of the castle rose around them as they worked their way down into the dark valley below. It was shadowed and grey, and soon they were lost in the gloom.

Mav caught Solanji looking back at the castle. The only lights twinkling in the valley came from the imposing structure sitting on the ridge high above. They had been travelling for two days, only stopping for the beasts to graze and for them to grab some travel rations, and they could still see the silhouette perched on the ridge. Exhaustion threatened to overwhelm him, but he wouldn't stop for longer; he knew Julius would be desperate to find him. In fact, he was still suspicious at how easily they had escaped. Where had the seraphim gone? Where were Julius' guards? And who was the woman who had rescued him?

When they finally stopped under a copse of leafless trees set back off the road, Solanji slid to the ground like a block of wood. She groaned as she rolled over, and he grimaced as he gingerly dismounted. Hissing under his breath, he hung onto the calope as his foot touched the ground. His knee was on fire and wouldn't take his weight. Pain shot through him, and he rested his head against the saddle as he settled back down. Sweat prickled his skin, and he inhaled, deep and slow.

He shuffled around and leaned on the calope as he observed the girl. For someone so small, she could make a lot of noise. "Sorry," he huffed out. "Forgot you hadn't ridden much. You should have reminded me." She glared at him from under her messy mop of brown curls, and for the first time in years some of the coiled tension within him eased, and a slight smile tugged at his lips as she stiffly rose. "I'll rub some of that salve you picked up on your backside if you like. It'll help for tomorrow." It wouldn't do much, but it would ease the aches for now.

She snorted and untied the bedrolls.

He unsaddled the beasts, stacking the saddles near a tree, and then hobbled the calopes so that they wouldn't stray, but they were well trained and just dropped their heads to graze.

Spotting a wiry bannen bush covered in feathery, silver leaves, Mav stooped to collect a few of them and awkwardly dug about for a woody root just beneath the surface of the soil. The spicy scent drifted under his nose, and he inhaled and sighed as his head cleared.

Aware of Solanji's knowing gaze on him, he rose and limped back to the camp. "Here, add these to the water. Make it taste better," he said, dropping the leaves into her hand.

Solanji sniffed the spicy scent and her eyes widened. "Bannen leaves? Do you know how much they cost?"

Wincing, Mav eased himself down to the ground. "Freely available in Eidolon, so make the most of it." He peeled the root with his belt knife and, cutting a piece off, began to chew as he loosened the tourniquet around his leg. The blood rushed through his veins, and he gritted his teeth as his knee pulsed and he started to sweat, even though he'd released the tourniquet periodically as they rode. Leaning back against the tree, he concentrated on chewing the spicy bannen root. As his greying vision sharpened, he focused on his knee. The towel was blood-soaked, and he slung it aside.

He inspected the damage, sinking his senses down to the bone, and he shuddered. It was unrepairable. Being able to heal himself seemed to be the only ability he had left, and even that was suspect and limited.

"How bad is it?" Solanji's soft voice made him start. He had been so focused, he hadn't heard her move.

Weariness dragged at him; he didn't have the energy for healing, even if he had the ability. "Beyond me," he said on a sigh. "I can knit the skin, seal the wound, but the joint is smashed. I can't repair it."

He spat out the remains of the bannen root and took the mug of steaming bannoe that she handed him. Solanji had proved adept at digging the fire pit and starting the fire.

She eyed him as he sipped the scalding liquid and relaxed against the tree. "I didn't realise the bannen leaves came from Eidolon. Must be why they are so expensive. What does the root do?" she asked as she pulled out a couple of strips of dried meat for supper.

Mav sighed. "You can steep the roots into a more pungent brew. Very strong, can knock a person out. The roots help alleviate pain, a natural pain relief. Best used in small doses though, as you can become reliant on it. Fortunately, the leaves are not so potent and are more widely used to make the popular drink you know as bannoe."

Chewing on a fragrant strip of dried meat, he concentrated on his knee. If he repaired what he could, he would be useless for the remainder of the night and probably the next day as well. A bout of dizziness made him pause and just breathe; he badly needed time to rest and recover. Travelling for miles across dangerous country wasn't the best plan, but he didn't see an alternative.

How had he gotten in such a mess? You'd have thought

he'd be more prepared after all these years, but he still wasn't. That unexpected betrayal caught him out every time. He was too trusting. And now he was in this woman's hands. She could knock him over with little effort, no matter what he portrayed. He wondered how long it would take before she realised it.

Taking another sip of his bannoe, he watched her hiss her breath out as she settled, her knives and a soft cleaning cloth in her lap.

"The offer stands. The salve will help with stiff muscles, and I promise I won't look," he said as his lips twitched at her expression. Quite rightly, she didn't believe him.

"Later. I need to clean these knives first. This damp air will corrode the metal if I don't keep them dry."

"Do you usually prefer knives?"

"Yeah, my father taught me how to use them when I was a lot younger, but my brother helped me hone the skill. He wanted me to be able to protect myself."

"Are you any good?"

Solanji flipped a knife over in her hand, caught it by the blade, and threw it at a tree across the clearing in one smooth motion. It pierced a darker patch of bark, and she raised her eyebrow. She retrieved it, returned to her bedroll and, spinning around, threw it again, and it hit the exact same spot.

"I see," Mav murmured as she walked over to retrieve her knife again. Her breath hissed out as she sat, but she diligently cleaned her knives, muttering under breath about how unbalanced they were.

She must have been in some discomfort because once she finished, she rummaged in her pack and produced a jar. When Mav took it from her, she turned her back and shrugged out of her leather vest and over-large shirt.

He smoothed the salve over the silky brown skin of her

back, rubbing in small circles, following the curves of her muscles. She was lithe and toned, and her skin was smooth and warm under his fingers. She groaned in pleasure as he continued rubbing. The aroma of pungent herbs drifted between them, the scent growing stronger as the heat of his hands on her skin released the perfume. His hands moved down, and she shifted so he could reach her lower back and her hips.

He was tempted to go lower, but he was quite proud of his restraint. She sighed when he stopped and replaced the lid. Shrugging back into her shirt, she concentrated on buttoning it up. "Thank you," she murmured.

"My pleasure," he replied. And it had been. It had been years since he had felt another person's skin beneath his hands. He'd forgotten the comfort that touching someone else brought. Her pleased groans had generated an unexpected warmth, which quested through his frozen core, trying to find a way in.

"So, how did you end up in the torture chamber?" Mav asked as he made himself comfortable on his blanket. He began trimming his straggly beard with a pair of spring scissors he had found in the saddle bag.

"I have no idea. This seraph accosted me at the divide. Accused me of touching his soulmist, even though I hadn't. Very bad-tempered."

"And is that what you can do, touch soulmist? Are you a SoulSinger?"

Solanji froze.

"Don't worry, I won't tell anyone. Is that what you were doing at the castle? Why we escaped so easily?" Mav was glad to have that anomaly explained, and some of his concerns about the woman eased. He began trimming his beard again.

"Yes, I persuaded the guards to go to sleep, or to go in a different direction."

"Persuaded?"

"When I touch their soulmist I can make suggestions."

"You can see souls. That's why you knew I didn't have one," Mav stated.

"Yes, I'm sorry I told him, but he wanted me to take your soul."

"I wonder who he is? I didn't recognise his voice. A seraphim prepared to get his hands dirty in Eidolon. Have many new angels risen in the last few decades?"

Solanji shrugged. "I don't know. I've never met one before. One moment I was eating my meal, the next I was being dragged up on a dragonair. She made me fall asleep."

Mav lurched forward. "A dragonair? In Eidolon? Which one?"

"I think her name was Xylvin. She put me to sleep, and I woke up in your torture chamber. How long had you been in there?"

"Xylvin?" Mav's heart beat so hard in his chest he thought he might have a heart attack. His oathsworn had been here? In Eidolon? Were they looking for him? How had she not sensed him? Taking a deep breath, he steadied himself. "Maybe we should go back to the crossroads if dragonairs visit there," he mumbled under his breath, ignoring her question. Scowling at the resultant pile of hair that he had cut off his face, he noted it was more grey than black. He ran his hands through his hair, wondering if it was also going grey. He was ageing, another sign that his abused body was failing him.

"I could retrieve my calope, if it's still there," Solanji suggested.

"Unlikely. Someone will have taken it by now." Mav dragged his gaze away from the physical proof of how dire his situation had become and stared at Solanji. "Which seraphim would be entitled to ride a dragonair?"

"I don't know. All I know is the dragonair was angry and said this was his last ride. The bastard blamed me for losing his transport, though it had nothing to do with me. I'd never even seen a dragonair before, let alone ridden one."

Mav smiled at Solanji's aggrieved tone. "Describe the seraph to me again."

"I told you, he was blond, blue eyed, lean, and elegant. Beautiful, arrogant, and very bad tempered."

That told Mav nothing. It could be one of many angels from the citadel. But this one was in league with Julius and Kaenera. "I wondered who would be working with Julius…" *to take my wings*, he thought silently. That was something he did not want to say out loud.

Mav waited for Solanji to roll up in her blankets and drift off to sleep. Once her breathing deepened, he struggled out of his trousers and, gritting his teeth, unwound the bandages stiff with his blood. His knee was a disaster, swollen and angry. He wasn't sure there was a knee joint left. As he hesitated, it throbbed in time with his faint heartbeat, the last sign that he was still hanging in there. Not for much longer, he feared. He had taken too much abuse for his body to sustain him.

Well, there were still a few things he needed to do before they claimed him for all eternity.

Jaw locked and tensing against the pain, he focused his thoughts on his knee. Delving beneath the surface, he winced as he concentrated on easing the swelling and removing the bone shards. Sweat dewed his skin as he did what little he could, but every delicate touch only aggravated the wound further. It took all night to clean out the shattered pieces of bone, to realign anything that remained, and to encourage the shredded tendons and muscles to repair.

Trembling with exhaustion, Mav struggled back into his trousers as the dusky predawn was lightening the sky. He eased himself flat on his blanket and stared up through the bare branches, trying to ignore the nauseous aftereffects of his attempted healing.

Solanji opened her inky black eyes, and just like that, she was awake. She tried to rise and then gave a heartfelt groan, and he chuckled. She scowled at him and staggered to her feet. "I hurt all over. Why does anyone want to ride those things?"

"Well, you could walk, but it takes longer."

"I think I might. At least until I loosen up."

"You repack and I'll saddle the calopes," Mav said, rising to his feet with difficulty.

She watched him. "Did you heal your knee?"

Mav tried not to limp. "As best I could."

"Good," she said and bent to pick up the bedroll and groaned again.

13

MAV

Mav shifted in his saddle for what felt like the hundredth time. His knee throbbed, the swelling tight against the material of his stolen trousers. Why he was annoyed at wearing someone else's clothes, when everything they had was stolen, he didn't know. Maybe his heritage was peeking through the years of strife and secrecy. He was supposed to be the one *helping* others, not taking from them. Though he didn't regret stealing from Julius or that seraphim at all.

He frowned in thought. Who had it been? They had never let him see anyone's face and he hadn't recognised the voice, though after so many years away from the citadel, that wasn't surprising. But that voice was now ingrained in his memory. He'd know when he met the seraphim again. That seraphim was his link to the citadel. Once more, he tried to piece together how he had fallen into his clutches.

Memories of his arrival in Eidolon were blurry. He didn't actually remember arriving. He just woke up one day, off kilter and confused. Fortunate to be taken up by a passing farmer and his wife, they had eyed him closely and then given him a knowing smile. "Just arrived?" they'd asked, and he had nodded. And then grabbed his head as the piercing pain threatened to split his skull in two.

Apparently, there was a certain look that a newly arrived soulless person had. Mav had come to the conclusion that it was an 'I've been bludgeoned and dumped' look, because that was how it felt. He had much to thank that couple for, giving him shelter while he recovered from his injuries, time to reorient himself in Eidolon, and a chance to wonder how he had ended up there.

Living a lie, he had pretended to be a drifter, moving from one farmstead to the next as the whim took him. Trying to stay out of trouble, though trouble had often found him. He seemed to attract it as if he had a sign on his forehead saying, 'Fallen Angel here. Come take your best shot while he's down.'

It was getting to the point where he no longer knew what was real and what was rumour. He thought he had successfully submerged himself into life in Eidolon, accepted that he could never return to Angelicus and that his family didn't want him. Well, if he was being honest, he hadn't accepted it as such but had grasped the opportunity that Eidolon offered to survive, with the desperate grip of a drowning man, clinging onto anything that might keep him afloat.

A memory stirred out of the horror of the torture chamber. Mav clamped down on the visceral flash of fear that flushed through him and focussed on the words Kaenera had said. Trying to divorce himself from the memory of the pain, he gritted his teeth and concentrated. Sweat dewed his skin as he hunted down their conversation, his stomach clenching no matter how hard he tried to ignore his racing heart. According to Kaenera, he had strayed where he was not wanted. What had he found that they didn't want him to know? And who had he stumbled across?

He lifted his head and stared around him, blinking away his musings and letting the memories go as he exhaled, trying to relax tense muscles. They were travelling through the vales of Eidolon. Grim and dreary, the grassy slopes were wreathed in layers of mist, leaching all colour and deadening the sound of the calope's hooves. They hid surprisingly warm and welcoming homesteads. There were a few distant lights of isolated farms or small hamlets. In Eidolon, people grouped together in villages and towns for safety. It was a shame people didn't look past the heavy clouds and uninviting outlook. The people of Eidolon had learned to laugh and enjoy life, even if a new path had been forced on them.

He glanced at Solanji, hunched in her woollen cloak as if the mist squashed her in the saddle. Straightening, he searched their surroundings. The light was unchanging, the mist thickening. It was time to stop for the night. The calopes needed to rest, as did they. Peering at the winterworn boughs of the trees looming overhead, he led the way into their damp embrace. Straggly branches sprung into their faces as they passed, leaving wet scratches and droplets of water in their hair.

Mav glanced around the small clearing. "We'll stop here for the night."

"Is it night? The sky doesn't change. There's no sun, no moon, just this depressing mist."

"We're too far north. The sun doesn't rise here. It'll get lighter as we travel south."

Solanji shivered, tugging her cloak tighter as she slid out of the saddle. She stretched her legs. "I hope so. I couldn't live in twilight all my life."

"It's not so bad. You get used to it."

"I prefer living in the sun all the time. Seems less threatening."

Mav grimaced. Just because it was light and sunny didn't make it any less corrupt. He gritted his teeth and slowly slid out of the saddle, balancing on his good leg. Heat flushed through him, chasing away the chill but leaving his skin damp with sweat.

He left Solanji to set up camp as he struggled with the saddles. He rested his forehead against the animal's flank and inhaled the comforting aroma of its musky coat. Once his tense shoulders relaxed, he limped towards the small fire she had lit.

"So what can we expect to attack us out here if everyone is afraid of leaving their homes?" she asked, poking a damp stick in her fire. The stick hissed and popped in protest.

"Whatever or whoever thinks they are stronger than you."

"Do you ever give a straight answer?"

Mav raised his eyebrows at her. The firelight burnished her brown skin to a warm copper, and her black eyes gleamed with twin pools of flame as she glared at him.

"I thought I had."

"It tells me nothing. Are there large beasts? Bandits? Rampant angels?"

"Angels rarely rampage, though I suppose there is always a chance," he mused. "They wouldn't bother this far north; too far to go home after they'd finished. You're thinking of the host. They're the soldiers. Though you don't want to offend the cherubim either. They are like a one-person army. And don't underestimate the cherubs. They may be small, but they are sneaky little buggers, catch you out every time." He blew his breath out as he tried to remember the last time he had seen a cherub. His eyes stung and his vision blurred, and he wiped his face, mildly surprised to see that he was sweating.

Solanji suddenly lurched to her feet, and the next

moment, her palm was against his forehead. "I knew it. You're burning up. Why didn't you say you had a fever?"

"I don't suffer from fevers."

"Well, you do now. Your cheeks are flushed and your skin is scorching, and you are talking nonsense. Here, drink." She shoved a water skin at him as she hunted in the saddlebags.

Mav suddenly realised he was parched.

"You need to eat something."

Mav ignored her outstretched hand. The smell of the dried meat made his stomach turn. "No, thank you, I'm fine. I'm not hungry."

Her eyes narrowed and then ran down his body to his swollen knee, straining against the material. "I thought you said you'd healed it."

"I said, I did what I could. There is nothing you can do, so there is no point worrying about it. I'll be fine."

Struggling to stay still under her searching inspection, Mav relaxed as she exhaled and sat back down. "Alright, tell me how you ended up in that torture chamber," Solanji asked.

"I've been trying to figure that out myself. A bit like you, I was in one place one moment and then awoke in chains."

"Do you know how long you were there?"

Mav was surprised to see concern in her expression. Why did she care? "No, and I'd rather not talk about what happened there, if you don't mind." He couldn't suppress the shudder, and Solanji nodded, keeping her eyes on him.

"Who are you, then? An angel? The seraphim said you had wings; you must be an angel."

Mav released a sigh of breath. "I was once. I'm fallen. Cast out. Almost forgotten, but not quite, it seems."

"What did you do?"

"It's been so long, I'm not sure I remember anymore. Whatever I did has been embellished out of all recognition over time. So, I try not to bring it up, else they'll kill me before I draw breath." He hugged his uninjured knee to his chest and closed his eyes as he rested his aching head against the tree trunk behind him. There was no doubt about it; he was desperate, about to exhale his last breath.

He couldn't wait any longer, he had to return to the citadel before it was too late. He would report what he had found out about the exploitation of the people in Eidolon, the desperate circumstances many people lived in and then leave, if that was what they wished. That was if they'd even let him enter and speak.

He rubbed his temple, trying to ease the ache. The thoughts rushed through his brain in an uncontrolled burst. One last attempt. One last throw of life's destiny. No matter how the dice fell, he would not be accused of giving up. What was left of him would go down blazing; *that* he promised.

"Where were you when they caught you? Is that where we're going?"

He rolled his head and squinted at her. His eyes hurt and his head ached. "You said you crossed at the divide. I assumed you were from Puronia and would want to go home."

"I live in the city of Puronia, but that's not where I'm from," she corrected him.

"The divide is a three-week ride south. You can cross back into Puronia there."

"What about you? Where are you going?"

"Haven't decided yet." He had three weeks to make that decision. It seemed like too much effort at this precise point in time. "Where are you from, if not Puronia?" he asked, closing his eyes again.

"Originally?" After a brief hesitation, Solanji continued, "Bruatra, down on the south coast. That's where my family lives. It's beautiful; blue seas, golden sands. My father and my eldest brother were fishermen. They always came home with full nets; kept my mother and I busy…"

Mav dozed, listening as her voice wrapped him in a warm hug, and sheltered by her caressing cadences, he fell asleep.

Solanji stopped speaking when she heard him snore. Just a tiny one, but she knew he was asleep. Relief that she could stop talking about her family rushed through her. She had managed to avoid mentioning her youngest brother, but it had brought all of her fears back to the fore. Was Bren alright? Were they keeping him in prison? Or had they let him go? Somehow, she didn't think Kyrill would be benevolent; he wouldn't release her brother until she brought Mav to him in Puronia.

Just the thought of handing Mav back over to such a monster curdled her stomach, but what was she to do? That was the only way she could save her brother. She wet a cloth and placed it on Mav's forehead. She almost expected it to sizzle, he was so hot. The heat radiating off his knee told her that nothing good was happening there, but she had no idea how to help him. His face was strained and tinged with grey, and he had eaten nothing all day. She should have noticed earlier that he was suffering and made him stop.

His shadows curled around him, and she reached, her fingers caressing them. They froze for a moment and then swirled between her fingers, cool and smooth and inherently Mav. They were *of* him, part of him, just as a soul was. Was it his soul? What was left of his soul maybe? No, surely not.

The shadows were tentative to begin with, keeping her away from him, but as she promised she wouldn't hurt him, they curled around her. Dark as the night, they absorbed all light, coaxing her soulmist closer. Her fingers tingled as the silvery sparks nipped at her skin. What were they? They pushed her away as she searched the shadows, trying to understand what they were.

Souls were normally golden swirls of light. They trailed after most people, humans and angels alike. Golden veils of vibrant life that she could thread her fingers through and cuddle and embrace and excite and use to bring her lovers to screaming climaxes that wiped all thought or memory of how they got there out of their brains. Well, until she had nearly killed someone and learned that it was best not to touch. They also gave her glimpses of the person's upper-most thoughts.

But not these shadows; they revealed nothing of Mav's thoughts or memories. No matter how much she probed, they told her nothing, and she was relieved. She didn't want to steal his memories, even if Kyrill was forcing her to. She would make some up. Kyrill would never know.

Mav's shadows were strong and dark, and they felt divine. Like plush fur or the softest wrap. She couldn't resist them and, ignoring her self-imposed rule not to touch, she leaned into them, embraced them, became one with them, exulted in the feel of them entwining with her soul light. They behaved like souls and they reciprocated. Oh my, did they reciprocate.

A sharp crack made her jerk, her head nearly twisting off her neck she turned so fast, and she swayed, feeling light-headed and giddy. She stilled, her heart racing as Mav gripped her wrist, and she met his amber eyes, which were soft and luminous. She gulped. She had forgotten the effect she could leave behind. If she felt languorous and decadent, what did he feel?

He rose swiftly, more in control of his emotions than she

was, and he pushed her behind him as he surveyed their camp. His sword was already in his hand, and Solanji fumbled for her dagger.

"What is it?" she whispered.

The thick bushes on the other side of the clearing shook, and a large beast emerged from its embrace and paused at the edge of their camp. Its huge eyes luminesced in the firelight, high in an elongated face. Shaggy fur in stripes of different shades of brown covered its body. Long limbs were tipped in vicious-looking claws.

Solanji hissed her breath out as Mav lowered his sword and moved towards the fire. "Mav," she breathed in warning.

"Not everything in Eidolon is dangerous," Mav replied. He stooped to pick up a saddlebag, and after a moment of rummaging, dropped it back on the ground. He approached the beast, holding out his hand. The animal whuffled, sniffed the air, and then shambled forward, and a large tongue licked Mav's hand and scooped up whatever he held. Solanji watched in shock as Mav scratched the creature behind the ear.

She flinched as a deep rumble echoed across their camp, and then she realised it was purring. Mav grinned at her, which eased the strain on his face, and he beckoned her over. "This is a demora."

"A what?"

"A demora. A creature of the night. They can only see in the dark. They bumble around in the day, so they don't often venture out of their caves. This far north it's not such a problem, but further south, you won't see them. I've always said this is where the word 'demon' came from, but these are big softies, nothing like a demon. Aren't you, fella?" he asked as he scratched the demora's chin. The rumble deepened to a vibration, and Solanji laughed.

The demora was huge. Mav barely came up to its shoulder, but he stood next to the gaping maw as if it meant nothing. Which from the way the creature was reacting, it didn't. Mav gave the beast a hug and then pushed at his shoulder. "Off you go. Not all camps will be as welcoming, so you be careful. Avoid the man people."

The demora grunted, dipped his head at Mav, and shambled off.

"Did you just talk to him? And he understood you?"

Mav glanced at her in surprise. "Of course. All beasts can understand you."

Solanji shook her head. "No, I'm pretty sure animals don't usually understand a word you say."

"Ah, but you're in Eidolon now. And the creatures of Eidolon are not the same as elsewhere. They are much more intelligent."

"But how? Shouldn't the creatures in Puronia, those under the aegis of angels, be the more intelligent?"

Mav's eyebrows rose. "Why?"

"Well, because they are angels, they know best. And it's brighter, warmer, more inclusive."

"Is it?"

"Yes! Here it's dreary, miserable, and oppressive."

Mav considered her. "I suppose you've only seen the castle and the local scenery. Not being in the sun's glare all the time gives others the chance to shine. You know," he said, waving a hand, "demoras are peaceful creatures, grazers. They may look vicious with those claws, but they are for stripping bark or digging up fungi or roots. The ground is often frozen up here in the north. Without their claws they would starve." Mav sheathed his sword and limped back to his bedroll. "You can't always judge things by what you see; you have other senses as well, you know. Get some sleep. We have an early start." He rolled up in his blanket and closed his eyes, leaving Solanji staring at him in shock.

"How do you know all this?" she demanded, but he didn't answer, and with some angst, she covered herself with her blanket and glared at him.

Mav's lips twitched as if aware of her glare. "You know, you could continue doing whatever it was you were doing before we were so rudely interrupted."

Solanji gasped as heat rose across her face; he had known! His grin widened, and she huffed and turned her back on him. She wasn't sure why she was angry at him. It wasn't as if he had done anything wrong. She heaved a deep sigh and rolled back over, snuggling into her blanket, her gaze resting on him. It was reassuring seeing him lying there. She fell asleep remembering the caress of his shadows, a slight smile on her face.

14

ADRIZ

A driz sighed out her breath and stroked the brush down the calope's back. Grooming the beast was soothing as hums vibrated up her arms and throughout her body. Fine hairs floated around her, glistening in the light of the glass lamp hanging from the rafter above her.

The land of Eidolon was such a contradiction. Dull and damp, with a nearly constant misty rain sifting from the heavy clouds, it hid fields of lush green crops and grass and hillsides covered in bannen plants, coveted for their roots and leaves. Beneath the green leafy carpet, a myriad of minerals lurked, only just being discovered. There was much that was rich in Eidolon, including the people.

Many of the people forced to live in Eidolon were here for minor discrepancies; falling into debt, crossing the wrong person, defaulting on a payment. Nothing that deserved such a permanent punishment, and yet the Justicers were relentless and unforgiving. A child caught stealing a loaf of bread, starving and desperate was treated as severely as someone deliberately causing harm to another person.

Adriz sucked in her breath at the number of young children she had seen on her travels, even more desperate and scared. And then you would meet a farmer or a homesteader or a small hamlet of families, and the expected brush off and belligerence were replaced by welcoming smiles and lavish, for Eidolon, meals.

The people were eager to hear of news from their old life, not quite ready to give up all hope of returning, and yet, if they crossed the divide without a soul, by the time they reached Angelicus they would have but a few hours to live. No one knew why. It was so unfair.

Her thoughts drifted to Felather, the reason they had stopped at this farmstead on the edge of a nearby village. He had succumbed to a heavy cold; the damp had clogged up his chest and he was tucked up in bed, frustrated that he couldn't heal himself. He could heal others, but that skill did not extend to his own ills or injuries.

Her lips curved as she imagined his flushed cheeks and feverish eyes. He looked so adorable and sweet burrowed in his bed, as if he was awakening from a night filled with adventure. Her fingertips tingled and she curled them in and out. She wished she could break down his barriers and crawl into his bed with him.

He had resisted her for years. Twisting her lips, she wondered why. She'd never seen him with anyone else, man or woman. She didn't understand his reticence. Chewing her lip, she frowned, remembering the time she had promised she wouldn't break him. Felather's embarrassed reaction had been priceless. She gave a low chuckle at the memory and then stiffened at a loud shout, edged with fear. She dropped the brushes and grabbed her sword, moving silently to the half open door at the side of the barn.

Peering through the gap, she frowned at the scene unfolding outside. Large, ill-dressed men were dragging the farmer and his wife out into the yard. More farm hands were dragged from their work and bundled into a group near a wagon. Her eyes narrowed as she saw a half-dressed Felather, a dark bruise already blooming on his pale cheek, struggling in the grip of two men. His foot lashed out and caught one of the men's knees. The man cursed as he staggered, releasing Felather's arm, and then he swung back round, a vicious fist catching Felather's jaw. Felather's head snapped back, and he slumped in the other man's grip.

Adriz's knuckles cracked as she tightened her grip, but she had to be sensible. She was one against a gang. She needed to see how many there were before they came to check the barn. At a sharp command, two men began to tie everyone up, wrist and ankle, even the unconscious Felather. Her jaw tightened as she watched a dark-haired man, with a hard face and hooked nose, ordering the men about.

Two of the men veered off towards the barn, their gaze vacant. Dybbuks! Kaenera's minions were far from home. What were they doing here? Adriz leaned her sword against the wall and pulled out her daggers before hiding behind the door. She had seen five men. Soon they would be three. A shout made her peer through the slats. They had stopped and turned, and Adriz cursed when they started walking back towards their calopes.

Sneaking out and around the side of the barn, Adriz winced as she saw the men swing Felather's body onto the back of the flat bed wagon. The dybbuks had moved quick, eager to be away with their booty. She wondered what they needed the men and women for and where they were taking them.

Farm equipment lined the edges of the open space, and Adriz crept from one hiding place to the next, working her way towards the wagon. But before she could do anything, the driver whipped them and urged them out of the yard. Her heart stuttered. Felather! She couldn't lose him as well.

A light scuff behind her had her spinning, whipping up her sword as she blocked a strike and she counterattacked, forcing the other man across the yard towards the house. He was sloppy and ill-trained, and she dispatched him in a few strikes, which left the black-haired leader, standing horrified on the step and Adriz not even out of breath.

"Who do you work for?" she barked, advancing on the man. "What do you want with these people?"

The man backed into the house, desperately glancing around him. As his eyes narrowed, Adriz lurched forward, a throwing knife already in the air. It thunked into the man's shoulder, and he stumbled out of sight. The cry of a child sent shivers down her back. She hadn't seen any of the children!

Adriz rushed through the door, and her lip curled at the sight of the man trying to shield himself with a terrified little girl. The farmer's daughter, Resha. His arm was wrapped around the child's waist to hold her in front of him as she struggled.

"So brave," Adriz crooned, taking a step forward.

"Stay there," the man shouted, his knife at the girl's throat.

"Tell me who you are working for and I'll make it quick," Adriz promised.

"I'll kill her!"

"But then you won't have a shield," Adriz replied. "Resha, close your eyes, my dear. It will all be over in a moment." The child clamped her eyes shut, tears trickling down her cheeks. "You chose the wrong farm," Adriz said, swaying to her left. The man swayed with her, and she leapt, closing the distance with unexpected speed, her hand clamping around the man's wrist and his neck. The knife clattered to the floor, and the man collapsed, releasing the child, who scrambled away. "Who do you work for?" Adriz squeezed his neck harder.

"He'll kill me if I tell you."

"And I'll kill you if you don't."

The man gasped, struggling to get enough breath. "H-he'll come for you. He'll get you all. He gets everyone in the end."

Adriz smiled but the man shuddered at her expression, and then a bone cracked and he went limp. She schooled her features before glancing behind her as she let go of him. Resha was huddled in a corner, her hands over eyes.

"Well done, Resha," she whispered as she gathered the child for a gentle hug. "It's all over now. I want you to go upstairs to your room and curl up under your blankets. Stay there until your mother comes to get you. Will you do that for me?"

Resha nodded.

"Do you know where your brother is?"

A shaky hand pointed towards the wooden table in the centre of the room, where a small boy huddled, eyes wide and fixed in terror and Adriz cursed under her breath. He had seen it all. "Benit, you're safe now. You can come out."

The boy licked his pale lips and held her eyes. "You killed him, with one hand," he whispered.

"I'm sorry you saw that, Benit. But he was a bad man."

The boy's nod was jerky. "He was going to hurt Resha."

"That's right, but he can't hurt either of you now. Can you come out, now? I need to know you're alright. He didn't hurt you, did he?"

Benit shook his head and after a moment crawled out from under the table.

"Can you protect Resha for me? Go up to your room and

hide under the covers whilst I go and make sure there is no one else outside?" Adriz asked.

"I'm bigger than he is. I should protect *him*," Resha announced, a scowl on her face.

Adriz smiled. "Why don't you protect each other?"

Resha nodded, grabbed Benit's hand and dragged him towards the stairs. They argued over who would protect who as they climbed. Adriz sighed out a breath and checked the yard. It was empty. Rushing over to the calope tied to the fence, she launched herself into the saddle and set off after the wagon and Felather.

Clenching her jaw so hard it ached, Adriz peered around her as she urged the calope faster. Tall trees lined either side of the road, branches extending over them like a wooden slat ceiling. The bare branches intertwined and met in the middle, forming a tunnel. Dim light shone through the gaps, a misty glow softening the edges. Relief flooded her as she heard the creak of the cart ahead and the sound of muffled animal's hooves in the silence that surrounded her.

"I can't get over how empty Eidolon is," Adriz muttered under her breath as she dismounted and led her calope to the bend on the road.

Cautiously peering around the corner, she observed the dybbuks. The driver and three guards plodded on mindlessly. She couldn't see Felather, only the farmer and his wife kneeling at the back of the cart. The dybbuks weren't concerned with anything surrounding them, just focused on the road ahead. She inspected them more closely as she followed. The dybbuks were muscular men, dressed in ill-fitting clothes that looked like they had been slept in, they were so creased. They slumped in the saddles, uncaring of what might approach them, and Adriz was tempted to attack them now. But Felather had become caught up in whatever was going on, and Adriz was not prepared to waste the chance to find out what they were up to.

A sense of expectation shivered through her at the thought that Mav could be imprisoned here, or in a place like this. There was a chance she and Felather would find something, give them somewhere else to look while they dismantled whatever was going on here. The people of Eidolon were not a free harvest to fill the bellies of greedy people, and Adriz was determined to cause a drought.

The presence of dybbuks suggested that Kaenera was involved, but the Guardian of the Oblivion Gate only cared about reaping a person's final moments, not the life they led before they died, or at least he never had before. She doubted he had changed. He had never struck Adriz as one who was interested in the details; he was above all that.

Not that she'd ever spoken to him, but Mav had, and from her silent position behind Mav's shoulder, she had heard plenty.

Anger stirred, and Adriz smiled. She was ready for a fight. It had been too long since she'd had a good sparring session, and she had a lot of pent-up aggression ready to be released. The thought of exercising her sword arm appealed and removing a few dybbuks appealed even more.

Adriz frowned as she tried to remember the map of Eidolon. There wasn't anything out this way that she could remember. Following, her senses on full alert, she cursed under her breath as she trailed after the wagon. Concern for Felather mounted. Was he still unconscious? Was anyone helping him? Starting as a bird's shrill call shattered the silence, she cursed again as she tried to control her racing heart. She would kill him! After she'd kissed him of course, but then she would kill him for scaring her so badly.

15

SOLANJI

The next morning, if it *was* morning, Solanji thought as she scowled at the light drizzle descending from the cloudy grey sky, they packed up the camp. "Is that all it does?" she asked, pointing upwards. "Dreary grey clouds and rain?"

"Pretty much," Mav replied as he cinched the girth tight and then tied the bedroll and travel bags behind it. Cupping his hands, he lifted her into the saddle. He pulled her cloak over the back of the calope to keep her bedding as dry as possible.

Pulling his calope over, he took a deep breath and briefly balanced on his left leg before hauling himself into the saddle. Solanji observed his pale face but there was nothing she could do to help so she led the way back onto the trail. Muddy puddles greeted them, and the calope sloshed through them regardless. Solanji peered at them. "Are they deliberately walking through the puddles?"

"Calopes love water, even if it's dirty. If we cross a river, make sure you keep the reins tight, else they'll be romping downstream before you know it."

"Are you feeling better this morning?"

"Much. I slept well. You?"

Solanji smiled and raised her face to the fine rain. She felt well too, content even. "It does seem to be a brighter morning."

"You were telling me about your family. Why did you leave home? It sounded rather idyllic." Her face fell, and he reached for her, his shadows questing. "I'm sorry. If you'd prefer not talk about it…"

"No, it's alright." She curled her fingers in his shadows without thinking, comforted. She didn't notice as he eased closer. "Even though my father was an excellent fisherman, even the best can get caught in a storm. His boat went down, and we were left without a father and destitute. My brother had to go work on another boat for someone else, and the catches never brought enough money. Not enough to support my mother, my younger brother, and me." She shrugged. "So I went north to the city, looking for work; one less mouth for my brother to feed. Only that wasn't as easy as I expected, either."

"Where did you go first?"

"Where else? The citadel."

"And how did that go?"

Solanji flicked a glance at him. "About as well as you are expecting. I'm sure you know it well enough."

Twisting his lips, Mav glanced around him as he replied, "Although it is a beautiful building, from what I've heard, it seems to have lost its sense of compassion in recent years."

"Compassion? They don't know the meaning of the word. The angels and seraphim may live there, but their guard won't let you past the gate."

"And yet they know best. Wasn't that what you said?"

"Of course they do. It's the guards that need re-educating."

"I suppose with so many requests for help, they must get a little brusque. It's difficult to feel sympathy for everyone, every hour of the day."

Solanji straightened in her saddle. "You don't like them much, do you?"

"No, I suppose not."

"Why not?"

Mav shrugged, causing the raindrops to run down his cloak. His black hair was plastered to his head, the silver threads hiding. "They are angels. They are supposed to help people. Protect them. Guide them. I think they've lost their way."

"Not surprising since Veradeus disappeared. It's been decades now, hasn't it? Do you think he will ever return?" Solanji's eyes narrowed as Mav stiffened beside her.

"I haven't heard that name in a long time," he said, his voice low.

She snorted. "Why would you? He's not here. Left his sons to rule while he went off searching for something. Isn't he supposed to know everything? Doesn't bode well if our God above covets something. I thought being covetous was forbidden?"

"If something is forbidden, doesn't it make it more tempting?"

A burble of laughter escaped, and Solanji rocked back in her saddle, her fingers still caressing his shadows. "You're asking me? You're the fallen one. What tempted you?"

"Whatever it was, I'm sure it was worth it," he replied, unconsciously leaning toward her. "What are you doing to me, Solanji?"

Solanji froze, and then released his shadows as her stomach dropped. She hadn't realised what she had been doing. "I-I'm sorry."

"Don't be. It's lovely. Reminds me of things I'd long

forgotten. I certainly feel better." He paused, his amber eyes unfocused and soft. "You make me feel more…real, maybe. I'm just worried that when you stop, everything will come crashing back down on me."

"I-I can't resist them." She curled her fingers tight.

"Resist what?"

"Your shadows."

"You see shadows around me?"

"Yes, in place of your soul light. They are black and they writhe around you; protecting you, I think. There are sparkles of silver throughout, and they nip."

"I am hurting you? I assure you, I am not doing it deliberately. You've stopped now, haven't you?" He shifted in his saddle.

"Yes, I'm sorry. And they don't hurt. It's nice. They like me."

Mav's rare smile flashed at her for a moment, and she caught her breath as it transformed his face. "I don't doubt it; *I* like you."

Solanji blushed. Oh glory be, he thought she was fishing for compliments. "You don't have to say that, it's probably just…" How should she phrase it? She couldn't tell him she was caressing his shadows, not to him; they hardly knew each other, even if she couldn't resist them. "It's just…"

"Soulbreathing? That's what it feels like. Your warm breath on my skin, caressing and silky-soft. It's like you are embracing me, touching me…" Mav paused and exhaled, "… everywhere."

Solanji flushed, her gaze flitting around them, avoiding him. His voice had dropped to an intimate whisper, and he was very, very close. She met his heated amber gaze and winced at the golden flames flickering deep inside. Like a fool, she had seduced him, and he had no choice but to respond.

"Do you want to embrace me?" he asked, his voice a low growl.

"Mav. I'm so sorry. I never meant to… to… without your consent."

"You have my consent now," he breathed.

She pulled her mount away from him, and the heat faded from his gaze, and he blinked.

A club swung from out of nowhere, hit him in the chest with a sickening thud, and he was swept from his saddle. Mav crashed into the muddy slush as high-pitched yowls and shrieks rushed towards them. Solanji's mount shied away from the noise, and she clung to stay on as Mav's calope shot back down the road, leaving him lying in the mud.

Solanji leapt down, hanging onto the reins, and knelt beside him. He was heaving and gasping for breath, his face pale and drawn. He had been so relaxed moments before, and she mourned the loss of that special glow she'd seen in his eyes.

Icy water seeped through her trousers. She was kneeling in a puddle, which meant Mav was just as soaked and uncomfortable. "Mav, are you alright?" Stupid, stupid question. Why did she always ask such stupid questions?

He wheezed in response.

She stood as their attackers approached, standing between them and Mav. They were short, and as they drew closer, she realised they were young, just kids. "What do you mean by attacking us?" she snapped. "We've lost our mount now; you'd better go and retrieve it for us."

"Toll. You gotta pay a toll before yer can pass," a skinny lad replied. His brown hair was matted and limp, his skin and clothes filthy.

"Couldn't you have asked first?" she demanded, clenching her fists to stop herself grabbing the child.

"You'da said no. Now we got what you want and you'll pay the toll."

"You hurt my friend."

The boy peered down at Mav still wheezing in the mud. "Nah, was just a tap; he's fine. Hey, you look familiar…" He narrowed his eyes as he squinted at Mav.

"He doesn't sound fine to me." Solanji wasn't letting him off that easily. "You ought to be ashamed of yourselves."

Laughing, the boy slapped his leg. He pointed at her as he turned to his equally ragged-looking friends. "Ashamed," he said, and the boys grinned. The skinny lad turned back and held out his hand. "Toll, four coppers for a friend of a friend."

Solanji crossed her arms. "I am not paying you anything. It will cost more than four coppers to get our clothes clean."

The boy shrugged. "Four coppers or you don't pass."

Mav heaved himself to his feet, and the boys backed away, their eyes widening. "And who is going to stop us?" he wheezed.

"We will," a deeper voice said. The boys jerked around as heavily armed men appeared out of the shadows and surrounded them. The boys were quick to scuttle behind Mav and Solanji.

Mav straightened, clearly assessing this new threat, and Solanji started as he gripped her arm. "And who might you be?"

"We've been looking for you. You left a bit abruptly. The seraphim was not finished."

"I beg to differ."

"You stole his favourite calope," another sterner voice said, pushing past the men. He faced Mav, a grim smile curving his lips.

"I always had good taste," Mav replied, shifting his

stance to face the officer glaring at him. "Don't you have anything better to do?"

Solanji scowled at the men. What was Mav thinking? They were outnumbered and out-armed. Each man had at least three weapons that she could see, gleaming with sharply-honed edges, and they had souls. Nice, golden souls that trailed after them, if she could reach them. She willed him to keep talking as she extended her soul fingers.

She brushed by his shadows, a couple of which entangled with her as she extended further, and Mav stiffened.

"You'll have to advise your pet seraphim that I decline his invitation. One visit was enough," Mav said.

"It's not a choice," the man said, stepping forward as he unsheathed his sword.

"There is always a choice," Mav replied as he raised his sword in response.

Solanji hesitated at the clash of steel, surprised that the other men waited as Mav and the officer began to fight. She extended further, grasping their soul trails and whispering suggestions. *You do not want to be here. A warm fire beckons you. Sheath your swords and find an inn. You are tired and cold. Enough for today, you deserve a break.* Her fingers combed through the golden light, relaxing a tenseness that she hadn't realised sat at her core.

The men sheathed their weapons, their eyes glazing. They drifted off, one by one encouraged by Solanji's gentle whispers. She turned her attention to the leader, the man currently pounding into Mav with powerful strokes. Mav deflected the strikes, but he was giving ground. Before she could intervene, he ducked under a swinging blade and struck back. Hefting his sword with two hands and hopping on his left foot, he pivoted into the man, taking them both down into the mud.

They grappled, both men of a size, and she hissed her

breath out as the flash of steel whipped between them. The man's lips were curled into a snarl, and he was gasping out words. "How… dare you… you're nothing… and no one… cast out shit… nameless… worthless… unwanted… fallen." It was like a litany, as if he was trying to convince himself. Mav was silent, his knuckles white around the wrist that held the knife.

Solanji yelped as she was jerked off her feet. One of the other guards had not left as she had suggested. "Think you can outwit us, do you?" he hissed in her ear. He struck her across the face, a stinging blow which knocked her off balance. Her cheek ached, and she gasped in shock, squirming in his grip as she grasped the dagger in her belt.

"You made a mistake helping him. Wrong bastard to help, only cause you trouble. Now, if you want to be nice to me, maybe I'll speak up for you."

Solanji struck upwards, a hard and desperate thrust; her dagger scraped off his buttons, jarring her wrist, and the man hissed, pushing her away. He looked down at the blade sticking out of his gut in shock. "You bitch," he snarled and tried to take a step forward. He staggered and went down on one knee. "What did you do?" he whispered as his eyes rolled in his head and he collapsed to the ground.

The dragon tattoo uncurled from her forearm and hovered in front of her. It flicked its snout towards the body with its shimmering soulmist hanging in the air above it and stared at her expectantly. Solanji stared at it, bewildered. Did the dragon expect her to do something? The little dragon huffed, and as faint whispers swirled around her, it inhaled the man's golden soulmist before it could dissipate, then slid back up her skin and solidified around her arm. Solanji's mind spun. The little dragon had collected a soul, though she had the feeling it had expected her to do it at first. Maybe she could give it to Mav, if she could figure out how.

Mav! She turned and froze. Mav was now on top of the man, the cords in his neck standing out as he forced down the knife in the other man's grip down, so slowly, inch by inch towards his chest. It was eerily silent, as if everything held its breath waiting for the end to come.

"Mav," the man whispered. "Why?"

And everything stopped. Just for a moment. Solanji was sure she had stopped breathing. They knew each other?

Mav couldn't kill his friend. That much she knew, even if he was trying to kill him in return. She stroked Mav's shadows and he shuddered. "I can put him to sleep," she whispered, holding on tight.

Mav bared his teeth. "Do it."

Solanji began whispering, stroking the man's trailing mist, encouraging drowsiness. As the man's eyelids fluttered and closed, Mav rolled off him and lay staring at the still drizzling sky, breathing deeply.

She dropped beside him, her hands fluttering over him. "Did he hurt you?" She couldn't see any blood, only grazes and bruises blooming on his golden skin.

He raised a shaking hand and cupped her aching cheek. "Are you alright?"

"I'm fine. Come on, we need to move before he wakes up." She rose and inspected the man. He was blonde-haired and had a strong face with a square chin. He was as tall as Mav and as broad across the shoulders. "You know him?"

"We were friends once. A very long time ago."

"Then it is better you don't kill him."

"I should have; he'll only be angrier when he wakes up," Mav murmured.

"That's his problem. You would have felt terrible."

"I'd feel worse if he'd killed me."

"No, you wouldn't; you wouldn't feel a thing, so no point

worrying about it." She helped Mav rise to his feet, though she wasn't much help really.

He looked around them and spotted the other body. "What happened to him?"

"I killed him," she whispered.

Mav gently gripped her chin and tilted her face so that he could see her cheek. "If he did that, then he deserved it," he replied and drew her in and hugged her. She inhaled the scent of him, vanilla and a hint of something warm and comforting. She snuggled into his shadows, feeling safe and protected.

His breath was hot on her neck as his grip tightened. He shivered, and she gave herself up to the moment until he sighed against her skin. "Much as I don't want to move, we need to," he murmured as he nuzzled her neck. She heard the smile in his voice, and an answering smile spread over her face as she looked up at him.

His heart skipped beneath her fingers, and she reached up on tiptoe, raising her face to his as she leaned against his hard body.

The sound of a throat being cleared made them spring apart. "Don't want to interrupt or nothing, but you still owes us four coppers," a young voice stated.

Mav exhaled and then rolled his eyes as he dropped beside his friend's body. He rifled through his pockets and rose, a purse in hand. He counted out four coppers, added a fifth and flipped them to the boy, one at a time. "I suggest you scarper before his friends come back."

The boy nodded. "I've placed you now. You set up Shandra's lot. She was pissed when you didn't come back. We found your calope. It's tied over there." Another coin spun its way over to the boy, and he grinned in delight and then scampered off.

Fortunately, Solanji's mount hadn't wandered too far, and

she went to fetch it as Mav stared down at his friend.

He stirred as Solanji returned and whispered, "Who is he?"

"Captain Julius Teravin. We were schooled together. Grew up together."

"Well, he's about the same size as you. How about you steal his clothes?"

Mav choked out a laugh. "He will definitely kill me next time if I leave him out here in nothing but his skin."

Solanji slapped his shoulder and was effusive in her apologies as he winced. "I thought you said you weren't hurt?"

"I'm not. Just bruises; they'll fade."

"Good. I meant steal the ones in his saddle bags. Clean clothes will feel much better."

Mav's eyebrows rose. "Nice thinking," he said and limped off to search for his old friend's mount. He found it in the copse of trees off the side of the road and brought it back, tethering it to Julius' arm. He stripped and changed, glad to be wearing clothes that fit for once, even a pair of socks, which Solanji had to slip onto his blistered feet for him. Julius' boots were a good fit, so he left his stolen ones next to him. Let Julius suffer for a while. Make him appreciate being alive.

Mav sighed as he stood. "You really don't appreciate good clothes until you've been deprived of them for a few years." He tugged the woollen cloak tighter and grinned as Solanji came out of the bushes, the dead guard's spare clothes hanging off her slim frame. She was busy rolling up the sleeves, but she had the cloak wrapped around her as well.

"I think it's time we moved on. Where did you send the guards?"

"To find an inn and go to sleep."

"Then let us get as far ahead of them as we can before they regroup and come charging after us."

"Do you think they will?"

"Oh yes. Julius won't forgive me for leaving him here."

Solanji pressed her lips together as she frowned in thought. "I don't see what else you could have done."

Mav chuckled under his breath. "Please make sure you are around to defend me when he turns up."

Solanji nodded firmly. "Be my pleasure," she replied as they remounted and set off down the road.

After a few miles of silence, Solanji spoke. "Who is Shandra?"

"Just a kid. You'll get to meet her soon. We'll stop at her den for a couple of days, throw Julius off our trail."

"He must know we are heading for the crossing. That will just give him more time to get ready for us."

"I need time to rest, as do you. We can plan our approach."

"What does he want of you?"

"Which he?" Mav asked, a dry twist to his lips.

"The seraphim? By what right did he treat you so?"

"He *had* no right, but then I am fallen, so I have no rights."

"He wanted me to take your soul. Why does he want your soul? Isn't his good enough?"

Mav hesitated for a moment and then said, "I think he'll find it won't do him any good."

Solanji grimaced. She flicked a glance at him. The shadows twisted and curled around him.

"Do you think the host will try to stop you crossing the divide?"

"Possibly," Mav replied.

"How much further is it?"

"Couple of weeks."

"Is that the only place you can cross?"

Mav nodded. "They closed all the other crossings years ago. They like to control entry to Angelicus."

Solanji considered his point. "How will you cross then? Will they recognise you?"

"Unlikely, but it doesn't matter as I'm not sure I *will* be crossing."

"What? Why not?" Solanji's heart fluttered at the thought of leaving him behind.

"I thought it was obvious why not."

"I might know of a different crossing we could use; one that will be safer for you."

"I can't cross without a soul."

Solanji wrinkled her nose. If you didn't have a soul, although you could cross you couldn't stay in Angelicus. That place was only for people with a soul. Funny how souled people could still cross into the dead zone. A bit unfair that. But she had a spare soul; her chest ached at the thought of the dead soldier and how the dragon had collected his soulmist. How would Mav react if she offered it to him?

"Can you borrow a soul?" she asked.

Mav heaved a sigh. "Only if it's freely given, and it will only last for a day or so. Seems a poor return for such a gift."

"So, it is possible?"

"For a SoulBreather. Maybe. But there hasn't been one of those for a long time."

"What is a SoulBreather exactly?"

"Someone who can manipulate and transfer souls. They can weave a soul back into the body."

"Like what I do?"

"From what you've said, I think you are a SoulSinger. You can touch and stimulate. It's different to weaving."

"Did you know a SoulBreather?"

"Yes. She was much sought after. So much so that, in the

end, someone decided that if they couldn't have her, then no one could." Mav's face was bleak as he finished speaking, and Solanji hesitated to ask further. Mav straightened. "There's no point going over it. I was stupid to think I could cross without a soul. If they arrest me, I'll die before I have the chance to speak to anyone."

Solanji stilled. Kyrill had been adamant for her to persuade Mav to return to the citadel. Her mouth went dry and it was difficult to speak. Was that what Kyrill wanted? For Mav to be arrested and incarcerated. For him to die in a cell?

Relieved he was finally answering some of her questions instead of deflecting them, Solanji asked the question that haunted her, even though she knew she shouldn't, her voice tentative. "What happened? To your soul I mean." She was quick to add as his shadows stuttered, "Only if you want to tell me."

He eased his shoulders and shrugged, casting her a suspicious glance. "I don't know, but the citadel has a rule. Without a soul you can't enter."

"Into Puronia, you mean?"

"You can enter Puronia, travel into Angelicus if you desire, though your stay will brief. But you can't enter the citadel."

"How long have you been here?"

"Too many years to count."

"Why did he capture you now, then? After all this time."

An arrested expression stole over Mav's face as he considered for a moment. "I have no idea."

Solanji wasn't satisfied with his answer, but then it was obvious that neither was he. There was more going on than either of them knew.

They fell silent as they encouraged their mounts to pick up speed, both resisting the urge to look over their shoulders.

16

FELATHER

F elather groaned as he regained consciousness sprawled in the back of the wagon. His jaw ached, along with his ribs as he twisted, trying to ease the strain of his bound arms on his body.

"Stay quiet," a low voice hissed. "Don't let them know you're awake."

The stench of fear and sweat pervaded the air, and Felather cracked an eye open, squinting at the browbeaten people huddled next to him. Bruises bloomed on pale skin, dark shadows ringed their eyes. He didn't recognise them, and his breathing quickened as he searched for Adriz. Then he saw the farmer, Benjamin, who shook his head as Felather's panicked gaze met his, and Felather closed his eyes in relief. A pissed off Adriz was a dangerous Adriz, and he knew she would be following. Of that, he had no doubt.

The cart rumbled down another track, and the wooden fence of a compound came into view. Drawing to a halt, a guard jumped down and unlocked the gate, swung it open far enough to allow the cart through, and then shut it again.

Felather peered around him with interest as they passed a

row of one story rectangular buildings stood along one wall, the lack of windows unnerving. Opposite them was a series of square structures with windows. Offices maybe?

The cart came to a halt, and the backboard was undone. One of the dybbuks climbed up and kicked them to move. Felather relaxed into a slump as the others dismounted. "Get out," the dybbuk said and kicked Felather in the side. When he didn't move, rough hands grabbed him and hauled him out of the wagon and slung him onto the floor in one of the dim windowless buildings.

Men and women crowded in behind him, shocked and bewildered as the door slammed shut, enveloping them in complete darkness. "What do they want with us?" a woman asked, her voice trembling with fear.

Felather wriggled about and, after a brief struggle, managed to thread his bottom and then his legs through his bound hands. Sitting up, he rolled his head, relieving the tension in his shoulders. Oh, for one of Adriz's lovely massages. Reaching down to his boot, he slid out a narrow blade and cut through the rope. He briefly wondered why Kaenera preferred such stupid followers. They hadn't even searched him.

"I'm sure we'll find out soon enough," he murmured. "Benjamin, are you and Elisa unhurt?"

"Yes, just bruised. What about you?"

"Other than a splitting headache, I'm fine. Did you see how many other guards were in the compound?"

"There was one by the cave entrance," a younger voice said. "The track led to a deep crevice in the rock face. And one of those brutes stood guard. There are watch towers around the perimeter, but I couldn't see if anyone was up there."

"A cave entrance?" Felather asked. "Benjamin, are you still tied up?"

"Yeah."

Felather crawled towards Benjamin's voice and sliced through the ropes. "How about anyone else?" he asked.

"Shouldn't we stay tied up?" the youngster asked.

"I don't think they'll notice," Felather replied as he crawled towards the boy.

Light flooded the room as the door was wrenched open, and those who could, shielded their eyes. A large dybbuk filled the doorway. "You mine for ore. Take a shovel and a basket. No ore, no food." The dybbuk stepped back, beckoning them out. They shuffled towards the door, eager to be out of the dark, though Felather thought it was probably safer in the hut.

"You have no right to make us work here. This is slavery and unjust," one of the men shouted as he shook his bound hands at them.

The dybbuk unsheathed his dagger and plunged it into the chest of the woman standing next to him. She inhaled on a shocked gasp, shuddered, and then went rigid as the dybbuk pulled his knife back out. Blood spurted from her chest as she slowly collapsed, her eyes wide and fixed. A man screamed in horror and dashed to her side, clasping her in his arms. He began to keen as a trickle of blood escaped from the corner of her mouth.

"You refuse, you lose woman," the dybbuk grunted and gestured to the stack of tools. "Choose."

The subdued group dispersed, grabbing a basket and a spade; even the children, who looked around them with wide-eyed terror. In a ragged line they entered the dark opening. The dead woman was pulled out of the man's arms and the man was forced into the cavern with the others.

"Dig ore," the dybbuk said, gesturing at the tunnels and then he left. The dybbuks remained outside, guarding the entrance. It seemed no one would be allowed out without filling their basket with ore.

Felather searched the cavern. It was empty but for three narrow tunnels, the rough rock walls lit by a burning torch. He darted down a dim tunnel. It ran straight in to the cliff, no deviations, and after about a hundred paces, he reached the rock face. He touched the wall, and the material crumbled under his fingers, dry and friable. He glanced up in sudden concern and was relieved to see some wooden braces holding the ceiling up. This rock was brittle and would easily collapse. Felather stored the thought and returned to the main cavern.

A quick count revealed that there were eleven adults, twelve including him, and three children. He was determined he would get them all out before even more joined them.

"Let's split into groups of four adults and one child. Take a tunnel each. You need to fill all your baskets with ore or they won't let you out for food. You need to keep your strength up, so go slow and steady."

"How do we know what the ore looks like?" a small woman asked in a tremulous voice. She was gripping her basket so tight, her knuckles gleamed white.

"Your name?" Felather asked with a smile.

"Ria."

"It will have a metallic sheen like this." He handed round a fragment of rock he had picked up. "It will be easy to mine; the rock crumbles at the touch. Fill your basket and no more. Help the children."

"What about the possibility of the roof collapsing?" Ria asked, and everyone looked up.

"A possibility, so go careful. Don't dig too deep."

"Who are you? How do you know all this?" the man with the black eye asked. "Terril," he said when Felather looked at him.

"I've travelled a lot, seen many different places and arti-sans. I'm called Felather."

"What should we do? If we are going to try and escape, isn't it better to do it now while there are only a few of them?" Terill asked, glancing behind him.

"We can't," Ria said. "You saw what they did. They'll kill us all. Women first!"

"Let's lull them for a bit. Make them think we are cowed. Observation is key. When we get out of here watch what the dybbuks do. We need to make sure it's just the three of them before we decide to do anything, and it's better that we wait until they are not paying so much attention to us. For now, everyone, go fill your baskets," Felather said, and then led the way down his chosen tunnel. "We'll take turns at digging out the material, and searching for the nuggets." Felather began attacking the wall with his shovel. Rock and debris clattered down around his boots, and another man scraped the mate-rial away toward the woman and child, who started combing through the rubble. After an hour of back-breaking work, the adults swapped places. They had filled half a basket between them. There was not as much ore as they had hoped.

Two hours later, their first basket was full and Felather was doubting there was enough ore in the ridge to fill four baskets. Felather scooped up the basket. "I'm going to check what is happening outside," he said.

The other man wiped his brow and nodded. "I'm surprised they haven't been in to check on us. I'll come with you."

"It's safer if you stay here. I'll just see what they are up to," Felather said as he left.

The clatter of shovels echoed down the other tunnels, so the others were struggling to fill the baskets as well. Did the dybbuks know? Was it a way to keep them contained and out of the way? They'd been here a couple of hours and not a single guard had come and checked on them.

Felather peered out the entrance. A guard paced back and forth in front of the mine entrance, and Felather scanned the rest of the compound. It appeared deserted, but he was sure it wasn't. Shoving the basket into a shadowy corner, he slid his dagger out of his boot, and after another quick search of the compound, leapt for the guard. Covering his mouth and stabbing his blade up under his ribs, he dragged him into the cave. The man twisted, his hands shoving up between Felather's and pushing him off, and then he grunted and fell to his knees, his hand holding his side as his eyes widened in shock before he slumped to the ground.

Felather exhaled before slipping out the cave and skirting the buildings. He silently approached the one square building with a light glowing in the window. Listening intently, he heard nothing, so he slowly depressed the handle and eased open the door. The room was empty. At a scuff behind him, Felather spun with a curse, both hands rising to block the blade slicing down at him. He had been so focused on the building he hadn't sensed the person sneaking up behind him.

His dagger caught the blade, the shock juddering up his arm and pausing its descent long enough for him to twist away. The man grunted and followed. A meaty arm grabbed for Felather's neck, his sword thrusting forward. Off balance, Felather tried to swipe at the man's legs, but he was like a tree, unmoving, and it was Felather who landed on the ground. The man stood over him, his sword pointed at Felather's chest, and Felather scrabbled back until he hit the office wall, cursing himself for his stupidity. The dybbuk sneered at him and thrust. Felather rolled and hissed as the sword scored his side, the bite of steel enough to clear his mind of his self-recriminations. The dybbuk stiffened as the tip of a sword protruded from his chest. Felather watched the man sway, eyes wide in surprise as he slumped to the ground. Inhaling deeply, he froze as a large figure loomed over him. His heart stuttered in his chest and he let his breath rush out.

"Why didn't you wait for me?" Adriz snapped as she grabbed him. She smoothed a finger over his bruised face. "Are you hurt?"

Felather shook his head. "I'm fine, I promise. Just a scratch."

"Good."

"Where is everybody?" he asked.

"The dybbuks left about fifteen minutes ago. I was just checking the watch towers, but they all appear empty," Adriz replied, still inspecting him.

"They only left two guards. What were they thinking?"

"They're not. They're idiots. How did you get free?" Adriz asked as she tugged up his shirt, investigating the source of the blood.

"They didn't search us," Felather said, holding up his bloodied dagger. "I was the first to venture out and see what was going on," Felather replied.

"Typical," Adriz muttered, tugging out a piece of cloth and a bandage from her pocket. "I knew you'd get into trouble." She folded the pad over the wound and started bandaging him up. "I assume there are no guards now? You didn't even leave me one to play with?"

Felather grinned and, after Adriz was sure he had no further injuries, led the way back towards the cave. "Start searching the offices while I tell the others to run while they can," Felather said as he hurried back into the mines. He soon returned, followed by a line of worried people, who bolted for the gate when they saw it was open. "Stay off the roads. They are searching for more slaves," Felather called after them.

"The children?" Elisa gasped as she rushed up to Adriz as she came out of one of the buildings. "Did they take the children?"

"They were fine. I told them to stay in the farm house and wait for your return," Adriz replied, clasping the woman's hands.

"Oh, thank the lord. Thank you!"

"Go on ahead. There's a calope in the barn. Take it. We'll follow you after we've taken a look around. We need to pick up our things and Felather's mule."

"Of course, thank you," Benjamin said, and he led his wife away.

Adriz rotated, scanning the compound. "This looks new. I assume they are just populating it. No doubt why there are so few guards."

"Then let's see if they've left anything incriminating," Felather said as he walked back towards the office with the light still glowing inside.

Adriz huffed and reluctantly agreed. "Fine. But only for ten minutes," Adriz warned.

He entered the office building with a wave of his hand and was immediately drawn to a map on the wall. Frowning at the strange markings, he hesitated for a moment and then pulled it down and folded it, before rifling through the desk, where he found sheaths of paper filled with illegible scrawls. He slipped the papers in his waistband and continued searching.

Adriz appeared in the doorway. "There's nothing here," she said. "Quite boring in fact. Empty sleeping huts, empty offices, little in the way of food or stores. We should leave."

"Then let's burn this boring place to the ground. One less place to exploit these people," Felather said.

"My pleasure," Adriz replied and hurried back out the door.

17

SOLANJI

The scent of burning wood drifted in the air and combined with ash and grit. Solanji observed Mav's tense expression and knew it wasn't just a road side camp fire. Cutting across an empty field, he led Solanji down another muddy track, the acrid aroma catching the back of her throat.

"Try not to breathe in the fumes," Mav said as he reached behind him into his saddlebag and grabbed a piece of cloth that he held to his nose and mouth.

"What do you think has happened?" Solanji asked as she copied him.

"Nothing good, I'll bet," Mav replied as he urged his calope onwards. Splashing through the puddles, they approached a burnt-out collection of buildings. Blackened beams lay smouldering on the ground, the only remnants of the structures left.

Dismounting, he led his calope through the ruins. "This was deliberate," Mav murmured. Even the perimeter fence had burned. Wood that would have been waterlogged after all the recent rain had still gone up in flames. Who could have ensured such complete destruction? And why?

Mav inspected the blocked cave entrance. A new rock fall by the looks of it, the debris clean and bright, not yet weathered. He turned the loose rocks over with toe of his boot and bent down to pick up one that glinted. Solanji squinted at the rock in his hand. Some type of mineral? He threw it back on the pile and returned to his calope.

"Best we don't linger here. Whoever owned this is not going to be happy to find it's burned down," Mav said as he remounted. "There's nothing left to tell us anything. I expect whoever did this was very thorough."

"Vengeance?" Solanji asked, a thrill of fear fluttering in her stomach.

"Maybe. At least they won't be able to use it for a while."

"You think they'll rebuild it?"

"If they want what's under that ridge, they will." Mav retraced their route back to the main road and they continued their journey.

A few days later, Mav consulted his compass, and they turned off the muddy track and cut cross country. How Mav knew where to go was beyond Solanji, but after being drenched in a sudden downpour, they arrived at a homestead with a dilapidated house, surrounded by a surprisingly well-kept veranda and a sturdy fence.

Within the fences, the ground was sectioned into rough rectangles and huge squashes and pumpkins sprawled in patches between rows of leafy vegetables and prickly fruit bushes. The fragrant scent of herbs drifted on the air, softening the underlying aroma of waterlogged mud.

The muted sound of hammering came from the adjacent barn. Dismounting, Mav led his calope towards the red painted building, bright against the dreary backdrop. The door slid open, and the nose of a loaded crossbow greeted them.

"How many times do I have to tell you not to point that thing at people?" Mav asked.

The crossbow dipped, and a small child, grimed in grease and dust from head to foot, peered out of the door. "Mav?"

Solanji gaped as a huge smile spread over the child's face, but she still paused long enough to unload the bolt and carefully hang the bow on a hook. And then she was in his arms, laughing and crying as she hugged him.

Leaning back, the child stared at him. "Shandra is so pissed at you."

Mav grimaced. "So I heard," he replied and waved a hand at Solanji. "This is my friend, Solanji."

Enduring a sharp inspection, Solanji stared right back at the child, who, although small, was older than she had first appeared. Bright blue eyes observed her before nodding. Strawberry blond hair was tied into a ponytail, most of which had escaped and wisped around a delicate face dusted with freckles. "This is Kiara." Mav jerked his head towards the barn. "What are you working on?"

"Fixing the plough. The soil is too heavy and it keeps breaking."

Mav nodded. "I'll come take a look after I've spoken to the others."

"I'd 'preciate it. Any help is welcome. Let me take your calope. Shandra probably knows you are here by now."

Heaving out his breath in a deep sigh, Mav handed over the reins and started walking towards the house. Solanji hurried to catch up with him.

"Who is Shandra? You never said."

"She's a kid I took in about five years ago. She's one of

the oldest, so she became the house mother. Don't underestimate any of them. They are all sharp, smart, and capable of looking after themselves and each other. They've had no choice."

He hesitated a moment outside the door and then rapped on it before opening it and walking inside. Solanji frowned as she followed. The room was dark and empty. A square wooden table was adorned by an unlit candlestick, and the fireplace was stacked with freshly cut wood. The fresh woody scent mingled with the dust.

"Kerris? It's Mav." Skirting the table, Mav crossed the room.

Solanji gasped as the rug began to rise on its own, and Mav bent and flipped it back, revealing a trapdoor. A shock of brown hair popped out of the hole, and hard black eyes in a round brown face raked Mav and then her.

"Where have you been?" the boy asked, scrambling up the steps and not taking his eyes off Solanji.

"I was unavoidably delayed," Mav replied.

"For over a year?" the boy asked, a note of disbelief in his voice.

Solanji shivered. He'd been trapped in that hell hole for a year?

Mav shrugged. "Not all plans work the way you expect. Did you get everyone out?"

"Of course we did," a much sharper voice replied as a slender young girl rose out of the hole. She inspected Mav, and her mouth tightened. "Don't you ever do such a fool-brained thing, ever again," she said, tucking a strand of blond hair behind her ear.

"No, ma'am," Mav replied.

She pressed her lips together. "I am so mad at you," she said, trying to keep the quiver out of her voice.

"Please forgive me. I never meant…" Mav didn't have a

chance to finish his sentence before the girl, Shandra, Solanji supposed, launched herself at Mav, and he staggered back under her weight. The boy relaxed, and his teeth gleamed white in the gloom.

"We nearly lost Muntra. We thought we had lost you," Shandra snapped at him.

"You knew the plan," Mav said, as he rubbed her back. "And you're all here, so you followed it. You managed to get all the kids out through the tunnels, and you all arrived here safely without anyone following you."

"That is not the point," Shandra replied, her voice muffled in his chest.

Mav exhaled. "I know it wasn't easy, and I'm sorry I brought trouble down on you."

"Where have you been?"

"I'll tell you, but we need to dry off first. We're dripping everywhere."

Stepping back out of his embrace, Shandra wiped her cheeks. "Seeing as you are here, the kids might as well come out. It's time for the youngsters to get some air before dinner." Her glance skittered over Solanji.

Mav was quick to introduce her. "This is my friend, Solanji. We're travelling together. Solanji, this is Shandra and Kerris."

Shandra gave her a nod. "Any friend of Mav's is welcome here," she said. "Hang your cloaks up. Kerris, light the fire." She called down into the dark hole she had climbed out of. "Bailey, send the kids up then start dinner."

The room was soon full of young boys and girls, all under the age of ten, Solanji thought, brimming with energy and laughter. Shandra and Kerris didn't look a lot older, maybe mid-teens? Solanji wasn't sure, but she smiled to see such high spirits.

"Out. Out all of you," Shandra said, sweeping them out

the door. "You have until first dark, then in for dinner." The kids ran out, calling to each other.

"Is it safe?" Solanji couldn't help asking, as she peered out the door after them.

Shandra shrugged. "Muntra is on guard. He'll keep an eye on them."

"You've collected a few more," Mav said as he eased himself into one of the chairs around the table and straightened his leg out. Rushlights were lit, and the room was transformed from grey gloom to warm wooden walls and a soft golden light. The aroma of roasting meat pervaded the room, along with mint, as boiling water was poured over mugs filled with dried leaves.

"Sit," Shandra said as she tugged another chair out with her foot and pushed a mug over to Solanji. She sat next to her. "Where did you meet Mav?" she asked as she leaned back.

"Up north," Mav replied. "We were fortunate enough to cross paths on the road and decided to travel together."

Shandra raised a cynical eyebrow at Mav but concentrated on her mug instead of calling him on it.

"How many children live here?" Solanji asked as she cupped her mug and inhaled the sweet, minty steam.

"There's twenty-three of us right now. We're about full. Mav, your signs are too clear; they keep turning up. I worry the wrong people are going to find them."

Wrinkling her nose, Solanji asked, "What signs?"

"Kerris and I came up with some markers to direct those needing shelter here," Mav replied. "Over the years, I've started rumours about where to look, embedded it in nursery rhymes and children's folk tales. We tried to make them discreet, but as you can see, the kids are finding them." Mav rubbed his face, his stubble rasping. "There are no guarantees. This is the most secluded place we've managed to set up. If this isn't safe, then nowhere is."

Solanji gaped at Shandra. "You are responsible for twenty-two kids?"

Mav laughed. "Don't let the lads hear you calling them kids. They do men's work and more, as do the girls."

"We've got twelve below the age of ten. Everyone else works the farm." Shandra flicked a glance at Mav. "I need you to talk to Muntra. He wants to go to the crossroads and find work. I keep telling him it's too risky, but it's getting to the stage where he won't listen to me. He thinks he knows better."

"I'll speak to him," Mav promised, and Solanji wondered what he would say. Life in Eidolon was not easy. These children had no soulmist; even the young ones who had rushed out to play. Shandra didn't look old enough to run such a large household, and yet she was authoritative and the children obeyed her requests without question. No doubt they were all relieved to have found a safe place to live.

Solanji's stomach churned at the thought that Brennan could be one of these kids, and that was only if he was very lucky. He would have no idea how to find a place like this. What had they done to be banished so young? The question was on the tip of her tongue when Mav leaned forward. "I can't make any promises though. He is getting to the age when he wants to strike out on his own. It's not fair to any of you to be stuck here, looking after young'ens."

"There's nowhere else to be. And anyway, you're back now. He'll listen to you."

"I can't stay. I'll only bring more trouble like before. I wanted to make sure you were all set."

Shandra jerked forward. "You're not staying?"

Solanji's eyes narrowed as she thought she saw a swirl of agitated shadows around the girl.

"I have some business to sort and then I'll come back for you. Even in Eidolon there is more to life than hiding, and none of you deserve that."

"You promise?"

"I swear. There is a place for you at my side if you want it."

Shandra blinked.

"And for Kerris, and Muntra, if he keeps his nose clean," Mav added.

"Tell him. It might make him think before he acts." Shandra placed her mug on the table. "You'll stay for tonight, though, won't you?"

"We'll stay a couple of nights, if you'll have us. The calope need resting. We've been travelling for over a week or so."

Nodding, Shandra rose, and there, Solanji was sure dark shadows undulated around her as she rested her slender hand on Mav's shoulder. His sparkling shadows extended to caress hers as she bent and kissed his cheek. "It's good to have you home," she murmured and left to oversee the kitchen.

"Muntra killed one of the chickens. He must have known you were coming," Kerris said from his lean against the wall.

"One chicken won't go far," Solanji said and then clapped a hand over her mouth. "Sorry, but it won't feed twenty-five people."

"Bailey's a magician in the kitchen, you wait and see," Kerris said. He slipped into the seat next to Mav. "Those men that attacked us that day you disappeared. They tracked you to us, didn't they?"

Mav stilled.

"They knew who you were; I overheard them talking," Kerris continued.

Closing his eyes, Mav inhaled. "You can't believe everything you overhear."

"I haven't said anything to the others." Kerris shrugged his shoulders. "I didn't want to worry them. But I can see you've been hurt, and you haven't..." His brown eyes, soft with concern, flicked to Solanji. "Mav, you can't ignore it, it won't go away on its own. Let me help you."

Mav gripped his shoulder. "I'll be fine."

"No, you won't," Kerris replied. "I can feel the heat from here."

This time there was no doubt. Solanji watched the shadows billow around Kerris, strong and determined. They extended to wrap around Mav's knee, and Mav hissed his breath out as his shoulders dropped, and Solanji realised how much pain he must have been in for him to have relaxed so visibly at whatever Kerris had done.

"I meant what I said to Shandra, Kerris. If you want to be one of my... uh... want to stay with me, there is a place for you."

"Then let me help you now. You need to rest. And your leg should be raised. There's a bed in the back room. You can lie down until dinner." Refusing to listen to Mav's protests, Kerris escorted him to the room at the back of the house and returned alone. His shoulders drooped as he sat opposite Solanji. "What happened to him?"

Solanji leaned forward and kept her voice low. "Apparently, a seraphim shoved a spear through his knee. Mav said he had repaired it as best he could."

Kerris' lips tightened. "It's infected."

"How do you know?"

"I just know. I drew some of the heat off, but it will return unless he sees a healer."

"Aren't you a healer?"

Shaking his head, Kerris slouched in his chair and stared

into the fire. "I know some basics, but not enough to help him. Him being a…" He glanced at her.

"An angel," Solanji supplied.

Kerris relaxed. "He should be able to heal himself."

"Even though he's fallen? He's not a true angel anymore, is he?"

"If you think that, then you are a fool. And I didn't take you for a fool," Shandra's voice said from behind her, and Solanji flushed.

"I meant no disrespect. I don't understand why he is here in Eidolon."

"Helping the likes of us, that's why," Shandra replied, placing a large tureen on the table. "Set the places, Kerris, while I call in the kids."

Kerris set six spoons on the table and left a pile by the tureen, and then he disappeared to return with a stack of bowls in his arms. He was followed by a slim young lad with a halo of soft blond curls framing his delicate face. None of them had any fat on them. They were all lean and underfed, but this boy was dainty, like fine china. He carried a plate piled with what looked like flat breads.

Dishing up the soup, he moved with an understated elegance, out of place in this rough household. Solanji wondered who he was as she watched him give a bowl, a spoon, and a flat bread, accompanied by the sweetest smile to each child who entered, who beamed back at him and scurried to sit on the floor and eat their dinner. The tureen seemed never ending, and every child received their bowl before Kerris went to wake Mav.

Solanji nibbled at the bread, surprised at the rich, nutty flavour. The soup was also full of vegetables and spicy flavours, and it was very filling. She eyed the young people around the table. Bailey, the unusual cook, Shandra, Kerris, Kiara, and Muntra. All had swirling black shadows, all of which quested towards Mav as he entered the room. Had he done something to them? Infected them with whatever he was infected by?

None of the other children had the shadow mist, which was what Solanji decided to call it, though it wasn't really a mist, more like strands. Just the five seated at the table with them. They were animated, all trying to tell Mav what they had been doing at the same time, all vying for his attention. Mav listened to each of them, praised them, offered advice when asked and when he wasn't. She couldn't help smiling as she watched him. He looked so relaxed in the middle of these children, and the children were open and happy to see him.

It was one of the most enjoyable meals Solanji had ever experienced. It reminded her a little of Georgi and Brennan when they had vied for her father's attention. The atmosphere around the table was one of happiness, and the smaller kids bathed in the overflowing good cheer, smiled and hugged each other. Warmed by the camaraderie and glad to be sitting next to Mav, she relaxed into his shadows as he chatted with his kids. Just his nearness was comforting.

Everyone had a job to do once dinner was finished. Clearing the table, feeding the livestock, preparing the youngest for bed, until finally, it was just Solanji and Mav and the four eldest left seated around the table.

"You going to tell us what happened to you?" Shandra asked.

"I fell afoul of the wrong people," Mav said.

"Powerful people," Kerris murmured.

"Unfortunately," Mav agreed. "I have unfinished business with some people in Puronia. I need to try to contact some friends who may help me. Worst case, I might have to figure out how to cross the divide and visit the citadel in Puronia."

"What?" Muntra gasped, sitting up from his slouch. "Are you mad?"

Mav grimaced. "Probably. But the seraphim that captured me has a seat in the citadel. If I can prove he is the one behind the disappearances, behind the attacks, then maybe I can stop them."

"Prove it how?" Kerris asked, his brown eyes gleaming.

"That's the crux of the matter, isn't it? Proving it."

"Well, you have a witness." Kerris nodded at Solanji. "She rescued you from their clutches, didn't she?"

Solanji raised an eyebrow. "I never said that."

"It's obvious you know what happened to him. You've been hovering over him just as much as Kerris has," Shandra said with a grin. "It's sweet." She laughed as heat flooded Solanji's face.

Solanji avoided looking at Mav. "I don't think my word against a seraphim will hold much weight," Solanji said. "And anyway, what is it you think the seraphim is guilty of?"

"Exploitation, trading people as slaves, encouraging an atmosphere of fear, and driving protection rackets, to name a few," Mav said.

"How do you know that's happening? I haven't seen any indication of slave trading."

Mav huffed out a laugh. "You haven't been afraid since you arrived in Eidolon?"

"Well, yes. But not because of slave trading."

"Even though you were plucked off the street and imprisoned against your will? And no one said a word?"

Solanji paused and stared at him, her mind spinning. "If you put it like that…" she said as, in agitation, she caressed the soulmist that the tiny dragon had taken from the dead soldier; it was becoming a nervous habit. The soulmist soothed her. As much as she wanted to caress Mav's shadows, she shouldn't. She was afraid of accidentally seducing him again, and as much as she wanted to trail her fingers through them, it wasn't right. Strangers would never know; she didn't feel guilty about skimming their soulmist, but Mav was becoming more important to her, a friend. And you didn't intrude on a friend's thoughts without permission.

"Considering how many people are supposed to live here, don't you think it's a bit empty?" Mav asked.

"I have no idea how big Eidolon is, and there were plenty of people at the crossroads," Solanji replied.

Kerris snorted and leaned forward. "That's the problem. Few go any further than the crossroads. They think the crossroads *is* Eidolon, when there is so much more." He held up his hand and curled his fingers over. He pointed at his thumb. "If that is Angelicus, then the rest of my hand," he spread his fingers wide, "is Eidolon."

"And some view it as a threat to be suppressed and others an opportunity ripe for the plucking," Mav said.

After that, everyone fell silent, and then they all dispersed to find somewhere to sleep.

18

SOLANJI

E arly the next morning, Solanji watched the children gravitate around a transformed Mav as he helped Kiara fix the plough and any other odd jobs Shandra gave him. It was as if he was a different person, relaxed and carefree, a smile not far from his mouth at all times. The brooding, silent travelling companion had been replaced by the kindest, most affection person she had ever seen.

Kerris shadowed him, imploring him to rest, to slow down, and Mav laughed. Solanji thought it might have been the first time she had heard him laugh, and it was a beautiful sound.

Bailey kept to himself, saying little, though he observed from a distance, his gaze following Mav a little wistfully.

"We're only here for a day or so. Make the most of me. There are some things you need help with. We really need to find you a guardian, someone you can call on when needed."

Kerris bristled immediately. "We manage fine on our own."

Gripping his shoulder, Mav shook him. "I know you can.

But you need someone you could contact in an emergency. I don't know when I'll be able to return, and I don't like leaving you alone. What I can do is give you a name. If you get desperate, there is a friend I know at the citadel you can contact. A last resort, but I would feel better if you had someone."

Snorting, Kerris peered out the barn and searched the surrounding area. "We managed so far. This farmstead is secluded, and no one knows we're here. We're safe. Muntra will ensure it."

"I know he will."

"Then stop worrying."

Mav's low chuckle surprised Solanji. She didn't see how one boy could protect them all, but Mav relaxed and slung his arm around Kerris' shoulders. "I know, he showed me his back up plans. Pretty impressive. You are all impressive, and don't you forget it."

Solanji grinned at the boy's expression. It was amazing what a few well-chosen words could do. Thrusting his chest out, Kerris preened for a moment, though he took the scrap of paper Mav offered and tucked it away. Mav took the opportunity to straighten up a fence and stooped to wedge a rock against it. Solanji wondered who Mav knew at the citadel.

As Solanji drifted back towards the house, she inspected the homestead in turn, her gaze pausing on the younger children playing in the dirt.

"Pitter patter, little feet," young voices chanted, and Solanji smiled at two tiny girls as they clapped each other's hands in rhythm to the words.

"Playing hide and seek.

Searching high, and searching low,

Looking for a treat."

Lifting her eyes from the girls, she realised that the

compound was actually well maintained, and there wasn't much that Mav needed to help with. He was just going through the motions, praising and recognising their good work and leaving a sense of pride and satisfaction in his wake. Solanji watched him with growing respect; not that she hadn't respected him before, but it was deepening. A warmth spread through her every time she caught his eye, and he flashed his gorgeous grin at her, enveloping her in his unconscious good spirits and inherent loving care.

"He really likes you, doesn't he?" Shandra asked as she paused on the veranda surrounding the house, a basket clasped in her arms.

Solanji stiffened, debated about denying it, and then sighed out her breath. "You think so?"

"Oh, definitely. Whenever he enters a room, you're the first person he searches for."

Heat flushed Solanji's cheeks as her gaze automatically returned to the barn, where Mav was still speaking with Kerris. Shandra's low chuckle made Solanji drag her gaze back to the girl.

"Oh, you've got it bad." Shandra shook her head and set her basket on the floor beside the small bench. Children's squeals made her smile as she placed a clay jug on the bench. Stacking a pile of rushes beside it, she began cutting them in half with her belt knife. "I don't think he realises it, but his expression softens when he watches you."

"He hardly knows me," Solanji said, and warmth filled her at the idea that Mav might like her as much as she liked him.

Shandra shrugged.

"He's probably looking at the kids. He cares for you all very much." Solanji licked her lips. "How did you first meet him?"

Shandra handed Solanji a handful of rushes and pushed

the jug closer to her. She began dipping the rush into the liquid. Wrinkling her nose, Solanji peered into the jug.

"Animal fat," Shandra said. "Dip the rush in and place it on the dish to dry. Once they set, we dip them again. Cheaper and easier to make than candles."

Solanji selected a rush and dipped it into the animal fat. She thought Shandra wasn't going to answer her question, but Shandra slowly began speaking. "Must have been about five years ago. My father and I were travelling home from the market when we were set upon." Her mouth tightened. "Mav appeared out of nowhere and helped my father fight them off. He stayed a few days with us and then left, returning every few months as if he was keeping an eye on us. It was comforting. Mav has the ability to make you feel safe." She stared at the pile of rushes in the dish. "My father never recovered from his injuries, and he died. Mav arrived with a group of kids. It was as if he had known. He suggested we keep the place running as a shelter for orphans. He stayed for a month and helped us set everything up. He brought us animals and seeds, enough for us to survive on our own. Taught us how to make rushlights and other things we could sell at market.

"We haven't seen him for over a year. Our old place was attacked." Her face tightened. "Mav was our last line of defence. He held them off long enough for us to get all the kids out safely, but he didn't follow us as planned. We saved all the kids and made it here, but we didn't know where he was. I've been so worried. They knew who he was. He was deliberately hunted down."

Solanji's chest ached. Her gaze found Mav's handsome face again. He still hadn't spoken of his torture, and she didn't think he ever would. Why had Kyrill wanted her to help him escape if they had gone to so much trouble to capture him in the first place? Mav still had something they wanted. No matter what they had done to him, they hadn't been able to get it. What could he possibly have that they wanted so badly?

"He spends all his time looking after others, but he deserves to be happy too," Shandra said softly.

Solanji nodded, her throat so tight she couldn't get the words out.

———

The evening meal was raucous and loud. All the children relaxed and buzzed around Mav like bees to an exotic flower full of nectar. Shandra shooed them away to bed, and finally the four eldest sat with Mav and Solanji at the table.

Kerris glanced around the table and then leaned forward. "If you are going to Puronia, then I am going with you."

Solanji noticed that none of the other children were surprised by his statement. And she thought, if they could, they would all have offered. At some point during the day, they had met and discussed this.

"I appreciate the thought, but this is my mess to clean up. I'll do it alone. I'll not risk any of you in Puronia."

"But you'll risk yourself?" Shandra asked, her voice as sharp as the newly fixed plough.

Mav shrugged. "I can't clear my name without returning. Until I do, I can't protect any of you."

"It's no safer here than with you in Puronia, and you'll not get far on that leg if you don't let me come with you. You need to see a healer, and until you do, I'm your best bet," Kerris argued.

"Shandra needs you here," Mav replied.

"We all support Kerris' decision," Bailey said, unexpectedly joining the argument. "It's the least we can do after all you have done for us."

Mav held Bailey's gaze as if considering the request and then shook his head. "No, you need him here, just in case. You've all done so well; I will not make it more difficult for you."

"It's my decision," Kerris said, scrunching his face in concern.

"No," Mav replied. "I appreciate the offer, but we'll leave first thing in the morning. You are needed here."

Wrinkling her brow, Solanji observed Kerris, and by the stubborn cast to his face she didn't think he would take no for an answer, but he remained silent, and Solanji rose as they all prepared for bed.

Solanji scrunched up her face as she studied the cracks in the ceiling of the room she shared with the girls. A blanket on the floor and a lumpy pillow for a bed. She had never considered the people who lived in Eidolon before. Not as people, with rights and hopes and dreams. Not children like Shandra, Kerris, Bailey, or Muntra, and they *were* children, forced into adult roles through no fault of their own.

Heart aching, Solanji wished she could help the children in some way. It could so easily have been her family banished to Eidolon. Since her father had died, they had teetered on the edge of poverty for years. A wave of homesickness swept through her. She wanted to feel her mother's warm arms around her and to hear her brothers' voices.

Fear prickled her skin. She had to find a way to protect them from Kyrill. He wanted her to persuade Mav to cross the divide into Puronia. That wouldn't be difficult; Mav had already half-decided that himself. But Solanji didn't want him to cross. If the seraphim wanted him to cross, then it was a bad idea. Mav didn't have a soul. If he was trapped there, he would die. The thought of Mav dying was like a physical pain in her chest.

Curling a lip, she snarled at herself. Why did she care so much what happened to him? She had to protect her family. Her brother was more important than a man she barely knew. And then she remembered that warm amber gaze and the way his eyes softened when he looked at her, and she groaned. It was clear he felt something as well. Whether it could be more than friendship, only time would tell. The problem was that their time was running out.

They all deserved so much more. These children, her family, Mav, and all the people living in Eidolon.

The children were fortunate they had Mav looking out for them, and her thoughts drifted to how they flocked around him and how good he was with all of them, how his voice softened as he spoke with them, giving each the attention they deserved. His beautiful smile had been prominent most of the day. He had even flashed it at her on occasion, making her smile back foolishly as her heart rate quickened.

She had spent the day yearning to touch him, to caress his shadows, but she had kept her distance, not wanting to get between him and his children, for they *were* his, and his love for each of them had been clear. She mused on the conundrum that was Mav. To have suffered as he had, as he still suffered, yet not show a sign of it today.

Wondering how they had all ended up in Eidolon, she fell asleep, twirling the spare soulmist between her fingers.

19

MAV

Mav rose early the next morning. Collecting his clothes, he silently dressed in the kitchen and slipped out of the house. He walked around the fence, checking for signs of visitors. He flexed his right leg. It was stiff but not painful. Kerris had some strong healing skills. The lad should be safe in Mav's fledgling hall, tucked under Felather's wing and learning how to control and grow his abilities. Instead, he was hiding in the shadows of Eidolon, helping to protect a flock of children younger than him.

Ignoring the twinge of regret and loss that the memory of his friend, Felather, had caused, he stared out over the lush green fields. These children were so vulnerable, and he hated leaving them so exposed. They had concealed the homestead as much as they could, but it was impossible to hide it completely.

Fortunately, they were a few leagues north of the cross-roads, far enough away to be out of sight of the merchants and travellers, but close enough to the local village to be able to get supplies.

His breath plumed in the cool morning air as he sighed. He hadn't slept well. Just the suggestion of returning to the citadel had dredged up some memories he preferred to leave buried.

Stroking the red stone at his throat, he knew deep down that it was related to the death of his close friend, Athenia. Red vendetta stones were for avenging untimely deaths, and Athenia's death should never have happened. Images of her blood-drenched body flashed through his mind, and he bit his lip. He hadn't been able to save her, and the knowledge tortured him. The worst part was that he didn't know who *had* killed her, and, without any other suspects, he had been blamed.

Should he return to the citadel? Reclaim his seat and protest his innocence?

Cursing under his breath, he began walking again. What was the point? He would be incarcerated as soon as he set foot over the divide. He needed to get a message to his oathsworn, Felather or Adriz. He shouldn't have stopped trying to contact them, but the lack of response had cut him deep, and in his vulnerable state, he had given up. But it had been so stressful waiting for a response that never came, beggaring himself just to get someone to carry a message over the divide and not knowing whether it would be delivered to the right person.

Deep in his gut, he knew the citadel and his angelic brethren were exploiting Eidolon. Someone had brokered a deal with Kaenera for him to ignore their activities, or even to help them. The dybbuks had grown more active over the last decade, stealing people away from their families.

Mav froze for a moment, ice slithering down his spine. Kaenera was waiting for him to fall. Why? Why was Kaenera interested in him? How had he even known he was in Eidolon? Was that why Julius had been hunting him all these years? Had someone promised him to Kaenera in return…for what?

Rubbing his face, Mav struggled to make sense of his tumbling thoughts. He had to unravel the clues, make sense of it all if he was going to survive.

Families across Eidolon deserved to live in peace. People who deserved a second chance and certainly shouldn't be soulless. Horror curdled his blood that the Justicers still used SoulSingers to remove souls, even when they knew there was no reversing that action.

His gaze slid over the misty landscape, not really seeing the rolling hills covered in clumps of bracken.

The last time he had spoken to his father and Athenia, the plan had been to reunite Angelicus and Eidolon, to remove the divide, but there was no sign of that happening. He stilled. Had someone in the citadel orchestrated his downfall and Athenia's death to stop it happening? No, that couldn't be it. He was being paranoid. Life didn't evolve around him. His father would have continued his plans without him. Maybe they had decided on a different strategy. The issue in Eidolon was more localised, someone taking advantage of a perceived weakness.

In nearly fifty years, he still hadn't discovered any solid proof of who was behind the slow disappearance of people, but he had his threads now. He had pieced together what was happening in Eidolon, found the roots, and disrupted the network where he could. Kaenera had intimated he had found out something he shouldn't have so he was on the right path. No doubt that was one of the reasons Julius continued to hunt him down. But now he had a seraphim. If he could identify him, it would lead him straight to the top. It all led back to the citadel, if he could find the courage to risk returning.

His gaze narrowed as he realised what he had been

staring at for the last few minutes, and he froze. Movement had caught his eye, and he had been unconsciously watching a small figure creeping along the verge of a thick hedge which bordered the empty heath land that butted up to their homestead.

The child, it had to be a child, stopped and peered over their shoulder. Mav followed the child's gaze and swore softly under his breath. Dybbuks! This was bad. His hands dropped to his waist, and he cursed again. He hadn't strapped on his sword belt. He was getting careless.

Bending low, he darted back towards the barn. Reaching the door, he tugged on a rope that was slung across the yard and into the house. A muted chime drifted on the air, quiet enough not to be heard across the fields, but loud enough to wake Muntra.

A quick search of the barn found plenty of sharp utensils, and Mav selected a few. Spotting the jagged discs that Kiara had been greasing in preparation for reassembling some piece of machinery, he swept them up, and hefted one in his hand.

Muntra appeared in the doorway, followed by Solanji. "What's up?" Muntra asked.

"Dybbuks! North of the plantain field."

"Shit!"

"Keep the kids indoors. Tell them to bar the door." Before Muntra could protest, Mav continued. "Take position at the first post. We have to stop them even discovering this place. Don't let them get past you!"

Muntra nodded, his determined expression making him look older. He darted back across the yard to the house.

"Solanji, we need to lead them away and stop them. You up for some target practice?" He had been impressed by her knife skills; she had a better aim than him. He held out the metal discs, and a grin spread over Solanji's face.

"Anytime," she whispered as she took them.

"There's a child heading this way. They are stalking him across the heathland, north of here. I'll try to distract them, lead them towards you."

Solanji nodded, flicking a glance towards the house and back to Mav.

"How many?"

"I only saw two, but there could be more." Mav led the way out of the barn and pointed across the fields. "I'll go east and drive them towards that copse of trees. That's the only shelter around here. Think you can get there before them?"

"On my way." Solanji ran, skirting the house.

Taking a deep breath, Mav started up the muddy trail that ran along the edge of the field and across the heathland to join the wider track that led towards the nearest village. Keeping to the dim shadows at the edges, Mav ran down the trail, his heart thumping loudly in his chest.

Pure chance; that was all it took and these children would be at risk. Nowhere was safe! He gritted his teeth, ignoring the ache starting in his knee as he crouched low. Hurrying up the trail, he skirted the field, scanning the bracken for movement.

There! The child was well-camouflaged in the drab rags he was wearing, but the bushes around him trembled as he crawled through them. "Stay down," Mav muttered under his breath as he searched for the dybbuks.

A sharp shout made the child jump to his feet, and Mav groaned. Men broke through the treeline and ran after him. The child fled, zigzagging through the brush, and Mav tried to close his distance. Sheer terror plastered the boy's face as he spotted Mav, and he veered towards the copse of trees, his pale face dominated by large eyes and a gasping mouth.

The dybbuks were closing in on him, and then they saw

Mav. "Get him!" the first man yelled, pointing at Mav, not changing his direction as he pelted after his quarry. Mav spotted a third dybbuk exiting the tree line and swore as he began to run.

Mav didn't wait for the man running towards him to get close. He flicked his wrist, and the disc flew through the air, glancing off the man's shoulder. The dybbuk cursed as he grabbed his arm, his hand coming away red, and he charged for Mav.

Ducking the swing, Mav followed the knife arm, gripping his wrist as he twisted his body inside and ramming the steel rasp into the man's gut. Good for filing down rough edges, it also made an excellent dagger. The dybbuk grunted and slumped to his knees, his hands wrapped around the hunk of metal protruding from his stomach.

Mav grabbed the dybbuk's fallen dagger, ran it across the man's throat and wrenched the rasp back out. Kiara would want it back. Using his foot, he pushed the dybbuk over, and the man collapsed into the bushes, hidden. Mav started to run towards the copse of trees.

The child was no longer in sight, and the first dybbuk had reached the trees. The running dybbuk suddenly jerked and faltered. Dropping onto one knee, he jerked again, his arms flailing as his head was flung backwards.

The second man skidded to halt beside him, mouth open in horror as he stared at the piece of metal protruding from the other man's forehead. He reacted too slowly, and he in turn lurched as a metal disc thunked into the side of his head. His eyes rolled as crimson blood poured down his face, and he folded into the prickly bushes surrounding him.

Mav spun, searching for any other movement, but all was still. The heath empty. He breathed heavily as he tried to slow his hammering heart. The threat was over—for now.

Slowly approaching the men, his rasp gripped tight, he

checked for a pulse. Solanji's aim was lethal. Thank goodness. He limped towards the copse of trees. He shouldn't
have tried to run. The pain in his knee had roared back to
life, the sullen ache replaced by sharp stabs of agony which
brought him out in a cold sweat.

"Solanji? Is the child alright?"

"Mav?" Solanji's anguished voice had him hurrying
forward.

"What? What happened?"

He stumbled to a halt when he saw Solanji kneeling on
the ground, rocking the small body in her arms. No! It
couldn't be.

"How? I didn't see them throw anything at him."

"I think it was sheer terror," Solanji said, her voice
muffled in the child's hair. "He grabbed his chest and made a
weird groan before he collapsed. There was nothing I
could do."

Mav sat beside her and reached over to wipe a tear off
her cheek, his fingers lingering on her skin, and then he
tugged the child into his lap. The boy was so light and frail,
and so nearly safe. His pale skin was almost translucent, the
blue veins running across his cheek and down his throat.
Dark lashes carved shadows under his eyes. Such a delicate
face framed by straggly brown hair.

Mav pressed his fingers against the child's neck, but there
was no pulse, no life. He traced callused fingers over smooth
skin, and his throat tightened as tears prickled behind his
eyelids. He had failed again. Failed to protect an innocent
life. Another child lost to oblivion and Kaenera.

Curling over the child, he couldn't prevent the low keen
that left his lips as he drew the child close to his chest. It
shouldn't have ended like this. Why couldn't he do anything
right? He wished he could turn back time and shelter the
child, prevent the horrors that had taken his life. His heart

cracked as he visualised his glorious white wings unfurling, but they weren't white, they were dark and brooding and full of shadows. Drawing them around his shoulders, he rocked the small body in his arms.

He pictured the Oblivion Gate. Tall double doors standing in the centre of a large cavern lit by a soft green glow emanating from the walls. Intricate swirls and patterns of gleaming black obsidian was inlaid in the carved grey stone. Stern and unforgiving, the entrance represented the oppressive nature of his uncle. Mav wasn't sure if the gates ever opened or how Kaenera allowed people through, but the thought of this innocent child making that journey alone made his heart ache.

He doesn't have to make it alone, Kaenera's voice whispered in his mind. *You know I'm waiting for you. Take my hand and I'll guide the way. Look.*

Kaenera coalesced before the gate, as green flames flared in the sconces either side of the doors. Elegant and suave, he was dressed all in black. A long black coat moulded to his body and soft ruffles fell from his throat. His face, so like Mav's father's, had a hard edge to it and his green eyes reflected the flame of the torch. Slender fingers grasped an ivory cane. The other hand beckoned.

Mav shuddered as Kaenera's regard passed over him, a watcher in the shadows, complicit as the Gate Keeper coaxed the child's essence closer. Kaenera opened his arms and the essence shivered and flowed away back towards Mav.

For a brief moment, Mav froze, torn between two places at once, standing at the gate and kneeling on the ground. The child's life flashed before his eyes, but he tightened his embrace against the fear and terror that the boy had experienced in his brief few years. A sense of desperation impinged on his senses and Mav bowed his head before the weight of the petition. He was the son of God, if he didn't help this child then he couldn't help anyone. Sighing out a breath, he extended his hand, much as Kaenera had and accepted the child's plea, allowing his essence to flow into him.

Offering the boy peace and love, Mav caught his breath against the sudden pain in his chest, and then it passed as he let all the images go, like water flowing through his fingers. As he kissed the boy's forehead, Kaenera roared in anger and fury, a threatening rumble in the distance like an approaching storm. Mav flared his wings in response as the image of the Oblivion Gate and his furious uncle faded, and a new silver sparkle gilded the edge of one his black feathers.

He ground his teeth as his wings faded and fury slowly replaced the grief. Enough! He would stop this or die trying. He would take his accusations to the citadel and force them to listen to him.

That evening, they buried the child within the copse of trees. Sheltered and protected from the weather, if nothing else. The children were sombre and wide-eyed, huddling together for reassurance.

Mav had spent the day searching the surrounding area for signs of dybbuks, or anyone else for that matter, but the area was deserted. The lack of riding beasts niggled at Mav. The men must have come from somewhere, and they wouldn't have walked. Had there been a fourth man? One who had fled with the animals?

He didn't know and worry gnawed at his belly. His children could be at risk and there was little he could do about it. Except return to the citadel and end this filthy business once and for all.

Muntra helped him dig a larger grave for the dybbuks,

out amongst the bracken, concealed from view. After that, they returned to the homestead to wash off the dirt, sweat, and grief.

When they entered the house, they found Solanji cuddling some of the smaller kids, offering comfort and no doubt receiving it. Bailey came out of the kitchen and thumped a large bowl of mixed berries onto the table, followed by a steaming jug. His bright blue eyes surveyed the room, and then he grinned, a splash of brilliant light driving away the shadows.

"Your favourite," he announced to the room and began dishing up bowls of fruit and pouring the thick, creamy sauce over them.

Children's heads popped up, eyes bright with expectation, and Mav smiled as Bailey drove away the quiet tension that had been hovering over the room and replaced it with gentle laughter. The children relaxed and began to chatter. By the time they went to bed, happy smiles graced their faces and the horror had left their eyes.

The next morning, Mav reluctantly saddled their calopes. He didn't want to leave, but if he didn't, the danger would never end. Solanji strapped on their bedrolls and travel packs, a similar reluctance in her movements.

Leading the beast out into the yard, he dropped the reins at the sight of his fledglings standing in a line waiting to say goodbye. He strode over, clasped Kerris behind the neck, and tugged him into a fierce hug. "Remember, it's never cowardice to fall back and regroup. Use your brain, not your anger."

Kerris nodded into his chest, his voice muffled as he replied, "Please come back, Mav." He pushed a sturdy stick into Mav's hand. "Use it," he said, his voice unyielding.

Mav's lips twitched, but he held Kerris' eyes as he said, "I promise. I'll come back for all of you. I swear it."

Releasing Kerris, Mav swept Kiara into his arms and swung her round. "I'm sorry for messing with your machine," he whispered. Small arms tightened around his neck. "You found all the bits, so I forgive you," she muttered against his neck, and his heart clenched as he felt warm tears on his skin. He kissed the top of her head and put her back down, and she stepped into Kerris' side as he wrapped his arm around her shoulders.

Mav clasped Muntra's arm, his hand gripping just below the young man's elbow, and Muntra's eyes flew to his face as he clasped Mav's arm back. "I would be honoured to have you by my side. If you still wish it, I will find a way to enrol you in the training academy."

The grin that spread across Muntra's face was worth it, and Mav nodded. He turned to Bailey, standing in Muntra's shadow. So ethereal and delicate beside the larger lad. He cupped Bailey's beautiful face and stroked his fingers lightly across his cheeks. "Look after them for me."

"Always," Bailey replied. In return, he reached up and cupped Mav's face. "Make sure you look after yourself as well. We'll be waiting for you."

Mav kissed Bailey's forehead, too choked to reply. Bailey snuggled into Muntra's side as Mav turned to Shandra. She flew into his arms, and he breathed in the comforting scent of her hair. "I am so proud of you," he whispered.

Her arms tightened around him. "I don't want you to leave," she said into his chest.

"I don't want to go either, but I promise…"

"Don't," Shandra interrupted him, looking up as she placed her hand over his mouth. "Don't make promises you can't keep." Her deep blue eyes searched his face, and her lips pinched. "We'll be here when you are able to return. Our home is your home."

Throat tight, Mav nodded as he hugged her tight and

then released her. Dashing his hand across his eyes, he slid the stick Kerris had given him under his saddle and concentrated on mounting his calope. Easier said than done. He huffed his breath out as Kerris shoved a wooden box in front of him and slapped him on the shoulder.

Using the box to mount, he waited for Solanji. All the younger children climbed up on the fence, hands waving above their heads as they shouted their goodbyes. Mav smiled at them all, raised his hand in farewell, and led the way down the muddy trail, leaving a piece of his heart with his fledglings.

20

SOLANJI

Solanji eyed Mav as they rode. He loved those children. It had broken his heart to leave them, but she recognised a new sense of determination. A hard line to his jaw, as if he was gritting his teeth. Had he made a decision? She thought he had. Especially when they turned south towards the crossroads and the road that led back to the crossing at Puronia.

Indecision warred within her. Mav was a good man. Everything she had seen him do had been to help others. Her gut told her he really *was* Demavrian, the fallen archdeus, no matter how fantastical it sounded. He had this sense of power and presence about him, and he was so goddamn gorgeous.

She wanted to help him. She fully supported all he had said in defence of the people living in Eidolon. But first, she needed to make sure her family were safe and get out from under Kyrill's control. The man owed her three halos, and she was going to make him pay.

She bit her lip as she stared at Mav's back. Just watching him comforted her. It would be so easy to fall in love with

Mav. And his shadows! She almost groaned out loud. They were so tempting and felt so divine, but she mustn't. Not unless he agreed, and for that, she needed to talk to him.

They had travelled in silence all day. At first, she had given Mav space, because the leave-taking truly had been a lot more emotional than she had expected. Those kids had inveigled their way into her heart as well. Concern for their safety hovered at the back of her mind, a constant worry. Not surprising Mav was silent.

And then there was that boy who had died. She wasn't sure what she had seen in that copse of trees. Finding the right words was proving difficult. Mav's shadows had coalesced into the most gorgeous night-black wings. Long, silky feathers had draped around him and the child like a curtain. But not before she had seen his pain-filled face. Did he blame himself for the child's death?

His strained face had glowed with an inner beauty and strength as he had…done what? She wasn't sure what he had done. The wings had shielded him, but when they had faded away, his expression had smoothed and he had found peace with whatever decision he had made.

Solanji was still shocked by the memory of Mav's wings. The shadows had formed into long, sleek feathers that she had been dying to stroke. They were so magnificent and impossible. Protective and impenetrable. A bright sparkle had caught her eye as they began to fade, one long feather edged with silver, and then the feathers had dissolved into the shadowy strands she had become so familiar with.

Her gaze narrowed on his back again, and wondering what was running through that intelligent mind, she urged her calope forward. When she drew level, she said without any preamble, "You've decided to cross into Puronia, haven't you?"

Mav switched his gaze to her face and slowly nodded.

"How will you get past the guards at the crossing?"

Mav shrugged. "It's been fifty years. No one will remember me."

Somehow, Solanji doubted that. Even with his beard, he was so distinctive. People looked at him even if they weren't sure who he was. The guards would recognise his presence as being angelic, and that would drive questions.

"I'm not convinced that would be the best plan," she said, and Mav huffed.

"No, but I don't have time for anything more elaborate."

"You have time to make sure you don't get killed. You can't save your fledglings if you're dead."

Mav flicked a sharp glance at her and sighed his breath out. "I know it's a lot to ask, you've done so much for me already. But…would you carry a message to the citadel for me?"

Solanji's heart expanded in her chest, and her cheeks ached she was smiling so hard. "Of course I will." And then her smile faded. Maybe he shouldn't trust her. What if Kyrill found out? What if Mav found out that she knew who the seraphim was and she hadn't told him? She should tell him. But she couldn't. She had to save Bren first. She couldn't risk failing her brother. A small voice piped up in the back of her mind. By then, it could be too late for Mav.

Mav was nodding. "Thank you. I have some friends in the citadel, though I haven't had much luck getting in contact with them. If you could go and speak to them, explain my situation, they can help find a way for me to cross safely. Maybe even arrange some meetings so I can work out the best time to cross so I can return the same day. If we get it organised in advance, it should be possible." He fell silent, a frown on his brow as he stared at his calope's ears. "Though how will I know when to cross until you return? No. That won't work. Maybe they need to come here first."

Solanji was sure he was reviewing different plans and, by his expression, disregarding them just as quickly. By evening his face was tense and his eyes heavy. He'd thought himself into a raging headache by the looks of it. Solanji knew how he felt. Her head thumped, a result of the constant uncertainty over what she should do.

Spotting a likely campsite, Solanji pulled over. "We're stopping here," she said, urging her calope into the screen of trees and then sliding off. "You need to stop thinking and relax."

Mav grimaced and rubbed his temple, but he didn't argue.

Solanji dug the fire pit as Mav scavenged for wood, and between them, they soon had a fire burning and a pot of water heating. Mav sank to the floor and stretched out his legs with a groan. Frowning, Solanji pointed at his knee, which was swollen and straining against the material.

"What did you do? I thought Kerris healed it?"

"Running after those blasted dybbuks," Mav replied.

"You should have said. We could have stopped earlier."

"Wouldn't make any difference, and it would only slow us down." Mav scowled at the fire, and after a moment, Solanji moved behind him and began massaging his shoulders. Mav let out a low moan and dropped his head.

Solanji smiled as the shadows curled around her fingers, teasing and nipping. She continued kneading, folding the shadows in, and a rumble sounded in Mav's chest. He felt so good under her fingers. Damn, even his moans and groans made her skin tingle and her core tighten.

Sweeping her hands down his back, she slid her fingers under his shirt and pressed hard as she dragged them back up. Mav hurriedly removed his shirt and leaned further forward. She could work with this.

Hesitating, she traced the fine scars lacing his back, and

he shivered. Not wanting him to dwell on bad memories, she chased tense muscles and stroked soft, heated skin. Treasured and caressed and then kissed. She knew she shouldn't, but the heady pleasure floating between them made her forget why.

Mav froze as her lips touched his skin, the salty taste pleasant. He lifted his head and stared at her over his shoulder. Solanji blushed. "Sorry," she murmured. "Got carried away." She dropped her hands and he half-turned. His heated gaze met hers, and when Solanji licked her lips, his eyes followed the tip of her tongue.

Heat built in her core, tight and eager. He had felt so good under her hands. His rippled skin soft and warm. She wanted more.

Mav tried to rise and cursed as he winced, pure agony flashing across his face. That blasted knee! He rolled back with a groan, kneading his leg as if he could rub away the pain. Sleek muscles rippled over his chest as he lay back and closed his eyes, a crease between his brows.

Solanji rose and searched the area quickly for a bannen bush. Breathing a sigh of relief, she grabbed a few leaves and rummaged to reveal the roots, before cutting a section off. Returning to the camp, she saw Mav had put his shirt back on, and Solanji sighed out her regret for the lost moment.

"Here," she said and offered Mav the root.

"Thanks." Mav popped it in his mouth and began chewing, the relief easing the lines on his face almost immediately.

They avoided each other's eyes for the rest of the evening, and they soon rolled in their blankets and tried to sleep.

A week later, Solanji was so relieved when they finally reached what looked like a reputable inn on the main road leading towards the divide that she could have burst into tears on the spot. After long boring days with them both tussling with their thoughts, and neither really finding any solutions, Mav had withdrawn behind a wall of reserve, keeping Solanji at a distance, and she wasn't sure why. It made the evenings awkward as they set up camp, and the result had been that they had both become irritable and short-tempered.

They had begun to pass the odd traveller. Morose and unfriendly, they tended to give Mav and Solanji a wide berth.

"Why are they so afraid of us?" Solanji asked as another traveller chose the muddy margins furthest from them.

Mav shrugged, his mind obviously elsewhere. "No one trusts anyone in Eidolon anymore."

"You mean they did once?"

"Oh, yes. This was never meant to be a place of punishment. It was supposed to be a place for redemption."

Solanji wrinkled her nose. "Redemption?"

"Mmm. A place to take a moment and breathe and figure out how to turn your life around."

"So the people in Eidolon should have been able to return to Angelicus?"

"Of course."

"But why is there a divide?"

"Good question," Mav said. "There wasn't always one. It seems to have solidified over the last few centuries." Mav straightened in his saddle and eyed the approaching inn. "You know this will probably take our last coin?"

Solanji didn't care. It had been Kyrill's coin anyway. Everything they had stolen from the castle was his. "Just one night. A hot bath. Please?" Solanji wheedled, and she led the way to the barn at the sight of Mav's resigned smile.

They had barely entered the inn when Mav was almost taken off his feet as he was tackled by one of the largest women Solanji had ever seen.

His shocked exclamation of, "Eladriz!" was lost in the litany of questions the woman was firing at him.

Solanji gaped as the woman steadied Mav with a frown. Her stomach curdled as she recognised her and her swirling soulmist. She was the large woman from the mis-matched couple at the campfire on the way to the crossroads. She was glad Eladriz hadn't realised it yet, so focused on Mav as she was. Eladriz was bound to recognise her. Her penetrating gaze had dwelled on Solanji for far too long for her not to.

Eladriz's scintillating soulmist writhed around her in agitation. How did she know Mav? What were they doing here? The woman hugged Mav, pushed him back to inspect him, and hugged him again, all the time muttering curses. "Demon's teeth, where have you been? I can't believe we've found you. We've been searching everywhere for you." She shook him. "I can't believe you're here!" Her eyes suddenly narrowed. "What have you done to yourself? You look terrible."

"If you'd let him go and stop asking him questions, he might be able to answer," a voice drawled from behind them. Her slender companion stood in the doorway and winked at Solanji. His words belied his own concern, for he inspected Mav just as intently, and his face tightened at what he saw.

Solanji wasn't surprised. Both she and Mav looked wrecked. Their clothes were worn and muddy after a week or so on the road, both with grimy faces and the odd abrasions. It was surprising they had been allowed into the tavern at all. As the woman smoothed gentle fingers over Mav's face, Solanji realised he hadn't healed himself. She hadn't noticed, with the layer of grime covering his skin. Had that been deliberate?

"I'm fine," Mav managed to reply as he gazed at the woman in shock. His face had paled alarmingly. "How did you get here? How did you find me?"

The woman ignored him and raised an eyebrow at the young man in the doorway, who shook his head. "No, you're not fine," she said, her voice sharp with concern. Her presence filled the room. Intricate leather armour, adorned with gleaming buckles and straps, covered her chest, back, and forearms. It moulded to her body, like a second skin. Well-worn and well-looked after. Solanji wouldn't be surprised to find out the woman slept in it.

"Not here," Mav replied with a glance around the taproom. It was dim, lit by a few glass lamps hanging from the thick, black beams above. A large fire roared in the grate opposite the entrance, a square mantel framing it. Wooden tables surrounded by spindly chairs filled the room, most of which were occupied. The occupants were staring at them. Men in homespun clothes with pipes in their mouths had small smiles tugging their lips.

"We've got rooms. Upstairs." The man pointed towards the ceiling. "Give Adriz your bags and let's go."

Mav didn't argue. He gestured for Solanji to follow the man, and he and Adriz trailed behind. Solanji dragged her eyes from her inspection of the fine clothes the man wore and flicked a glance behind her as Adriz hissed. Mav was pulling himself up the stairs, one step at a time, unable to bend his knee.

In the dim light of the stairway, lines she hadn't noticed before fanned out around his eyes and she was sure around his mouth under his beard. His beautiful face was strained and grubby. He waved her on and she continued up the stairs. The young man waited for her and then led the way to the wooden door at the end of the dingy corridor. Mav's irregular footsteps echoed noisily, the woman's large bulk behind him silent.

The room was larger than expected. A rumpled and unmade bed ran along the wall. Opposite, two spindly wooden chairs sat either side of the banked fire. The walls were lined with brown paper, which was cracked and peeling. The window was so crazed from wind-blown weather and leaf debris that they couldn't see out and little light could get in. Adriz pushed Mav into a seat as soon as he cleared the door, and he groaned slightly as he stretched his right leg out before him. He closed his eyes as the young man busied himself with the fire.

Solanji hovered by the wall, eyeing the merrily burning wood with some longing. She was chilled, damp, and hungry.

Mav waved a weary hand, not opening his eyes. "This is Solanji. She helped me escape." He pointed towards the woman, "Adriz." His hand moved again to the young man. "Felather. My friends."

His friends had souls. They curled around them tightly, glowing bright and alive. So alive. She wanted to touch them; she was desperate to touch them, but daren't. She hadn't missed it when they weren't there, but now the golden light teased and taunted, and she clenched her fingers against the temptation.

Adriz frowned at her. "I know you," she said slowly. "It will come to me." Her bright blue gaze slid back to Mav, and Solanji breathed out a sigh of relief. At least the questions would come later. Felather crouched down beside him and ran his hands, featherlight, over Mav's right leg.

Mav stiffened even though Felather barely touched him. "Later," he said through gritted teeth.

"No," Felather replied. "I'm sure Solanji would love to have a bath, get clean, and warm up. Adriz, can you show her the way? You strip. Now."

The sound of a hot bath was irresistible, and Solanji

eagerly followed Adriz as Mav tried to resist Felather. Somehow, she thought Felather would win. She had thought him gentle compared to Adriz, but the determined expression on his youthful face was anything but.

The hot water was pure luxury. Even if the bath itself was chipped and cracked and the room grimy. The water was clean and hot, and that was all she cared about. Adriz had given her a bar of soap, and she scrubbed every inch of her skin, hissing as the cuts and scratches stung. Her hair took two washes, but the dirt was now in the water instead of on her, and as she stood, she winced at the sight of the filthy water and pulled the plug out.

The towels were rough but clean. She eyed her clothes with distaste, but they were all she had, and she shook the shirt out and began scraping off the dried mud. A tap at the door made her stiffen, and Adriz's voice muffled by the wooden door said, "Solanji? I have some clean clothes for you."

Solanji peered around the door and the woman handed her a bundle of cloth. Adriz eyed her as if deciding something and then nodded once. "Felather is more your size. You can thank him. Food's ready when you are." And she was gone.

When Solanji slipped back into the chamber, the air was much warmer. The fire was blazing, the flames flickering in their own merry dance. Mav was lying in the bed. He was so still and lifeless, he could have been dead. Her heart sputtered and she started towards him, but Felather grabbed her arm. "He's sleeping. Leave him be."

"What did you do to him?" Solanji inspected Mav's pale face, her heart rate slowing as she realised he *was* just sleeping. The slow rise and fall of his chest was reassuring. She wondered when Mav's welfare had become as important to her as her own.

"What little I could," Felather said, and she glanced at him as she heard the sorrow in his voice. He smiled gently and fine lines creased his face. He was not as young as she had thought. His slim form and youthful voice had misled her. "We have some food; you must be hungry." In agreement, her stomach grumbled loudly, and he chuckled.

She sat by the fire and toasted her bare feet, accepting the bowl he offered. The soothing aroma of cinnamon and porridge soon had her eating.

"Where did you meet Mav? And how did you rescue him?"

The spoon clattered in the bottom of the empty bowl. She had forgotten he was still there, and the question asked in his gentle voice had surprised her.

"I have no idea," she said, startled into honesty. She stared at Felather. Where Mav was pure muscular perfection, and what you saw was what you got, this man was lithe and softer. He seemed the gentler, friendlier one, but there was a core of steel somewhere and a sense of purpose. He would get his answers one way or another. She could feel it. Placing the bowl by her feet, so her shaking hands wouldn't betray her, she tried to think up a plausible excuse.

He quirked a blond eyebrow at her, and she flushed.

"An angel detained me for…for SoulSinging."

Felather whistled. "You can see souls?"

Solanji nodded. "His soul trailed around him, it was difficult to avoid it, but this man said… said me touching his soul was a violation of his rights."

"By law he is correct, but there are so few people who can see souls let alone touch them, that people don't usually worry about it. I expect most aren't even aware that people like you exist."

The words curdled the food in her stomach. *People like me.* It still hurt; she supposed it always would.

Gentle hands gripped her arms. "I meant no offence," he said. "Please forgive me."

Solanji stared into the dancing flames and slowly nodded. He continued speaking, his voice low. "You are very rare. You shouldn't speak of it if you can avoid it."

"I wouldn't have, but he knows." She jerked her head towards the bed.

Felather smiled. "Of course he does. So how did you end up rescuing him?"

Twisting her fingers in her lap, Solanji explained her unexpected trip. "One minute I was at the crossroads minding my own business and the next, this blond-haired seraph transports me on a dragonair to a…a dungeon in the middle of nowhere."

Adriz snapped her fingers. "You were in the wagon train. Travelling on your own to the crossroads."

Solanji nodded. "I was doing some courier work but that angel lost me my commission, and he dragged me up onto that dragonair."

Felather snorted. "A dragonair? Now how does a lowly seraph rate a dragonair?"

"She was beautiful, but she put me to sleep. I missed the whole ride!" An expression of annoyance flitted across Solanji's face.

Felather grimaced. "Maybe she thought you weren't coping too well. Most people don't when introduced to a dragon. Did the seraph tell you why he took you there?"

"He said I had to wait for Mav's wings to flare and then take his soul." Solanji faltered as Felather hissed and Adriz clenched her fists.

"What did he do to him?"

Solanji licked dry lips. "He was chained, hanging from the ceiling. He…he'd been there for a while. They tortured him…"

"Whipped him, repeatedly, by the scars all over his body," Felather snapped.

Solanji nodded, her gaze distant, and she shuddered. "So much blood," she whispered.

"And did you take his soul?" Adriz demanded, her voice harsh.

"No! He didn't flare his wings, and..."

"And what?"

"H-he doesn't *have* a soul."

There was a fraught silence. "What?"

"He doesn't have a soul."

"That's not possible," Felather said.

"No one in Eidolon has a soul," Solanji pointed out.

"No, but Mav isn't from Eidolon, nor was he sentenced...before he left. He should still have his soul."

"I can't see one. You and Adriz have one. They curl tightly about you, as if you know how to control them. Most people, the soulmist trails after them like ribbons of mist. Yours are the only ones I've seen since we left the castle and the guards behind, except for Julius and his men."

"You met Julius?" Adriz asked, her voice sharp.

Solanji nodded. "He's been hunting Mav for years, or so Mav said."

"Did you tell the seraph that Mav didn't have a soul?" Felather asked.

"Yes, but he didn't believe me. They waited for his skin to heal and then they flayed him again. They said it would make his wings flare, only they didn't. They said they had before. Every time." She stared into the flames. "So much blood," she whispered, remembering the horrific injuries Mav had sustained. He still hadn't mentioned them, not once.

"Does Mav know? That he doesn't have a soul?" Felather suddenly asked.

Solanji nodded. She didn't mention Mav's plans. They were for him to share, not her.

"What happened to his knee?" Adriz's voice cut through her thoughts, and Solanji flinched.

"There was a spear pinning his knee to the rock floor when I first saw him. I don't know how long he'd been suffering, but the seraphim taunted him because he couldn't get it out, because he couldn't heal himself."

Felather strode across the chamber and back again, his youthful face strained, his eyes burning with anguish. "And the wound in his side?" he hissed as he collapsed in the other chair.

Solanji flinched back from his barely veiled anger. "Another spear," she whispered.

"How did you escape?" Adriz asked, and Solanji stilled as the large woman pinned her with a predatory stare.

"They were so busy hurting him, they forgot to chain my hands. I managed to unlock my ankle restraints and release his. I pulled the spears out of his body, but he couldn't completely heal himself." Solanji shuddered at the memory of Mav collapsing. She twisted her fingers together, resisting the urge to go over and touch him, to make sure he was alright.

Felather was on his feet, striding over to the bed. He hovered over Mav, his hands clenched into fists. At that moment, Solanji realised he was much older than he looked. The shadows accentuated lines that creased his face as he looked down at the sleeping man.

Solanji looked away from the raw emotion on Felather's face and dragged her gaze back to the far more dangerous Adriz. Her face was pale, and her eyes hooded as she glared at Solanji as if it was her fault. "After that, when he came to, we walked out. He said he couldn't fly. We stole some calopes and rode away. I guess the seraph was absorbed in something and didn't notice."

The fire crackled in the silence.

"Mav was an angel, wasn't he?" Solanji asked.

"He still is," Adriz growled.

"What did he do?"

"It doesn't matter." Adriz stalked over to the fire. She stared into the flames, much as Solanji had. "If he doesn't have a soul, that's possibly why Xylvin didn't sense him," she said almost to herself. Solanji didn't think she realised she'd said it out loud. Adriz suddenly looked up. "How long will he sleep?"

"Not long enough," Felather replied.

She nodded. "We move in the morning then. We can't remain here." Her eyes strayed to Solanji, and Solanji stiffened under inspection. "What to do with you?"

"Show me how to get back to Puronia and I'll be fine," Solanji said.

"She's a SoulSinger. She can touch souls. Maybe she should stay with us until we find out what happened to Mav's soul?"

Adriz's gaze sharpened. "How do we know we can trust her?"

"We don't. But she's the only SoulSinger outside of the citadel we've come across in the last fifty years. If it's true, and Mav's soul is gone, then we'll need her help to get it back."

"Depends if she wants to help. Do you?"

Solanji gaped at them. God above knew if she could help or not, but the thought of leaving Mav now made her stomach crawl. And even though she wasn't forcing Mav to go to Puronia, maybe the fact that she was with him would mean Kyrill thought she had done as ordered and would release her brother. And anyway, she had already agreed to help Mav. She had already made her choice. "I helped him escape, didn't I?"

21

MAV

Mav regretted waking up that morning. As he lay against the pillows, he debated about never waking up again. Every morning was an effort, and his body dragged him down. The abuse it had taken was paying him back in full. The fire running through his veins was an echo of the agony his body remembered. But he smothered the flames, shuddering at the loss, unable to relive the last moments yet another time. He felt empty, adrift.

"Mav?"

He opened his eyes, and Felather's concerned face hovered over him.

"Let me help you," Felather whispered.

"You can't," Mav replied, bracing himself to get out of bed. Felather helped him sit up and gently embraced him when he swayed. Mav felt like Adriz had trampled all over him in the sparring ring and then come back and done it again, repeatedly. His knee was on fire, a burning he was unable to quench.

"What happened, Mav?" Felather asked. "How did you get two vendetta stones?"

Mav's fingers strayed to the stones around his neck. Of course Felather would have seen them. One red, for Athenia, one blue for…he still had no idea.

"Nothing you could have prevented." He almost snorted. If *he* couldn't have stopped it, then there was no one else who could have, except one. And he was long gone. "The red one is for Athenia, I think. To avenge her death. The blue, I'm not sure, but I think it may have to do with Eidolon."

Felather frowned at him, and Mav nearly laughed. He was supposed to know the reason he had a vendetta stone, else how was he supposed to fulfil it? If he didn't know what the wrong was, how could he right it?

"We've been searching for you for so long. I thought we'd lost you," Felather admitted in a low whisper. "I still can't believe you just walked through that door yesterday."

"Neither can I." Mav inspected his friend. The relief of seeing a familiar face almost brought tears to his eyes. "I've missed you."

"I've missed you too."

"At least I lasted longer than anyone gave me credit for."

"Don't say that." There were tears in Felather's voice, and Mav regretted voicing his fear.

"I'm not done yet," he said, hugging his friend. "You'll have to put up with me a bit longer." He looked around the shadowy room. "How long was I out?"

"Just the one night. You should have slept a few more hours."

"We don't have time. We need to find out what the citadel is up to and why now. Where's Solanji?"

"She's with Adriz. They went down for food."

"Then maybe we should join them."

Mav couldn't help the limp. Each step, pain shot through him. And he was aware that Solanji watched his every wince with tight lips and burning eyes as he crossed the room. The stairs were his personal form of hell, and he decided he wasn't going back up them. One of the others could collect their things.

He eased into the seat opposite Solanji and grinned at her. "Sleep alright?"

She shrugged her slim shoulders, dwarfed by the woman sitting beside her. "As well as I could with all her snoring."

"You should have told her to roll over; she would've stopped," Felather said, taking the chair next to Mav.

"I couldn't move her, she's solid."

"You just need to tell her; she's well trained," Mav said, as he reached for a slice of the coarse bread.

Adriz snorted and carried on eating.

Tapping the table with her spoon, Solanji stared at her companions. "What's the plan?" she asked.

"Nervous about something?" Mav asked as he stilled her hand.

Solanji flushed and put the spoon down. "I'm not one for keeping still for long." She sipped her mug of bannoe and then started twiddling the buttons on her leather vest.

"Well, you get to ride your calope again, so that should be fun!" Mav said with a smile.

Solanji groaned, and Felather grinned at her. "Not a fan?"

"No."

"I'll swap my mule if you like. She is so smooth you won't notice you are riding," Felather offered.

Solanji stopped twiddling her button and glared at him. "How do I know you are telling me the truth?"

Adriz laughed and pointed her knife at Felather. "Feather here couldn't lie himself out of a slip knot."

"Feather?"

"He's as soft and silky as a feather, aren't you, my love?"

"Yeah, right," Solanji said under her breath, and Mav

grinned into his mug, inhaling the spicy aroma of bannen-root that Felather must have added.

Felather drew himself up as he flushed bright red. "I'll have you know I am nobody's plaything."

"But you could be," Adriz purred.

Felather tilted his head, a teasing gleam in his eye. "You offering?"

"Not at the table, children, we are eating," Mav said, and they all laughed. "I'll start saddling the animals. You all collect our gear and meet me in the stables. We'll head for the crossing."

They fell silent, and Solanji tapped her foot on the floor as if unable to sit still. She stopped when Mav shifted his outstretched leg, which had been next to hers.

Mav watched her for a moment. She seemed on edge, nervous. Was she still worried about him crossing? "It will be fine," Mav said, gripping her knee under the table. "Felather and Adriz were the ones I wanted you to contact for me. We'll make plans on the journey. We still have time." He could hear the 'yeah right' as if she had actually said it. He stood and, gritting his teeth, limped out of the room.

"He should be using his stick," Solanji said, and the others stared at her.

"He used a stick?" Adriz asked.

Felather cursed under his breath and quickly followed Mav out of the room.

Adriz scowled after him. "I guess that means we're on clean up duty. I wish you'd mentioned that earlier, Solanji."

"Why?"

"It means something is more wrong, if that is even possible. He is not healing as he should. We thought it was just a relapse from your skirmish, but if he's already accepted…" She bit the words off. "Angels should heal within hours of an injury; within a day of the injury at the latest. If it takes longer, then it isn't likely to heal."

"He said he was drained from too much healing. It would just take time." Solanji stared at her plate. She lifted her eyes to Adriz's. "We've been travelling for weeks," she whispered.

Adriz's hand clenched, but all she said was, "Come on, let's get our stuff. Felather will deal with him."

When they reached the stable, Mav was already mounted, idly waiting for them. Felather had the other three mounts ready. "Your choice," he said, indicating a sturdy mule or Solanji's previous mount. They didn't look much different, except the mule was rounder. Solanji chose her own calope. She ought to be used to it now. Mav was silent as they tied on their saddle bags and mounted, and then he led the way down the road.

Felather and Adriz peppered Mav with questions about his time in the castle as the miles passed, and Solanji hung back, listening intently as she pretended to inspect the rolling grey-tinged fields, which rose and fell around them. She felt quite sorry for Mav as he answered some questions and deflected others. Finally, he snapped. "Enough. I don't how why Julius handed me over to that seraphim. I didn't see him, only heard his voice, and I didn't recognise him. I have no idea what they think I have that they want, but I wouldn't have lasted much longer." He stopped and then whispered, "They drained my ability to heal."

Felather and Adriz had been glaring at him, not satisfied with his answers, but at that soft whisper, they fell silent, their anger dissolving into a concern so raw it made Solanji's chest ache.

Reaching for him, Felather said, "Mav." But withdrew his

hand as Mav stiffened. Solanji observed his shadows roiling around him, thick and dark and very defensive.

Felather and Adriz fell back, leaving him to brood as his calope walked through the filmy mist slinking along the edges of the hedgerows and trailing around the calope's legs, swirling away as they passed through. Drops of water fell on her from the branches above, making her flinch; they were so cold.

The sun that constantly bathed Angelicus was absent; no golden light, no warmth. The grey, clouded sky was depressing and felt like it pressed down on all of them. A dull glow provided the light; a non-shadow but not a light exactly. An absence of shadows maybe. She pondered on the idea. That there were shadows or not. Angelicus had few shadows; they were all here, and they gathered around Mav.

Instead of a bright glowing soul like the others, his roiling shadows caressed him and blurred his edges if she looked too hard. Even in the short time she had known him, he had changed. The shadows were thicker, silver threaded his hair, and his limp was more pronounced. She noticed his stick had been fastened under his saddle flap.

She had deliberated about riding next to Mav, not because she wanted to ask him anything, but to avoid those glowing souls. Her fingers yearned to touch them, to caress and play with them; to wrap them around her soul and absorb their light. She gritted her teeth and stared ahead. Her knuckles gleamed as she clenched her reins, trying to curtail the need that bubbled through her, and then she was suddenly aware that she had caught up with Mav and he was asking her a question.

"What?" she snapped and took a breath as he recoiled slightly.

"I asked if something was the matter. You seem tense," he said.

"No, nothing. I'm fine."

"We won't be attacked again, if that is your concern. We have Adriz in full armour to scare them off."

Her lips twitched, and she relaxed a bit. "They would have to be mad to take her on," she agreed. A soft snort from behind her told her any conversation would be overheard, but the question was burning up inside her, and she couldn't hold it in anymore.

"Why do you have shadows instead of a soul?"

Everyone stiffened, and she knew she shouldn't have said it out loud.

"I suppose something has to fill an empty space," Mav said eventually, "and if the light is gone, it only leaves shadows and darkness."

She kept going, now that the first question was out. "But the other soulless typically don't have shadows. They are empty. No light, no dark."

Mav shrugged. "You can still see the shadows?"

"Yes, they are getting thicker. Darker. Even in this last week."

"What happened, Mav?" Felather asked, moving up beside him.

Mav didn't answer, just stared ahead.

Solanji faltered, not wanting to mention Shandra and the children if Mav didn't. She resorted to one thing she did know. "They took his wings," Solanji whispered, knowing it for truth.

Felather hissed, as did Adriz. "Mav, why didn't you tell us?"

"It won't bring them back." Mav's voice was dead. Not an inkling of emotion coloured it. Solanji shivered as his voice reverberated on the damp air.

None of them knew what to say.

An angel without wings.

An angel without a soul.

An angel who could not heal himself.

Was he even an angel anymore? And if not, what was he?

"God, Mav. If we get hold of the seraphim that did this, I'll rip *his* fucking wings off," Felather said.

"He's mine." Mav's voice was hard as steel.

Vengeance wasn't a trait an angel usually had either. But then, if you had been tortured like Mav had, couldn't they give him a little leeway before they started calling him a monster? Solanji hoped so. If they began calling him a monster, he might start to behave like one. And she liked the Mav that she had helped rescue from a dungeon, even if he was all shadows. She curled her fingers, itching to touch them.

22

SOLANJI

The camp was quiet. Adriz had led them to a small cave off the trail, only large enough for them and their bags. The calope grazed on the sodden grass and flicked their tails in silent protest.

It had been difficult to find any wood dry enough to burn, though Adriz had found some tucked in a dryish corner, and the resultant fire crackled and hissed. They huddled around it in their damp clothes, more for the comfort of the dancing light than any expectation of drying out.

Solanji watched Mav, the flickering firelight casting his drawn face into shadow. More shadows curled around him as if trying to keep him warm. He had fallen silent after she had blurted out her questions about his soul. Though if she was honest, he was often quiet, introspective. She supposed he had much to think about. Meeting his old friends must have stirred some memories he would prefer to forget, and then being tortured for months... how was he still sane?

That quiet 'why' Julius had said in a voice of such pain, all those weeks ago, niggled her. What had Mav done to hurt his friend so deeply? An event that, even after many years, had not been forgotten. That still drove a man to try to kill him.

Adriz and Felather chatted quietly as they cleaned their weapons. Mav rubbed down his calope's tack, meticulously cleaning the metalwork. The pile of tack beside him slowly diminished as he worked. Solanji couldn't take her eyes off his hands, so competent and sure.

She flushed when she met his gaze, and she realised he had been watching her watching him. She smiled at him and dropped her eyes back to her own work, trying to clean off the mud from her favourite leather jerkin.

Felather rose and tossed a small tin in her lap. "Use that, it will help protect the leather."

Solanji smiled her thanks, and Mav grinned as Felather returned to his log. "Is that your famous all-in-one polish?"

"Yes, and you can't have any."

"Why not?"

Felather paused in his cleaning and stared at Mav. "Because you didn't take us with you."

And there it was, voiced, hanging in the air between them. The unspoken anguish, the anger, the hurt and disbelief that Mav had not trusted them, had not let them help him, had left them behind. Solanji felt it all, in the swirling emotions and the agitated soulmists that surrounded Adriz and Felather.

Mav's face blanched as he stared at them. "I couldn't," he said, a tremor in his voice.

"Yes, you could, and you should have," Adriz replied.

Mav swallowed. "You don't understand."

"Then explain it to us," Felather said, "so that we do."

"I can't."

"Can't or won't?" Adriz asked, sliding the whetstone down her blade.

Solanji shivered as the stone swished, an unspoken threat.

"It's been over fifty years, Mav. We've been searching for you for five decades. Don't you think you owe us an explanation as to why?" Felather asked, unable to keep the hurt out of his voice.

Solanji sat up. They had been searching for how long? To be so long-lived and not look it, they must be immortal. They were not only Mav's friends but something more. Were they angels as well? She had always thought that was a myth; only the gods were immortal.

"It's not that simple, and this isn't the place for it," Mav replied.

Adriz flicked a glance at Solanji. "Very well, but you will explain before we cross. You owe us that much."

Mav nodded. "I will."

"Damn right you will," Felather growled and strode off into the gloom. After a slight pause, Adriz followed him, and Mav heaved a deep sigh and stared into the flames.

Solanji squirmed in her seat, aware that her presence prevented this old friendship from resolving their differences. The issues between them were beyond her comprehension; that they would search for him for so long and were obviously concerned about him and for him. Everything they did was for him. Who was he to garner such devotion?

"I can leave if you need to speak to them," Solanji offered.

Mav lifted his head, his amber eyes deep pools of regret. "No, they'll be back. There will be time to speak to them before we cross."

He was still determined to cross the divide. Her stomach tightened. It was a mistake, she was sure. Before she could say anything, the others returned and all conversation died out, and by tacit consent, everyone rolled up in their blankets and tried to sleep. The dripping of wet foliage was soothing, the patter of rain on leaves filling the silent night. Night scents of damp stone and waterlogged grass pervaded the chill air.

Solanji gazed at Mav, unwilling to let him out of her sight. Her eyelids drooped, but she still stared at him. He wasn't happy. Of course he wasn't happy; there didn't seem to be much he could be happy about. Solanji wanted to hug him, comfort him, offer him solace and relief from whatever was worrying him. Her soul fingers extended, and she caressed his shadows, soothing, offering peace.

Mav's half lidded gaze locked onto hers, and she snuggled deeper into his shadows, wrapping them around her as she hugged him close. She soothed him, offering to ease his pain, and she latched onto his shadows. Flickers of images came into focus. A large building lined with white columns, white marble floors and steps, a trail of blood, bright red and vibrant against the white stone, and a woman collapsed across the stairs. She recognised the room, from where she couldn't remember, but she had seen this room before. It wasn't her memory; it must be someone else's that she had seen within their soulmist.

The injured woman was dressed in golden robes, a circlet of gold filigree in her strawberry-blonde hair, which curled down over her shoulders. An angel; she had that beautiful inner glow that all angels seemed to have.

Mav knelt next to the woman. As he gathered her in his arms, his anguish was visceral, and Solanji caught her breath. Bright crimson blood gushed over his clothes from a gaping wound in her chest, and he clamped his hand over it, though it made no difference. He hugged her close, rocking back and forth. The woman's hand rose, visibly trembling with the effort, and cupped his cheek, and Mav stilled.

They stared at each other for a moment. She truly was exquisite, and Solanji felt a stir of envy that Mav had loved someone so deeply. The woman mouthed the word 'go' but Mav shook his head and voice shaking said, "I won't leave you." He held her as the light in her eyes faded, the glow diminishing, their gaze never leaving each other, until her hand fell.

A tear rolled down Solanji's cheek, but she wasn't aware of it as she grieved with Mav for the loss of his friend. She held him as he had held the woman, offering comfort, as he railed against her death, anguish and anger rising at his failure to save her. But the comfort was shattered as loud voices and clattering feet stormed the hall. Shouts of horror and accusation. The woman's body was torn out of his arms, the shock of grief and loss immobilising him as rough hands grabbed him, and then a fist connected to his jaw, and darkness descended.

"Mav, come on lazy bones, it's time to wake up," Felather said the next morning once the camp had been struck. "And you Solanji."

Solanji embraced his shadows, rocking him gently, soothing the pain and the anguish and the self-recriminations. *"It was not your fault,"* she whispered.

"I should have helped her. Instead, all I did was hold her," he replied, bitter regret in his voice.

"There was little you could do; she was already bleeding out when you found her."

"I should have done something, called for help."

"You did what she needed. You stayed with her; your face was the last face she saw, and she was glad."

"No, I should have gone for Julius…her partner."

"Even if Julius had been there, he couldn't have saved her either,

and you would have left her to die alone. It's better she was with a friend."

"Come on, Mav, we need to get on the road." Felather crouched down beside him and shook his shoulder. He scowled at the lack of response and then looked at him closer. "Mav?" He gripped Mav's shoulder harder and jerked him upright. Mav sagged against him, the gleam of his half-lidded eyes the only sign of life.

"Adriz! Get over here! Mav won't wake up." He glanced at Solanji and nudged her. "And nor will Solanji."

Adriz hurried over. "What?" She gripped Mav's shoulder and stared at his face. "Mav? Can you hear me?" She shook him. "Demavrian?" She peered down at Solanji. "Do you think it's her? Is she doing something?"

Felather shrugged. "It could be Mav. I mean, with everything that's happened to him, he is different. Though why she is affected as well, I have no idea."

"Which makes me think it's to do with her. She said she could see shadows around Mav. She's a SoulSinger. Maybe she touched his shadows and caused a reaction or something?" Kneeling beside Solanji, she shook her shoulder. "Solanji! You must stop. Wake up." There was no response. Adriz frowned in thought. "We'll have to shock them out of it."

"Shock them?"

"We'll try icy water first. Go fill a feedbag from the stream."

"Hush, you must stop blaming yourself. You didn't kill her, someone else did." Solanji considered what she had just said. *"Someone else did. Mav. We need to find out who did. What else do you remember? Was there anyone else in the hall?"*

"No, it was empty. Sounds echo in that hall. I would have heard them."

"Was it usually that quiet?"

"No, not really. The citadel is a busy place."

"But only you found the woman."

"Athenia, yes. Everyone blamed me. Said that I killed her, I couldn't save her."

"It was not you who attacked her. Mav, listen to me, you did not kill her, you hear me? Did Athenia say anything? Did she see who attacked her?"

Mav was silent, and he shuddered as his memories played through the scenes again. Solanji soothed away his anguish, murmuring in his ear.

"He's spasming," Felather said as he dumped the icy water over Mav's head.

"Not *his* head, you fool, *her* head. We have to break her connection to him. Stop whatever she is doing to him."

"Adriz, if he can't keep her out of his head, how will he keep anyone else out?"

"We'll worry about that later. Let's wake them up first. Fill another bag."

Felather hurried back to the stream.

"What did she say, Mav? She spoke to you. What did she say?"

Solanji woke up gasping, her connection to Mav wrenched away by the icy water cascading over her head. "What the fuck?" she gasped as she lurched up, shaking the freezing water out of her face and hair.

"What did you do to him?" Adriz demanded, her knife at Solanji's throat.

"W-what?"

"Mav won't wake; what did you do to him?"

"N-nothing, I swear!" Solanji swayed towards Mav's limp body, still cradled by Felather. She halted as cold steel met skin, and Adriz's voice whispered in her ear, each word slow and distinct and laden with threat.

"What...did...you...do...to...him?"

Water dripped from Mav's hair and drenched his shirt,

but his eyes were still half-lidded, his face strained and pale as he relived his worst nightmares. On his own.

"He was having a bad dream; I was trying to help," Solanji said hurriedly. "I swear, I would never hurt him."

"Can you wake him?" Adriz asked, not moving.

Solanji was already reaching for him. *Mav? It's time to wake now.*

Images flickered past, faster and faster, a constant flow of horror and torment. He was remembering the torture chamber, his exquisite white wings flaring and going up in flames, his anguish like a knife thrust through her chest as the feathers curled and shrivelled in the heat, and Mav moaned.

"He's stuck in a nightmare," Solanji gasped. "He's remembering the torture."

"Get him out of it." Adriz's face darkened as she towered over her.

"Mav? It's Solanji. I'm here to help you escape. I've released the chains, Mav, you are free. Come with me, please, Mav. Solanji is here to save you. Here to protect you. Come with me." Solanji eased past Adriz and dropped beside Mav. Felather moved out of the way, and she took Mav's face in her hands, and after a moment, she kissed him. He didn't wake.

"Tell him to stop the pity party," Adriz growled in her ear.

"Mav? You're scaring Adriz. You need to wake up."

"Kiss me again and I'll consider it."

Solanji exhaled. *"One kiss and you open your eyes."*

"Only one? Are you rationing them?"

She leaned over him and gently cupped his face and kissed him again. Mav's arm snaked around her waist, and he kissed her back. "You feel so nice," he murmured and reluctantly opened his eyes. He stared at her, his eyes dark as the bannoe he liked to drink, and then his eyes widened as he saw Adriz and Felather standing over them.

"Why do we have an audience?" he asked.

Adriz hissed out her breath. "Because you wouldn't wake up, you fool."

Mav pondered that and then met Solanji's eyes.

"I'm sorry," she whispered. "You were having a nightmare about Athenia. I was trying to help you lay it to rest."

"I was remembering…" Mav broke off, and his eyes darkened until they were almost black.

"You didn't kill her, Mav. You found her like that. Why wouldn't they believe you?" Solanji asked.

Felather knelt back down beside Mav and helped him sit up. He kept his arms around him. "What did you remember, Mav?"

"I found Athenia dying in the citadel, and I couldn't save her."

"Athenia was an Archangel. Why didn't she save herself?" Adriz asked, her voice gentle and unthreatening, so unexpected that Solanji stared at her, but Adriz was focused on Mav.

"She was nearly unconscious; she had lost so much blood." Mav looked at his hands, and Solanji knew he could see it. "It was everywhere."

"She spoke to you. What did she say?" Solanji asked, and Felather's eyes widened as he stared at her.

"She told me to go. But I couldn't leave her, not like that, not to die alone. So I stayed."

"Did she say who attacked her?" Adriz asked in that gentle voice.

"She just kept repeating 'go', over and over." Mav dropped his face in his hands, and Felather tightened his embrace.

Adriz scowled at him. "We've lost half the morning. We need to get on the road, and we need to reach an inn tonight; fresh cooked food and a comfortable night's sleep will be good for all of us. And you," she pointed at Solanji. "Stay out of his head."

Solanji flushed. "I'm sorry, I was just trying to help."

"He doesn't need help like yours," Adriz growled.

"Why am I wet?" Mav asked as he slicked his hair back out of his eyes.

"I dumped a bag of water over your head. Be thankful you woke before Adriz suggested fire to try and wake you," Felather grinned.

Mav shuddered and avoided Solanji's eyes, and Solanji knew he was remembering his wings going up in flames. The loss in his expression was heart-breaking. "Thank god for that," he murmured as he stood.

23

SOLANJI

Solanji stared at the escarpment that filled the horizon. The sheer wall appeared impenetrable, and she wasn't looking forward to climbing it. Maybe the tunnel wasn't so bad after all. Bleak grey stone rose so high it met the clouds and was lost within them. Half the journey would be traversed in a thick mist, making it even more treacherous. A deterrent against daily crossings.

Musing on that thought, she followed Mav down the road that led to a sprawling settlement at the base. Another week passed before they reached the divide, and she knew no more about her travelling companions than when they'd first met, apart from the fact that they were extremely competent, well-travelled, and they rotated around Mav, even if they were upset with him. They seemed to have relaxed into a familiar, to them, travel routine, camping each evening to rest their mounts and rising every dull morning to continue their journey.

After the accidental lock, Solanji had kept her fingers to herself. The conversation had steered clear of souls, and they threw banter between them like shrugging on old jackets, easy with each other, and she had felt quite honoured to be included.

The current conversation swirling around her, almost too fast to follow, was about nicknames. She nibbled on the end of one her curls as she listened, and Mav leaned over and pulled her curl out of her fingers. "You'll ruin your lovely hair," he said.

Solanji tilted her head. He thought her hair was lovely? This curly old mop that always got snarled and tangled?

"We'll call her Anji the curl-biter," Felather said with a wicked laugh, and Solanji wrinkled her nose at him.

"You do that and I'll be calling you Featherweight," she replied.

Adriz snorted. "Nice one."

Felather rolled his eyes and pointed his finger at her. "I'll call you Drizzle!"

Mav chuckled, and Solanji's grin widened. Mav had been silent for most of the journey, lost in his own thoughts. He had sparred with Adriz on occasion, using his stick for balance and as a useful weapon. It seemed it was here to stay.

The murky landscape, although quiet, felt oppressive and threatening, even though Mav said the people were just like those in Angelicus. They wanted a peaceful existence. Not a life; the soulless did not 'live'. They could not procreate. There would be no children here unless they came soulless to start with. Solanji shuddered at the thought that anyone would condemn a child without giving them the chance to redeem themselves. An image of her brother, short and sturdy, bright brown eyes full of mischief, hung before her, and she clenched her teeth. Then she thought of Shandra's den and all the innocent youngsters under her wing. It was so unfair.

She stilled. Mav would not be able to have children. She

wasn't sure if the seraphim *could* procreate. They must be able to. Another thing he had lost, and her heart ached for him.

"What sad thought just passed through those beautiful eyes of yours?" Mav asked, his voice low.

She smiled at him sadly. "You don't want to know."

"It's better to talk about things instead of bottling them up."

"Pot, black." Felather called from behind them. His hearing was impressive. Mav cast him a scowl, and Felather laughed.

Solanji thought that he was some sort of squire to Mav. He was always on hand to help Mav dismount, set up camp, pass him a bowl of gruel or whatever they had managed to catch. Adriz was the bodyguard. She was a warrior, but everything she did rotated around making sure Mav was safe. They were his two-person army, and she so wished she could make it a three-person army. She would happily die for him.

Thinking that through, she wondered when he had slipped past her guard. She couldn't die for him; she had others to protect. Clamping down on that stray thought, she tucked it back in its box before anyone could pluck it out of the air. She hadn't seen any sign of mind reading in her companions, but some angels had that power.

The escarpment drew closer, blocking their way.

"How do we cross that?" Solanji asked, peering upwards.

"With difficulty," Mav said with a sigh. "But tonight, we have a bath and sleep in a bed for once."

Solanji bit her lip as the argument raged around her. They were stuffed in a room at the top of the building. The only room available in the inn that Felather had led them to. One double bed took up most of the space, and Solanji was curled up on it as she watched Adriz and Felather gang up on Mav.

For about the twentieth time Mav said, "I have to cross. I need to speak to Amaridin."

"We need to cross first," Felather insisted yet again. "We need to speak to your brother. See if we can get him out of the citadel."

Mav scowled. "You think the citadel will refuse me?"

"Why would the citadel refuse you?" Solanji asked. She was now certain Mav was the missing Demavrian. Being Archdeus Amaridin's brother confirmed it and that made what Kyrill had done to him even worse. A seraphim had tried to kill an archdeus and had dragged Solanji and her family into his schemes as well.

"We don't know for sure, and we're not risking you to find out," Felather snapped. "We're not attempting to enter the citadel. Amaridin will have to meet you elsewhere, and I need time to set that up. It's safer if you wait here with Adriz until I can confirm time and location."

"What if Amaridin refuses? Or doesn't believe I'm alive? I bet he believes I killed Athenia." Solanji winced at the rasp in Mav's voice. They had been arguing for hours.

"There was no evidence against you, except you were found at the scene of the attack. You had no weapons on you; none that would match the injuries Athenia received. Only your running painted you guilty," Felather said.

"I didn't run," Mav said, dropping his head in his hands.

"How did you escape your cell then?" Adriz demanded.

"I don't know! Julius knocked me out in the citadel hall. When I awoke, I was in Eidolon, being cared for by a farmer. He said he found me collapsed beside the road, obviously just arrived and without a soul."

"How did he know you didn't have a soul?"

"Apparently, you look glazed, bludgeoned. I certainly felt

like I had been wiped out. I couldn't remember who I was or how I had got there. Took a few years for it all to settle and for my memories to return."

"Are you sure you don't have a soul?"

"Definite. I felt it leave me."

"When?"

"With Athenia; she took it."

"But why?"

"I don't know. Maybe she was confused, distraught."

"Athenia would never hurt you, just as you would never hurt her," Adriz said, her voice softening as she stood by his shoulder. "We need to be cautious, let Felather make plans. Otherwise, we'll never find out what happened, and whoever *did* hurt her will continue to get away with it. Solanji can help you figure out what happened; she can help you remember."

"Was Athenia the SoulBreather?" Solanji asked, hesitant to interrupt but desperate to find out more about the woman who haunted Mav's memories.

"The only SoulBreather in recent history. She could remove souls but also return them. With her death…" Adriz faltered. "She could weave the soulmist back into a soulless person; offer them the chance of redemption and returning to the light."

"Athenia was our friend," Mav growled.

Solanji gasped. And someone had murdered her? "But why would someone kill her?"

"No one knows. But since her death, anyone who loses their soul won't ever get it back." Adriz scowled at Mav. "Unless he crosses the divide and returns to the citadel, we'll never find out who *did* kill her, and he can't enter the citadel without a soul."

"That's never been proven," Felather started to say, and Adriz cut him off.

"We are not testing it with him; we'll have to find him a soul he can borrow."

"How do you borrow a soul?" Solanji asked.

Adriz scowled at her from where she leaned against the wall, her arms crossed over her ample chest. "We need to find someone dying, already beginning the journey, and you will have to convince them to give their soul to Mav. It has to be given freely."

"What? Me? There's no one here with souls except you two." Solanji's heart stuttered as her stomach dropped. The stolen soul curled within her, mocking her. It hadn't been given to her freely; she had taken it.

Adriz hissed her breath out. "At worst, we'll have to cross and come back."

"And how long will that take?" Mav asked, raising his head at last. "The longer I stay here, the more likely someone will recognise me."

"So? There is a reason we found you now. After all this time, do you think we are going to let you fade back into the shadows? The citadel needs you. *We* need you," Adriz said.

"I am no longer what I was."

Solanji cringed at the lack of emotion in his voice.

"No," Adriz agreed. "You are much more. I know you haven't wasted your time here."

"I am an Eidolon now. Soulless. The citadel will not allow me entry."

"You don't know that. There is no reason for the citadel to deny you. And if it does, then at least it will put you out of your misery!"

Mav huffed out a laugh.

"You speak of the citadel as if it is alive," Solanji said carefully.

"No, not alive as such, but it does have an opinion on occasion," Mav said.

"Then why doesn't it reject the person who attacked Athenia?"

There was a short silence, and Felather heaved a sigh. "Everyone believes it did by forcing Mav to leave."

"But you just said there was no proof," Solanji said.

"There isn't. But unless Mav walks through those doors, the popular opinion is that he can't," Felather replied.

"What a mess." Mav ran his hands through his hair. "If I can't enter the citadel, how do I prove my innocence?"

"If lacking a soul is the reason you can't enter the citadel, and you say Athenia would never hurt you, why did she take your soul? *How* did she take your soul?" Solanji rubbed her temples. "This doesn't make sense. Did something else happen?"

"Is being accused of murder and lacking a soul not sufficient for you?" Mav asked.

"Neither of which were your fault."

"How do you know that?"

"Adriz and Felather know it's not. They wouldn't have been searching for you for years—"

"Over five decades." Adriz's voice was cold.

Solanji scowled at Adriz at the interruption. "—for over five decades if they thought you were a murderer."

"You know better than that. Friendship doesn't negate guilt," Mav said.

"Why did you never send us a message? You know we would have come running to help you," Felather asked.

"I did," Mav replied, his voice tinged with exhaustion.

"When?" Adriz snapped, straightening out of her lean.

"About three years after I arrived. It took that long to earn enough money to bribe someone to cross the divide for me."

"We never received a message," Felather said.

"I sent another five years later. Each time it took all the

money I'd earnt and made me destitute again. The waiting was crippling, wondering if you or the Heavenly Host would turn up and arrest me again. But no one came."

"We never received any messages from you," Adriz said. "They never reached us."

Mav rubbed his face. "I gave up after that. There was no way to know why you didn't come. Whether my messages weren't getting through or if you…" Mav's voice faded, and Adriz was across the room and pulling him into her arms.

"We never gave up on you," she said into his hair. "Neither did Ryvalin or Xylvin. They've been searching Eidolon for years, taking on deliveries, transporting seraphim. But there was no sign of you."

"Xylvin?" Solanji whispered to Felather. "Isn't she the dragonair?"

Felather nodded. "Her rider, Ryvalin, is Mav's captain."

Mav moaned into Adriz's chest, and her grip tightened. "We never gave up on you and we never will," she repeated as she closed her eyes and hugged him tight.

After a short silence, Felather cleared his throat. "The seraphim that Julius handed you over to. Any idea why he didn't give you up to the citadel? Why did he torture you? What did he want?" Felather began pacing.

Solanji bit her lip. She wanted to say his name, to tell them everything, but she couldn't. She couldn't risk them not crossing. Brennan was depending on her. "He wanted your soul. That's what he wanted me to take. Why didn't you tell him you had already lost it?" Solanji asked.

"I didn't want him to know I couldn't return to the citadel."

"So, you were still planning to return." Adriz pounced on him.

"No! Yes! I don't know, one day. Maybe, if I could figure out what happened."

"In all this time, you've not come up with any ideas?" Adriz asked.

Mav stared across the room at her and didn't answer for a moment. Then he deflated as he sat on the end of the bed. "I believe Julius and others are working to exploit the minerals recently discovered in Eidolon. Someone is stealing people from their homes and turning them into slaves. I don't know how far it goes up in the citadel." He rubbed his face. "That's why I need to speak to Amaridin. I don't know who else to trust."

"Which is why I need to go first. Amaridin hasn't left the citadel in decades. Probably not since you disappeared," Felather said carefully, his eyes on Mav. "I need time to convince Amaridin to meet you, and even then you may have to enter the citadel."

Round and round they went, Solanji thought, back to the lack of a soul and the risk Mav took if he crossed the divide and couldn't return before he dropped dead. The brilliant soulmist she still held within her roiled for a moment, and she opened her mouth to speak, but Felather continued. She was forgotten as these age-old friends continued to discuss what to do next.

"Adriz and I investigated one of those mining compounds run by the dybbuks."

"You're such a damn fool, you nearly got yourself killed," Adriz snapped, her eyes flashing.

"No I didn't. You're just jealous that I got inside and you didn't." Felather smirked.

Adriz cursed under her breath until Mav raised his hand. "What did you find?"

Felather began pacing as he quickly recounted his brief incarceration in the mining compound and what he had found. "I've been studying the map. I think there are at least twenty other compounds across Eidolon. This is not a small operation." Adriz grabbed his arm and halted him. He huffed and then said, "The other paperwork I haven't been able to decipher yet. I'm still working on it. The handwriting is atrocious. None of which matters if we can't find you a soul to get you across the divide and into the citadel."

"That's still only a temporary fix. It will only last for a day or so, even if you do find one, and then I'll be exposed anyway for the fraud that I am."

"For God's sake, Mav. Would you at least try? Your father would want you too." Adriz glared at him.

Mav's laugh was harsh. "Yeah right. My father's not been seen since…oh yes, since I fled. Hid his face in shame, did he?"

Adriz stared at him. "We were hoping you would be able to tell us what happened to Averdeus."

"Oh, great, that's been laid at my door as well, has it?" Mav dropped his face back in his hands. His voice was muffled as he said, "God, what a mess."

Solanji's gaze jumped from one to the other; she was lost. What were they talking about?

"Mav, it has to be connected; it all happened at the same time," Felather said in a soft voice. "We have Solanji now; she can help you unravel your memories, see if there's something you buried that could help us."

"If there was anything to find, don't you think I would have found it by now?" Mav asked, suddenly rising and limping across the room. Adriz and Felather exchanged glances. "It's been fifty years. Fifty! What makes it any different today versus yesterday? It's just the same. Another dreary day to survive. Another day to pretend all is well. Another day to…"

"Stop it, Mav," Adriz said.

"Or what?" Mav whipped around and staggered as his leg gave way. His derogatory laugh cut through Solanji. "I have no soul, no wings, no nothing. I can't even heal myself anymore. One good thrust and you could finish me off. I am nothing." He ran his hand through his silver frosted hair. "What are you expecting me to do? Even if I manage to cross, what *exactly* do you expect me to do?"

Adriz gripped his shoulders and physically shook him. "Be the man you are," she said, and Mav fell silent.

Felather waited, anxious, across the room. Solanji was sure he was holding his breath, just as she had as Adriz's quiet words hung in the air.

With or without a soul, Mav was still an archdeus, and he lived, even if he lived in the shadows. The silence stretched, and Solanji exhaled.

"I might be able to help with the soul, though it might not work," Solanji said into the awkward lull, and three pairs of eyes swivelled to her. She flushed.

Releasing Mav, Adriz turned on Solanji, and Mav sank back onto the bed as if exhausted and covered his eyes. "What do you mean?" Adriz demanded as she approached the bed.

"I-I have a soul Mav can use."

Adriz scowled. "You'd give him yours?"

"N-no, I mean, I have a spare one he can use."

"You just happen to have a spare soul on you?" Adriz snarled, throwing her hands in the air. "Since when?"

"Umm, since those guards attacked us when we escaped. I took the soul of the one who died."

"Took?" Adriz repeated.

Solanji shrugged. "It was hovering there, as if I was supposed to collect it. So, I did."

"It has to be freely given," Mav whispered.

"It is. I am freely giving it to you."

"But it wasn't given to *you* freely."

"That had nothing to do with you."

"She's right. The legend only says it must be freely given to the recipient," Felather said.

"Legend?" Solanji asked.

Felather shrugged and then leaned against the wall as he watched Mav still lying across the bed. "Well, it's been a while since anyone's managed to transfer a soul. It's all myth and legend."

"That's the only problem. I don't know how to give it to Mav."

Adriz narrowed her eyes. "How did you collect it?"

Solanji hesitated then pushed her sleeve up her arm. "The dragon inhaled it. I saw it." It had been the only thing keeping her sane over the last week or so. Being able to trail her fingers through it, cuddle it. It had eased the need to caress Adriz's or Felather's soul and lessened the temptation to embrace Mav's shadows.

Staring at the tattoo on her arm, Mav sat up.

"Souls don't normally 'keep' as such," Felather said hesitantly. "When transferred, they only last for maybe a day before they are released."

"Says who? I've had this one for over two weeks, and it looks just as bright to me."

Mav slowly raised his head and met her eyes.

"What?" she asked, licking her lips at the intensity of his gaze.

"Who are you?" Mav asked.

"I told you. I'm from Bruatra…"

"When did you first start SoulBreathing? Does it run in your family?"

"No. I'm not a Soulbreather. I can't transfer…" she faltered, not sure what he wanted.

"How did the seraph find you? What did he say he wanted of you?"

"H-he wanted a SoulSucker. He wanted your soul."

"That's not what he wanted," Mav said. "He never mentioned my soul. Not once, in all the years——" He cut off what he was going to say. "It was my wings he wanted and finally got."

"No, he wanted me to wait for your wings to flare and then take your soul. If he managed to take your wings, he didn't know it. That's what he said."

"And what did you get in return?" Adriz asked, her voice tight.

"They'd leave my family alone and let me go."

"As if!" Adriz huffed. "There's been no one like you in centuries. He would never let you go."

Solanji shrugged. "That was the deal."

Adriz's eyes narrowed as she observed Solanji. Trying to keep her expression calm, Solanji ignored Adriz's suspicion and focused on Mav. He grounded her, kept her safe. Uncertainty flooded her. Was she doing the right thing? Was she trusting the wrong people? Should she tell them all that she knew? What would they do if they found out what she was really capable of? That she could influence people's actions, read their thoughts, that she *could* SoulBreathe. Would Mav look at her the same way?

Calming herself, Solanji cleared her throat. "How do I transfer a soul to you?"

"I don't know," Mav said.

Adriz threw her hands up in the air. "Anyone would think you don't *want* to return."

"Return to what exactly?" Mav asked with a wry twist of his lips. "Blunt accusations? Suspicions? Being put on trial?"

"Rejoin your family? Your friends? Amaridin has mourned your absence," Adriz said.

"So much so I hear he is replacing me."

"It's been nearly fifty years, Mav."

"So once we are past the mandatory mourning period, it's a free for all? I was deemed dead as soon as I fled?"

"I didn't say we thought you were dead," Adriz said, coming to stand before him. "I would never..."

Mav held up his hand to stop her. "I'm sorry. I never meant to question your loyalty. The fault is mine. I stayed away."

Eyes flashing, Adriz hissed her breath out. "Without us."

Mav flinched, her anger a sharp blade.

"I don't think we should be discussing this here," Solanji said, drawing Adriz's ire to her. Mav looked distraught enough already without Adriz pummelling him.

Adriz glowered at her, and Solanji regretted opening her mouth.

"You will transfer the soul tonight. Tomorrow, we cross the divide, together. Felather will meet with Amaridin and, if necessary, Mav will enter the citadel and prove his innocence. Amaridin will have to meet with him after that." And then she stomped out of the room. Felather cast Solanji an apologetic glance and skittered after Adriz.

Mav exhaled and carefully moved over to the worn bench on the other side of the room. He stretched his legs out, leaned back, let out a long breath, and waited.

Solanji fidgeted as she sat next to him.

"Do you know how Athenia did the SoulBreathing thing? How can I give you the soul?" Solanji twisted her fingers, and Mav captured them as he observed her with tired eyes.

Shaking his head, he said, "I believe it was instinctive."

"So if I try to give you the soul, it should automatically try and find a new host?" She extended her soul fingers to soothe the shadows that flicked around Mav in agitation. She tilted her head as she observed them, silver flashing as they writhed. "Your shadows don't seem pleased at the idea."

"Is that why I feel unsettled? As if something is not quite right?"

"Maybe," Solanji said. "What if your shadows are a type of soul?"

Mav's eyes widened. "Is that even possible?"

Solanji shrugged. "I have no idea, but they behave similar to the soulmist. If a little more antagonistic," she huffed, snatching her fingers back as they nipped her.

The shadows writhed around Mav as if creating a barrier. Silver sparkled in a haze of shimmering smoke.

"You know, however this is supposed to work, I don't think they will allow a soul to join them," Solanji said. "They seem a bit defensive."

"Yet we have no way of proving that these *shadows* as you call them will behave as the soulmist does in Angelicus."

Solanji heaved a deep sigh. "I suppose we can but try."

"I can't feel my shadows. I can't tell them what to do, but I thank them for protecting me as they have," Mav said. He flicked a glance at Solanji, who gave him an encouraging smile. "I've been lost for many years, trying to survive, to accept. Maybe that seraph did me a favour." He paused as Solanji gasped, and he gave her a feral grin. "He made me see that I have unfinished business in Angelicus. If he'd just let me be, he may have gotten away with his plan to replace me. My life may be in Eidolon now, but I should at least clear my name and provide Athenia some peace. She deserves to rest," he said, fingering the red vendetta stone around his throat.

Solanji hesitantly touched the second vendetta stone, the blue one. "What is that one for? Who gave you that one?"

"I'm not sure. It was there when I woke up."

"So you gained it between Athenia's death and waking up in Eidolon? What else could possibly have happened?"

"I have no idea. I was unconscious. Julius knocked me

out, remember?"

"Julius did?" Solanji gritted her teeth. "You should have killed him."

Mav laughed, and his shadows danced.

Narrowing her eyes, Solanji extended her soul fingers. "Please," she whispered, she wasn't sure to who, "will you at least let us try? Do you know if you can sustain Mav in Angelicus?"

The shadows wriggled around her fingers, playfully nipping. The shadows obviously thought they could. Her forearm burned as the dragon unravelled and slid down her skin, making Solanji shiver. It reformed in the air before her, huffing out a spark of red glitter and fluttering its eyes. Mav jerked back. "What the…" His face paled, and Solanji thought he might faint.

"She latched onto me in the curio shop in Puronia."

"That…That is…" Mav's voice failed as he stared at the little creature.

"It's what?"

"Athenia's," he whispered. "Or maybe the SoulBreather's?"

"There was a gold ring in the cabinet. I couldn't leave the curio shop without taking it. When I touched it, it evaporated and changed into a mist that became the tattoo around my arm."

"Athenia's ring. That's right, she was wearing it the day she died," Mav said, his eyes glazing.

"Why was it attracted to me? I'm nobody."

"You are a SoulBreather. The only one in existence. You are certainly not a nobody," Mav replied. "Of course it would want to find its way to you. How it ended up in the curio shop," Mav paused and shrugged, "who knows. I imagine it's been trying to find you ever since you were born."

Solanji stared at the little dragon still nosing Mav's shadows. "Who would have wanted to kill Athenia?"

"What?"

Solanji frowned. "Mav, are you alright?"

Mav was staring off into the distance. The dragon snorted, and a fine mist spewed out into the air, and it glittered, golden and bright and brilliant as it swirled closer. Solanji looked more closely. That was not the soulmist she had collected from the soldier. This was scintillating, crackling with energy and life. She swallowed. Was this Mav's soulmist? Stored in the ring all this time?

Mav's shadows stiffened and then flared into his gorgeous wings. The strands of shadow mist solidified into a barrier of interlocking feathers. Silver and darkest night slotted together in an impenetrable mosaic. Beautiful yet adamant. The soulmist could not find a way through, and the tiny dragon sighed. The dragon eyed Solanji and she scowled. "What?"

The dragon flicked her head at Mav as if expecting Solanji to do something.

Solanji spread her hands. "I have absolutely no idea how to get through them."

The dragon huffed and stalked forward, as if such a tiny creature could stalk. She butted her nose against a black feather. The feather dissolved into a fine mist and she sucked it in, tasting it. Exhaling the gold mist, a golden feather formed in its place. The dragon inhaled another feather. Only the black ones, Solanji noticed, not the silver edged ones. She huffed out a red-gold mist and it formed into a golden feather before another black one could form in its place.

Solanji rubbed her fingertips together as they began to tingle. Extending her soul fingers she stroked a golden feather and smiled as an image of a sunny, book-filled room with comfortable chairs to snuggle in flashed through her mind.

The little dragon continued until maybe a third of the black feathers had become golden, and then she burped and Solanji chuckled.

The scintillating soulmist was now golden feathers interwoven with the shadows, entwined and complete. The dragon had returned his soulmist, though to be honest, Solanji still didn't think he needed it. The shadows were his soul, and they were still predominant, the golden feathers accentuating what he had become instead of replacing it.

As Adriz had said, Mav had become more than what he was. Whatever he had been doing in Eidolon had changed him. She suddenly realised Mav had said very little about where he had been in all the years he had lived in Eidolon. Except for the children she had met at Shandra's place, she knew nothing about him.

That wasn't quite true. She knew he was Archdeus Demavrian, son of the god, Veradeus. That alone was mind-blowing. She was helping a fallen angel retrieve his soul. Well, watching a soulbreathing dragon do all the work. She frowned, looking down at her tingling fingers. Shouldn't she be doing something? Would the dragon teach her how to be a SoulBreather?

The dragon faltered a moment, fluttered up to stare into Mav's glazed eyes, and then nodded before dissolving into a fine mist and swirling around Solanji's wrist and up her arm and settled into the golden tattoo with a weary sigh that resonated through Solanji. She wilted as exhaustion hit her as if she *had* been the one doing the work.

Solanji slumped against Mav, curling into his glittering gold and silver shadows. Mav shuddered out a breath as his eyes cleared. "What just happened?" he asked. But there was no answer. Solanji was fast asleep.

24

MAV

The next morning, Solanji was silent and pale, and Mav eyed her with concern. They had awoken with stiff necks after sleeping uncomfortably on the bench all night, Mav scrunched up at one end and Solanji curled up, head resting in his lap. Adriz and Felather had claimed the bed.

Mav knew Solanji was more than he had originally thought. Amazement and a thrill of excitement flushed through him at the knowledge that a SoulBreather was in his presence. She had Athenia's dragon tattoo. The one that came alive. He had only seen the tiny dragon briefly, but Mav had recognised it. With a SoulBreather, they could reverse some of the damage inflicted on the people of Eidolon. That thought was swiftly followed by the realisation that no one could know. If someone wanted the Soul-Breathers dead, then Solanji's life would be at risk.

The connection to Athenia and his absent soul was frightening. Had she returned his soul? All he knew whatever Solanji had done had made him feel unbalanced. Out of sorts. And he was foul tempered as a result. The fact that he was contemplating returning to a place that promised certain death had nothing to do with it.

Vague memories teased his brain, shadowy and indistinct. There was something, just on the tip of his tongue, but he couldn't remember what it was. Something to do with Athenia's death. If he returned to the halls of the citadel, maybe that would jog his memory. He stared across the room, considering who could have killed Athenia. His stomach stirred queasily as he realised in the recesses of his mind that he knew who it was.

Breakfast was a tense affair. Felather was frowning over some papers in front of him as he absently ate a piece of bread. He pointed to a word. "Do you think that seraphim at the castle could be Kyrill?" he asked.

Mav shrugged. "I don't remember Kyrill that well. He must have been quite young when I left."

"Tall, good looking, blonde hair, blue-eyed," Felather rattled off.

"Sounds like any angel," Mav replied.

"He would fit the description," Solanji said.

"Kyrill looks to Golaran. He is the citadel's golden boy. His star is ascending, the most likely to rise to Archangel," Adriz said. "I can't see him risking that."

"So he would visit Eidolon often?" Solanji's voice was eager. "Didn't you say Golaran ran the projects in Eidolon?"

"Yes, good point, Solanji," Felather replied. "He represents Golaran as he prefers not to travel, so he would fit, and we saw him a few weeks back travelling to the crossroads. I am sure this says Kyrill, but I can't make out the context. I'll keep working on it."

Mav was glad when Adriz and Felather left to prepare the calope and Solanji left to pack up her things. Alone for a moment, Mav scowled into his mug. The scent of bannen leaves spiralled up with the steam, and he rubbed his throbbing temple. He didn't want to go back to the city of Puronia, back to the stifling expectations, the rigid hierarchy, the minute inspection of every action and reaction.

Eidolon had been freeing, if he was honest. Difficult and challenging, but endearingly honest. The people lived here because they had to. All pretension was stripped; what you saw was reality.

He held his head in his hands. His heart was in Eidolon with his fledglings and the people who had wormed their way into his affections, and he couldn't desert them. They were good people who didn't deserve to be left to struggle on their own. They were entitled to their chance at redemption, as originally intended. Whatever his father had planned to do, Eidolon had the right to have a say, and he would be their voice. He had responsibilities, and soul or no soul, he had to honour them.

The arrival of his oathsworn had Mav rising. Adriz wore her ornate leather armour, and Felather had changed back into his finer robes. Mav had chosen a pair of dark grey, wide-legged trousers that would hide his stick if he should need it. Even when his station had demanded it, he had never worn white. He supposed he had always lived in the shadows.

He had made his decision, and if Solanji had been there, she would have seen his shadows standing to attention. Limping out of the tavern, he was relieved to see Solanji mounted and waiting in the courtyard. She appeared a bit strained, her face taut, but Mav supposed they were all tense and on edge. Even if he was able to cross the divide, they would be on tenterhooks for twenty-four hours. He might just expire on the spot. Though deep down, he didn't believe he would, even if the others were concerned; not with Athenia's dragon involved.

Puronia was his home. Yes, he had allowed himself to be

banished. Maybe he had been punishing himself for not saving Athenia? But he wasn't prepared to allow a lowly seraphim to wipe him from the history books.

Drawing his calope over to the mounting block, he ignored Adriz's concerned expression as he lurched onto his mount. He still couldn't bend his knee properly and he accepted that he probably never would. He gave his companions a bright grin and gestured for them to lead the way. Felather took point. Adriz fell in behind him, a familiar presence, and he relaxed.

The road towards the escarpment was busy. Wagon trains rumbled down the road, followed by herds of livestock roped together. Small stalls, a concoction of wooden boxes, offered refreshments, a mug of bannoe brew, some type of cake, the chance to replenish your water, all before you began the ascent that would take half a day, even riding a calope. Mixed aromas teased their noses, the strong, comforting scents making their mouths water.

Solanji suddenly pulled her calope in front of Mav's. "I don't think you should cross here," she said in a rush, her face heating and then paling as she twisted the reins between her fingers.

Felather pulled up beside them. "Why not?" he asked with a frown. "We agreed we'd all cross together last night."

"But what if Mav gets stopped or arrested? Could you prevent that?"

"That is going to happen at some point," Mav pointed out. "Preferably not as soon as I cross the divide though."

"I might know an alternative route." Solanji stared around her as passing travellers jostled her. "But we can't discuss this in the middle of the street."

Adriz rolled her eyes. "Why didn't you tell us this last night?"

"I don't know! We were all so focused on Mav's soul, it was never the right moment."

"Let's stop at that water station. We can discuss whatever your plan is there," Mav suggested, urging his calope forward and waving his hand at the people complaining behind them.

Once they were out of the road and clustered around Solanji, she exhaled. "I know another way to cross the divide, only I don't think we can all use it."

Mav raised an eyebrow. An alternative route? "Go on," he murmured.

"There is a crossing under the divide," Solanji said.

"What?" Felather asked on an explosion of air.

"There is a tunnel under the divide, avoiding all guards and checkpoints."

"How do you know of this?" Adriz asked, suspicion clear in her expression.

"On occasion I'm a courier for…questionable goods. For the more important items, a token for a crossing under the divide is included. I used one to enter Eidolon, and I have a return trip left. Only we can't all go as the token is only for one person. I can probably take Mav. I doubt you'd fit, Adriz. It is quite a narrow tunnel."

"There is no way I'm letting him go through some tunnel on his own with you," Adriz said straight away.

"Where does it come out?" Felather asked with interest, ignoring Adriz's outburst.

"In a shop in the Shambles," Solanji replied.

Felather's mouth dropped open. "Really?"

"Yes, it's very discreet; we wouldn't be seen. Only, it's quite a strenuous climb. The tunnel gets steep in places, and there are some twisty bits where we'll have to crawl. It will take a few hours. I'm worried Mav's knee will be a problem."

Felather narrowed his eyes as he stared at Mav. "I could

give it some reinforcement. Strap it up so it's supported. Though once it all wears off, you're going to be in agony."

"You are not seriously considering this?" Adriz asked on a horrified gasp.

"The element of surprise is our greatest advantage," Felather began.

"No! We only just found him. I'm not losing him again," Adriz replied, her tone uncompromising.

"It would give you two time to cross and to advise our allies that I'm coming," Mav said. "You could also see if you can speak to Amaridin and arrange a time for us to meet. We would be more prepared to strike when I arrive," Mav said, keeping his voice calm and reasonable.

Adriz glared at him, and Felather jumped in. "You know it's unlikely Mav will get through the checkpoint," he said, "and if Xylvin is there, she'll go beserk. We need to warn them."

Adriz hesitated, and Felather pressed on. "It will give Mav time to readjust to Puronia. He's been gone a long time."

"We can go to my room. It will be safe. No one knows where it is. You can bring us word when you have the meetings set up," Solanji said.

Mav stirred. The more he heard the more he liked the plan. The thought of barrelling straight into trouble at the checkpoint had been worrying him. "It makes the most sense. I'll go with Solanji, and you two cross here. Where is the tunnel entrance?" Mav turned to Solanji.

"It's about two days ride south of here," Solanji said. "If we time it to arrive in the early hours of the morning, no one should see us enter Puronia."

"Give Felather your address. Felather, don't come to us until the morning three days hence, which will give you time to speak with with Amaridin. There's no point risking anyone following you and drawing attention to us."

Felather huffed. "As if I wouldn't know I had someone behind me."

"Let's not take the risk," Mav replied. "We've only got one shot at this. Once I'm in their hands, the citadel will be in control."

"I don't like it," Adriz said.

"It's no worse than me crossing here," Mav said.

"I suppose," Adriz agreed, begrudgingly.

Mav gave her a grin and a quick hug and then moved behind the calope using them as a screen. "Felather, do what you can for my knee. It has to last through the tunnels, and I need to be able to bend it."

"Try not to. The more you bend it, the more damage you'll do."

"Do you have any pain relief for when it wears off?"

Felather shook his head. "I'm completely out. I'll get some in Puronia for you."

Mav leaned against his calope and unbuckled his trousers as Felather knelt beside him and laid his hand on Mav's knee. Sweat sheened Mav and Felather's skin by the time Felather finished and began winding a wide bandage around the still swollen knee. Felather looked up at Mav in concern. "There is so much wrong with your knee, I don't even know where to start. You could do irreparable damage and not realise it. I've completely numbed it. You won't feel it for a couple of days, but it will wear off."

"It's already irreparably damaged. It won't make much difference," Mav replied.

"It will increase the amount of pain you have to suffer in the future," Felather said under his breath, and Mav squeezed his shoulder as he rose to his feet, tugging Mav's trousers back up.

Rebuckling his belt, Mav sighed out his breath as for the first time in weeks, he was pain free.

"Still use your stick when you can," Felather warned. "Remember, it is not healed, only numbed."

Mav nodded and, with Felather's help, remounted.

"We'll see you in Puronia in three days," Mav said with a small smile and gestured for Solanji to lead the way south. A quick glance over his shoulder revealed his oathsworn still standing forlornly by the side of the road.

25

FELATHER

Adriz and Felather watched until Mav disappeared from view, and then Adriz hissed her breath out. "We're really going to stand here and let him ride off?" she asked, her face tight.

"But this time we know he is alive, and we know where he is going," Felather replied.

"We know little about that woman, and he's not at full strength. How do we know she's not a threat?"

"If she was, she would have killed him by now. She's been travelling with him for weeks. She would've had plenty of chances." Felather turned back to the escarpment and the winding track that climbed it. The cliff was sheer, a wall of grey stone that rose into the thick clouds above them.

"I still don't like it," Adriz muttered, and Felather gave her a fond smile. Adriz had been Mav's cherubim for years. It was her job to protect him. Of course she wouldn't be happy letting him out of her sight now that she had finally found him. He was surprised she had so easily agreed to him going through the tunnel. But then, the risk of him being arrested at the crossing had been extremely high. The sooner they returned to Puronia and arranged for Mav to meet his brother, the sooner she would be back at his side.

Felather sighed out his breath. "Come on, it'll take us all day to climb that escarpment. And just think, you'll have the pleasure of telling Xylvin you've found your wayward archdeus!"

"If she's there," Adriz grumbled as she pulled her calope around and remounted.

Reaching the base of the escarpment, they joined the queue to pass the checkpoint so they could climb the trail to enter the city of Puronia, the gateway to Angelicus. The checkpoint had been moved to the bottom of the cliff as there had been a few altercations when travellers, who had climbed all the way to the top, were denied entry, turned away and sent back down. They had responded with fists and knives.

The queue was slow moving as the guards checked papers and searched wagons and bags. Felather had always wondered what they searching for, because although it happened on occasion, it was rare for people to be refused entry. He thought maybe they performed the checks to spread the travellers out so they weren't clumped together on the trail. The checks were briefer when you left Angelicus to enter Eidolon.

"Reason for travelling to Angelicus?" the guard demanded in a bored tone of voice as she held out her hand.

"I'm returning home after a business trip," Felather replied and handed over his papers.

The guards skimmed the papers and then reread them again, before raising her eyes to meet Felather's. "And what business would that be?" she asked, her mouth thinning into a hard line.

Felather just managed to hold back the 'None of yours' retort that was on his lips and smoothed his expression into one of amused interest. "My business? Well now, I have an investment in a wool merchant in Jinnel, to the east of the crossroads. The wool he harvests is the finest in Eidolon. The finest threads for the best materials."

The guard scowled. "Enough of your drivel. I know you're Demavrian's scribe. Where have you really been?"

Felather straightened and looked down on the woman. "*Archdeus* Demavrian to the likes of you."

The guard stiffened, and Felather continued. "As you know, my archdeus has been absent these many years; therefore, I have to fill my time with something. I chose wool." He smiled, and narrowed his eyes. "And as you are well aware, an oathsworn cannot denounce his position, so I have to return to Puronia and manage my master's affairs in his absence."

Snorting, the guard shook her head. "Maybe you'll find there is no longer a need to bend your knee to one who chose to forsake those he was responsible for or to manage his..." she paused and tightened her lips, "affairs any longer."

Felather's smile grew frigid. Was this woman really trying to suggest that Mav had voluntarily deserted his responsibilities? "I would suggest that is not a comment you repeat too loudly," he said as Adriz stepped to his side. The guard visibly gulped, obviously well aware that she had just insulted Archdeus Demavrian before his cherubim. Felather wasn't sure how the guard had missed Adriz standing behind him, but maybe she just had a death wish. Anger vibrated through Adriz, and her hand gripped her sword so tight, her knuckles gleamed white.

The guard hurriedly shoved the papers back at him and said, "You may pass."

Felather's lip curled as he took his papers and pulled his calope towards the trail. The guard waved Adriz past and proceeded to ignore them.

Worry gnawed at Felather's gut as they began to climb. If lowly guards were beginning to publicly denigrate Mav, then someone was already actively besmirching his name. A guard would not dare to insult an archdeus unless the citadel had already begun to do so.

Exchanging anxious glances with Adriz, he clamped his lips shut and concentrated on leading his mount up the slowly steepening slope. Although some rode their beasts, it was quicker to lead, and Felather had the feeling that time wasn't on their side.

It took all day to climb the winding trail up to the escarpment, looping back on themselves at each switchback. The view over Eidolon, a patchwork of grey and green fields interspersed with darker clusters of trees, was lost in the gloom as they slowly rose until they reached the actual clouds. Cloying mist trailed swirling fingers of dewdrops over everything it touched, a clammy embrace that neither welcomed nor deterred, just was.

Adriz wiped the sheen of moisture off her face and peered through the gauzy air at Felather. He was hunched over in his saddle, one shoulder raised in defence against the chill. His face was pinched with concern. The fine lines around his mouth and eyes were deeper, more pronounced, and she wanted to smooth them away, along with his worries.

What she really wanted to do was punch that smarmy guard who had dared suggest that Demavrian had deserted and betrayed them. She restrained her simmering anger and quietly released her breath.

"Not much further," Adriz murmured and pushed through the misty heaviness until they burst into the brilliant sunlight on the other side. Felather straightened in his saddle, unfolding like a flower questing towards the light. He slicked his damp hair back and blinked as his eyes watered in the golden glare.

Adriz had forgotten how bright the sun could be. Shielding her eyes, she relaxed as the warmth chased away the tightness across her shoulders and the resentment in her breast.

The city walls rose around them, gleaming in the golden sunlight, and as they passed through the open gates, the pleasure of returning home flushed through Adriz. The familiar streets, the hum of voices, colour and sun and warmth all bombarded her, telling her she was home, and a slow smile spread across her lips.

Wending their way through the vibrant city, inhaling the warm aromas, the rich scents, and the happy vibes that the smiling people of the city shed without thought, Adriz edged forward and took the lead through the tightly packed buildings, jostling for space on the road.

Golden stone and red roofs interspersed with vine-draped courtyards, and open squares helped project a more spacious mien to the city, but as the road widened and the buildings became grander and further apart, it was obvious where the wealth was situated; at the feet of the glistening citadel rising above the city. Its presence even overpowered the majestic mountains rising behind it, drawing the eye to the perfection of the gilt domes, of which there were more than one, and the slender spires. The home of the angels.

A huge dragon, her iridescent scales gleaming in the sunlight, guarded the citadel gate, making the accompanying guards superfluous. The sharp spines decorating her back were all raised and polished to a shine. Her long body and tail curved through the gates and around the ornate fountain in the courtyard.

Adriz knew she was basking in the fine mist drifting in

the warm air. Three exquisitely carved cherubs with their tiny wings adorned the fountain, one with a bow and arrow, another with a harp, and the third holding out its hands. A spray of water gracefully arched from their open mouths into the shallow basin beneath them.

Relief flowed through Adriz at the sight of the amazing creature. That meant Ryvalin, Mav's Captain of the Host was in Puronia. The impressive dragon, Xylvin, rose as soon as she saw Adriz and Felather riding up the wide road. She forced everyone out of the way, blocking the entrance until they had dismounted so she could inspect them. The calope and the mule attempted to bolt, and it took a moment to control them and then to allow the eager stable lads to take them off to the stables.

"Welcome back. Any news?" Xylvin asked as she always did, the warm greeting tickling Adriz's mind.

Adriz had missed the mind speech all the time they had been in Eidolon. It was so convenient, but they needed Mav to enable them speak mind to mind, and she faltered as she realised that not once had Mav spoken into her mind. Had he tried and she hadn't heard him? Her stomach dropped. Would he think she had blocked him? She didn't know. *"No, but we'll come and have a chinwag once we've cleaned up,"* she replied, trying to keep her concern out of her voice.

Xylvin tilted her head, and Adriz knew she had failed, but the dragon nodded and said, *"Be quick about it then, for we have news too."*

She had definitely failed, but Xylvin surprised her by calmly returning to her curl around the fountain, as if nothing had occurred.

Adriz continued into the citadel, followed by Felather, eager to wash off all the road grime before the hard work began.

26

MAV

Mav followed Solanji down the road, turning her revelations over in his mind. A tunnel under the divide? He wondered how many people knew of it. Not many for it to still be secret. So who was Solanji really? To be one of the honoured few who knew.

Observing Solanji as they rode, he knew she was a rarity. A SoulBreather, even if she didn't know all the workings. He wracked his brain, trying to remember what Athenia had told him, but whenever he thought of her, he became mired in grief and loss, and it hurt too much to remember.

He had failed so many people. Spent far too many years hiding in Eidolon when he should have returned and cleared his name. A low snarl vibrated in his throat. It wasn't that simple, and he knew it or he would have returned before now. Walking into a situation blind and unsupported, especially with such high stakes, was foolhardy.

His fledglings needed him. He couldn't afford to get himself killed. He would return for them; that he vowed. Someone in the citadel had been very busy in his absence.

Well, now he was returning, and they would soon regret every move they had made against him.

The day passed slowly. They travelled in comfortable silence, sharing soft smiles when they met each other's glances, and Mav relaxed in the company of someone who wanted to be with him for who he was, not for what he might be. He remembered the feel of her lips on his, her gentle caresses that she thought he didn't notice, her anxious concern for him, and he knew with certainty that he wanted more of her. Waking up and not meeting those soft black eyes across the campfire every day filled him with such a sense of loss that he gritted his teeth to keep in the moan.

The escarpment towered above them like some brooding threat. Grey stone rose in sheer columns, adorned with swathes of green and yellow and deep, shadowed crevices, which might have been impressive but for the fact that it guarded the entrance to Angelicus.

They camped near a small stream, and Mav took the time to wash some of the grime off his skin and soak his feet. The cold water refreshed him, and for the first time, some of the tension eased from his shoulders and he slept reasonably well.

The next morning, they were back on the road, speaking little as they both contemplated their return to Angelicus. Solanji had awoken short-tempered and heavy eyed as if she hadn't slept well. Fidgeting with her buttons, she avoided his eyes, and he wondered what was worrying her. She had said she'd lost her commission and the payment. What would that mean for her? She hadn't spoken of any other means of income, and weren't her family dependent on her as well?

He owed her much for helping him escape. If that seraphim hadn't dragged her to his mountain retreat in the first place, Mav would still be incarcerated, too weak to escape and slowly dying. Shuddering at the possibility, Mav thought about his fledglings instead. Those kids were an inspiration, and their belief in him filled his chest with warmth.

After a few hours, Solanji turned off the road onto a much smaller lane that led them into a picturesque hamlet that butted up against the escarpment, which filled the horizon.

Solanji suddenly halted. "I can't do it," she said, her shoulders bowing as she slumped in her saddle.

"Can't do what?" Mav asked, scanning their surroundings for a threat.

"Lead you to your death!"

"You're not. This is my choice, and I don't believe the citadel will reject me."

"No. I haven't told you everything." Solanji faced him, and his heart clenched at the distraught expression on her beautiful face.

"What haven't you told me?" he asked, a sudden rush of adrenalin clearing his mind.

"The seraphim's name *is* Kyrill. He looks to Archangel Golaran. Kyrill knows I can touch souls, because I accidentally brushed through his soulmist and he felt it," Solanji said in a rush. "My brother was caught stealing and sent to the Justicers. He's only nine. They were going to send him to Eidolon, abandon him there. I went to the Justicers office and pleaded for his life, offered to do anything to save him. Kyrill was there and recognised me." Tears poured down her face, and Mav reached for her, unable to bear her anguish, but she put up her hand to keep him away. "Let me say this," she said, sniffing.

"Kyrill said that if I did a task for him, he would make sure my brother wasn't sent to Eidolon. He wanted me to take your soul, discover what you had found in Eidolon, help you escape, and persuade you to go the citadel."

"And did you do any of that?" Mav asked calmly, assimilating the sudden rush of information, his flash of anger at the seraphim's continued depravity, and the hurt that ached in his chest at the idea that Solanji had considered betraying him, returning him into that man's control.

"No!" The word burst from Solanji and then her shoulders sagged. "Not to say I wouldn't have, but you didn't have a soul so I couldn't see your thoughts, and when I saw what he had done to you, I didn't want to. I thought I could just make something up. Though I did help you escape," she said with another sniff.

Mav's lips twitched at her need for complete honesty and some of the hurt eased. She hadn't been able to betray him. She had instead consigned her brother to a life of fear and uncertainty, and the anguish and despair in her expression stirred his anger. That she had been forced to even consider one life versus the other made him want to gut Kyrill. He controlled his growing fury and said, "For which I thank you every day."

"You don't understand," Solanji said, actually wringing her hands. "He made it simple for us to escape. I don't know why he couldn't take you to the citadel himself or why he wanted me to, but if he wants you to go to the citadel, then it's a trap, and you can't go."

"But they won't know when we return or where we are. We have the advantage of surprise."

Solanji rocked in her saddle. "You can't go back." Her voice shook. "You'll die. Your fledglings need you. I'm so sorry I didn't tell you before; I didn't know what to do. At first, I didn't know who you were, and I didn't think it would matter, and then later, when I got to know you…Brennan is only nine."

Mav moved his calope next to her. "Solanji, stop beating yourself up."

Solanji raised her tear-stained face. "I betrayed you. I'm so sorry."

At that, Mav reached for her and dragged her onto his lap as his calope jinked under the extra weight. "No, you didn't. You were in an impossible situation, and I know for a fact that I would never have got this far without your help. Your brother is very fortunate in his sister, but you have to realise that it is unlikely Kyrill has the power to stop any deportation, nor does he have any intention of doing so."

Solanji buried her face in his neck, and he tightened his embrace. "The more I thought about it, the more I wondered," she admitted against his skin. She inhaled and then kissed his neck as if she couldn't help herself, and he shivered at her touch.

"We will find him, and luckily, I know a beautiful Soul-Breather who can return his soul if necessary."

Solanji stiffened in his arms, and Mav grinned. She hadn't realised what she could do. He lifted her chin and dropped a soft kiss on her parted lips. "Can't you?" he asked.

"I-I never thought," she whispered staring at him with wide, black eyes. Tears glistened in her lashes, and he kissed them away before returning to her lips. "But I don't know how to return a soul."

"Then we'll figure it out, together," Mav said.

"Mav?" Solanji whispered against his lips.

"What?" he murmured, more interested in kissing her.

"Will Adriz kill me?"

Mav jerked back as a laugh escaped him. "She may be angry, but I think I can talk her down."

Solanji exhaled and relaxed against him. "Good." She kissed his neck again. "You smell so lovely," she said.

"So do you," Mav replied, "but I think my calope is about to collapse, and we need to climb a tunnel."

Solanji chuckled and looked around for her mount. It

hadn't strayed far, and after another lingering kiss, she clambered back on to her calope. "There's a hostelry at the end of the street," she said as she pointed down the road. "We can stable the animals there."

"Don't the people think it strange that so many travellers visit this hostelry?" Mav asked as he drew close enough that their legs rubbed, and she smiled at him.

"They are paid not to look," Solanji replied with a slight shrug, which explained why the village was so well maintained. It would not have looked out of place in Angelicus, with the pruned hedges and well-kept fences.

"How has no one found this place before?"

"It is not so easy to find if you don't know it's here. And as I said, no one looks. It is probably the safest village in Eidolon." Solanji dismounted as they reached a tall wood-clad building with large double gates. One wood-barred gate swung open as she flashed something that she held in her hand, and they entered the dim interior.

The warm aroma of livestock and leather assaulted his nose, long used to the scent of waterlogged vegetation. He inhaled the familiar smell.

"Stable your calope in that stall. The man will take care of them," Solanji said and then waited for him as he removed the saddle bag and his stick. She entwined her fingers with his, and he smiled as she led the way to the back of the barn. She released his fingers with a quick squeeze, dropped her saddle bag to the floor, and began rummaging. "We need to travel as light as possible. Just take your canteen, weapons, and your stick. Leave the rest here. It will just weigh you down."

Mav did as she said. He didn't have much anyway. Most situations he found himself in tended to strip him back to nothing. A test in resilience, he supposed. Had he passed yet? How many more times was he to be tested? Somehow, he didn't think he was anywhere close to an end. He did slip his flint and compass in his pocket. They were not so easily replaced. Grabbing his stick, he followed Solanji into the darker shadows at the back of the barn, where it morphed into a stone cavern between one step and the next. Mav gaped as he followed. The barn was built into the escarpment.

Solanji disappeared into the darkness, and Mav hurried to keep up. He found her scooping a cup of water out of a barrel. "Drink. It gets hot down below and you'll need it. Fill your canteen. It's the only water station for the next six to eight hours. It will be late by the time we reach Puronia."

Silently, Mav filled his canteen, suddenly aware that he was completely at this woman's mercy. Could he trust his innate reaction to her? How he wanted to be with her, to see her wicked smile. Especially after all her revelations? The answer was an unequivocal yes. He wanted to spend whatever time he had left with her. She had made him feel alive for the first time in years.

"This is the worst direction to travel," Solanji said, her voice a warm caress. "The tunnel will slope down to begin with, but then it's all upwards. It will get very narrow in places and extremely steep. There are steps cut in the rock in places; at others you'll have to pull yourself up by rope."

"Why didn't you say before? You could have just magicked the guards at the check point, and I could have ridden up the escarpment."

White teeth flashed in the gloom. "I considered it, but I wouldn't have been able to persuade them all quickly enough. It was too risky. This is safer, though more strenuous."

"Then we'd better begin. Is there any light in the tunnel?"

"Very little. Most of it will be travelled via touch. I'll warn you of obstacles when I can."

"Thank you, Solanji. I do appreciate you offering to show me this secret route. I was surprised when no one protested against you bringing me with you."

"I encouraged them to forget you were here, but they'll scratch their heads when they find two calope in their stables, so we'd better get moving."

"You are amazing. You do know that, don't you?" Mav said, following Solanji's appreciative chuckle which led him through the open cavern and into a smaller enclosed space. The mineral infused tang of water and stone brought him to an abrupt halt. His fingers tightened on his stick as he leaned heavily on it. His brain went into a frenzy as images flashed, the taste of blood flooded his mouth. His muscles tightened: flee, run, get out!

"Mav?" Solanji was back. "What's the matter?" Cool hands cupped his heated cheeks. "Shit, I didn't think," she said. "You're safe, Mav. Solanji is here, and I promise no one is going to hurt you."

A tremor shuddered through Mav. *She lies. No one can protect you. Run.*

Soft lips kissed along the ridge of his cheek and then warmed his lips, and he tensed. "I promise, I will protect you. You are safe. I swear no one will ever harm you." Her warm breath thawed his frozen muscles.

He cleared his throat, surprised at her words. "You swear? You would swear your oath to me?" It was too dark to see her, but her lips smiled against his skin. She was so close.

"You would accept my oath?" she asked.

"Instantly," he replied, the truth of it shocking him. Was it her oath he wanted? Or something else? She had slipped under his guard, eased into a trusted companion without hesitation. Their silences were comfortable, her presence comforting. Her company over the last few weeks had become as important to him as anything else he could imagine. "But I would want you to appreciate what swearing your oath to me means, especially as it may not be the safest path at the moment. So I would understand if…"

Those soft lips kissed him again, and he forgot his line of thought as the kiss deepened. He opened his mouth as her insistent tongue demanded entry. Heat washed through him as she pressed against him, waking thoughts he had long consigned to the discarded pile.

"The choice is mine, and I choose you," Solanji breathed into his mouth as she slid her hands around his neck, pulling him close. "I will always choose you. No matter what others say, you must always believe that."

Her touch tingled all over his body, driving away his fear, and he took the opportunity to gasp in some air. He shivered, filled with the need to touch her, so he did. Running his hands over her back and up to her shoulders, he gently clasped her neck, smoothing his thumbs along her jaw and back down her smooth throat. He tasted her mouth, pleased at the responsive tremors he could feel beneath his fingertips. "I would promise to protect you always, but my promises are hollow, and I am unable to keep them."

"Your promises are not hollow, and I would hold you to them."

Mav leaned his head back, giving her room to kiss his neck, his throat, and he shuddered as she parted his shirt and ran warm hands over his skin. "I know I'm going to regret saying this, but are you sure you want to do this here?"

"If we are going to swap oaths, don't you think we should celebrate it?" Solanji asked, her voice a husky rasp.

Mav slid his hands down to her waist and pulled her tight against his throbbing body. "You would choose me? When tomorrow may be my last day?"

"Tomorrow will not be your last day, and I told you, I've already made my choice and you will not change it."

Tears sprung into Mav's eyes, that someone would believe in him so completely and utterly and at such a moment. "Truly?" he whispered, still not quite accepting it.

"Truly," she whispered back and attacked his buttons. Before he knew it, she was sliding his shirt off and light kisses peppered his heated skin, smoothed his taut muscles, followed the contours of his stomach, and brushed through the thicker hair that led further down beneath his waistband. He groaned as quick hands unbuckled his trousers, and he realised Solanji was way ahead of him in the removing of clothes.

Reluctantly, he stayed her hands. "You know who I am? You know what swearing your oath to me entails?" he asked, wanting to be sure.

"Demavrian," Solanji said deliberately, and Mav relaxed. "You are the angel I believe in and would swear my life to protect. I want you!"

Mav's doubts faded, and he felt for the fastenings on her vest and then her shirt and pulling the laces loose, he swept it over her head. He fumbled for the buckle at her waist, shuddering as her cool fingers cupped him, stroked him, set him on fire.

"Take the weight off your knee, and lie down," Solanji whispered in his ear, the heat from her skin touching his, and he awkwardly lay down. Her warmth chased away the chills from the cold stone that now pressed against his back. Mav liked this demanding Solanji, especially when she was demanding his body. She lay on top of him and forced his mouth open, her tongue questing, tasting, tangling with his. He couldn't prevent the upthrust of his hips, the urge to be inside her, to move with her, to be wrapped in her, driving his need.

He thought he might explode when she slid her hand down his shaft and guided him to her entrance. He was so hard, and she was so wet and inviting and encompassing him. Ecstasy flooded through him, and he swore it lifted him off the floor as his back bowed. Solanji cried out as she moved with him, their speed quickening. His mind spun off as sensations cascaded over his skin, through his body, and then whited out his brain.

Soft panting greeted his ears when he regained his senses, the cold stone reminding him where he lay in complete disarray. She had undone him and put him back together again. "I accept your oath," he whispered against her damp skin. "As I hope you accept mine."

"Always," Solanji replied, raising her head and kissing his nose. "You are an amazing man, and I have come to the realisation these last few days that I just can't live without you. I am so sorry I lied to you."

Mav tightened his embrace, relishing the feel of her skin against his. "You didn't, not really. You told me all I needed to know when I needed to know it, and it was your decision to tell me. You do know you've aligned yourself with a notorious fallen angel, despised by all of Angelicus?"

"No, I've aligned myself with the Archdeus Demavrian, the kindest, most thoughtful man I've ever met, who shines even under the worst kind of duress and, if he can find his clothes, will now climb through this awful tunnel with me."

"Hmm," Mav replied, kissing her shoulder and clinging to the last blissful sensations of being wrapped in her heat. "Clothes might be a problem."

"For an archdeus?"

"I'm no longer an archdeus," Mav murmured as he felt around him for his shirt.

"They can't take away who you are," Solanji replied,

"and you," she prodded his chest as she sat up, "are definitely archdeus material."

"I think these are your trousers," Mav said as he grasped cloth. He winced as she climbed off him and searched around her.

"Here's your shirt," she said, and soft cloth smacked him in the chest.

He took it and searched for the arms. Nope, wrong way round. He tried again. "You do know we're going to find our clothes are inside out when we finally reach some light."

"At least when we put them on the right way, they'll be clean. Hey, saves on laundry," Solanji said with a laugh as she passed him his trousers. "Have you found my shirt?"

Trousers went on easily, and he shuffled around, hunting for more cloth and his sword belt. He found his stick instead, and he used it to extend his reach. "You do know that swearing your oath to an archdeus has ramifications," Mav said as he found her shirt and a canteen.

"Is it official then? I thought there might be some ceremony or something you have to do in public to seal it."

"I am not repeating what we just did in public," Mav said, as he slung his canteen crosswise over his body.

Snorting, Solanji stepped into him and wrapped her arms around his waist. Laying her head on his chest, she murmured, "I promise I never used my skills on you. I only caressed your shadows, I swear."

Mav lifted her chin, even though he couldn't see her. He slid his finger along her jaw, and she shivered. "I never thought you did. I don't need any 'persuading' to make love to you, Solanji. What we just did was the most enjoyable experience I've ever had, made more special by your faith in me. I fully intend to repeat it, many times and in much more comfortable locations, when we can actually see each other.

You made your oath of your own free will. I couldn't persuade you or anyone else to do that."

Solanji kissed him and then stepped back out of his embrace. "You could persuade me to do anything, but we need to go."

Mav heard the reluctance in her voice, but she was right; their moment was over and they to needed move.

27

SOLANJI

The tunnel was pitch black. Only the rope she was clinging to kept her moving into the inky depths, and the fact that Mav was following her, trusting her soft directions as he blindly scrambled down the steep slope.

Heat flushed her cheeks, and she was glad of the darkness as she replayed their lovemaking. She couldn't believe she had been so forward, but Mav's fear had sent her into a frenzy, determined to ease that horror-filled tension from his body. To remove him so far from those terrible memories and replace them with love and compassion.

She had wanted to prove that not everyone was out to hurt him, and in so doing she had pledged herself, heart and soul, to him, and she didn't regret it for a moment. Her hands slid on the rope, and she hissed her breath out at the burn. She should have wrapped their hands in cloth, but the thought hadn't crossed her mind.

Her head had been full of Mav, the feel of him inside her, against her skin, wrapped around her. His deep voice blurred with emotion, his honesty. Her heart skipped a beat, and she knew she was lost. The man had stolen her heart in a few short weeks, and the thought of losing him filled her with terror.

"Rest a moment," she called, bracing her knees against the tunnel floor. "We're about half way down. At the bottom are tunnels. We'll have to crawl through some of them."

"I'll manage," Mav reassured her, his calm voice a balm to her worries. Her lips twitched. In fact, he still sounded a bit blissed out. It had been out of this world sex, and she had done that to him without manipulating anything. She hadn't needed too. And her own reactions had been just as surprising. She had never felt so complete and comfortable with anyone.

"Tell me how your soulbreathing works." Mav's voice was above her and she realised he was right next to her. She hadn't heard him move.

"I'll tell you as we descend. We'll rest again at the bottom. In return you can tell me what the ramifications of being oathsworn to an archdeus means."

Mav huffed his breath out. "A bit late to be asking."

Solanji shrugged against his leg, which had somehow wrapped itself around her. He felt the need to touch her as much as she needed to touch him. It reassured her. His swirling shadows reached for her, glittering in the darkness, open and accepting, and a rush of warmth sped through her as she welcomed their caress. "I have no idea what it means for you to be oathsworn to a SoulBreather," she said, finally accepting that was what she was.

"I suppose we'll learn together," he murmured, his voice a soft embrace. "But I would hope it means we're a damn good partnership."

"I know one thing we're damn good at," Solanji replied and then slapped her hand over mouth as Mav laughed. It was a sound of pure joy, and she couldn't help but grin. She gripped his thigh in appreciation and then began climbing down the rope again.

"I don't know when I first realised I could touch soulmist," she began.

"What does it look like?" Mav asked. "How do you see it?"

"Soulmist is golden, a swirl of golden mist that trails around a person. Sometimes it's wrapped tight around them, as if they know how to control it, like Felather or Adriz. For others it trails loose behind them and it's difficult to avoid."

"And to you it is physical? You can touch it?"

"Yes, I can comb my fingers through it. I can even extend my reach, soul fingers I call them, and touch it from a distance."

"Like you did with Julius, when you sent him to sleep?"

"Yes, soulmist can be influenced. I can suggest a person do something and they do it. I don't do it often, only when I'm desperate. Part of touching a person's soulmist means you see their uppermost thoughts, and sometimes they are not particularly nice."

"A bit like a cherub then," Mav said.

"Can cherubs touch soulmist? Adriz never mentioned it."

"Adriz is not a cherub, she's my cherubim, my bodyguard. She is one of my oathsworn, as is Felather, and now yourself."

"And Xylvin? How did a dragonair become your oathsworn?"

"That is a story for another day, but yes, Ryvalin and Xylvin are also oathsworn to me. But we were talking about cherubs. Cherubs can sense history through touch. When they touch something, they see how it was made, or its recent history. They can also regress that history to see what happened in the past. It is a difficult skill and one much sought after by the citadel. A cherub is a point of truth, and their word is unassailable."

"Wouldn't a cherub be able to see what happened to Athenia?"

"One would need to have touched her before she died to see who attacked her. They can only see a history once it's happened. She died in my arms, so I know one didn't, especially seeing as I'm still believed to be the one who murdered her."

"What if a cherub touched you?"

"I wouldn't wish myself on any cherub. Once they see a history, they can't unsee it."

"But to prove your innocence?"

"It's a possibility, if we can get a cherub to agree to regress."

"I'm at the bottom. Be careful you don't jar your leg as you step down," Solanji said, as she reached up to guide him down. She slid her arms around his waist and inhaled his slightly sweaty scent. He smelt so good.

"We'll rest here, and you can tell me about the ramifications of being an oathsworn. Drink some water."

"Yes, ma'am," Mav replied, reaching for his canteen. "If everything was working properly…"

"Oh, I can assure you, everything is most definitely working," Solanji interrupted with a laugh as she settled between his legs and leaned back against his chest. He began massaging her shoulder, and she sighed.

"You are so good for my self-esteem. But as I was saying, if everything was working, we would be able to speak mind to mind."

"Wow, really?"

"Yes, typically if we're in the same room, and sometimes over longer distances. But it's not working at the moment.

Xylvin acts as an amplifier. She can broadcast over longer distances than I can."

"That's right, she spoke straight into my mind when I met her at the crossroads. It was Xylvin who transported Kyrill and me to his castle." Solanji twisted around and placed her hand on Mav's chest. "Why didn't she know you were there?"

Mav shrugged. "I don't know. As I said, I haven't been able to project, not that I was in any state to project anything."

"If I get the chance, I'll kill that seraphim," Solanji said viciously. "He threatened my family, he hurt you. He doesn't deserve to be called an angel."

Mav rested his chin on her head. "I won't argue with you on that, but we need to use him to find out who he is working with first. This is so much bigger than them just trying to get rid of me. They could have killed me many times over, so why didn't they?"

"I'm so thankful they didn't. But I thought you were immortal? I thought you couldn't die?"

"I'll live forever, but I could be killed, if someone was determined enough. If I was unable to heal myself quickly enough, like Athenia, I could still die. More importantly, my oathsworn inherit my immortality."

There was a short silence. "They what?"

"My immortality. You will age slower, and I am very glad to say that it is a lot more difficult to kill you now."

"I thought that was just a myth. You mean it's true?" Solanji's voice came out as a squeak.

"It's true. Is that a problem?"

"Well, no, but…"

"But what?" Mav clasped her to his chest. "But what?" he prompted again. His breath hot on her ear.

Solanji shivered and shook her head. Mav lurched back

as her hair slapped his face. Before she could apologise, he pushed it aside and he bent to kiss her neck. "There are few benefits to being oathsworn to me, but that is one of them," he said into her skin.

"Stop that. There are lots of benefits to being your oathsworn. I get to see your beautiful face every day, for one. When we're out of this tunnel, of course. But, immortality? I thought only gods had that."

"I *am* a god."

"*Son* of a god," Solanji corrected. "Don't get big-headed."

Mav laughed. It was freeing. His laugh filled Solanji with joy, and she revelled in it. She squeezed his arm. "Come on, let me entice you through the tunnels."

"How could I resist such an invitation?" Mav asked.

The tunnels passed by in a flurry of laughter and conversation as Mav and Solanji crawled through the narrow passages. Solanji described her hometown of Brurata, and Mav shared some of his favourite places in the citadel. When one of them faltered at the thought of the oppressive tunnels closing in on them, the other was there to chase the fears away.

"We've reached the stairs," Solanji said when she stumbled across the warning ridge. "Let me know if you need to stop and rest."

"I can't feel any pain. I'm fine."

"You won't be tomorrow. Remember Felather said he numbed your knee, but the pain will return. Let me splint your leg with your stick so you can't bend it."

"It's fine. I had to bend it to get through those tunnels. It couldn't be helped. I'll see if I can climb the steps backwards. Give my knee a rest. Depends how steep they get."

"You go first, then I can catch you if you slip," Solanji

said, and when Mav sighed his breath out, she grimaced. "As your oathsworn, you will do what I tell you."

"I'm pretty confident that's not how it's supposed to work," Mav said.

"It is now. I'm taking lessons from Adriz."

Mav groaned. "No, please don't."

Solanji laughed. But Mav did crawl around her, and she shifted as his long legs stretched out beside her as he sat on the first step. She reached for him, placing her hand on his chest as he braced his left leg and then lifted himself up a step. She wrapped the rope around her left wrist and followed Mav up the step. It was slow and more tiring than she had hoped. When Mav's breathing became more laboured, she made him stop, more often than he wanted too, but he listened to her, to Solanji's surprise.

After three punishing hours, a cool breeze wafted through the tunnel, and a dull glow illuminated the tunnel walls. Solanji looked up into Mav's exhausted face, and she smiled as she made out his features for the first time in hours. "Nearly there," she whispered. They were covered in dirt and grime and they both needed a bath. Together would have been perfect, but Solanji clamped that thought down before she got carried away.

Once they reached the top, and Solanji was sure Mav was securely wedged on the final step and wouldn't fall, she fumbled for her token and pressed it into the circular depression in the centre of the door. There was a metallic click and the door swung open, revealing the collections of glass and china ornaments piled on the tables of the curio shop.

28

FELATHER

PURONIA

A s they crossed the training courtyard a shout jerked Felather out of his thoughts. "Hey, Eladriz, still haven't found your vagabond, then? You've only wasted, what, fifty years?"

The man didn't even see Adriz move, but her dagger was at his throat and her voice was hissing in his ear. "You ever speak of Archdeus Demavrian with disrespect again and your head will be in the dirt with your boots, understand?"

There was an abrupt silence as all the men stopped sparring, and then a soldier stepped forward. "Cherubim Eladriz, he meant no disrespect. Please, lower your blade and accept our apologies," he said.

"Say it," Adriz hissed as she pressed the dagger into the soldier's throat so the edge bit his skin and drew bright red blood.

"My apologies, Cherubim Eladriz, I meant n-no disrespect n-now or at any other time." The man's voice shook as he stuttered out the words.

"Good." Adriz withdrew her blade and held each man's

eyes until they dropped their gazes to the ground. She nodded and stalked out.

"Brant, you fool, you got shit for brains. Why'd'ya take her on? She'd have you in ribbons before you took your first breath."

"I thought she'd take it as a joke," Brant whined.

"She's a cherubim; she'll never take anything about her angel as a joke, you idiot."

Felather exhaled as the soldiers resumed their sparring, and he scurried after Adriz, glad to reach the plain white marble corridors that led to the wing with their rooms and Mav's apartment.

He had fought so hard to retain Mav's rooms, and he detoured to check that they were still secure. Many archangels had grown covetous of those rooms over the years, even though they were supposed to be above such thoughts. As a result, Felather had bound Mav's apartment up in so much bureaucratic tape and misleading regulation that most scribes had given up trying to untangle them.

Breathing out a sigh of relief, Felather was glad to find the rooms untouched, though he feared they would soon be defending them against a new assault with the growing anti-Demavrian fervour. The apartment was calm and peaceful. Floor to ceiling shelves covered the wall on his left and the one opposite, even framing the door to Mav's bedchamber. The shelves were filled with books, all with different coloured leather covers and golden lettering on the spines. A large wooden desk and matching chair sat at an angle between one wall of books and the tall windows to the left.

Bright evening sunlight shone through the glass, warming the room with a golden glow. Dust motes sparkled in the slow-moving air, and Felather frowned. He'd have to arrange a cleaner without arousing anyone's suspicion. Thank goodness he had periodically had the rooms cleaned over the years so it wouldn't be that unusual a request.

Walking across the room, he opened the bedchamber door and halted on the threshold. It was silent and still. Lifeless without the charismatic man who should have been in there, and he quickly shut the door.

He was suddenly struck by an image of Mav leaning over to pull some tome or other off the shelf, and he caught his breath as he realised the man in his imagination looked nothing like the exhausted man he had left in Eidolon that morning. Another image, of Mav sitting in the comfortable chairs gathered around the fireplace, talking long into the night. He looked so young and vibrant. The images were so clear. His throat tightened as more memories tumbled through his mind, and he abruptly left the room and relocked the door.

Walking to his own rooms down the corridor, he noted the steam creeping out of the bathing room that he and Adriz shared. Adriz wouldn't take long, and then he could wash all the sweat and grime off.

His saddle bags were already in his rooms, leaning against the wall, but he ignored them, stripping off his road-begrimed clothes as he crossed his room to the cupboard. Pulling out shirts and jackets, he tossed them on the bed and then stopped, gripping the wooden door.

Mav's strained face swam into view, the lines of pain on his skin, the new creases around his eyes and mouth, the silver streaks in his once black hair, the grime covering his skin. Eidolon had not been kind to Mav, and Felather dreaded what he had seen and what he had experienced in his years there.

The sudden realisation at how reticent Mav had become struck him as tears filled his eyes. Mav had said enough to answer their questions, to fill some gaps, but there were gaping holes he was going to have to fill, and Felather was not looking forward to hearing it. That was if they could even get Mav to tell them everything. He was no longer the man they remembered.

He startled as Adriz rapped on his door, indicating that she had finished in the bathing room, and Felather closed the cupboard door, wiped the tears from his eyes, and grabbed a towel from the basket on the floor.

Wrapping it around his waist, he hurried to the bathing room and locked the door. The aroma of lemon and lavender filling the steamy air helped him relax. Adriz's favourite and, ever since he had known Adriz, his as well. He pushed the lever that started the water and stepped under the shower, reaching for the bar of soap.

Feeling much better for being clean, Felather followed Adriz as she climbed the stone steps to Xylvin's eyrie set into the face of the mountain behind the citadel. Both he and Adriz had been quick to dry off and dress. They didn't have time to waste.

They hurried up the steep steps, curving around the citadel wall, rising above the spires and finally reaching the ledge that marked the entry to Xylvin's lair. Felather was panting by the time they reached the top. Adriz just raised an eyebrow, not even out of breath. It was easier, though he had to admit scarier, when Xylvin gave them a lift to the ledge.

"You're out of shape," an amused voice said from the dim interior. "Those steps shouldn't affect you. You need to be running up and down them every morning."

Felather held up his hand and wheezed. "Thank you, but no thank you. We don't have time for that."

"Make time," the woman grunted as she stepped into the glow of a lamp. Ryvalin, Xylvin's rider and Mav's Captain of the Host, was grey-haired and had the most vivid blue eyes that bored into Felather and then Adriz before she led the way back into the eyrie.

She moved with fluid grace, covering the ground much faster than the still winded Felather, and, he ruefully realised, she had been right. He had skipped too many training sessions.

Xylvin was curled up in her nest at the back of the cavern, her wings folded, her tail wrapped around her body, and her chin lying flat on the stone, pointed towards the entrance. Her faceted eyes flashed as she watched them approach. Ryvalin paused beside her, patting her scaly cheek before indicating the chairs arranged in front of the dragon and sitting in one.

"You have news," Xylvin said without preamble, her soft voice projecting into all their minds.

"We found Mav," Felather replied.

Xylvin's roar deafened them, and Ryvalin leapt to her feet, trying to calm her. "You idiot," she growled at Felather as Xylvin's chin slowly returned to the floor, though her eyes flashed with reds and oranges.

"Where is he?" Xylvin demanded. *"Where did you find him? Does he need help?"*

Felather raised his hands against the torrent of questions. "He's fine," Felather said and then cringed. "Well, as good as can be expected. We found him in a tavern a few miles north of the crossroads."

"North?" Xylvin asked in surprise. *"But I left…"* Her voice stopped suddenly, as her eyes flashed red again. *"What do you mean as well as can be expected?"* she asked. *"What's wrong with him?"*

"He has injured his knee and he hasn't been able to heal it. His healing ability seems drained, which means he's had to use it constantly for a period of time, but he wouldn't say why." Felather sighed. There was no getting around it. Xylvin would know as soon as she saw him. "He has aged and he is…different."

Smoke drifted from Xylvin's nostrils. *"Different?"*

Felather shrugged. "He's quiet, reticent. His hair is going grey, his face is lined, he has a limp. He's not the same Mav we lost fifty years ago."

A low rumble started in Xylvin's gullet, and Ryvalin leapt to her feet. "Just because he's suffered, doesn't mean he has to continue to suffer," she snapped. Her blue eyes bored into Felather. "Where is he?"

"Apparently, there's a crossing under the divide. He's with a guide who is showing him the way," Felather replied.

"What? Since when?" Ryvalin gasped. "That's a serious security breach!"

"For centuries, so I'm told. It's a smuggler's route. Fortunate for us, it's a way of getting Mav into Puronia without anyone knowing. In the meantime, we need to arrange for him to get in to see Amaridin, without Serenia or the council finding out," Felather said.

Ryvalin shook her head, still grappling with the idea of a secret tunnel into Puronia. "Not possible. Amaridin doesn't sneeze without Serenia's permission. He won't meet Mav on the sly." Then she glared at Adriz as she sat back down. "You found Mav and you let him go again?"

Adriz held her eyes. "It is the safest way to get him into Puronia. There is no way he would have made it through the check points. This way, he enters anonymously and can hide in the city until we get him an audience. If Mav enters the citadel, they'll arrest him on sight! We have to get him an audience with Amaridin or Serenia, or both. He has information they need to know."

"They won't listen. There is a constant barrage of anti-Demavrian sentiment in the citadel. Someone has demolished his character

completely. Julius is a raging lunatic, ready to kill on sight," Xylvin said.

"Why rile everyone up now?" Felather asked with a frown.

Ryvalin sighed heavily. "Ever since Amaridin announced Mav would be declared dead, there's been a scramble for his position. The more they denounce him, the easier it is for them to replace him. He was formidable, remember? Unassailable."

There was a short silence.

"Someone assailed him," Felather said, his voice hard. "He doesn't remember how he ended up in Eidolon. He doesn't remember anything after Athenia dying in his arms on the steps and Julius knocking him out."

There was another silence, and Xylvin's tail slithered around her with a soft rustle. *"It must have been a deliberate move against him. Just their luck he was found holding Athenia and they could accuse him of her murder,"* she said.

"He can't come back unless he can prove who did kill her." Ryvalin walked towards her dragon and leaned against Xylvin's head as if for comfort. "Does he know who killed her?"

Felather shook his head. "No."

"How can he not know?" Ryvalin erupted and began pacing again.

Felather rubbed his temple and wished he could pace with her. He glanced at Adriz, who had been unusually silent. She was watching Xylvin with a strange expression on her face. She leaned forward. "Xylvin, do you know something we don't?" she asked.

Xylvin raised her head and hesitated. *"No,"* she said, her voice a soft whisper, and for some reason, Felather was sure she was lying.

There was no point pressing Xylvin. She was as stubborn

as Mav was. But Feather filed the anomaly in his brain for further investigation. He filled the awkward moment by saying, "Mav believes the people of Eidolon are being exploited, and I believe he is right. We found proof of slave camps and dybbuks stealing innocent people from their homes. He believes a seraphim from the citadel is involved. I think it might be Seraphim Kyrill, though we have no direct proof. Mav says he will recognise his voice when he hears it."

Ryvalin was shaking her head. "That is not a lot to go on, and it's not as if every seraphim is going to speak so he can hear their voice."

Adriz rose to her feet. "Mav is on his way to Puronia, now. We can't delay or stop him. He is depending on us to find a way for him to present his suspicions."

"Accusations more like," Ryvalin said with a frown.

"Accusations, then. Felather and I can corroborate the people stealing and the slave camps. Felather was abducted by dybbuks and held in one. Mav was captured by Julius and handed over to a seraphim to be tortured instead of being handed over to the citadel. They are after the minerals that are rife under the sodden dirt of Eidolon. Someone is out to make a lot of money," Adriz said.

"Dybbuks? That involves Kaenera. No one will be prepared to speak against him," Ryvalin stated.

"We have to find a way for Mav to be heard. If he can denounce those enslaving the people of Eidolon, it will give him some credibility. They will be more likely to listen to his side of the story regarding Athenia. No one's heard it yet," Felather insisted.

Ryvalin dragged her fingers through her short hair and paced back to Xylvin. She scratched Xylvin's eye ridge as she frowned in thought. She lifted her head. "What about Archangel Golaran? He is the citadel's most vocal supporter of the people of Eidolon. He's the one behind most of the projects. Unless he is mired in perfidy, he will be horrified by any suggestion that the citadel is exploiting the people of Eidolon."

Felather nodded, his eyes distant as he scrolled through everything he knew about Golaran. He pursed his lips. "That might work. He is senior enough that others would listen to him."

"Has there been any hint who is expected to step into Mav's position?" Adriz asked.

"*Serenia, surely,*" Xylvin said with a snarl.

Felather's eyes widened at the unbridled contempt in Xylvin's voice. "You think it's a done deal?" he asked.

"*Don't you?*" Xylvin replied with a bite to her voice.

Felather wondered when Xylvin had taken such a dislike to the archangel who had controlled the citadel for centuries and why.

29

FELATHER

F rustration gnawed at Felather as he battled his way through all the bureaucracy to meet with Archangel Golaran. It had taken the rest of the previous day just to get on his schedule. It didn't bode well for him meeting Mav.

Seated on a plush sofa, Felather frowned at the wall opposite him, not seeing the floor to ceiling length painting hanging on the wall. The vibrant colours were a blur as he chewed his bottom lip, worrying about how far Mav and Solanji had travelled. Had they reached the tunnel yet?

He had also spent time digging into the seraphim, Kyrill, following his gut reaction that the seraphim was involved somehow. He had been horrified to find out he owned a castle in the north of Eidolon, matching the description of where Mav had been held. Ryvalin had been distraught when she realised Mav had been incarcerated in the castle when she and Xylvin had last visited. He licked dry lips wondering if he should confront Golaran with his seraphim's activities.

One of his many other worries was how they were going

to prove Mav's innocence. Mav may be more concerned with stopping the exploitation of the people in Eidolon, but they couldn't return to any semblance of normal without proving who did kill Athenia and why.

Athenia had been one of the sweetest people, Felather knew. Always ready to listen, supportive, a friend. Could Julius have killed her in a fit of jealousy? Was that why he was so frantic to kill Mav? Remove Mav from the equation and it would be more difficult to prove he wasn't the murderer.

Felather swallowed. He didn't have many friends anymore. Mav's oathsworn had been slowly ostracised, as Mav had. Pressure for them to switch allegiance, to abandon Mav, had been growing. Only his oathsworn remained; all Mav's other staff had long moved on, and he couldn't blame them. They needed to earn to support their families. Not that Felather had refused to pay them, and Mav's coffers were deep so he could, but they couldn't handle the sneers and insults. A frisson of fear rushed through him. Would they try to confiscate his estate? His brain began calculating ways and means to protect Mav's inheritance.

A man softly cleared his throat, and Felather looked up, so deep in thought he hadn't heard him approach. "If you would follow me, sir," he said, and Felather rose. His boots sunk into the deep red carpet as he crossed the large antechamber and entered Golaran's office. The aroma of polish and the subtle scent of violets hung in the air as Felather observed the portly man standing behind his desk.

Golaran was a large man, broad across the chest and stomach. Smartly dressed in deep blue collarless jacket and trousers, he waited calmly as Felather entered, his shrewd grey eyes watching Felather as he crossed the room, hand outstretched.

White haired and red cheeked, Golaran was one of the

older Archangels. No one knew how old, but it was said he was a contemporary of Averdeus and his wife, though he never spoke of it.

"Sir," Felather said as he clasped Golaran's hand. "I appreciate you taking the time to see me."

"Not at all, my boy, I have been expecting you."

Felather stiffened. "You have?"

"You've taken longer than I expected, but that does you no ill in my eyes. Shows dedication and loyalty, important traits."

"I don't understand, sir,"

"Sit." Golaran moved to his seat behind his imposing desk. "I apologise for the formality, but I have meetings all day, and you were insistent on meeting as soon as possible."

"Thank you, sir. I wanted to discuss your opinion on a matter concerning Eidolon." Felather paused as the manservant placed a mug of bannoe before him and silently disappeared.

Golaran raised a bushy white eyebrow. "In Eidolon?"

"Yes, sir."

"I thought you were here looking for a new patron."

"A what?" Felather sat flabbergasted. His brain froze in shock. That anyone would ever believe he would disavow Demavrian...he couldn't process the words. He sat there with his mouth hung open.

"Drink," Golaran said, wrapping Felather's hand around a glass and guiding it to his mouth. The liquor made him inhale, and the world straightened and he breathed again. Golaran stood over him, watching him in concern. "My apologies. That was insensitive of me. But with Demavrian's demise, I thought it only logical that you would be looking for..." his voice trailed off at Felather's horrified expression. "I see I was mistaken. If I instil a fraction of your devotion to Demavrian in my oathsworn, I shall count myself fortunate."

He returned to his seat and picked up his mug, sipping his bannoe to give Felather time to recover.

"So," he said slowly, "what is this matter in Eidolon you wished to discuss?"

Felather gathered his scattered wits and, after rubbing his aching chest, took a deep breath. "Someone is exploiting the people of Eidolon. Abducting innocent people, incarcerating them in inhuman conditions, working them to death, so that they can reap the rewards."

Golaran's benevolent expression hardened. "I don't take lightly any accusation that I am exploiting those people. My projects provide much valued work and reward appropriately."

"I wasn't accusing you," Felather said in a rush, raising his hands. "Your projects are an example of what *should* be happening, but others have twisted your idea and are using people as slaves instead."

"What?" Golaran barked.

"Cherubim Eladriz and I have been travelling Eidolon searching for Demavrian, but in doing so, we found evidence of slave compounds run by dybbuks. I was abducted off the road and thrown in with a group of people, expected to mine ore for food. The conditions were basic, the threat real. They killed a woman because one of the men protested against our treatment."

"Kaenera would not involve himself in petty profit."

"No, which makes me think that someone with a lot of power has promised him something he wants in return for his support."

"Who?"

"I believe your Seraphim, Kyrill, is involved."

"I don't believe it. Kyrill has worked the hardest to ensure my projects are a success. What proof do you have for such a libellous accusation? You are treading on thin ice here, Felather."

"Sir, I do not say these words lightly. How often have you visited your projects? Seen where Kyrill spends his time?"

"I am too old to jaunt around the country. I trust Kyrill."

"I'm sorry, sir, but I think you have placed your trust in the wrong seraphim. Did you know he has a castle in the mountains north of Eidolon? A castle where he incarcerates those he wants to torture?"

Golaran rose to his feet. "I don't believe it. I will not listen to any more of this slander. I think it's time for you to leave."

"There is someone who can prove this, who has suffered at Kyrill's hands. Would you meet with him and listen to what he has to say?"

"And who might that be?"

"Someone who has lived in Eidolon for many years. Seen the rise in abductions, the plethora of compounds being built, fought to protect the innocent."

"What's his name?"

"It's safer not to say. This is explosive information, and there are many who would prefer to kill him than let him reveal it. There are huge amounts of money at stake, and that means people are more prepared to kill than wait and ask questions."

Golaran considered him for a moment. "If what you say is true, then I could guarantee his safety, provide an escort. The people of Eidolon deserve better than how we treat them. You know I would support a proposal to remove any threat against them."

"I appreciate the offer, and after you've spoken, if he agrees, I would gladly accept it, but he is of Eidolon, and although he is prepared to come to Puronia to meet with you, he cannot stay. I would need your guarantee that you would allow him to leave."

"A soulless would travel to Puronia? He would take such a risk?"

"He wants to help the people of Eidolon. He believes the citadel continues to use SoulSingers only to populate the land with more potential slaves. There is no reason to continue to condemn every unfortunate person to cross the Justicers and lose their soul."

Golaran's mouth tightened. "Citadel policy is not up for discussion."

Felather bowed his head and gritted his teeth. "Of course, but maybe you should visit Eidolon, see how many homeless children there are, and then tell me the policy is humane." Felather fell silent, regretting his heated outburst. But how could Golaran of all people not question such a policy?

After a short silence, Golaran spoke. "When would your man be able to cross the divide?"

"I could get him here to meet you by eleven tomorrow morning, though I would prefer if you met away from the citadel."

Golaran nodded thoughtfully, his eyes never leaving Felather's face. "I'll reserve a chamber at the Three Cherubs. Would that suffice?"

"That would be perfect," Felather said, suddenly feeling light-headed. The tight band constraining his chest relaxed, and he breathed easier. The Three Cherubs was located in the quieter suburbs and well away from the citadel and all its guards. He would give Mav time to cross and then go and tell him he had been successful.

"Thank you, sir," Felather said as he rose.

"We'll see if you're thanking me tomorrow. You'd better

have proof or I'll be locking you up for defamation of character and making sure you won't be able to do it again."

"I understand."

Golaran grunted. "I know you do, which is the only reason I'm agreeing to this. Be careful, Felather. If what you are insinuating is true, then the fewer people who know the better."

Felather couldn't agree more. He left Golaran's office and returned to his rooms. Mav would have one chance to present his case. He hoped he was ready.

30

MAV
PURONIA

Mav followed Solanji through the dim curio shop, his gaze darting around the glass cabinets and the odd items piled upon wooden benches; opaque glass vases, ornately decorated boxes, twisted pieces of metal he didn't have time to identify, before Solanji dragged him out the door, and then the brilliant light outside captured his attention and he halted just over the threshold as he gazed at the sunrise.

It was beautiful, so vibrant, *so alive!* The sky was clear of clouds, rising unimpeded above him. Reds, oranges and yellows blended in streaks across the vast expanse above him, fading into a pale blue, which darkened the higher he gazed. The rich colours spreading across the horizon became more vibrant as the sun rose.

The urge to spread his wings and fly consumed him, and he only just kept his feet on the ground, even though he knew his wings were no longer what they were. He wasn't sure what was left would hold his weight. He hadn't flared them since the child had died at the dybbuk's hands a few weeks ago.

Mav stood with his face raised towards the exuberant light show, absorbing the colour and heat as if he'd never seen it before, and Solanji stared at him as if experiencing the sunrise through his reactions and appreciating it all the more.

"Mav," she said, touching his arm. "We need to get off the street."

Dragging his gaze from the sky, Mav stared at her for a moment and then followed, though he couldn't prevent his eyes from returning to the colour-streaked display as he walked. Golden walls reflected the light, vibrant red tiles adorned the roofs, such rich colours for ordinary things. Solanji led him through open courtyards decorated with tall cylindrical pots containing orange and pink flowers. Flowers! Mav couldn't remember the last time he had seen a flower planted purely for enjoyment.

Following Solanji, Mav couldn't have said where they went. He didn't recognise this part of town. She stopped at a building and slotted a key in a drab wooden door and dragged him inside. He followed her up the stairs and into the single room that took up the upper floor. One wall was lined by a long counter inset with a shallow sink, a stoppered water pipe jutting out over it. An iron-framed fireplace was inset against one wall, with a plain square mantel over it. Opposite, a bed was curtained off in its corner, and a table and chair stood in the centre.

Mav hesitated as Solanji scanned her room. "It's not much, but it's home," she said after a short pause. "You should rest, and I'll go get some food. There's nothing here. I've been gone a while." She picked up a clay pot from the counter and tipped out a few coins as Mav slowly moved towards the curtained off corner. He was exhausted, and he knew he was about to crash as Felather's treatments faded. He needed to sleep before the pain hit him.

"I won't be long," Solanji said as she edged towards the door, her forehead creased in a worried frown as she watched him.

"Don't worry. I am so tired, I'll not hear a stampede of demoras," Mav replied as he swept the curtain aside. The bed lured him forward and exhaustion consumed him as he dropped his bag to the floor, along with his sword belt as he unbuckled it, and then he flopped face down onto the bed and let the darkness consume him.

———

That comment didn't reassure Solanji, but there was little she could do, so she left and headed back down the stairs, determined to be as quick as possible. Leaving Mav alone in her room didn't feel right. She needed to protect him, injured as he was.

Twisting her lips into a wry grimace, Solanji knew she was lying to herself. It wasn't just his injury; there was a vulnerability about the man that tugged at her heart. She had seen him at his very worst and he had still tried to protect her. It was inherent in the way he was made, the need to protect others.

And for that, he was accused of murder and had lost his soul. How he had created his own soul of shadows and those graceful wings she didn't know, but he *was* the son of a god, and he had comforted and supported the people of Eidolon in life and in death. If anyone deserved a soul, it was Mav.

Few shops were open this early in the morning, but a local bakery began baking about now, so Solanji headed there, intent on at least getting him something to eat. Anxiety gnawed at her belly. Was he alright? Had anyone seen them? There was no reason for anyone to be interested in them, but she worried all the same.

An oppressive weight settled on her shoulders, and Solanji wondered if this was what Mav felt all the time. The pressure of expectation and accusation, the fear of being caught. The constant glancing over your shoulder. It was enough to make you turn tail and bolt. She could see why he had changed his mind about returning to Puronia so many times. Wanting to do the right thing but terrified of being tortured again. If she was honest, Solanji couldn't blame him. She would have been petrified as well. She wasn't sure she was as brave as Mav, but she would do her best to help him.

If she could help him prove his innocence, then Mav could help her find Bren. Where these amazing soul-breathing skills had come from, she didn't know, but she had to learn how to transfer souls so she could return Bren's if the Justicers had taken it. There were so many other people she could be helping as well. All those abandoned children in Eidolon. Maybe Mav and Felather could tell her more about soulbreathing. If there was the slightest chance she could rescue her brother, she would take it. Her chest ached. Her baby brother was possibly stranded in Eidolon and for all she knew he could be dead. The uncertainty was excruciating and she could do nothing about it. She had no idea where to look.

Mav was her best bet. He would get Felather searching the Justicers records to see what had happened to Bren. If she kept Mav safe, and helped him clear his name, he would have unlimited resources to help her find her brother. Mav was an archdeus after all. He had a Dragonair as his oathsworn. They should be able to find anyone. Carefully ignoring the fact they had been unable to find Mav, she straightened her shoulders and lifted her chin.

If they could solve Mav's problems, and rescue her brother, they might have a chance to nurture their relationship. They had a strong connection, if only they had the opportunity to build on it.

Entering the bakery, Solanji inhaled the comforting aroma of yeast, freshly baked bread, and a heady mix of pastry and spices. Unable to resist the mouth-watering scents, Solanji chose a loaf of cinnamon-infused bread and two pies stuffed with meat and cheese. She hurried back through the empty streets, the warm packages clasped to her chest.

After a couple of detours and doubling back on herself enough times to confuse anyone who might have been following her, Solanji darted back up the stairs and rushed into her room only to find that Mav hadn't moved since she had left. He hadn't even taken off his boots.

Shaking her head against all that wasted anxiety, Solanji dumped the bread and pastries on the counter and unwrapped one of the pies. Taking a bite, she groaned in pleasure and then crossed the room and wafted the pie under Mav's nose.

He twitched, inhaled, and then opened his beautiful amber eyes. They were tired and bloodshot, but Solanji loved the deep, rich colour. The grey-flecked stubble covering his chin combined with the dark shadows under his eyes and the lines of strain made him look ill and old. Mav tried to sit up and then groaned as he flopped back down, his fists clenching in the blanket beneath him.

Solanji had forgotten that all the relief Felather had provided would have worn off, and she had nothing to ease his pain. "Eat it while it's hot," she said instead, offering Mav the second package, and he rolled over and levered himself upright. Once he took the pie, Solanji filled a jug with water from the pipe jutting out over the small sink. Replacing the stopper in the pipe, she poured the water into two clay mugs and offered one to Mav.

Sitting in the only chair, Solanji smiled as Mav demolished his pie. It reminded her to eat her own. The cheese oozed out the edges as she bit the pastry, and she hummed in pleasure at the explosion of rich and comforting flavours.

Mav laughed at her. "I have to agree. That was one of the best pies I've ever eaten."

"Fresh out of the oven. Always the best," Solanji agreed, and she took another bite.

Mav leaned down and began unlacing his boots, groaning as he eased his feet out of them. "I thought they were permanently attached to my feet," he said, carefully swinging his leg onto the bed and shuffling up so he could lean back against the wall.

Solanji grimaced at the sweaty odour that wafted across the room. "I don't have a shower. The public baths are a couple of streets away. We can get cleaned up there on the way to the citadel."

Mav's lips twitched. "Are you telling me that I stink?"

"I'm sure we both smell," Solanji replied with a grin, able to relax now that she knew he was safe and well. "But that will have to wait. How long do you think it will be until Felather will come?"

"This evening at the earliest. It will take time to arrange meetings, and then he has to persuade them to speak to me." Mav frowned at the wall. "That's if he is successful. It is possible they will refuse. Until I can prove my innocence, we are always going to be on the defensive."

"How do we prove you *are* innocent? Do you have any idea who could have killed Athenia?"

"I was hoping you had some ideas. You being a Soul-Breather and all, maybe you could trawl through my memories again and see if there's anything that can help me."

"Now? What if we get stuck again?"

"When Felather gets here. I'm too exhausted now, I doubt I would be any use. Let's catch up on some sleep, then

we'll worry about it." Mav shuffled over to the other side of
the bed and beckoned. "Come on, you look just as wrung out
as I feel. We're safe enough. No one has any idea we're
here."

Solanji stared at him for a moment, her heart racing. She
bent over and unlaced her boots, wrinkling her nose at the
unpleasant odour. She padded over to the bed and climbed
in beside Mav and moaned a little as she stretched out beside
him, her joints cracking and muscles aching.

Her bed wasn't very big, so she turned on her side, facing
away from him, and her back was enveloped in his heat as he
snuggled up to her, his arm draping over her hip as he
tugged her back against him. "Sleep well, my amazing Soul-
Breather," he muttered into her hair as he inhaled deeply
and then exhaled, his hot breath on her neck sending tingles
racing across her skin. She smiled. She was a SoulBreather,
and together they would figure it all out. Resolutely closing
her eyes, she counted to ten and relaxed and then drifted off
to sleep in the safety of Mav's arms, aware of his shadows
curling around them both, protectively.

Solanji woke abruptly as her front door was kicked in, and
Mav lurched upright, unceremoniously dumping her on the
floor. Before she had a chance to assimilate what was
happening, her dagger was in her hand and she was scuttling
back out of reach of the large men who stormed into her
tiny room.

Somehow, Mav had his sword in his hand. Had he slept
with it? She hadn't seen him grab it off the floor where he
had dropped it. It was instinctive to fight, but there was
nowhere for them to go. They were trapped, and Solanji saw
the moment Mav realised it as his shoulders sagged.

He stepped back and spread his hands. "If you'd knocked first, none of this would have been necessary," he said, eyeing the armoured guards as they crowded forward.

One grabbed his sword arm and forced him to his knees, wrenching the sword out of his grip and twisting his arm behind his back. Mav grunted, his face paling.

Solanji snarled as she faced the men. "By what right do you destroy my property?"

"By order of the citadel and all that is good and true," the officer who had entered the room behind his men replied. "Now drop your weapon and don't try anything funny or he gets hurt."

Solanji growled as the guard holding Mav pressed a blade against his neck. "On what charges are you arresting me?" she demanded as she dropped her dagger.

"Aiding and abetting a known criminal and resisting arrest," the man said. "Restrain her," he snapped, and a guard tied her wrists behind her back. He grabbed her arm and tugged her towards the door.

"I need my boots," she protested, twisting to see Mav. It had all happened so fast and there were so many of them. There was nothing she could do.

"You won't need boots where you're going," the guard replied as two other guards hauled Mav to his feet. His arms were also tied behind his back, and, bootless, he was forced down the stairs and into the street.

"We should have got the bath first," Solanji muttered under her breath as she stumbled after them with her own escort. Her shoulders ached and her feet hurt as she trod on sharp pebbles and uneven cobble stones. She was sure her arms would have finger-shaped bruises left by the guard's tight grip.

People stopped in the street to stare as they were hurried past. Whispers of conjecture and suspicion followed them, along with a growing crowd of followers, eager to find out who they were and what they had done. The guards were tight-lipped and ignored them, but they picked up the pace, and Solanji struggled to keep up with their strides.

She was relieved when they left the cobbles behind and reached the smooth wide road that led to the citadel. Though the imposing building no longer looked benign and welcoming, it rose above them like a restrained monster straining at its leash and ready to eat them whole. An icy flash of fear shivered through Solanji as they approached. Mav was limping badly, at times even being dragged as the guards ignored his low pleas to slow down.

These people had no intention of treating them with any care or consideration, especially not Mav. In their eyes, he was already guilty and therefore was treated no better than some rabid beast about to be put to death.

Gritting her teeth, Solanji stiffened as they waited for the tall golden gates to be opened. Mav was silent as he watched them swing open, and he took his first glimpse in nearly fifty years of what used to be home. Solanji's heart twisted at the sight of his expressionless face. Was he expecting the citadel to reject him? What would happen if it did? He stood tall and straight as the guards either side glanced nervously at him as if expecting him to do something. The urge to grab him and bolt as far from the citadel as possible flashed through her, and she ground her teeth as she realised how helpless she was. Some oathsworn she was.

A servant waited inside the courtyard and spoke hurriedly to the officer before bowing and darting away. The officer swore and then rapped out an order. "Make yourselves presentable. He is being honoured with an audience before the assembly, and then he is to be taken to the cells."

Solanji swallowed. The full assembly? Did they mean her too? They clearly did, because after the guards straightened their uniforms and rubbed their boots on the backs of their trousers, they were both marched through the imposing arch and into the candle lit interior.

Mav cocked his head as if listening for something, but as his glance flitted around them, Solanji was sure he hadn't heard something that he had expected. She had no idea what that was, and she didn't have time to wonder as they were marched into a tall chamber with high ceilings and elegant candle-festooned chandeliers hanging from golden chains.

Gleaming white marble covered the floors and walls and sparkling crystal inclusions glittered under her socked feet. She skidded as the guards pulled her forward. The long hall led to a circular chamber, at the head of which stood a raised platform with two golden throne-like chairs.

Mav faltered at the sight and then stiffened again, a muscle jumping in his clenched jaw.

Solanji hissed her breath out, relief making her knees weak as Mav seemed unchanged by entering the citadel. The citadel had accepted him. What did that mean?

Rising either side of them were tiers of seating, currently filled with red robed councillors, grey robed administrators, blue robed angels, and golden robed archangels. Solanji had never seen so many angels in one place, and they were all staring at her. No, not at her, at Mav.

Voices rose in exclamation as the guards drew to a halt in the centre of the room and pushed Mav and Solanji to their knees. *Keeping us in our rightful place*, Solanji thought with a wry twist to her lips. Mav hadn't made a sound, though she knew from the fine sheen of sweat on his face that he must be in agony.

Silence returned to the hall as a soft chime sounded, and then a tall, elegant woman dressed in golden robes walked out from behind the dais, her hand resting lightly on the arm of the blonde-haired man beside her. He wore white robes, and the cast of his face reminded Solanji of Mav. This must be his brother, Archdeus Amaridin.

That his brother would treat Mav in this way, arresting him and then dragging him through the streets in restraints. An attempt to humiliate him? An accusation of guilt before they had even heard Mav speak? Solanji ground her teeth. This perfect couple were not surprised to see them. It was almost as if they had been expecting them. How could they have known?

The archdeus barely glanced at his brother kneeling on the floor. He waited for the Archangel Serenia to be seated, for that was who she had to be. No other archangel would be treated like a consort. Amaridin sat beside her.

"So, the absent son returns," Serenia said in a melodious voice. "Have you finally come to face the results of your actions?"

"And what actions might those be?" Mav asked. His voice shook with barely restrained anger. Solanji sneaked a glance at him in surprise. He had been so contained, until now.

A slender eyebrow rose. "You need me to tell you?"

"Seeing as the citadel has allowed me entry, dispelling one of your myths, and the fact that I found Athenia on the steps and didn't kill her, it may be best if you state what you are accusing me of." He shrugged his shoulders. "I would not like to waste my time defending myself against the wrong accusation."

The audience stirred, a hum of conversation at his words, and Serenia raised her hand for silence. "Apologia has been invoked. You are accused of four counts."

Mav lurched to his feet and took a step forward. "What? Since when?"

The guards grabbed him and forced him back to the floor, pinning his face to the cold marble.

Serenia continued, her voice hardening. "You are

accused of four counts. Failure to defend any of those counts will result in you forfeiting your life. The counts are as follows." She raised a ringed forefinger, the opal stone glinting with a rainbow of colours. "First count, the murder of Archangel Athenia Demois, our one and only Soul-Breather; second count, explain the absence of Deus Veradeus to the council's satisfaction; third count, lack of a soul; fourth count, inability to flare wings and therefore no longer a divine, blessed angel."

Solanji froze. They were accusing Mav of what? She didn't know how Mav felt, but she wanted to scream at the injustice of it all. And they weren't even allowing him to respond. He was rigid under the guards.

"Allow him to rise," Serenia said.

"Prove it," Mav said when he lifted his head. Solanji didn't recognise his voice, it was so cold and harsh.

Serenia's smile was pure evil, and Solanji was shocked at seeing such an expression on an archangel's face. "No. As the accused, you must defend yourself against the counts. The Apologia has been initiated. You have four days to prove the four counts false. The first count for you to defend is the lack of your soul. After that the order of your refutations is your choice. Failure of any count forfeits your life." Serenia returned to her seat. "Who is the girl? Your whore?"

"Archangel Serenia. If you please, I claim her as my fledgling. I reserve the right to deal with her," a blond-haired seraph stated as he rose from his seat in the middle of the tiers.

"I am not his fledgling," Solanji shouted. "Kyrill abducted me off the street and threatened my family. You are all just bullies, out to get what you can from innocent people. And you call yourself angels." Solanji curled her lips as a loud murmur rose from the ranks of administrators, and Serenia rapped her gravel on the arm of her chair.

"Enough, take her to the cells for now. We have more important matters to discuss."

Solanji snarled as the guards closed in on her, but there was nowhere to go, and Mav was still braced against the floor, unable to move. Nothing she did would be able to help him. She would only make matters worse.

"The girl is working for me. She was instrumental in bringing Demavrian before us today. I have been watching for her return to Puronia. Had her rooms under close watch. That is how the guards knew where to find them."

"You promised you'd release my brother if I did," Solanji gasped out, risking a glance at Mav. He was rigid and silent. "Did you?" she challenged, knowing that Mav had been right. Kyrill hadn't even thought of her brother. He looked at her blankly, not acknowledging what she was referring to.

"You bastard," she hissed, white hot anger flashing through her. He hadn't even made the effort to save her brother. "You'd condemn a child without thought just to get what you wanted. None of you have any honour. The only person with honour in this building is Demavrian."

"Take her away," Serenia said.

"You ought to be ashamed of yourselves. Your behaviour is an embarrassment to all. Your lack of humanity is a joke," Solanji screamed as she struggled against the guards hauling her from the room. Hard fingers bit into her arms as she twisted, the guards struggling to shut her up. "You call your-self true and good, but you don't know the meaning of the words," Solanji shouted, attempting to trawl her soul fingers through the guards' golden soulmist, to suggest a delay, but there were too many of them and they dragged her out and her shouts were cut off as the chamber doors slammed shut.

Serenia barely glanced at Kyrill. "You claim such a harlot? Then you can pay for her release fees." Her cold stare raked Demavrian, still pinned to the marble floor by two guards.

"Is there anyone left who will speak for you, Demavrian?"

Mav's mind was still spinning at the speed of Serenia's proclamations. It was as if she knew he would be returning this very day. How? How could she be so prepared? And so ready to believe him guilty. He had recognised Kyrill's voice, and it sent ice through his veins. How dare he claim his oathsworn? Solanji was his.

"No one?" The derision dripped from her voice and Mav stiffened.

"My oathsworn," he whispered to the floor.

"Who? Did he say something? Let him rise." The pressure on the back of his neck released, and Mav lifted his head, though he didn't attempt to rise. He glared up at Serenia, met her cold blue eyes, and was satisfied when her eyes widened at whatever she saw in Mav's expression. Hatred? Determination? Fury? Or even vengeance?

"I said," Mav bit the words off. "My oathsworn will speak for me if needed."

"But they are not here," Serenia purred. "Where is your scribe, Felather? Or your Cherubim Eladriz? Your captain of the host, Ryvalin? None of them are here when you need them. Maybe they have found a new purpose, a better purpose."

"They would have been here if you had informed them that you intended on grabbing me off the street and invoking Apologia."

Serenia tilted her coiffured head and smiled. "Don't be over-confident, Demavrian. Allegiances change over time, especially when those who should know better betray them."

That shaft hit home hard, and Mav struggled to disguise

the flinch. By Serenia's widening smile, she knew she had hit her mark, and she waved a negligent hand.

"Apologia commences at nine tomorrow morning, if you're still here. Don't be late or your absence will be taken as proof that you have no soul and you didn't survive the night. And Apologia will be proven. Take him away." Serenia turned away to speak with Amaridin, ignoring Mav as if he was a stain that her guards could wipe off the floor. Grinding his teeth, Mav swore she wouldn't get rid of him that easily. Stains were stubborn, and Mav would be the most stubborn of all.

31

MAV

The march through the citadel corridors seemed to never end. Gleaming marble mocked him, the reflection of him restrained and bracketed by guards demeaning. The citadel guards were eager to lock him up, and when he stumbled, they thought he was trying to delay them. A sharp jab to his ribs left him gasping, partly in shock that they would lay a hand on him. He was, after all, still an Archdeus; once one of their supreme commanders. Not that it seemed to mean anything, anymore.

Excited whispers followed behind him, echoing in the high halls. Wide eyes, more interested in gossip and conjecture, watched him. He didn't see any horror or sympathy, and his chest ached at the general acceptance that he was capable of such heinous actions.

He needed time to assimilate what had just happened. For the guards to stop for a moment and for him to be able to think. The citadel had allowed him entry, but the expected welcome had been absent. Relief that he hadn't expired on the spot bubbled through him, but the gut-wrenching fury at Serenia's declaration of Apologia wiped it out.

Panic fluttered in his belly. Serenia didn't know where Veradeus was? How was that possible? Was he one of the last people to speak to his father? He had assumed his father had accepted the accusations against Mav and supported his banishment. He should have known better. And that meant not only had Mav and Athenia been incapacitated, but his father had as well. There was only one person who had the power to even attempt a confrontation with his father and that was Kaenera. The situation was worse than he had ever imagined.

Agony shot through his right leg by the time they reached the bottom of the stone steps, a radiating pain that ran through his bones and collected in his ruined knee. When the barred door to the tiny cell swung open, he forgot the pain.

"No," Mav snarled at the sight of the shackles hanging on the wall. Gut tightening, jaw clenching, he came to an abrupt halt.

His guards kept moving, dragging him forwards, and he tried to twist out of their grip. "A cell is sufficient. There is no need for restraints," he said, trying to keep the panic out of his voice. His brain was shrieking at him to run, but the guards tightened their grip on his arms. "I still have rights. I have not been proven guilty of any charge," Mav exclaimed, again trying to slow their progress.

He didn't stand a chance, restrained as he was. Struggling only made it worse as the guards forced him into the cell. Blows rained down on him, forcing him to curl up to try to protect himself. He grunted as the beating continued, pain flashing through his abdomen, his back, and then their boots joined in, and he could no longer protest. The only thought running through his brain was that they would kill him and he would never even make the trial.

Solanji's voice, muffled by the stone cell walls, shrieked at them to stop. The sound of his oathsworn's pleas penetrated the haze of pain surrounding him, and the guards suddenly stopped their attack. Mav wasn't sure if he was glad or not. Maybe death would be better. At least the agony might stop. He didn't resist as they pulled his limp body to the wall and raised his arms to shackle his wrists, which set off a different spike of torment from his ribs, and then his head was jerked up as a leather strap was fastened around his neck. "Enjoy your stay! Make the most of it. Murderers are not welcome here," the guard hissed.

Mav squinted at him through swelling eyes and didn't respond. He could barely breathe. The guards left, and the barred door clanged shut. Blessed silence descended, except for his belaboured breathing. Cold, grey stone surrounded him, pressing in on all sides, relieved only by the narrow door which had floor to ceiling metal bars that allowed the guards to watch his every move.

All his weight rested on his left leg as he tried to ease his position, but it didn't help. His brain raced, pulling up flashes of his torture, the flaying, the scent of his blood, his wings going up in flames. Leaving him a heaving mess, driving him towards panic, escape, run, get out! That was all he could think of as he gasped for air, and his body shook.

"Mav? Are you alright?" Solanji's voice was full of concern. Alright? No, he didn't think so.

"Don't answer that, of course you're not. I'm so sorry. I thought my rooms were safe. I didn't know they had found them or that Kyrill would be watching."

Why had Kyrill been so interested in her? Oh yes, she was a SoulBreather. A rare and wonderful creature, his oathsworn. She could be Eidolon's saviour; she could be his saviour. The thoughts swirled around Mav's mind. If anyone found out she was a SoulBreather, her tenure might be short lived. At least being his oathsworn extended her some protection against those who would attempt to kill her. After all, he was supposed to protect the SoulBreather. That was a joke, he couldn't even protect himself.

"Mav?"

He had failed her at the first hurdle. She was incarcerated in a stone cell like he was, and he couldn't protect her. Not from Kyrill, not from anyone, and she needed to find her brother. She had thrown her lot in with him and lost. Not replying, he slowly relaxed in the restraints, hanging limp. A low moan escaped from his lips as his body protested against the new position.

He was on his own.

Run, flee, look out for himself, forget everyone else. No one cared if he lived or died. Deep down, Mav knew that wasn't true, but he ignored the flash of conscience and wallowed in his misery. Would he even make it to the first count of his trial?

"Mav? Can you hear me? Speak to me."

Mav couldn't even remember what he was supposed to prove. He fumbled for the word, ignoring the woman's voice that continued to plead for him to reply from the adjoining cell. Apologia. That was it. Didn't being under Apologia give him some rights? Felather would know. It hurt too much to think, and he moaned again. Images flashed through his mind; so much blood, the remembered metallic taste filled his mouth, and it made him heave. His inability to heal and the sheer despair of being back in shackles overwhelmed him. His inner voice taunted him with his failures, dragging him into deeper despair, filling his head until he heard nothing else.

At the sound of Mav's pain-filled moan, Solanji fell silent. She had promised to protect him, to keep him safe, and she hadn't. Her hands shook as she grasped the metal bars set into the door. Mav's grunts of pain as the guards attacked him, the smack of their fists on unprotected skin, had made her want to vomit. Desperate to make sure he was alright, she began shouting at the guards.

"He needs help. Get him a healer." She rattled the bars. "Do you hear me, you ignorant bastards? Get him help, now."

An exasperated guard yelled back, "If you don't shut up, woman, you'll get a beating as well."

"You brutes deserve a whipping. He is an archdeus. How dare you beat him up."

"And you are a prisoner, with no more rights than he has, so belt up!"

"Yeah? Come and tell me that to my face," Solanji challenged.

The guard stomped down the stairs and stood well away from the bars of her cell. Someone had warned them of what she could do. "You really want to do this?" he asked.

Solanji smiled and extended her soul fingers to caress his golden soulmist. They didn't know *all* that she could do. "Oh yes. Come open the door and I'll show you how much."

The guard blinked and then opened her cell door and, with Solanji's encouragement, the door to Mav's cell. Her heart stuttered as she took in Mav's limp body, hanging in much the same position as she had first seen him. Though this time at least he was dressed. Solanji's stomach clenched. Oh god, what had they done to him? "Release him," she whispered. And then she repeated it more firmly. "Release him!"

The guard fumbled at Mav's throat, unbuckling the leather strap around his neck and then the iron shackles, and Solanji caught Mav as he collapsed to the floor. She twisted, trying to cushion his fall. "Mav? Oh god, Mav? Can you

294 | HELEN GARRAWAY

hear me?" She smoothed gentle fingers over his bruised face, over his swollen lip and the cut under his eye.

Mav didn't respond, and she knew he was lost in his memories, fighting his own demons. He had never talked about what had happened to him in the year he had been incarcerated, but the scars marking his skin, the state of him when she had first seen him, and his reaction in the tunnel had told her enough of the story. She extended her soul fingers and caressed his shadows. But they were wrapped tight around him, a protective shield.

Trailing her fingers through the guard's golden soulmist, she snarled, "Go and find the scribe, Felather, and bring him here." Once the man had left, she focused back on Mav, cradling him in her arms, his head against her chest. "You are not what they say you are. Do you hear me? You are so much more. Shandra, Kerris, Muntra, and Bailey are waiting for you. They believe in you. *I* believe in you. The people of Eidolon need you. Mav, please don't give up on them." She kissed his cheek, his cold lips, the edge of his bruised jaw.

The thought that she might lose him had her reaching for his shadows again. She pushed and stroked and petted. He was mired in a situation so far out of her experience that it wasn't surprising he was so defensive. But she didn't care. She would never give up on him, just as he had never given up in those he had sworn to protect. Mav had demonstrated his care for the people of Eidolon many times over, and she knew he would never shirk his duty. He had promised to help find her brother, and she knew he would keep that promise. She would help him battle his demons, she swore. Together, they would prove how wrong these people were.

Mav shuddered in her arms, and she kept talking. "Remember Kiara trying to fix that plough, even though she was a fraction of its weight? The kids so happy playing in the dirt? Or Bailey cooking a meal out of nothing?"

Mav stirred and groaned.

"Or Shandra, so stern, when all she wanted was to hug and play with the kids? Please don't give up on them."

"Who said I was giving up?" He rasped as he squinted up at her, and she tightened her embrace. Mav drew in a deep breath and exhaled it on a groan, clasping his side as his face paled.

"I thought you were lost," she whispered as she covered his face in kisses.

"Never," he replied.

"The guards are very lax these days, aren't they?" a light, cheery voice said from above them, and Solanji tightened her arms around Mav as she looked up. The cutest, baby-faced boy hovered above them. Tiny golden wings sprouted from his back and fluttered to keep him in place. Vivid blue eyes sparkled with mischief. In his hands, he held a golden bow and arrow and as he observed them, he raised a blond eyebrow and smirked. At that moment, Solanji realised he was older than he looked.

"Who are you?" she asked, her voice hard as she clutched Mav to her body as if she could shield him from whatever threat now hovered over them.

"A friend."

"Says who?" Solanji asked as she extended her soul fingers towards the scintillating mist surrounding the tiny creature with the golden wings.

"Don't touch him," Mav whispered.

"Who is he?"

Mav squinted. Solanji was sure his vision was blurry, his eyes were so swollen. "A cherub."

"Tch, tch, Demavrian, my dear boy, what have you gotten yourself into?" the cherub asked.

Intelligent blue eyes inspected them, and Solanji was surprised to see an expression of sympathy and compassion on the cherub's angelic face. Soft blond curls covered his head like a halo, and he had a cream and peaches complexion that would make many young girls jealous.

"Sero?" Mav rasped. "What are you doing here?"

The cherub huffed out a laugh. "I could ask you the same thing. I couldn't believe my eyes when you were dragged into the hall like some desperate criminal. Where have you been?" The cherub's voice held a note of interrogation as he pointed his tiny bow and arrow at him.

Mav grimaced and winced as he held his jaw. "In Eidolon."

"Doing what?"

"Surviving."

Sero snorted. "Is that what you call it? I would suggest you haven't got the hang of it."

"Why thank you, Sero. I didn't think you cared."

The cherub narrowed his vivid blue eyes. "I don't. But you've been missed." He gave a sharp nod and fluttered his wings.

Solanji tightened her embrace as Mav tensed, and she wondered why he was so surprised at Sero's reply.

"At least someone's missed you," she whispered.

Mav snorted and then groaned as he clasped his ribs. Pinning the cherub with a glare, he said, "As you can see, I'm not at my best at the moment, so you'll just have to come right out and say whatever it is you came to say." Mav glanced up at Solanji. "Typically, cherub's like to make mischief, but for Sero to go out of his way to give his opinion, and to find me in my lovely cell when he could have ignored me completely, is highly unusual."

"There is much I have to tell you, but I won't if you're not going to be nice."

"Being nice is not at the top of my list of priorities right now," Mav replied.

Sero tilted his head and then nodded. "I'll give you that one. Things have gone from bad to worse here in the citadel. You need to fix it."

"Fix what exactly?"

"The citadel. It's not responding."

Mav shivered as an expression of uncertainty flickered across his face.

"What is wrong with the citadel?" Solanji asked as Sero fluttered out of the cell and returned holding a thin blanket, which he dropped in Mav's lap.

"Thank you," Mav murmured. "I don't know what's wrong with the citadel, but it didn't greet me when I entered. There is no connection, no heartbeat, but I haven't had a chance to search for it. After my reception in the chambers, I thought that everyone had already given up on me, including the citadel," he said, closing his eyes. The lines on his face deepened as he took a careful breath. Solanji rubbed his back, offering comfort and silent support, reminding him she was there and that he wasn't alone.

"Not those with brains," Sero snapped. And Mav flicked his eyes open. The little cherub was pointing a finger at him. "Don't you go giving up when things get hard."

Mav chuckled and pulled the blanket closer. "This is nothing," he replied and closed his eyes again. Solanji hoped Mav's sluggish healing powers had dampened some of the pain he must be in. Where was Felather? He was taking his time.

Watching the cherub closely, Solanji scowled as he descended and hovered in front of Mav and then extended his hand. Mav flinched when Sero's fingers touched his brow. "I thought you were supposed to ask permission," Mav said.

The horrified expression on Sero's face was just wrong, but it convinced Solanji he had seen Mav's uppermost thoughts. She was sure Mav was still consumed by memories of the torture chamber. Solanji supposed that was why cherubs had a reputation for being so aloof. If they embraced everyone they met, they would be bombarded by unwanted thoughts and histories.

Sero hissed his breath out. "Who would do such a thing?"

They were interrupted by the sound of feet clattering down the stairs, and Felather entered, an expression of horror on his face. "Dear god above," he exclaimed as he rushed to Mav's side and dropped to his knees, hands hovering in front of him as if he wasn't sure where to begin.

Mav gave him a lopsided grin. "Well, my arrival didn't quite go to plan."

"How did they know where to find you? I don't understand how they caught you so easily."

"Don't worry about that now. Patch him up. He's got a big day tomorrow. It's his only chance to state his case," Sero said.

"There are four counts," Mav said, frowning at Sero.

"Not if you fail the first one," Sero replied.

"Ah, there's that vote of confidence." Mav shifted on the cold stone, and Felather finally laid his hands against his ribs.

"If you could see yourself, you'd understand why," Felather muttered under his breath. "Sero, could you see if you can get some water?"

"I'm not some lackey," Sero grumbled, but he did flutter out the open cell door.

"Drink this," Felather said, handing Mav a phial, and Mav drank it without asking what it was. Solanji watched him with suspicion, not that she expected one of Mav's oathsworn to try and kill him, but if it was poison, she supposed he would soon be out of his misery. If it wasn't, then hopefully, it was for the pain.

Felather moved down Mav's body, pausing over his

kidneys and then moving down to his knee. He shook his head and moved on after a moment. "There's nothing I can do to disguise the bruising. They'll fade in time, but you're going to look a sight tomorrow."

Sero returned with the bucket, the water sloshing as he struggled with the weight, and Solanji rose to take it. Folding a pad and wetting it, she gave it to Felather, who started dabbing at Mav's blood smeared skin.

Felather pursed his lips as he worked and then looked at Solanji as if he was making a decision. He exhaled. "Mav asked me to see if I could find out what happened to your brother," he finally said.

"What? When?" Solanji exclaimed as she grabbed his arm, her throat so tight she could barely get the words out.

"The night before we crossed the divide."

"Did you find him?" She shook him, unable to wait to hear his response.

"I'm sorry, Solanji, but what I found isn't good. They soul stripped him and transferred him to a transit house in Eidolon. I haven't had a chance to trace him any further."

"But he's alive? He's alright?" Solanji's heart stuttered in her chest. Bren was alive!

"As far as I know, yes, but it's been over two weeks since he was shipped out. He could be anywhere now; anything could have happened."

"How did you find him so quickly?" Tears welled up and Solanji brushed them away.

Felather squeezed her arm. "We haven't. But I called in some favours at the Justice office, and they are following up some leads for me."

Solanji grabbed his face and peppered him with kisses and then she did the same to Mav. "Thank you so much. You don't know how relieved I am."

Mav smiled up at her a little groggily. The draught must

have been for the pain, because Mav had relaxed and he looked like he was drifting in a haze of fluffy confusion.

"We haven't found him yet, Solanji." Felather's voice was loaded with warning, though a small smile tugged at his lips.

"I know, but at least we know where he went. We can follow him." Solanji smiled up at Sero in giddy relief. He raised an eyebrow in response and tapped his cheek as if he wanted a kiss too.

Head spinning, Solanji stroked Mav's face. That he had taken the time to start the search for her brother, amidst all his troubles, was incredible.

"How long is he gonna be out of it?" Sero asked peering at Mav. "Because we need to get out of here and plan his defence."

"We?" Felather asked.

"Yes, we," Solanji said.

Mav chuckled, his voice slurring as he said, "A scribe, a cherub, and two prisoners went to the citadel."

"Sounds like the beginning of a bad joke," Sero muttered, though he smiled.

"The joke will be on them, then," Felather said. "Because we are not alone."

Xylvin's distant roar punctuated his words and Sero's expression grew calculating. "So his oathsworn stand firm? We may have a chance." He tapped his chin as he stared at Mav, battered and bruised, and now slumped against Felather. "*He* may have a chance, after all."

Solanji silently exhaled. She would take any chance the cherub was offering, if it meant she could save her brother.

The End

Continue the adventure and find out if Solanji and Mav can stay alive long enough to prove his innocence and help her master SoulBreathing so they can save her brother and the people of Eidolon, in DragonBound, book two of the Soul-Mist series which will release in 2023.

If you have a moment and you enjoyed reading Soul-Breather, then please do leave a review and tell other fantasy readers what you enjoyed. Reviews are so important to independent authors to drive visibility and to help us to continue publishing our books.

Sign up to my newsletter via the link on https://linktr. ee/helengarraway to find out more about my books and download a free novella set in the world of Remargaren, the setting for my epic fantasy Sentinal series.

Novella: Book 0.5: Sentinals Stirring

Thank you for your support.

Helen Garraway

www.helengarraway.com

GLOSSARY

Angels

Demavrian (duh-MAV-ri-un) Archdeus

Amaridin (a-MA-RI-din) Archdeus

Veradeus (v-AIR-ad-ay-us) God, father of Demavrian and Amaridin

Kaenara (k-AY-er-nar-a) Veradeus' brother

Serenia (s-REN-i-a) Archangel

Athenia (a-th-eh-ni-a) Archangel, SoulBreather

Goloran (go-law-ran) Archangel

Capt. Julius Teravin (t-air-a-vin) Captain of the Heavenly Host

Eladriz/Adriz (el-a-driz) Cherubim

Felather (fell-a-th-ur) Scribe

Sero (s-air-ro) Cherub

Ryvalin (riv-a-lin) Captain of the Heavenly Host

Xylvin (SHIL-vin) Dragon

Kyrill (k-i-rill) Seraphim

Mortals

Solanji (so-lan-j-i) Mortal
Brennan/Bren (bren-an) Solanji's younger brother
Georgi (j-or-gi) Solanji's elder brother
Jolee (jo-li) Madam of the Strutting Peacock
The Fixer (FIX-er) Shady dealer
Faythe (fae-th) Shop owner
Joran (j-or-an) mortal

Kerris. (k-air-riss) Orphan
Shandra (sh-an-druh) Orphan
Muntra (mun-truh) Orphan
Bailey (bay-li) Orphan
Kiara (key-ar-a) Orphan

Locations

Angelicus (an-zh-el-i-cus) country
Puronia (p-roh-ni-a) Capital city of Angelicus
Bruatra (bru-ar-tra) Town in south Angelicus
Eidolon (Eye-d-oh-lon) Country
Merapol (m-air-a-pol) town
Jinnel (j-in-eh-l) town

ACKNOWLEDGMENTS

I am so excited to have finished the first book in a new series. Breaking new ground and venturing out of the world of Remargaren has been exciting as well as a little scary!

SoulBreather is the first book I've written to an external deadline, and was originally published as part of the USA Today Bestselling Realm of Darkness anthology.

I have to thank Maddy Glenn, my editor, for making me dig deep and split my original story into two books. Delving deeper into the world and my characters has made for a much richer story. I hope you agree! The benefit to my readers is of course this series is now at least a trilogy instead of the duology I had planned.

My thanks also go to Michael, Daisy, Karen and Rosalyn who beta read and found some of the typos. If you do still manage to find any typos, the fault is all mine!

My wonderful team of ARC readers continues to grow. Thank you to each of you for joining me on this journey, I really appreciate all your support, comments and feedback. If you would like to join my ARC team, you can find the link via linktr.ee/HelenGarraway.

Congratulations to Blitz Abrego, who entered my Soul-Breather cover reveal competition to win a book dedication in SoulBreather. See! If you enter, you can win amazing prizes! Make sure you sign up to my newsletter to be notified of any future competitions.

For those who love the #topsyturvy writing prompts on Instagram, you'll find a nod to one of my scenes from the

#TopsyTurvyWhatsMyLine challenge. Did you spot it? If not, a clue - It was from day five!

I love my cover. Seeing my characters brought to life is such a great feeling. The cover was designed by the Ukrainian creative company MiblArt, who have continued to support their authors through very difficult times. My thoughts and prayers go out to all of you.

Thank you all.

Helen

ABOUT THE AUTHOR

USA Today Bestselling and award winning author, Helen Garraway, has been writing about the world of Remargaren, a fantasy world of her creation since 2016.

Sentinals Awaken was Helen's debut fantasy novel published in 2020 followed by three further books and three novellas in the Sentinal series.

An avid reader of many different fiction genres, a love she inherited from her mother, Helen writes fantasy novels and also enjoys paper crafting and scrapbooking as an escape from the pressure of the day job.

You can find out more about Helen's work on Patreon, Sign up to her newsletter or on Social media.

Patreon

Join Team Arifel, Team Darian or Team Sentinal and get access to the first chapters of my new books first, free bookish downloads, polls, early sneak peeks and for Team Darian: a Sentinal mug and free ebooks, and for Team Sentinal: a signed paperback of new releases and a patreon exclusive Sentinal hoodie.

patreon.com/HelenGarraway

instagram.com/helengarrawayauthor

twitter.com/HelenGarraway

facebook.com/helengarrawayauthor

bookbub.com/authors/helen-garraway

SENTINAL SERIES

Interested in my epic Fantasy Sentinal series? Then keep reading to sample the first two chapters of Book One, Sentinals Awaken.

Available in the format of your choice:

- Audiobook
- Ebook
- Kindle Unlimited
- Paperback
- Hardcover

Sentinals Awaken is the first book in the saga of Remargaren, a vibrant, ancient world of high fantasy suffused with magic and adventure.

Remargaren is a vibrant, ancient world. With Goddesses, Sentinals, Rangers and Ascendants all trying to protect or attain that which is important to them.

Join me on the journey, as we meet Jerrol Haven, a King's Ranger, who is destined to become Lady Leyandrii's Captain. A role lost in the mists of time after her last Captain spectacularly disappeared with her when she sundered the Bloodstone and banished all magic from the world.

Throw into the mix some magical creatures, magic seeping back in, an insidious disease affecting the Watches of Vespiri and the tall sentinal trees, the only reminder of the Lady's Guards, her faithful Sentinals, and we have the Sentinals Series.

We travel deeper into the world of Remargaren as the battle between the Ascendants and the Sentinals continues...

Book two takes us to the deserts of Terolia, Book three to the frozen wastes of Elothia and Book Four to the island archipelago of Birtoli.

ONE
THE SENTINAL SERIES

SENTINALS AWAKEN

HELEN GARRAWAY

SENTINALS AWAKEN
BOOK ONE OF THE SENTINAL SERIES

Chapter One

Lady's Temple Gardens, Old Vespers

The sword missed his nose by an inch, if that. A momentary relief as solid steel thunked into the ground and Jerrol jerked back like a snake about to strike and then slithered away, inhaling the scent of soggy grass, dirt and roses. Roses? His brow wrinkled in confusion as he scuttled away and regained his feet. Backing towards the tall sentinal tree arching over the Lady's temple, he strained to see his assailants.

He leaned against the trunk as he scanned the gardens. He would have to apologise later; staying alive was more important than the sanctity of the temple gardens. There were three guards, large and brutal: chancellor's men eager to deliver him up more dead than alive.

The complaint of him snooping around the chancellor's business would be enough to get him placed on report, if not demoted. He wasn't supposed to be near Chancellor Isseran, let alone follow him.

Gritting his teeth, Jerrol considered his options. He couldn't kill them, not on the Lady's soil, yet he couldn't let them report back, either. The satin-smooth bark of the tree beneath his fingers warmed for a moment as he hesitated. The image of a tall, black-haired man stood before him. This apparition wore a silvery green high-necked uniform that glimmered in the swirling mist. He was striking to look at, unnaturally pale with distinctive features and straight, black eyebrows over silver eyes that gleamed in the dim light.

Jerrol gaped at him, unable to stop staring. It wasn't possible. Lady help him, it wasn't possible, was it? He recoiled as the man spoke.

"Captain? Is it time?" the man asked, his silver eyes burning bright.

He was young—younger than he was, Jerrol thought. Yet his expression was grave. There was a sense of a burden understood and accepted, of experience over youth. He had a sword strapped to his hip and a bow across his back, and he looked like he knew how to use them.

Jerrol frowned. *"Time?"* he asked, and the image faded. He took a deep, steadying breath and turned into one of the guards rushing him. Blocking the blow, he spun towards his attacker instead of away. Deep grunts and the thwack of punches broke the silence of the garden. Jerrol twisted out of the man's grip and drew his knife.

He hesitated, remembering he was on the Lady's ground, and instead landed a punch that dropped the man as he retreated. More men arrived, crowding the gate. Jerrol flinched as something buzzed by him, and one of the men grunted in pain and fell back. Audible thuds followed, and the men jinked back from the gate.

Jerrol took the opportunity to fade into the night, circling the temple and up towards the Justice buildings. The tower chimed another hour. The sky was beginning to lighten to a steel grey. If he didn't return to the barracks soon, it would be evident to everyone that he had been out that night.

Keeping to the shadows, he made for the rear wall of the garrison. The small pack still nestled at the foot of the oak tree where he had hidden it. Assessing the height, he pulled the grappling hook out and slung it over the wall. The soft clank was loud in the quiet night air. He pulled it tight and was over before anyone noticed him; gathering up his rope, he dropped to the ground behind the stables.

Jerrol reached his room undetected; as a captain of the King's Rangers, he rated his own space. Sometimes he missed the camaraderie of the shared sleeping quarters but not on nights like this, when he was returning from an unsanctioned venture, battered and bruised.

He dropped his bag in the corner and lit the lantern with the candle he had picked up from the hallway. Fishing the notebook out of his pocket, he shed his clothes, lay down on the bed with an exhausted sigh and began flipping through the pages. His fingers slowed as he realised it was the chancellor's handwriting. He recognised the looping tails Isseran used. A list of names and words. Nothing else, nothing to explain what they meant. Most of the names in the book were known to him, a scattering of administrators, lords and courtiers, as well as high-ranking officers from both the rangers and the King's Justice.

He snapped the notebook shut and lay frowning in thought as the sky lightened. Had he seen a man in the sentinal tree? Legend said that Lady Leyandrii's Sentinals, her personal guards, had all vanished with her when she sundered the Bloodstone and brought down the Veil nearly three thousand years ago. The trees appeared at the same time–it was said in memory of them–and that's where the name came from. Some said the guards slept inside them, unable to cross the Veil with the Lady.

No, it couldn't be true. It was all myth and legends.

Shrugging off the possibility, his thoughts returned to his unsanctioned foray into the warehouse district of Old Vespers which raised more questions than answers. If Isseran was involved in smuggling goods across Vespiri, then they were in more trouble than he had realised. According to the notebook he had found, the chancellor was colluding with a network of influential individuals.

Rising before sixth chime, he showered and dressed in the grey and black of a King's Ranger. The only visible sign of his overnight excursion were his reddened knuckles, and a slight bruise discolouring his right cheek. At least they could be explained easily enough. Everyone gained bruises in the sparring ring.

Commander Nikols was in his office when Jerrol arrived. Nikols was a career soldier; he had risen through the ranks uninterrupted and had been tenured as the Commander of the King's Rangers, and Jerrol's commanding officer. He was a large man, towering over Jerrol's slight stature, and twice as wide.

He was also intelligent. Jerrol respected the sharp mind that sat behind the piercing brown eyes that saw through every ragtag, desperate excuse. He could cut through bull faster than any commander Jerrol knew. Nikols was a staunch supporter of the Lady and Jerrol trusted him.

Nikols' brow darkened as Jerrol reported. He glared at Jerrol as he took the notebook he offered him. Jerrol knew the names, having memorised them during his sleepless hours. He stiffened under Nikols' inspection and knew his nondescript appearance, slight build and brown hair belied his competency. After all, he had been on Isseran's detail because he was tenacious and discreet. The tenacious piece was the part that got him in trouble, and that usually meant trouble for Nikols.

Nikols flipped through the notebook. "This doesn't tell us much. It certainly wasn't worth drawing Isseran's attention to you any more than it already is. You're not supposed to be anywhere near him."

"I didn't expect him to be there, sir. I left him in the arms of his latest floozy. He should have been there for the night."

Nikols glanced up from the notebook and Jerrol winced.

"If the chancellor is at the root of our recent troubles, then we have no choice but to go to the king," Jerrol said, watching his commander. "If these people are his supporters, then most of the administration is corrupted."

"If you can get through the Crown Prince first. He guards his father's peace with a tenacity equal to yours."

"Depends if the king wants it guarded so," Jerrol said, considering the astute monarch that ruled their kingdom. He didn't think the king would accept his son's scheming for long.

"Unless he says otherwise, that is what we have to accept." Nikols glared at Jerrol in warning. "Do not offend the prince, Haven. Your life will become much more difficult if you do. You think Isseran is a pain? Kharel would be ten times worse."

"But it's not like the king to allow others to speak for him," Jerrol argued.

Nikols shrugged. "It's time the prince was more involved, and I expect Benedict is preparing him for the throne."

"Still, it doesn't seem right to me."

"Good job it's not down to you, isn't it? Leave this with me. I'll see if I can get an audience with the prince. Keep your head down. You're supposed to be off Isseran's rotation, so stay away from him. Let's not rile him any more than necessary. Keep to the barracks." Nikols stood and leant on his desk. "Understood?"

"Yes, sir." Jerrol saluted and left the office. He didn't

think arguing would get him anywhere. He knew Isseran was up to no good—look at his attempts to lose Jerrol. If he didn't have anything to hide, he wouldn't try so hard. His turning up at the warehouse, which was totally unexpected, sealed it for Jerrol. He wondered why Nikols wasn't so sure.

The days passed, and Jerrol kept to the barracks, leaving once to visit the Lady's temple to apologise for fighting in her gardens. When he arrived, a young man was kneeling before the altar and Jerrol halted in surprise. The white marble was shimmering; it solidified as he watched, and soft voices drifted on the air.

"Dearest Birlerion, please, be a diversion, protect him."

"But my Lady..." The man broke off as he looked around, aware of someone behind him. He rose in one fluid motion, bowed towards the altar and turned away, keeping his eyes downcast as he left the temple, but Jerrol recognised him even without his bow strapped to his back. The glimpse of silver eyes and the archaic uniform—those were distinctive.

"Hey, wait." Jerrol ran after him, but he had disappeared; the gardens were empty. Returning to the temple, Jerrol knelt before the Lady's altar. He stared at the lifelike statue of a young woman, standing barefoot by a stream surrounded by flowers. The Lady Leyandrii, the deity who helped create the world of Remargaren.

The white marble gleamed in the soft light of the temple, the statue shimmered, and the flowers rustled, giving off a heady scent.

"You are late, my Captain."

Jerrol stiffened, glancing around the empty temple, and his stomach fluttered as he stared at the statue. *"Late?"*

"Events quicken, and we are unprepared."

He swayed, grappling with her words. *"Unprepared for what?"*

"The forgotten stir. It is time."

Jerrol braced a hand on the stone step. What was going on? Was he hallucinating? He flicked another glance around him and back to the statue. *"The forgotten?"*

"They wait patiently, my Captain."

"Who does?"

A tinkling laugh filled the air. *"Who do you think?"* The shimmering statue solidified, and the laugh faded. The statue gleamed in the subdued light, watching him.

Jerrol rose, staring about him wildly, his heart thrumming in his chest. He backed away from the altar and hurried out of the temple. He stopped before the tall sentinal. It couldn't be, the myths could not be real. The silvery trunk glistened in the sunlight, and he placed a tentative hand against it. Nothing happened.

He shook his head. He was an idiot. What had he expected to happen? Did he really think a man would step out of the tree?

The sentinal stood as it had for the last century and more. Records stated that the temple had been buried beneath the land for nearly three thousand years, and all that time the sentinal had been sheltering it. As the soil was excavated and the temple revealed, the sentinal had slowly straightened, its pointed leaves reaching for the sky. One of many sentinals scattered across Remargaren, though the only one in Old Vespers.

Deep in thought, Jerrol paused at the entrance of the Chapterhouse. After a fleeting glance back at the temple, he entered and approached the duty scholar.

"History of the Sentinals? First floor, section twelve, you

won't find much though. No one's been able to explain them," the duty scholar said, pointing the way.

———————

Jerrol leaned back in his chair and scrunched his face up. His eyes were sore from trying to decipher the faded text in the oldest document he could find. According to the dusty journal, the Lady Leyandrii had called forth her Sentinals in 1122, and nearly one hundred men and women had responded, committing their lives to her. Then she had dispersed them throughout Remargaren. She had kept an arm at the palace. An arm? He frowned at the unfamiliar term and returned to the parchment, searching for references to an arm.

He stilled as he read the list of twelve strange names that comprised the 'arm': the Sentinals posted to the Lady's Palace. His breath hissed out as he found what he was searching for. The name he had heard for the first time only a few hours earlier. "Birlerion," he whispered.

As Jerrol returned to the barracks, his mind was spinning. Questions spangled off one another, and there were no ready answers. He wasn't sure if the Lady had spoken to him, or if he had imagined her and the man. Could a man exist within a tree for three thousand years? And if he could, why had he awoken now? And a more disturbing thought, were there others?

Chapter Two

Rangers Garrison, Old Vespers

It was much later by the time he slept, and early when a tapping woke him from a dream about the Sentinals, the

Lady's Guard. Tall, silver-eyed men and women lost when the Lady banished all magic from the world, immortalised by the silver-trunked trees which had appeared overnight in their place. The Sentinals awaited his command.

A young page in palace livery stood outside his door, a missive in his hand. "Captain Haven? Message for you."

Jerrol pushed his hair out of his face and flipped open the note. The page waited, trying to suppress a yawn. The king expected his presence in the throne room, immediately. As he dressed, he speculated on why King Benedict of Vespiri was granting an audience at this late hour. The page led him to the dimly lit courtyard, where horses waited patiently in the darkness.

On arrival at the palace, a sleepy groom took his horse, and the page led Jerrol through the silent corridors to the throne room. King Benedict was already seated on his throne when Jerrol arrived, which was unusual. He was also unattended.

Behind the king, engraved in the wall, were the words of the King's Oath. The oath that bound the king to the Lady and the Land, and the protection of his people. A gleaming mosaic of a sentinal tree and a crescent moon covered the floor.

Jerrol entered and knelt before the king. He bowed his head, waiting for permission to rise. It didn't come, and he remained kneeling, getting stiffer as the minutes passed. He swallowed; was the king that angry with him? He reported what he found. It was not his fault if it wasn't what the king wanted to hear.

As he continued to wait, he realised the king was muttering to himself, but he couldn't make out the words. The mosaic floor began to burn his knee, and he squirmed into a more comfortable position, but it didn't help.

He hadn't seen the king for a few weeks; his last report

had not been received well, and the king had not been pleased. Discreetly peering up at the king, Jerrol could see those few weeks had not been kind to him. He looked as if he had lost weight, and Jerrol's frown deepened in concern.

"Do your Duty. Never Falter. Never Fail."

Jerrol jerked his head up as the first line of the King's Oath rang around the throne room. He inhaled sharply as the words vibrated in the air. Was the king trying to invoke the Oath?

He stared at the king, noting now how dishevelled he appeared. King Benedict was usually immaculate no matter the hour, but now his shirt was wrinkled; his brown hair looked as if he had dragged his hands through it a few times, and his face was lined and pale. He mumbled under his breath; he seemed agitated and not quite himself.

Jerrol held his breath as King Benedict's unwavering eyes stared into his. The king rambled about oaths, the King's Oath in particular. He kept changing topics: he talked about the Watches and his responsibility, and then back round to his Oath before he veered off talking about his concern for the guardians, the tall sentinal trees that were located across Vespiri. The king struggled with himself, and then he spoke again. "Lady, Land and Liege obey."

Jerrol gasped out loud, recognising the second line of the oath. The king's eyes bore into his as he gripped the arms of his throne. He looked, dare Jerrol say it, a bit desperate. The king was rambling about time when he cut himself off and started to speak the third line. "All are one, entwined ascend..." The throne room doors crashed open and interrupted him, and a stocky young man in an ornate uniform of navy blue and gold trimmings entered.

"Father." The king's eldest son, Crown Prince Kharel, strode up to the throne. The king faltered, the words dying on his lips.

Jerrol flinched as a loud crack ricocheted around the throne room and the floor trembled. Jerrol caught the king's eye. "Sire, if it is your wish, I accept your oath. I will guard the Watches for you."

The king dipped his head in what Jerrol hoped was acknowledgement rather than despair. Jerrol was sure the words of the Oath flashed as he spoke.

Prince Kharel grabbed Jerrol roughly by the shoulder and spun him around. His numb legs failed to take his weight as he tried to rise. Staring at the wall, the prince growled, "Haven, you are under arrest for treason."

Jerrol struggled to his feet and glared at the prince. "For what?" A shiver of fear flashed down his spine.

"For plotting against the Crown and the Administration," the prince replied, his face stern. "Guards, arrest this man."

Jerrol turned to the king, who leaned back on his throne and closed his eyes as if exhausted. "Your Majesty, I swear, I have done no such thing."

"All lies," the prince said. "Take him away." He waved the guards forward, and they gripped Jerrol's arms firmly between them. Jerrol had no choice but to let them steer him out of the throne room; their grip was unyielding. The prince was telling his father he had it all under control as Jerrol was escorted away.

Jerrol sat on the floor of the cell and stared at the bare rock wall opposite him. It was good for interrogations, he assumed, as he'd collected a few cuts and bruises as the guards bounced him off it when he first arrived. They weren't taking any risks. He must have quite a reputation for being difficult.

Not only had they shackled his hands behind his back,

but his cell was also on the lowest level. A solid oak door barred his escape. His lips twitched. He had to admit he had been a thorn in Chancellor Isseran's side; this must be payback.

He frowned in thought. Was the prince's action connected to Isseran? It must be. Nikols must have gone to the prince with the notebook. There had been more than enough time for the prince to speak to Isseran, and the prince must have believed his lies. There was no other reason to arrest him.

The situation was far worse than he had reported if the Crown Prince supported Isseran. After the king, they were the two most powerful men in the Kingdom of Vespiri. The prince had moved fast. Nikols could only have shown him the notebook in the last few days.

He sighed as he tried to get more comfortable. His shoulders ached along with his head as his mind spun, trying to figure a way out. Why had the king not spoken up for him? Why would the king try to invoke an oath that as far as Jerrol knew had never, ever been invoked, and yet allow the person he was entrusting it with to be arrested? It didn't make sense.

The cell door rattled as it was unlocked. It opened, revealing Commander Nikols. Jerrol struggled to his feet as his commanding officer raked him with a no-nonsense glare and folded his arms as the guard locked the door behind him. It was clear he wouldn't be amused by Jerrol's bloodstained jacket and bruised face.

"You are a disgrace to the uniform," Nikols began, his voice deep and hard, just as Jerrol had expected. "That a King's Ranger is arrested for treason, manacled as a common criminal—words fail me."

Jerrol grimaced; he wished they would.

"Look at me when I am speaking to you."

Jerrol raised his eyes to his commander's furious brown ones.

"The prince has ordered you executed at dawn. I wonder at his eagerness, but from his reports, you have been stringing us along for months. Your actions have finally caught up with you." The commander's eyes flicked down to his hands, and Jerrol's eyes followed. He was holding a set of metal lock picks in front of him.

"I don't know whether to beat you myself or offer you to the dogs, but I suppose the prince has made that decision for me." He leaned forward and slapped the wall, before pushing Jerrol back against it. "You are no longer a King's Ranger. Maybe that will remind you not to embarrass me before the king." He slapped the wall again as he lent over Jerrol and stuffed the bundle of metal down the back of his trousers. He stood away as Jerrol slid down the wall. "You're not worth the effort," he spat, turning back to the door. "Open up; this reprobate won't even make the first dawn."

The door rattled, and the commander left. Jerrol lay stunned for a moment, the picks digging into his back. The guard leered at him before locking the door again. Jerrol considered what his now ex-commander had said; he had to get out before dawn. Trying to ignore the creeping sense of failure, he worked the picks out of his waistband and felt the thin metal rods to find which would be best to unlock his manacles.

Shucking the manacles off on the floor, he rubbed his wrists and rolled his shoulders, easing the tension in his muscles. He froze as a sharp voice penetrated the wooden door. "A cat? You've had your nose in too many jars, mate."

"I swear, a black and white one, with... um... with wings! It just flew down the steps."

"Yer having a laugh. Try and pull the other one."

"I swear, I saw it. It appeared out of thin air. A cat with wings."

The other guard burst out laughing. "You think you can gull me? You'd have to come up with something better than that."

There was a clatter of boots as one of the guards clumped down the stairs to the lower level–presumably to chase the cat. Jerrol grinned at the thought. The guard slid the peephole back and peered in; he saw Jerrol laid out on the floor and turned back to the hunt. Boots clattered back up the steps. "Did yer see it? The bloody thing's greased, slid right out of my hands it did."

"There's no such thing as a flying cat."

"I swear, look, it's over there."

There was the echoing sound of a chair falling over. "Bleeding 'ell. Well, catch it then you idiot; it can't stay down 'ere." Muffled curses floated down the stairs.

The older guard groaned. "Only you could make such a ball ache out of it. It's just a bleedin' cat."

"Well, you catch it then." The younger guard sounded annoyed.

"If this costs me my rotation, you'll regret it. I've got just one more watch, and I'm out of 'ere. One more soddin' night of making sure locked doors stay locked and you have to find a bleedin' cat..." His grumbling voice faded as he climbed the stairs.

Jerrol peered through the peephole; the younger guard had his back to him, and at an exclamation from above, he climbed the first few steps. "Did you get it?"

Jerrol knelt by the door and selecting his picks, set to work. Sliding out of the cell, he shut the door behind him, and as he crept along the wall, he listened. The older guard cursed. "The bastard's slippier than the first frost. Get up 'ere. I'll chase it to you, and you grab it."

The guard on the stairs hurried up, and Jerrol silently followed. Chairs scraped across the floor as they shoved furniture out the way. "There it is, go on, chase it up the stairs, quick. It's just a cat. It ain't got no wings; you need to get yer eyes checked."

Jerrol peered through the doorway. Both guards were herding a small black and white cat up the curved stairway to the upper level. He squinted at it. He was seeing things. It did have wings, and a scaly tail which was flicking in agitation. Jerrol hid behind the desk, rubbing his eyes.

"Which idiot let it in? That door shouldn't be open," the older man said, stomping back down the stairs. "Whatever next. You go down and check the lower cells. I'll do this floor." The guards dispersed and Jerrol fled up the stairs. His eyes widened as he reached the top; the door was open again.

He eased out of the opening and after a quick scan of the dark expanse of the parade ground, he shut the door behind him and knelt to lock it. He didn't hesitate; he straightened his jacket and strolled towards the outer wall of the palace, the darkened parade ground behind him.

A low hooting, like that of an owl, made him stop and peer up at the wall. A knotted rope dropped down, almost braining him. He tugged it and climbed up and onto the gantry and then, flipping the rope over the wall, down the other side. He peered around for his helper, but he couldn't see anyone.

The torches lining the palace walls flickered as patrolling guards moved in front of them. Jerrol waited, counting as the guards reached the end of their patrol, and as they exchanged words, he slid down the steep slope into the scrub.

He waited, expecting a hue and cry as they realised he had escaped. But the night was silent, and after a moment to calm his racing heart, he worked his way deeper into the bushes and retreated into the murky darkness. He made slow progress across the shadowed landscape, listening for whoever had helped him, but there was only his heavy breathing, loud in the silence. He worked his way towards the edge of the city as the faint grey dawn began to steal across the sky.

You can find Sentinals Awaken and the rest of the books in the series on Amazon: https://www.amazon.com/Helen-Garraway/e/B08JQPPK3Z/

Sign up to my newsletter via helengarraway.com and download Sentinals Discovery, the first few chapters of Book one, Sentinals Awaken, from Sentinal Birlerion's POV for free.